RECUSAL

RECUSAL

BOOK ONE IN THE RECUSAL SERIES

Donald Catalano

coffeetownpress

Kenmore, WA

coffeetownpress

A Coffeetown Press book published by Epicenter Press

Epicenter Press
6524 NE 181st St.
Suite 2
Kenmore, WA 98028

For more information go to:
www.Camelpress.com
www.Coffeetownpress.com
www.Epicenterpress.com
www.donaldcatalano-author.com

This is a work of fiction. Names, characters, places, brands, media, and incidents are either the product of the author's imagination or are used fictitiously.

Cover design by Scott Book
Design by Melissa Vail Coffman

ISBN: 978-1-60381-743-1 (Trade Paper)
ISBN: 978-1-60381-744-8 (eBook)

Printed in the United States of America

To my friends and family who always lend their support and love.

ACKNOWLEDGMENTS

THANK YOU TO MY CARING AND diligent literary agent, Barbara Hogenson. Many thanks for the imparted knowledge to my Coffeetown Press editor, Jennifer McCord. Much appreciation to my personal editor, Katherine Greenslade, who makes all my novels better. Thank you to my friend, Keith Stolte, whose law review article inspired this novel.

CHAPTER 1

Tʜᴇ ᴡᴀᴛᴇʀ ɢᴏʙʟᴇᴛ sᴍᴀsʜᴇᴅ onto the mahogany desk and splintered glass in many directions. A knock on the heavy oak wood door went unanswered, as did yet another.

"Justice Martin, are you alright?" The law clerk opened the door to find her mentor slumped over in his leather chair. She raced to his side, while shouting, "Someone call for an ambulance!" The clerk reached for the Justice's wrist in an attempt to discern a pulse. Without success. Justice Martin did not appear to be breathing, as the clerk began to sob in panic and desperation. She implored, "Someone please help!"

Tʜᴇ ᴡɪɴᴅ ᴡʜɪsᴘᴇʀᴇᴅ ᴛʜʀᴏᴜɢʜ ᴛʜᴇ ᴄʏᴘʀᴇss ᴛʀᴇᴇs as twilight began to overtake the horizon on the shores of Lake Pontchartrain. The old woman opened her satchel and carefully removed the contents and laid them out onto a ragged wool rug of concentric designs. Once the ceremonial gris-gris were in place, Queen Rita fastened the wanga amulet around her neck. Her deep set dark eyes stared off into the distance. The other women dressed in long black skirts each wore a headdress. They lit candles as the men began beating their drums and chimes. A small fire illuminated their gathering. Chants and prayers to Loa Ghede, the family of Loa embodying the powers of death, were recited by the women as they swayed to the rhythmic beating of the drums. Papa Levi reached down and opened the latch on the old wooden box. He removed the chicken from its cage, as Queen Rita blessed with words and then heated over the small fire, the sickle knife she held in her right hand. The chicken thrashed in Papa Levi's secure grip as the drum beats gained volume and speed and the chants grew in intensity. The women hiked up their skirts to their knees dancing and swaying with their eyes looking up to the heavens as the repetitive synchronized thumping of the drums grew to a crescendo. The chicken flapped its wings and cackled wildly as one swift motion of the knife whooshed through the night air. And then, suddenly there was silence. The chants, the drum beats, and the cackles of the chicken ended abruptly. Queen Rita slowly turned to her assemblage and solemnly declared, "Now, it is done."

THE WIND CONTINUED TO WHIP down the National Mall lending an even chillier atmosphere to the bleak gray sky on the 20th day of January. The red, white, and blue bunting on the Capitol Building's west front flapped with vigor as the crowd awaited the inauguration of the next President of the United States. Supreme Court Chief Justice Mitchell Keith took his position at the dais along with President-Elect Andrew Cochran and Mrs. Cochran.

Mrs. Cochran extended her hands which held the well-worn century old Cochran family bible. President-Elect Cochran placed his hand on his family's bible and repeated the oath recited by the Chief Justice.

"I, Andrew Jackson Cochran, do solemnly swear that I will faithfully execute the office of President of the United States, and will to the best of my ability, preserve, protect, and defend the Constitution of the United States, so help me God."

As President Cochran reached out his hand to shake the hand of the Chief Justice, the United States Marine Band struck up four ruffles and flourishes and performed "Hail to the Chief," while a 21-gun salute was fired from artillery pieces of the 3rd United States Infantry Regiment. The northerly wind howled through the leafless trees on the Mall. A frosty chill swept the Capitol.

THE TUXEDO DRESSED WAITER APPROACHED the familiar customer at his accustomed table. "A pleasant good evening to you, Justice Winchester. It's a pleasure to see you again, sir."

"Lucius, how many years have I been coming to Arnaud's?" Justice Winchester asked slowly with a heavy drawl.

"Well, sir, for at least as long as I've been a waiter here, so for some fifteen years, I recall," Lucius politely answered.

"And, in those fifteen years, how long have I been asking you to call me by my Christian name, Stanford?"

"Most probably all of them, Justice Winchester."

"You see there, Lucius, you're just trying to get my goat, ain't you?"

Lucius slyly smiled, "You know I don't feel comfortable calling you by your Christian name here at Arnaud's, sir. Besides the management requires that we treat all of our customers with the utmost respect and dignity, sir."

"Alright, Lucius, now that we've played our little customary name game, do tell me how your lovely wife is doing?" Justice Winchester asked.

"Oh, Bessie is just fine, sir, and she sends you her best," Lucius responded grinning ear-to-ear. "In fact, we were watching the inauguration of President Cochran on television the other day and Bessie was wondering if you were in Washington attending the inauguration?"

"Well, you be sure to send my love to Bessie, and you can tell her that it takes more than a Presidential inauguration to get me to leave New Orleans to go to Washington, D.C. in the middle of January. Did you see how cold those folks were shivering in that wind?"

"Yes, sir. It did look cold. I don't know how them northern folks can stand it," Lucius replied.

"I don't know either, Lucius. You've got to have been kicked in the head by a mule to live in those conditions. Us southern boys just aren't made for those kind of frigid conditions, are we?"

"No, sir, we surely aren't, we surely aren't," Lucius repeated with a smile and a laugh. "Would you like to start off with a Sazerac, sir, as usual?"

"C'mon now, Lucius, do birds have beaks?" Justice Winchester asked with a hearty laugh.

"Oh yes, they surely do, sir, they surely do!"

Lucius returned with the cocktail, "Made just the way you like it, sir, with an extra dash of Peychaud's Bitters."

"Why thank you Lucius, you're the best," the Justice replied. "While I take my time with this here Sazerac, would you kindly put in my dinner order?"

"Yes, sir, my utmost pleasure to do so," Lucius responded.

"I'll start with the turtle soup, and then I'll have the Pompano Duarte, and let's finish up with some pecan pie. Even though the pecan pie is fine here, it still can't hold a candle to your Bessie's pie," the Justice said with a smile, while slowly sipping his cocktail.

"Now, I don't want Bessie fussin' over the likes of me, but I sure couldn't say no to Bessie's pecan pie, Lucius. Only an old fool would say no to that!"

SENATOR PERRY DOUGLAS PUSHED BACK and reclined in his leather chair as he put his feet up on his large ornate desk. He ran his hand through his graying dark hair and shook his head. He stared across the desk at his aide and sighed.

"I loved that old man, Aaron, and I will miss him dearly", Senator Douglas began. "Justice Martin will go down in this country's history as one of the finest jurists the Supreme Court has ever had. But he could have done his country and his party a huge favor and retired while the Democrats still held the White House. He was eighty-four years old, when is enough, enough? We knew his time was coming, he hadn't been in the best of health for a couple of years now. Yet, part of me thinks that that old man thought he was going to live forever. The same stubbornness that led him to push his reluctant colleagues on the court in a progressive direction has also put us in the position we find ourselves today."

"Yes, sir, it certainly was unfortunate timing," Aaron solemnly responded. "It would have been advantageous for the party if he had retired last year."

"Or died six months earlier," Senator Douglas responded. "What a shame and a horrible coincidence that Justice Martin died just days before the inauguration. I don't mean any disrespect, but it didn't have to be like this. The first thing this new Republican President gets to do is make a Supreme Court nomination, while he's still in his honeymoon period with the American public. As Chairman of the Senate Judiciary Committee, my job just got a helluva lot harder. Have you heard any scuttlebutt about who might be on Cochran's short list for the nomination, yet?"

"No, sir, but I'll check around and see what I can come up with," Aaron replied.

"The sooner the better, Aaron. We know the usual suspects that the Republicans push for when a vacancy comes up. Let's try to find out if there are any surprise names that they add this time around. It's been eight years since they held the White House, surely they've come up with more creative choices since their last pick. What a disaster that idiot turned out to be!" Senator Douglas stated with a sigh and a shake of the head. His once sparkling deep blue eyes were beginning to dim with a heavy weariness. Eighteen years of tireless Senate battles will do that to any man.

"Yes, sir, I'm on it," Aaron emphatically replied.

SENATOR PERRY DOUGLAS WAS BORN AND RAISED on the north side of Chicago. His father was an Anglican priest and his mother a professor of Political Science at DePaul University. He was an only child, who wanted for little growing up. Education was a priority for his parents, and Perry excelled in academics. He was a liberal arts graduate from Northwestern University and a high honors student and member of the Law Review at Yale Law School. As a young man, Perry melded his religious upbringing and liberal political views into a short career as a community activist, working with several neighborhood and educational associations in Chicago. After law school, he practiced as a general litigation attorney at a large prominent Chicago law firm. Following four years of practice, he left the law firm to pursue a career in politics running for a vacant Congressional seat.

Perry was an attractive man, with dark wavy hair and sparkling blue eyes. He possessed a fit athletic build and a charm and charisma that equally matched his attractive outward appearance. Perry had a flair for friendly interaction with people and was well schooled in interpersonal politics. He was a natural as a politician. He won the Congressional seat fairly convincingly without an incumbent to challenge his lack of experience. After serving two terms in the U.S. House of Representatives, Perry ran for and won the race for U.S. Senator from Illinois.

AARON ROSE, LIKE SENATOR DOUGLAS, was born and raised in Chicago. Born from a biracial marriage he grew up in Chicago's south side Hyde Park neighborhood. His African-American father worked as an aide to Chicago mayor Harold Washington, until his death. Aaron's Jewish mother was an elementary school teacher at a Hyde Park charter school. He had a fairly typical middle class childhood, with his parents and his four siblings. Aaron was a tough competitor in sports and in academics. He graduated with a Bachelor's degree and honors from the University of Illinois and a law degree from the University of Chicago, not an insignificant accomplishment. Aaron was smart, but he was also a battler. Politics were in his blood. He grew up with politics as he watched his father maneuver his way through the Chicago Democratic Party system. In Chicago politics, nothing is given to you, you fight for everything. Well, unless your last name happens to be Daley. Aaron fought for his success. No one handed him anything in life. And certainly not his position on the Senator's staff.

THE DRIED CHICKEN BONES WERE LAID OUT in concentric patterns on the sidewalk on Bourbon Street just to the left of the door stoop outside of Marie Laveau's House of Voodoo. Few in the boisterous crowd on the street noticed their existence. A discarded plastic beer cup was tossed inches from the delicate formation.

PRESIDENT COCHRAN AND THE FIRST LADY danced together on stage as the orchestra played the Harold Allen/Ted Koehler song, "I've Got the World on a String" at the Presidential Inaugural Ball. The crowd cheered loudly as the new President twirled his wife in rhythm to the music. After eight years of a Democrat as President, the assembled crowd was very enthusiastic to have a relatively youthful southern governor as their new President. The over-crowded warm room provided a welcome respite to the frigid outdoor temperatures as guests attempted to squeeze their way through the doors and the security detail to enter the ballroom and catch a brief glimpse of the First Couple.

JUSTICE WINCHESTER EXITED FRITZEL'S EUROPEAN JAZZ CLUB on Bourbon Street and walked towards St. Ann Street. The judge was an old friend of the owner and had stopped in to say "hello," listen to a little ragtime jazz, and have a nightcap after finishing his dinner at Arnaud's. He straightened his bow tie and buttoned his gray suit jacket as he left the establishment. He ran his hand across his receding hairline as he thought about his long past youth and how he took his then fiancée, LeeAnn, to Fritzel's to dance to the jazz music. The thirty-nine years of happy marriage to LeeAnn and the five years since her death had passed as quickly as the notes audibly racing from a Dixieland clarinet, the judge thought to himself as he stood on Bourbon Street.

Stanford Winchester came from a prominent New Orleans family. His father was a renowned surgeon, his mother's father had been Governor of Louisiana. High accomplishment was a family standard and Stanford was no exception to that rule. A graduate of Tulane University and Harvard Law School, Stanford worked for a short time with the Louisiana Republican Party before he decided to run for district court judge. He won his first election and after serving for four years, subsequently ran and was elected to the State Appellate Court and later the Louisiana Supreme Court. After serving for eight years on the high court in Louisiana, he was nominated and appointed to serve on the Fifth Circuit Federal Court by the Republican President of the United States at that time. Several years later he earned the post of Chief Judge of the United States Court of Appeals for the Fifth Circuit.

Stanford, and his wife of 39 years, LeeAnn Winchester lived in an opulent house in the Garden District of New Orleans. They were among the leaders of New Orleans high society. However, five years ago, LeeAnn succumbed to her lengthy battle with cancer. Stanford could not bear to stay in their family home after LeeAnn's death. He sold their house and re-established himself in a much smaller house located in the French Quarter. Now living alone, he believed that he needed the bustle and crowds of the Quarter to keep him from sinking further into despair.

As Stanford Winchester walked past Marie Laveau's shop, he glanced down and noticed the intricate intertwining of chicken bones and string. He paused momentarily, and bent over as he examined the symbolic structure. He had lived in New Orleans all of his life, the various practices of voodoo were not lost on him. Stanford raised up, straightened his suit jacket and proceeded to walk on, headed towards his home.

THE BRANCHES ON THE LEAFLESS CHERRY TREES near the Tidal Basin in Washington, D.C. rattled from the force of the wintry gusts. While the Spanish moss hung heavy as the gentle breeze whistled through the cypress trees in New Orleans.

CHAPTER 2

ALBERT MARTIN HAD A VERY LENGTHY and distinguished career as a Justice on the Supreme Court of the United States. He was born and raised on the tough west side of Chicago. An African-American youngster from a lower middle-class family, he had fought and scraped for everything he had gotten from life. But his tough hewn battler's instincts as a youth eventually evolved into a gracious gentleman's demeanor and a generosity of spirit and kindness that ultimately was his calling card after he was nominated and appointed to the position of Justice on the highest court in the country.

It was not an easy or convenient journey from under-privileged Chicago minority youth to Washington judicial elite. Albert Martin climbed that ladder with efficiency as well as a developed gentlemen's decorum. Though he held several positions during his career, he moved judiciously through the trial and appellate court levels. He often disagreed with his colleagues on the court, but seldom was he disagreeable with them. Long established convictions mattered to him. Martin fought for his beliefs and ethical standards, but he was not without the ability to acquiesce to compromise for the sake of prudence and progress. He had little respect for some of his more political colleagues who would eschew their beliefs with the shifting of the political tides. Justice Martin would occasionally inform his colleagues that "a house of reason built on a foundation of political expediency and popular whim often crumbles under the pressure and velocity of the shifting civic winds."

Albert's older brother Marcus helped keep him on a righteous path through a childhood that saw several of Albert's friends wind up on the opposite side of the judicial bar in a criminal courtroom. Albert battled against social and moral temptations for most of his life. Similar to most everything else he accomplished over his eighty-four years, he often came out of those battles victorious and unbent. A strong-willed, church-going mother and a present and hard-working father, who practiced and preached moral conviction, laid the foundation for Albert's growth and success. And to his mother, Margaret, and his father, Randolph, Albert devoted his life and career. Both tragically died in a devastating car accident when Albert was twenty-three years of age. They both lived long enough to watch Albert graduate Summa Cum Laude from Princeton University, but before he completed his Law Degree at Yale University, finishing first in his class.

Albert always considered himself so fortunate to have a mother, father, and brother who engendered within him a strong moral compass and a compassion for his fellow man. So many of his friends and schoolmates came from one parent or broken homes with questionable ethics and behavior and therefore, lacked the clarity of civic morality and the tacit acknowledgement of human frailty. Albert schooled himself observing others. He attempted to discern people's motivations and objectives in all of life's presented situations. It suited him well when he moved from a brief three year private practice with a Chicago law firm after his graduation from Yale, to pursuing his life's work in the state and federal court systems.

Albert was elected and served as a Cook County trial judge for six relatively short years before being appointed as a Federal District Court Judge for the Northern District of Illinois by the then seated Democratic President of the United States. During his six-year tenure as a Cook County trial judge, Albert crafted an impressive record for his judicial decision-making and temperament. He often received the highest scoring and praise from the local Bar Association and legal community. He received high praise from several Chicago newspapers, and his stellar judicial record and reputation did not go unnoticed by the Democratic Senator from Illinois, who had been following Albert's judicial career.

Senator Allen Blackman from Illinois had gained knowledge of Judge Martin when his cousin, Ralph, was before Judge Martin in a complex civil suit involving a real-estate development dispute. Blackman's cousin was taken by the Judge's fairness and even-handed temperament and reported such to his cousin the Senator. That led to the Senator tracking

Judge Martin's career and a subsequent meeting at a political event a couple of years later. Senator Blackman met and be-friended Judge Martin at that event, and later presented his name to the President for nomination to the Federal bench.

Judge Martin served for four years as a Federal Court trial judge before being nominated to sit on the United States Seventh Circuit Court of Appeals. His confirmation by the Democratic majority held U.S. Senate was swift and without conflict. After a heralded six-year term on the Court, Albert Martin was nominated, confirmed and appointed to the Supreme Court of the United States, at the remarkably young age of forty-seven. He was a liberal force on the Court for the remaining thirty-seven years of his life. A strong and unwavering voice for civil liberties and judicial social activism, Justice Martin was the principal voice for the majority on several landmark human rights decisions during his tenure.

During his years on the Court, Albert Martin mentored many law clerks who went on to have outstanding careers in both the private and public sectors. Among them was a fellow Illinoisan and Yale Law School graduate named Perry Douglas, who eventually went on to become a U.S. Senator from Illinois. Justice Martin developed personal relationships with several of his law clerks over the years, but the relationship between Justice Martin and his mentee, Perry Douglas, was something special. Justice Martin saw something he liked in Perry Douglas when he selected him straight out of Yale law to be one of his law clerks. A fellow Chicagoan with an aggressive intellect and a liberal commitment to social values, the Justice and his law clerk together were a formidable team. Perry possessed outstanding verbal and written skills and often drafted large portions of Justice Martin's opinions that went virtually unchanged or unedited by the Justice himself. Politically, ethically, and philosophically they were of one mind. They were committed progressives who saw the Court's role as one of judicial activism when it came to righting the civic wrongs of past decades. Justice Martin often railed against injustice. He contended that, "ignoble was a jurist who saw the rights of others being trampled upon and did nothing to hasten change."

Justice Martin and his law clerk Perry Douglas were not only an excellent pairing on the high court but off it as well. They socialized together when Perry worked for the Justice and became fast friends when Perry began his political career. While he did not become outwardly involved in Perry's political campaigns, the Justice lent his support and counsel to Perry behind the political scene. Socially, they both enjoyed attending baseball games together. Often in August when the Court was in recess and Congress was on its summer break, Justice Martin and Perry Douglas would meet up at a Cubs game on the north side of Chicago and spend a summer afternoon engaged in lively conversation over a beer and a hot dog. They cherished the limited time that they were able to spend together when both led busy lives on the Court and in Congress. Their yearly baseball games together continued up until the Justice's final year of life.

"He had just turned eighty-four a week before we attended the Cubs-Dodgers game together in mid-August," Perry related to his aide Aaron Rose, as they stood side by side at the funeral of Perry's beloved mentor and friend on that cold early January day in Chicago's Graceland Cemetery.

"Even though his health had begun to deteriorate, that didn't keep him from enjoying a few beers and a couple of hot dogs in the hot afternoon sun," Perry continued. "There was no slowing down for him, no taking it easy or planned retirement. He was looking forward to the Court's fall term. His mind and his spirit still soared even as his body began to fail him."

"He lived an inspired life, his legacy is vast and affirming to all of us," Aaron added.

"Truly," Perry replied. "And to think that this neophyte conservative darling of the religious right and big oil will be naming his successor is absolutely galling to me. Gird yourself for a battle, Aaron. We will not go quietly into the night while the Republicans attempt to undo all of the progressive good Justice Martin spent a lifetime achieving on the Court. I will not sit idly by and allow them to tarnish this great man's judicial legacy. Today, we are here to bid farewell as Justice Martin shuffles off his mortal coil, but tomorrow we begin the fight to preserve his well achieved moral justice."

CHAPTER 3

"**A**NDREW, ANDREW, HAVE YOU FINISHED YOUR chores yet? I see that the garbage hasn't been taken to the curb, boy," Grandma Blanche called out.

"I'm fixin' to get to that real soon," Andrew yelled back at his grandmother from across the backyard of his grandmother's house in Savannah, Georgia.

"There'll be no supper until your chores are finished, ya hear?" His grandmother bellowed in response.

"Yes, ma'am, I hear," twelve-year-old Andrew called back.

FORTY-SIX YEARS LATER, PRESIDENT ANDREW COCHRAN leaned back in his chair at his Inauguration Day dinner and recalled growing up with his grandmother in Savannah, and not being allowed to eat his supper until all of his daily chores had been completed. His melancholy smile belied the fact that Grandma Blanche did not live long enough to see her scrawny grandson, whom she fondly called "Tadpole," become the forty-fifth President of the United States.

Andrew Cochran's parents died in a house fire when Andrew was ten years old. The only reason that Andrew survived the fire was that he had spent that night at a sleepover at his friend Tim's house. A fact that never escaped his mind. Not even for one day.

A cold draft of wind circulated through the large hall as President Cochran pushed his dinner plate to the side. The drafty wind current extinguished a couple of candles cradled in an expansive and ornate candelabra that was carefully arranged on the President's banquet table. The acrid smell of the extinguished flames lingered in the air, as President Cochran lowered his head and recalled, in his mind's eye, the sight of the burned-out shell of his childhood home as neighbors struggled to keep the young Cochran boy from racing into the smoldering debris in search of his parents. He was inconsolable as he struggled against the grasp of his neighbor's restraining arms.

Only the arrival of and the comforting embrace of Grandma Blanche could quiet his anguished howls and calm his frenzied thrashing. President Cochran raised his head and stared far off across the large noisy hall as if he were looking for Grandma Blanche who would come to comfort him once again.

Grandma Blanche Bellamy was Andrew's maternal grandmother. She was a woman of simple means and customs. Born and raised in a lower middle class family in Savannah, Blanche learned the meaning of hard work at an early age. And the lessons she learned about diligence, effort and perseverance, she passed on to her grandson, Andrew. It took Andrew a while to appreciate the wisdom, work ethic, and tough love imparted by his grandmother. But once the message registered for Andrew, he used it to constantly push himself forward in all aspects of his life. He allowed his misfortunes and anger to motivate him to greater achievement. And now, on a cold, wintery night in mid-January in Washington, D.C., Andrew Cochran sat at a long banquet table as the most powerful man in the free world. "Tadpole" had learned his lessons well.

AARON ROSE HAD BEEN AROUND WASHINGTON long enough to know who had the inside scoop in the Cochran administration about the names of the potential Supreme Court nominees. He worked his sources for several days until he was certain he had exhausted every possibility and had an accurate list of potential nominees. Aaron handed his typed list of names to Senator Douglas.

"Are you pretty sure about this list?" Senator Douglas questioned Aaron as he surveyed the short list of names.

"Yes, sir," Aaron replied. "I'm pretty sure that this is an accurate list of who the Cochran administration is considering for the nomination."

Douglas sneered with a cynical chuckle. "Conway from the Eleventh Circuit, Brumfield from the Eighth, and Lewin from the Fourth Circuit, they're just the same old recycled names from the last Republican administration," Senator Douglas stated with a pro-nounced sigh. "Wait a minute, Stanford Winchester?" Senator Douglas questioned as he turned to his aide. "He's from New Orleans, Chief of the Fifth Circuit, isn't he?"

"Yes, Senator," Aaron replied. "He has an outstanding reputation down there. There's nothing terribly controversial about him that I know of."

"Well, let's take a closer look at him Aaron. Why did his name get included this time around? I want to know everything. Dig through his judicial history and see if there is anything there that we can use. He's not terribly well known and that fact alone scares me," Senator Douglas stated.

"Yes, sir, I'll get right to it," Aaron replied.

"Grab a couple of interns and staffers and carefully review his judicial record, and look into his political and personal history as well. Let's go through everything with a fine-toothed comb, Aaron. Got it?"

"Yes, sir," Aaron affirmed.

Lucius Collins was born in Alabama and moved to New Orleans at the young age of seventeen. His father and grandfather were share-crop-pers in Alabama. Lucius knew how to work with his hands, and he was a diligent and thorough worker. But, Lucius craved a life in the big city and had heard wonderful things about living in New Orleans. Beautiful women, world class jazz music, and food that delighted the palate and lifted one's imagination. While working sweeping the floors at Central Grocery, Lucius met his wife-to-be Bessie Albright. Young and pretty, with caramel-colored skin, Bessie didn't look like any of the girls Lucius knew in Alabama. She had a sophisticated elegance that you would not normally find in the cotton fields of Alabama.

Lucius presented himself well. A strong physique and a gentleman's manner is what drew Bessie's attention. Bessie worked in a women's clothing store in New Orleans' French Market area just a few doors down from Central Grocery. She would eat her lunch on a bench out-side of the tented French Market. Lucius would also eat his sandwich at lunchtime on a nearby bench. Interested glances between Lucius on his bench and Bessie on her bench soon elevated to polite small talk, shared stories of their childhood, and eventually a languidly paced but progressive romance. Much like his determined trek to New Orleans to live a more interesting and cultured life, Lucius knew what he wanted.

Sharing his life with Bessie was at the top of his list. He wanted to spend his days with a pretty young local product of the Crescent City. Gone were the days of chasing tadpoles in the pond behind his grandfather's farm in Alabama. Lucius had bigger fish to fry, and he wanted a woman like Bessie to be by his side.

CHAPTER 4

Aaron Rose assembled a small staff of interns and Senate aides tasked with thoroughly reviewing every decision that was rendered by Justice Winchester during his entire judicial career. The staff workers poured through the text of his state and federal court written orders and opinions. The logic and factual reasoning, as well as the application of the standing law and the tenor of the written opinions, were scrutinized by the staffers who were looking for errors in applying the law and inconsistencies in language and judicial temperament. Meanwhile, Aaron was occupied with talking to Senators who were part of the research process when Justice Winchester was vetted after his initial nomination.

Aaron spoke with Senator Henry Fitzsimmons, the senior Senator from South Carolina, and one of the few Democratic Senators who were part of the original vetting process for Justice Winchester prior to his appointment to the federal bench. Aaron knew that Senator Fitzsimmons enjoyed an excellent bourbon. So, he brought the Senator a bottle of Elijah Craig 21-Year-Old Single Barrel Straight Bourbon Whiskey.

"Aaron, this is a very generous gift," Senator Fitzsimmons stated as he opened the wooden case containing the bottle of bourbon. "Perry Douglas is either paying you too much or not enough if you can afford to give a $300 bottle of bourbon to a cantankerous old coot like me," Senator Fitzsimmons said with a chuckle and a wink of his eye.

"Nothing but the best for one of the most esteemed Democratic lions of the Senate, sir," Aaron responded with a cordial smile.

"Well, you have exquisite taste, Aaron. If you ever get tired chasing after Perry all day long, you can always have a place on my staff," Senator Fitzsimmons stated with conviction. "Now what can I help you with? You mentioned something about Stanford Winchester on the phone?"

"Yes, sir. You were a minority member on the Senate Judiciary Committee when he was vetted prior to his appointment to the Federal bench in Louisiana. Do you or does someone on your staff have any personal notes from the vetting process? There is only so much information that I can glean from a review of the full committee hearings in the Congressional Record. I was wondering if anything came up in subcommittee meetings or background investigations that caught your eye or drew your attention."

"There might have been a few minor questionable things that came up, as I recall, but after we're done chatting here, you should talk to my Chief of Staff, Clay Grover. You know Clay, right?"

"Yes, Senator, I know Clay very well."

"Clay can give you access to my notes and comments from when we first vetted Winchester."

"Do you have any substantive recollections about Justice Winchester or the nominating process at that time that might have caused you some concern?" Aaron inquired.

"Well, you know, you've got to take us aging traditional Southern boys with a grain of salt to begin with Aaron. Stanford Winchester is old school New Orleans. He comes from a very prominent family. He's a crafty politician and an outstanding horse trader. He can put a bug so far up your ear that by the end of the day you're paying him $10,000 for a broken down stable horse that can't run a lick. Smart and savvy with a gentlemen's charm, and charisma that goes on for days. But all those old established Southern families got enough skeletons in their closets to fill a two acre boneyard. I should know, I come from one of them," Senator Fitzsimmons declared with a broad smile as he lifted his crystal whiskey glass to his lips.

The Senator leaned back in his leather chair and momentarily closed his eyes. "I do vaguely recall that there was something about a couple of cases that Justice Winchester had presided over in the Louisiana Supreme Court that raised an eyebrow or two. One case that he wrote the majority opinion on involved numerous plaintiffs, two defendants, and claims of violations of the Fair Housing Act and housing discrimination. I believe that there might have been some questions about whether Justice Winchester should have recused himself because members of his family had a long-standing financial relationship with one of the defendants. I can't recall all of the specifics. Though I do recall asking him about the questionable relationship during committee hearings and he just looked at me like I had accused him of starting World War II. He sat up straight in his chair, attempting to fill the room with his Southern gravitas, and calmly replied, with his sweet as maple syrup heavy drawl, 'Senator Fitzsimmons, you know as well as I do, that that dog just don't hunt.' The next day, the committee was temporarily recessed as we were in the middle of one of our never-ending Middle East crises and I believe that nothing else came of it. Yet, there was something about his demeanor and answers to my questions that just stuck in my craw. But ultimately, we were in the minority back then and couldn't find anything that would stick and truly allow us to question and reject his nomination. Plus, everyone in the Senate was too busy focusing on our daily foreign policy problems to invest too much time in a federal bench appointment. But, do get together with Clay, he'll give you access to my notes and perhaps he can recall more than I can. I believe that he spearheaded my staff investigation at the time when he was an aide."

"Thank you for your time Senator, I'll give Clay a call," Aaron responded as he extended his hand to the Senator.

"Good seeing you Aaron. Give my regards to that old warhorse you work for, will you?" Senator Fitzsimmons requested.

"Of course, Senator," Aaron replied with a smile.

Aaron walked out of the Senator's office, while looking down at the notes he had scribbled on his legal pad. Aaron quickened his pace down the Senate office building corridor. He had work to do.

PRESIDENT COCHRAN SLOWLY AND GENTLY lowered his body into the leather chair positioned behind the desk in the White House Oval Office. He sat deeply into the chair and gingerly rocked back and forth. On the corner of his desk, in four separate shiny polished silver frames sat an old and faded photograph of his mother and father, a recent photo of his wife and his two children, a photograph from his college graduation with his arm around his college friend, Nathan, and a picture of his Grandma Blanche with both of her arms securely wrapped around a grinning thirteen year old "Tadpole." He arranged the photographs so that Grandma Blanche was front and center. After all, he knew that there would be no President Andrew Cochran without the love and strength of the most important woman in his life.

Andrew Cochran relied mostly on three people during his life. His beloved Grandma Blanche, his college sweet heart and subsequently his wife, Sue Lynn, and his trusted college friend and the man who would go on to be his campaign manager for all of his electoral battles, and now his White House Chief Of Staff, Nathan Bedford Forest Whitaker. Born and raised in Bedford County Tennessee and named after a well-known Confederate Civil War Lieutenant General, Nathan Whitaker met and befriended a shy teenager from Savannah, during their freshmen orientation weekend at Vanderbilt University. The two teenaged boys were roommates during their first year at college and bonded over their shared interest in Southern history and literature, and their love of Southern rock music.

Nathan was a gregarious and out-going young man, full of confidence and a touch of arrogance. Upon meeting him for the first time during Christmas break of Andrew and Nathan's freshman year at Vanderbilt, Grandma Blanche told Andrew, "That boy is smart as a whip, and will be a good and loyal friend to you, but he's got some of Lucifer's spirit in him as well. Best you be careful, Andrew, not to be chasing down the Devil's Tail too much with the wild child that is within Nathan." Andrew recalled his grandmother's warning and thought he knew how to control Nathan's impulsive, and at times, peevish nature. The young men became fast friends and shared many aspects of their lives together. But Andrew learned how to step aside or look away during times when Nathan was socially feeling his oats and seeking an adventure. Nathan's adventures were not always within the confines of the law, modest decorum and civil courtesy, or even common sense. Yet, Andrew understood his friend's occasional penchant for the dramatic or even the scandalous, and considered it just part of college life and something Nathan would soon enough mature out of and away from. Nathan always knew exactly where the line was drawn. At times, he just felt compelled to cross it, either as a lark or simply as an affirmation of life.

"Andy, you cannot attain boldness if you are only willing to peek over the side of the cliff. Sometimes you gotta just blindly jump," Nathan often told his friend as they sat in their dorm room at night sipping an excellent bourbon that Nathan had purloined from the professor's lounge earlier that day. Where Andrew cautiously peeked, Nathan without hesitation would jump.

CHAPTER 5

A LIGHT SNOW FELL ON THE NATION'S CAPITOL as Aaron Rose sat in a comfortable chair in front of Senator Douglas' desk, waiting for his boss to finish a conference call.

"What've you got for me, Aaron?" Senator Douglas asked while placing the telephone into its cradle.

"I've still got a bit of research I need to review, but at this time the most glaring evidence that we have to question the ethical behavior of Justice Winchester are two cases that he was a part of the majority ruling on while he sat on the Louisiana State Supreme Court. And then a case that he presided over and issued the majority opinion on during his second year on the Fifth Circuit Court," Aaron informed the Senator.

"Go on," Senator Douglas intoned.

"The Fifth Circuit case was *Happy Foods v. Lake Pontchartrain Brands*. At the heart of the matter, this was a case focused on trademark, false advertising and unfair competition claims. There were claims made by both companies about the 'heart healthy' and 'cholesterol lowering' effects they advertised for a particular brand of organic bean Cajun and Creole frozen dinners for consumers. Specifically, the suit centered on 'Queen Rita's Cajun Jambalaya' which was a product of Lake Pontchartrain Brands. *Happy Foods*, an American and Chinese based company, also had previously established similar claims for its product 'Uncle Keith's Creole Jambalaya.' Both companies sued each other under the Lanham Act. The lower trial court had ruled . . ."

Senator Douglas interrupted his aide. "For now, Aaron, spare me the litigious details, just give me the Reader's Digest version of how this impacts Justice Winchester's possible nomination to the Supreme Court," Senator Douglas asked while scanning the messages on his iPhone.

"It appears that an old family friend of Justice Winchester's was Jim Bob McCallum, majority owner of Lake Pontchartrain Brands. McCallum had been a lifelong friend and high school classmate of Justice Winchester's wife LeeAnn. The stock and sales implications of the verdict in this case alone had major consequences for both competitors. It seems apparent that Justice Winchester should have recused himself from presiding over this matter. Not only did his friend, McCallum own a portion of one of the parties companies, a newspaper article, in the 'Times-Picayune' at the time, reported that tax documents revealed that LeeAnn Winchester had significant holdings in Lake Pontchartrain Brands in a family trust fund. The 'Times-Picayune' covered the story for a couple days after the Fifth Circuit issued it's ruling in a 2-1 majority opinion written by Justice Winchester. One of the Louisiana Supreme Court cases was regarding a violation of the Fair Housing Act in which members of Justice Winchester's family had a personal and financial relationship with one of the defendants. When asked by the local press about the relationship, Justice Winchester said, "'My family has lived in Louisiana for generations. Our family tree's roots run deep and spread wide. If I recused myself from every case where there was some obscure tangential relationship between a party in a matter and a member of my extended family, I would never be able to sit on any case matters. I utilize my God-given ability to discern truth and fair justice and act accordingly.'"

Senator Douglas put his iPhone down on his desk and focused his attention on his aide. "Where did this all come from?"

"I met with Senator Fitzsimmons last week and he gave me the initial tip about the Louisiana Supreme Court cases from his recollection of the vetting process when Justice Winchester was nominated to the Federal bench," Aaron replied.

"Why didn't this become a bigger deal?" The senator inquired.

"The answer to that question is less obvious. Senator Fitzsimmons chalked it up to the Congressional focus on the wars in the Middle-East and a general lack of Democratic enthusiasm to go all-out on opposing a judicial appointment. The Senator also mentioned something about the skeletons in the closets of established Southern families, though he did not allude to anything specifically about Justice Winchester," Aaron responded.

"If anyone would know about Southern skeletons, it would be my friend Henry. His father monopolized the funeral home business in the entire state of South Carolina for decades. He made a fortune forcing small family owned funeral home business owners to sell their businesses to him or simply close or move. I believe that in South Carolina they referred to Henry's father as the 'Merchant of Death'," Senator Douglas stated with a sly grin. "Keep digging, Aaron, let's see what other skeletons you can unearth regarding good Justice Winchester. The Cochran administration is indicating that they have their short list and may make an announcement any day now. We want to be fully prepared with a file on each of their potential nominees. The Republicans can't wait to get their nominee confirmed and on the bench wreaking havoc. Let's be prepared."

"Yes, sir."

"NATHAN, GIVE ME A MINUTE WILL YA?" Andrew Cochran yelled to his Chief of Staff from outside the Oval Office.

"Yes, sir, Mr. President," Nathan Whitaker responded.

President Cochran entered the Oval Office, as Nathan Whitaker raised up from the couch to extend his hand to his long-time friend and now, President.

"My time is never my own anymore," Andrew Cochran lamented to his friend. "Speaking of, I've got to get Nancy to get a day long hunting trip with you on my calendar sometime before too long. I can see you grinning like a fool already Nathan. And no, I'm not gonna pull a Dick Cheney on you, and shoot you in the face, my friend."

"Reassuring to hear, Mr. President," Nathan replied with a chuckle and a sly grin.

"Let's see, it's Tuesday, so it must be Supreme Court nominee day, ain't that right?" President Cochran quizzed his Chief of Staff.

"Yes, sir. Here is our short list for prospective nominees," Nathan stated while handing the list to the President.

"Let's see, Carl Remington of the Fourth Circuit, Collin Brumfield of the Eighth Circuit, and Stanford Winchester of the Fifth Circuit. Where's Artemis Asburger's name?" President Cochran asked with a quizzical expression on his face.

"Respectfully, Mr. President, even though we both highly respect and admire Justice Asburger, we would not have much of a chance getting him through the Democratic majority in the Senate. He's just too controversial. And, do you really want to expend the political capital necessary to fight for Asburger this early in your administration?" Nathan politely inquired of the President.

"He is the best choice, hands down. Shouldn't I fight for the person that I think is best for the country?" The President countered.

"The Senate Democrats view him not as a conservative, but as being on the outer fringes of our party's policies. There is no doubt that he has some extremely controversial points of view. Not to mention his three marriages and his alleged infidelity to his second wife while she was on life support," Nathan responded.

"We should be choosing a nominee based on his judicial performance and record, his overall logical consistency, and his ability to interpret and apply the law fairly with an even-handed judicial temperament, correct?" The President asked. "Well, on that score you can't find a better person to be on the high court than Artemis Asburger. The man's personal life is just that, personal," The President insisted.

"Yes, sir, but one must pick and choose one's battles. I'm afraid sir, that this is a battle we would have a very tough time winning."

"Nathan, we both know a little about the Civil War, that's fair to say ain't it? In mid-July of 1861, Irvin McDowell marched his impressively large but untested Union army from Washington against the Confederate army which was drawn up behind Bull Run beyond Centerville. McDowell crossed at Sudley Ford and attacked the Confederate left flank on Matthews Hill. The fighting raged on throughout the day and the Confederate forces were driven back to Henry Hill. All appeared to be lost. No one would have given the Southern troops any chance to win the Battle of Bull Run. That is, until Thomas J. Jackson and his troops waged a vigorous fight and upheld the left flank. With the aid of Confederate reinforcements the South was able to extend and then break the Union right flank. The Federal retreat deteriorated into a full fledge rout. Thomas Jackson quickly earned the nom de guerre "Stonewall." People have been telling Southerners that they wouldn't be able to win certain battles for decades. Nathan, how can we win battles if we don't even engage the enemy?"

"Even Stonewall couldn't beat the odds all of the time, sir. We cannot win a battle supporting Justice Asburger. Each name on that list would prove to be an outstanding Supreme Court Justice, sir. I don't think that this is the time in your nascent administration to indulge in a Quixotic battle tilting at windmills," Nathan firmly but politely responded.

"Ah, Sancho Panza, my Chief of Staff," President Cochran stated with a smirk. So, whom should I pick?"

"Each and every name on that list is a renowned jurist in his own right. I don't think that there is a bad choice. However, I would highly recommend Justice Winchester, sir. We can further discuss his qualifications after you've had a chance to go through the dossier I've left with Nancy," Nathan energetically replied.

"Alright Sancho, we'll forego the windmills for now. We'll reconvene on this topic tomorrow morning. The press and the Democrats are getting antsy for a name," President Cochran stated with a slight shrug of his shoulders. Nathan Whitaker stood and walked out of the Oval Office. A slight smile creased his pursed lips.

THE SCENT IN THE SMALL SHOP on north Rampart Street became overpowering.

"I need to open a window," Papa Levi stated as he jostled with the rickety old sliding window pane."

"I'll soon be done. Where dat box come in from Haiti yesterday?" Queen Rita asked in her lilting French Creole mixed with Haitian accent as she scanned the countertop of the old shop.

"It tis over by the amulets. You put it there yourself when it come," Papa Levi pointed toward the box with his shaking right hand.

"Ya mon," Queen Rita responded as she carefully opened the box. She removed a small vial and a mojo bag containing snake fangs. She placed a few of the fangs in a mortar and began to crush them using a granite pestle.

"Is this potion for our friend?" Papa Levi asked.

"Help is needed, help must be delivered," Queen Rita stated solemnly while she continued her grinding.

"The spirits protect him," Papa Levi added in a hoarse voice barely above a whisper.

"Ya dat be done," Queen Rita quietly responded. "Dat be done."

CHAPTER 6

Aaron Rose spent hours poring over Senator Fitzsimmons notes from Justice Winchester's vetting process. Clay Grover had flagged and highlighted some notations that he thought Aaron would be interested in. Aaron had known Clay for a number of years. When he first came to Washington to be on Senator Douglas' staff, Clay was one of the first Senate aides to approach Aaron and attempt to make him feel comfortable and welcome. The clubbiness and decorum of the Senate not only applied to the Senators themselves, but at times, also to the members of their staffs. At least, on your own side of the aisle.

Clay had invited Aaron to join him and some of the other staffers in a weekly Capitol Hill basketball league. They played twice a week and the games were nothing short of physically brutal. They were all young aggressive adult alpha males in their physical prime, all serving in high pressure positions on Senatorial staffs, competing against one another for a couple of hours on a basketball court. The fact that an ambulance only had to be summoned once in a three-year span of league play was considered a Capitol Hill miracle. Capitol Hill security, on the other hand, had to be on call for most of the games.

Aaron Rose possessed a sinewy, muscled, six-foot, light caramel colored frame. His short afro haircut accented a squared jawed attractive face and brilliant green eyes. Aaron grew up playing basketball on the hard scrabble outdoor courts of Chicago's Hyde Park neighborhood. His father had been an All-State power forward at DuSable High School during their glory days. Aaron also played basketball in high school as a point guard but never replicated the accomplishments of his father on the court. Off the court was another story.

Clay Grover was six feet two inches of sculpted muscle. His blond shaggy hair, when not firmly affixed in place during the business day by an inordinate amount of hair gel, often fell into his dark blue eyes as he ran up and down the basketball court. Clay seemingly gleamed of attractive fitness. He may have been raised as an elite Southern gentlemen, attending an outstanding prep school and then on to Duke University for undergraduate studies and law school, but on the basketball court, his pointed elbows flew in an effort to ensnare the ball without any gentlemanly restraint.

With Aaron and Clay as the dynamic duo of their team's backcourt, their team won the league championship two out of three years. Clay was four years older than Aaron and was the self-appointed captain of the team. Aaron, always the team player, was more than willing to subjugate himself to Clay's leadership. Their time spent battling together on the basketball court eventually led to a warm and nurturing relationship off the court. The tough-minded biracial kid from the south side of Chicago and the privileged Southern boy from South Carolina became a close and formidable pairing on Capitol Hill.

PRESIDENT COCHRAN SAT ON THE COUCH in the Oval Office on Saturday afternoon, with the long legs of his six foot four body crossed at the knee exposing his brand new shiny black and candy red cowboy boots sticking out of his blue jeans.

"Nathan, how do you like my new kicks?" He asked his friend.

Nathan Whitaker studied the boots carefully before blurting out, "Well sir, with all due respect to your position as the most powerful man in the world, them boots make you look like a five dollar whore all gussied up to impress the new, young, good looking preacher at the Saturday evening potluck social. Sir." Nathan responded with a stone face and a matter-of-fact tone to his voice.

"Then mission accomplished! That was just the look I was going for," the President stated with a hearty laugh.

"Sir, you're a Republican President, with a not so distant history of another Republican President whose horrifyingly inaccurate claim of 'mission accomplished' will haunt him throughout the annals of United States history. You might want to choose another catch phrase," Nathan replied with a grin.

"Point taken, smart ass!" Andrew Cochran chortled. "Let's get down to brass tacks, I don't want to eat up too much of your Saturday afternoon. Your wife Posy already hates me enough for monopolizing your time!"

"First of all, that is a blatant falsehood, respectfully, sir. Posy loves and respects you almost as much as I do. Secondly, and of greater relevance, I serve at the pleasure of the President of the United States."

"Damn, Nathan, spoken like a true diplomat. I understand that the embassy in Iraq has an opening," President Cochran goaded his friend with a laugh.

"You know as well as I do, that we could go on like this for days. Heck, in college, that is exactly what we did. Always trying to be too clever and witty for the other fellow," the President reminisced. "But truly the only thing I wanted to make sure of today with you was that we have crossed all our t's and dotted all our i's on this Supreme Court nomination?"

"Yes, sir, I'm certain that we have the three very best candidates on our short list," Nathan stated with conviction.

"Alright, my friend, as long as we ain't jumpin' over a cliff without looking," the President replied.

"My cliff jumping days are over, sir. The list is solid."

"Well, then please give the nominees a call and let them know they've made it to the final three. Also have Lloyd leak it to the press in a day or two, will you?" the President requested.

"Consider it done, sir!" Nathan energetically confirmed.

STANFORD WINCHESTER ROCKED IN HIS WICKER CHAIR on the wrought iron and wood balcony of his home overlooking Royal Street and Ursulines Avenue. He watched as a bee flitted from one light orange blossom of his dwarf-braided hibiscus tree to the other. The warm sun caressed his weather-worn face as a good breeze altered the bee from its appointed honey-gathering rounds. His cell phone ring tone, programed by his law clerk, Susan, to the song, "When the Saints Go Marching In," suddenly interrupted the bucolic setting.

"Justice Winchester?" The voice on the other end of the phone questioned.

"Yes, this is he."

"Good afternoon, sir. My name is Nathan Whitaker. I am Chief of Staff to President Andrew Cochran.

"Yes, sir," Stanford Winchester slowly drawled.

"Justice Winchester, the President would be pleased and honored if you would consider allowing him to present you as one of three potential nominees for the Supreme Court to fill the vacant seat on the Court due to the unfortunate recent passing of Justice Martin?" Nathan solemnly and deliberately asked.

"Well, ain't that a kick in the head," Justice Winchester stated as he laughed to himself.

"Sir?" Nathan questioned.

"Sorry," the Justice intoned. "That's not something that I get asked every day. Or most days. Or any days as a matter of fact."

"It is a humbling honor for me to be able to pose that very question to you on this very day, sir," Nathan responded.

"When would you need an answer?" Justice Winchester asked.

"Well, sir, of course we want to afford you the time to think it over and discuss it thoroughly with your family. It is a life changing decision," Nathan politely responded.

"So, in Washington-speak that's about 3 days? Is that correct, Mr. Whitaker?

"Yes, sir, and please feel free to call me Nathan. That's about right. The press and the Senate are clamoring for our list of nominees. We would like to present something officially by mid-next week," Nathan offered.

"Well then, Nathan, would it be terribly impolitic of me to ask who the other two potential nominees are for the vacancy?" Justice Winchester slowly questioned.

"Not at all, sir, the other two candidates have already been informed that they are under consideration. One is Justice Carl Remington, who presides on the Fourth Federal Circuit Court and Justice Collin Brumfield who is seated on the Eighth Circuit," Nathan recited to the Justice.

"So, I'm the last girl waiting to be asked to the dance?" Justice Winchester quipped.

"Saving the best for last, sir," Nathan playfully replied.

"What about Artemis Asburger? I would have bet dollars to donuts that Artemis would have topped Andrew Cochran's list," Justice Winchester chuckled.

"No, sir, Justice Asburger is not being considered for the vacancy on the Court at this time," Nathan stoically stated after a brief silent pause.

"Alright, Nathan, I won't try to wrangle a real answer out of you. Please let the President know that I am honored to receive this esteemed acknowledgement. I will give it the sober and reflective thought that it fully deserves. Should I call you or someone else in seventy-two hours with my decision?" Justice Winchester asked.

"That won't be necessary, sir. I will personally call you back on Tuesday at 5 p.m. if that time is acceptable to you?

"That's perfectly fine with me, Nathan. I look forward to your call and I will have an answer for you at that time. Have a lovely weekend," Justice Winchester replied.

"Thank you again, Justice Winchester, on behalf of a grateful President. You have a wonderful weekend as well. Goodbye."

Stanford Winchester placed his cell phone back into his front pants pocket. He raised himself up from his wicker rocking chair and ambled through the screen door of the balcony leading into the front parlor of his home. He gently grasped a framed wedding picture of his deceased wife LeeAnn that was positioned on the center of the mantle of his fireplace. He lovingly held the silver frame with both of his slightly trembling hands. He stared at the photograph for a few moments before quietly stating, "LeeAnn, darling. You ain't gonna believe the phone call that I just received."

CHAPTER 7

ONLY THE DIM STREET LIGHT from the slightly parted curtains of the well-appointed room in the Ritz Carlton Hotel in DuPont Circle illuminated the naked couple intertwined on the king-sized bed. Two silhouettes maneuvered into position. The head of one of the participants slowly descended down the male torso of the other. Soft moans and a pronounced sucking cacophony constituted the only sounds emanating from the couple. Several minutes later, as one body bucked its hips to meet the full and attentive mouth of the other, and with the impassioned utterance of the words, "Yes, deeper . . . faster . . . take it!" Soon it was over. The sexual ballet of the darkened silhouettes ended. After several minutes of languid recovery, both participants arose from the bed and began the process of dressing.

The words, "Thank you, darling, that was wonderful," were spoken as perfunctory kisses were exchanged. Followed by the hushed phrase, "As usual, there is a Secret Service agent outside the door who will escort you out of the kitchen of the hotel to a waiting car that will drive you home." And with that, the encounter concluded.

Kate Wilson used the palm of her right hand to attempt to press the creases out of her wool skirt as she exited the back entrance of the hotel and into a waiting town car. This was far from the first time she had made this exact walk, and she knew in the back of her mind that it was probably far from her last. Having an affair with a powerful married man in Washington had its perks, but they were always nestled in between the constant overriding need for secrecy and the humiliating exits out of back doors into dimly lit alleyways.

Kate was a very pretty and smart twenty-eight-year-old woman. With flowing auburn hair and bright blue eyes she was more than attractive enough to gain the attention of most men. A Harvard Law School graduate, she was a law clerk to the Conservative firebrand on the U.S. Supreme Court, Justice Allen Sallis. Justice Sallis was the hero of the far right of the Republican Party. He was the unequivocal, unrelenting and passionate voice of the Tea Party and right wing libertarians. And Kate had served him faithfully for the last two years. She had a passion for the law and an intoxication for the realm of politics. She had no qualms working for a Justice who was unapologetic about his controversial viewpoints and his, at times, gruff and demeaning behavior. Justice Sallis exuded confidence and power. These were the aphrodisiacs for an ambitious woman like Kate Wilson.

AARON ROSE LOOKED AT THE LEAKED DRAFT of the White House press release with a proud smile creeping across his well-formed lips. No surprises, he thought to himself. Senator Douglas will be pleased. Carl Remington seemed like the hands-on favorite for the nomination. After all, the Cochran administration must be aware of the potential problem with Justice Winchester not recusing himself from the controversial intellectual property case, as well as the Louisiana Supreme Court matters, right? It hadn't taken Aaron that much time and effort to uncover the pronounced conflicts of interest. And, so early in their administration, certainly they wouldn't take the chance of jeopardizing their reputation and gravitas by defending a nominee with a handful of glaring examples of judicial misbehavior. Aaron continued to filter the logical rationale through his mind. He became more and more convinced that Justice Winchester's name appeared on the prospective short list only to make the obvious selection of Justice Remington that much more appealing. It was purely political gamesmanship, Aaron concluded.

IT WAS A GOOD MILE AND A THIRD WALK from the U.S. Appeals Court Building in New Orleans' Central Business District, winding through the French Quarter to get to his home on Royal and Ursulines. It was a journey that Stanford Winchester enjoyed making. It allowed him to clear his head from his daily duties on the Court and enjoy people watching as he made his way through the French Quarter. Every Wednesday, he would stop and have dinner at Arnaud's. He enjoyed eating at most of New Orleans fine restaurants. But, Arnaud's was his favorite. Since LeeAnn's death and his subsequent move from his home in the Garden District to the French Quarter, Stanford found himself eating out on almost a daily basis. Never one with any formidable talents in the kitchen, he eschewed his own attempts at food preparation to enjoy the vastly more talented skills of others. His housekeeper, Clara, would often leave him a casserole dish she had prepared or a homemade pie. Stanford appreciated her efforts and her kindness, but Clara was hardly a James Beard award winning chef herself. Stanford had become accustomed to exceptional New Orleans Cajun and creole cuisine prepared by award winning chefs.

As he made his daily walk through the French Quarter, Stanford thought about everything that he would be giving up if he were chosen and confirmed as President Cochran's nominee to the Supreme Court. So much of his life and his loves were deeply rooted in New Orleans. What was left of his family still lived in or near the "Big Easy." This is where all of his friends were located. He loved the music, the food, and the odd but homogenous mixture of Southern politics, deeply rooted religious beliefs, old world voodoo practices, and laissez faire debauchery. To sacrifice all that he had known and loved, and for what? Did his ambition and ego require that he attain the title of U.S. Supreme Court Justice? At the cost of giving up his way of life and the many loves of his life? This is what Stanford Winchester thought about as he slowly walked down Royal Street briefly peering into the windows of antique and art stores and giving a polite waive to the owners of the shops whom he had always considered to be amongst his friends.

"MY GOODNESS, PERRY, you look like something the cat dragged in," Katherine Douglas chided her husband as he entered the front door of their Georgetown condo.

"Good evening to you too, darling," the Senator sarcastically replied to his wife.

"Seriously, Perry, you look like you've been sleeping in your suit for days," Katherine further admonished her husband.

"Well, honey, this is my D.C. disheveled look. But I clean up pretty good when I get back to Chicago," Perry chirped with a devilish grin.

"Which is never quite enough," Katherine interjected. "Which is why I travel out here to spend some time with my husband who is never around."

"Katherine, you saw me plenty last year when I was running for a new Senate term. If I recall, we choked down some god-awful dried out chicken together at fundraisers for a good portion of the year. We crossed Illinois together side-by-side for months. But now that the elections are over and we are into a new year and a new administration, I'm going to have to spend more of my weekends here in D.C. Well, at least until we get the Senate leadership and committees squared away and teach our new Georgia peach of a president the ways of Washington," Perry said with a smile. "Now, stop grousing at me, and give your wrinkled warrior a big kiss."

Katherine Douglas complied and wrapped her arms around her husband's neck. The couple locked lips in a deep passionate kiss that lasted for a couple of minutes. "Well, you haven't lost your kissing ability. That remains wholly intact. But, my beloved, you smell as bad as you look," Katherine matter-of-factly stated as she stared into Perry's deep blue eyes and tousled his graying hair with her right hand.

"Well, then, how about we take a shower together and clean up this dirty boy?" Perry seductively asked his wife.

"Only if you promise to stay out of the office tomorrow and we spend some time together. After all it's God's day, Perry, and thou shalt not work on the Sabbath, or the Tea Party shall smite you down!" Katherine declared with a smirk and a short giggle.

"It's a deal!" Perry enthusiastically responded. "We can go see that movie you've been after me to take you to in the afternoon, and then Perry will take you to Perry's for a sushi dinner. How's that?"

"Ooh," Katherine gleefully replied. "Perry's is that cute place in Adam's Morgan, where we can curl up on the couch on the second floor and watch the people walk by while eating exquisite sushi, right?"

"One in the same," Perry declared. "And you know how much you love their large dragon rolls," Perry stated seductively as he took his wife by the hand and led her towards the master bedroom. "I just know how much you love Perry's dragon roll. You just can't get enough can you?" He whispered as he began to sensuously strip in front of his wife.

"WHERE HAVE YOU BEEN?" Posy Whitaker challenged her husband as he strode through the front door of their Arlington, Virginia home.

"Saving the free world," Nathan Whitaker offered back to his wife.

"Don't get cute with me, Nathan," Posy reprimanded.

"Easy there, girl, no need to get your undies in a bunch," Nathan replied in his best smooth bourbon Tennessee accent. "I told you, Posy, that there would be plenty of late nights in the early going. We've got one hundred days to make a very good first impression on the American people and set our administrative agenda. Andy's got one chance to have a political honeymoon with the public and the press while we push for our top priorities against a Democratic Senate."

"I thought the purpose of selling our house in Savannah and moving up here was so we could be together," Posy replied.

"It is, lamb chop, but as Chief of Staff, I've got to set the agenda and marshal the troops for this administration to be successful," Nathan replied as he took his wife's hand.

"Isn't that Andy's job?" Posy queried.

"Hardly," Nathan swiftly declared. "The President is the figure head, the titular leader of the country. The real politics and power play takes place behind the scenes. That is where I am most helpful to Andy. Sometimes, he can be just a bit too timid, too polite to get the hard work of politics accomplished. That's where I come in. I possess the temerity that Andy occasionally lacks. It's been that way since we were eighteen years old at Vanderbilt. Some things never change. So, if this administration is going to have a mind-blowing successful first one hundred days, I've got to step up to the plate and work my ass off and do whatever needs to be done. Surely, you understand that, my love?"

"I guess so, but that doesn't mean that I can't miss my attractive, well-built, blond-haired, blue eyed husband, does it?" Posy seductively said as she reached over and grabbed Nathan's firm buttock. "Fifty-eight years old and this ass hasn't sagged one bit," Posy declared with satisfaction.

"Darlin', you just grab hold, baby, and hold on tight," Nathan Whitaker moaned.

CHAPTER 8

I T WAS TUESDAY MORNING IN EARLY APRIL and Stanford Winchester sat at an outdoor table at Café du Monde as usual, one of the first customers of the morning. Clara, as she had done every weekday morning, had brewed the Chief Justice a fresh pot of coffee. And, as he had done every weekday morning for the past five years, Stanford had taken a couple of obligatory sips of the coffee, praised her efforts but placed the barely touched cup of coffee on the kitchen counter claiming that he was late and had to rush off to court. Then, on his meandering walk to work, with the guilt of a five-year-old boy who had just snatched a couple of pieces of candy from the drugstore counter without paying for them, Stanford Winchester would glance at the people around him and deftly sneak into Café du Monde to enjoy a cup of Café au lait, and a plate of buttery powdered sugar covered beignets.

Suddenly a shocking thought came to Stanford as he held the small deep-fried spherical pastry puff in his hand. Do they even know how to make beignets in Washington, D.C.? He took a bite and allowed the warm beignet to dissolve in his mouth. What is the price of glory? What would he be giving up if he was offered and accepted the nomination? But on the other hand, he recalled how proud LeeAnn was of him when he was appointed as Chief Justice of the Federal Fifth Circuit. She told him at that time, "Stanford, this is just the next step to you taking your rightful place on the United States Supreme Court. Soon, you will be considered one of the greatest jurists in this nation's history on the highest court in the land, and I will be the proudest woman on God's green earth."

Her words hung in his mind, as he took his last sip of Café au lait, paid his bill, and continued his stroll through the French Quarter, crossing Canal Street and ambling ever closer to the steps of the U.S. Appellate Court Building.

SENATOR DOUGLAS SAT BEHIND THE LARGE DESK in his office scrolling through the new emails in his inbox, as he sipped his cup of badly brewed coffee. His mouth seized up into a sneer by the sheer bitterness of the nasty hot brew. His right hand kept pressing the "delete" key as he wondered who you had to bribe to get a decent cup of coffee in the Senate Office Building. He came upon a memo sent by his aide Aaron entitled, "Cochran Administration Supreme Court Nominee." He stopped his rote deletion process and opened the email. As he began reading the text of the email, there was a knock on his office door.

"Aaron, what a coincidence, I just started to read your email," Senator Douglas stated as he spied his aide standing in his doorway. "I see you believe that the Cochran administration is tapping Carl Remington for the Supreme Court nomination, eh?"

"Yes, sir, I think that Stanford Winchester is just a smoke screen," Aaron replied.

"So, you think they know of the possible conflict of interest in that trademark case, or even care about it?" Senator Douglas queried his aide.

"It didn't take me long to uncover it, and it's fairly clear to me that Justice Winchester should have recused himself from presiding over the matter," Aaron responded.

"Aaron, you are giving the Republicans too much credit for caring about the perception or optics of things. This is a party that is operating in the 1950s on pretty much every major social issue of our time. They're against gay rights and gay marriage. They're against comprehensive immigration reform that shows an ounce of human compassion. They abhor women's reproductive rights. They're attempting to wholly destroy the Voting Rights Act. They demonize teachers and their unions. They refuse to provide a living wage to millions of Americans by refusing to raise the Federal minimum wage, and they do not care one iota about healthcare for the poor. Several Republican governors, including Andrew Cochran, turned away millions of dollars in Medicaid funding for their states to make a political point. Aaron, if you think that a possible conflict of interest in a trademark case will keep them from nominating who they want to nominate, you have not been paying attention to the craven, illogical, and at times inhumane policy behavior of our friends on the other side of the aisle. Don't try to insert logic into bloviated base pandering rhetoric," Senator Douglas concluded with a shake of his head.

"But why take the risk of public humiliation and a failed nomination when you can avoid it?" Aaron questioned.

"Good point, but your employing logic and reason, Aaron. What logic was there in Reagan's nomination of Robert Bork, or Bush senior's choice of Clarence Thomas and his pubic hair incidents, not to mention his own recusal issues? Or "W's" initial nomination of his buddy Harriet Miers? That was so preposterous, even his fellow Republicans were too ashamed to let that one go forward. Don't attempt to figure out an opponent that stopped making sense decades ago," Senator Douglas gently admonished his aide with a weary smile.

"But for now, come with me, Aaron," Senator Douglas stated while rising up from behind his desk and placing his arm around Aaron's shoulder.

"Where are we going?" Aaron inquired.

"Starbucks. This government issue swill is killing me!"

LATER THAT AFTERNOON, AARON MET CLAY GROVER for a late lunch at Bub and Pop's sandwich shop in DuPont Circle. The two friends gave each other a hearty embrace and greeting.

"I miss you," Clay stated as they sat at a small table across from one another.

"I know, me too," Aaron confirmed. "But between the campaign last year leading into the November election and then the holidays, it's been crazy. I spent far more time in Illinois with the Senator than I did in D.C. And now, it's been really busy as the new administration begins to put forth their agenda."

"Any word on their final three choices for the Supreme Court nomination?" Clay inquired.

"Not yet, though I hear it should be announced either later today before the five o'clock news or tomorrow morning," Aaron responded.

"Were Senator Fitzsimmons' notes of any help to you?" Clay asked.

"Yes, they were. Thanks so much for providing them to me so quickly," Aaron said with a wink and a smile.

"Anything for a close friend," Clay replied while staring into Aaron's brilliant green eyes and reaching across the table to brush his friend's hand. "So, who do you think their choice will be?" Clay asked.

"I'm convinced it will be Carl Remington. I don't think they'd take a chance with Stanford Winchester. His judicial behavior in the past has already raised flags in his previous vetting process," Aaron summarized.

"Yes, but he did get confirmed for the Fifth Circuit despite his prior indiscretions, right?" Clay questioned. "If those past cases didn't thwart his upward movement on the bench before why would they matter now?"

"Well, I would hope that it's because we are now talking about a life-time appointment to the Supreme Court of the United States where his judicial temperament and ethical standards will influence the interpreta-tion of American law for decades to come," Aaron replied with emphasis and conviction in his voice.

"I love how fired up you get, how you always demand fairness and jus-tice. It looks good on you, Aaron. But, unfortunately, this is Washington, and things aren't always done because they are fair or just. Usually, it's quite the contrary. Who do you know? And what can they do for you? So unless Carl Remington can do more for the Cochran administration than Stanford Winchester can, I wouldn't be so sure that Remington is their pick," Clay stated to subdue his friends vigor.

Aaron bowed his head and his shoulders slumped. "Don't you get tired of this game? Can't idealism get a little play?" Aaron asked, his voice less energetic.

"Your idealism is what makes you so beautiful. Well, that and your big, loving heart. Your trim athletic body and those gorgeous eyes, don't hurt either," Clay softly stated, as his eyes glanced around at the other tables of the sandwich shop. "Maybe it can change. Maybe that's why you're here, Aaron to help change it."

"LUNCH, SUE LYNN, I'M ONLY TALKING ABOUT an occasional lunch," President Cochran repeated to the First Lady. "You don't have to be best friends."

"There's no worries on that score Andy, that woman and I will never approximate anything close to even good friends," Sue Lynn Cochran emphasized to her husband.

"Look, I know she can be a little crass and vulgar at times, but she's not a horrible person," Andrew Cochran said as persuasively as he could muster.

"She's more than a little crass, Andy, especially around me, and she has been that way ever since Nathan began dating her over twelve years ago. I mean, there he was the forty-five year old Chief of Staff to the new governor of the State of Georgia dating a twenty-three year old Miss Peach Cobbler, or whatever her silly beauty pageant title was," Sue Lynn stated dismissively.

"Honey, they sold their Savannah home after we won the election. All of her friends and family are back in Georgia. Other than Nathan, who spends most of his days trying to help me get my act together and run this country, she doesn't know anyone else in Washington. She's bored and lonely. And Nathan's irregular schedule just makes things worse. All I'm asking is that if you could invite her over to the White House for lunch every other month or so. Perhaps when you have some celebrities or dignitaries over for a White House luncheon you can have your social secretary add her name to the invitation list?" Andrew asked his wife.

"And who am I going to sit her next to, Andy, at the White House luncheons? Reverend Carrigan, so that she can explain her boob job to him, or opera singer Carmine Solotso, who she can impress with her ability to play "Turkey in the Straw" with a comb and wax paper?"

"This isn't like you Sue Lynn. You're always so protective of and defending of other women. You're kindhearted and accepting of so many different types of people, which makes you an ideal First Lady," Andrew Cochran firmly stated.

"You're right, I'm being far too harsh," Sue Lynn relented. "There's just something about Posy Whitaker that sets me off. Always has been. I never understood what Nathan saw in her other than her far too obvious physical attributes. I'm just not used to being around women who are that crass and vulgar. My friends are Vanderbilt ladies or Sweet Briar women. I'm not sure what junior college Posy graduated from, do you know?" Sue Lynn challenged her husband.

"I thought you just said you were being too harsh?" Andrew quipped back to his wife.

"You're right, Andy. I apologize," Sue Lynn sighed in response. "She's lonely in a new place without any friends. The least that I can do is to attempt to make her feel more comfortable and welcome, and I promise I will."

"Now, that's my girl. I can always count on you to do the right thing and show that big heart that made me fall in love with you during our junior year at college," Andrew stated with a big smile as he reached out to hug his "First Lady."

CHAPTER 9

Nathan Whitaker paced around his White House office while he reviewed the draft press release. Earlier in the day, he had telephone conversations with Justice Remington and Justice Brumfield, who both accepted the President's request that they be named as potential Supreme Court nominees. It was 4:45 p.m., and the phone call to Justice Winchester was to be made in less than fifteen minutes. Nathan was optimistic but not overly confident that Stanford Winchester would say "yes." But if he did, Nathan knew that the Cochran administration would have their first appointee to the Supreme Court of the United States. And with Justice Winchester on the Court, the administration would have a friend and ally to return the country to Republican conservative values and promote the Cochran agenda.

Four hours earlier that afternoon Bessie Collins was carefully laying her towel wrapped pecan pie on the moving conveyor belt at the security check point leading into the U.S. Appellate Court Building in New Orleans. After passing through security she took an elevator up to the floor where the Chief Justice's office resided. Waiting at the open door was Chief Justice Winchester with a big smile spreading across his lips.

"Bessie, what a lovely surprise!" Stanford Winchester shouted as his friend approached. He took the still slightly warm pie from Bessie, carefully placed it on a desk top, and threw his arms around Bessie and squeezed tightly.

"I'll tell you right now, Bessie, and God will strike me down if I'm lyin', when I picked up the phone and the security guard from downstairs told me that you were here to see me and that you was carrying a pie, my mouth started to water something fierce. It was like the Mississippi River in my mouth bust forth over my dam lips!" Stanford chortled as he simulated wiping drool from the corners of his mouth with a handkerchief.

"How you go on, Chief Justice Winchester!" Bessie heartily laughed in return.

"Bessie, we've been friends for over fifteen years, would you please call me Stanford?" the Chief Justice beseeched.

"In my house or in your house or out on the street, it's my pleasure to call you by your Christian name. But, in this here Federal building where you reside over a powerful court, no, sir, I'm sorry I can't do it. Lucius would take a switch to me if he knew I called you by your Christian name in this fine building. He just wouldn't consider it proper, and neither do I. So respectfully, sir, in between these here walls, you are Chief Justice Winchester," Bessie firmly but politely stated.

"Well, I am too much of a gentleman to argue with a lady. But all I need say is that you and your husband are two of the most stubborn people I've ever met in my life. I could hear Lucius' voice as you were saying those words. That being said, I am honored to have two such lovely people in my life that would accord that kind of dignity and respect to an old broken-down sinner like myself," Justice Winchester said with whole-hearted sincerity as he took hold of Bessie's hands.

"Do you have a minute, can you stay?" Justice Winchester requested.

"Well, I surely don't want to get in the way. You got important work to do," Bessie stated with slight apprehension.

"I'm done with court cases for the day. I've got an administrative meeting at 3 p.m. and a call with a fella in Washington at 5 p.m. Other than that, my time is my own, and I'd love it if you'd come sit for a spell with me in my office," Justice Winchester stated.

"Well, if it's alright," Bessie hesitantly offered.

"It is indeed! Naomi," Justice Winchester beckoned to his secretary as he quickly snatched the pie from the desk top, "Would you be so kind as to round up a pie server, a couple of plates and forks, and brew a fresh pot of tea for Mrs. Collins and myself?"

"Why of course, Chief Justice Winchester, I'll do that presently," Naomi replied.

"Mmmmm, that is one fine pie!" Justice Winchester declared after forking a large portion of pecan pie into his open month. "I surely don't have to die to go to heaven, it's sitting right here on this plate," he moaned in appreciation.

"It makes my heart jump to know that you appreciate my pies," Bessie blushed in return.

"Bessie, you know I'm preaching gospel when I tell you that I've eaten at every fine eatery in this whole city. And no medal-winning, Food-Channel-celebrity chef, and I know a lot of them, can hold a candle to your pecan pie. God can't strike me down when I'm just telling the honest truth," Justice Winchester recited like a Sunday preacher with his hand held up to the heavens.

Bessie just smiled and blushed. "LeeAnn, God rest her soul, always told me that you could go on and on about how you enjoyed food," she stated.

"That's right," Justice Winchester agreed. "I loved to eat and LeeAnn loved to dance. We were a perfect match. We'd go out for a fine dinner and then go dance off the butter and fat. It's what kept us from becoming a couple of roly-polies, I reckon."

"But enough about me, how's your family, Bessie?" Justice Winchester inquired.

"Well, Lucius is fine. I know that you saw him at Arnaud's last Wednesday as usual. My mama and her sister, my Auntie Rita, are planning on taking a trip back to Haiti in a couple of weeks. They haven't been back to their homeland since they fled Haiti and came to New Orleans just over fifty years ago. My brother Cecil is doing well. He's still living in Baton Rouge and working in a fine restaurant," Bessie stated.

"How old is mama now?" Justice Winchester asked.

"She's about to turn seventy. She was nineteen when she fled Haiti with my Auntie Rita. If they had not left they would have been killed by the government like their brother was. A year later, she met and married my father here in New Orleans. Two years later she gave birth to my brother Cecil, and a year later, I come," Bessie proudly recited.

"Well, you make sure that you give her my best, would you please?" Justice Winchester requested.

"Of course, I will, sir," Bessie replied with a smile. "She can't believe that I have a friend who is such an important and powerful person in the government."

"You must be talking about another friend then," Justice Winchester responded with a hearty laugh.

"I'm sorry to interrupt, but it's almost time for your 3 p.m. administrative meeting," Justice Winchester's secretary Naomi stated as she stood in the doorway of the Justice's open office.

"Bessie, unfortunately duty calls. I can't tell you what a lovely surprise your visit and this delicious pie have been," Justice Winchester said as he reached out his arms to embrace his friend. "It truly means so very much to me."

Bessie politely nodded in return and walked down the Federal building corridor. Stanford Winchester looked down at the pecan pie sitting on his office desk, now missing a couple of slices, as a few tears welled up in the corner of his eyes.

THE FIRST LADY PUSHED THE SEATING arrangement plan across her office desk towards her social secretary, Antoinette.

"I've got no idea where to seat Posy Whitaker," she mumbled in frustration.

"How about next to the wife of the French ambassador?" Antoinette questioned.

"We don't need that illiterate blonde bimbo telling the French ambassador's wife that she likes to dip her 'freedom fries' into catsup," the First Lady scoffed. Then quickly added, "I never used the term 'illiterate bimbo' in reference to Mrs. Whitaker, understood?"

"Yes, ma'am," Antoinette replied with a sly smile.

"The President has requested that we occasionally include Mrs. Whitaker in a few White House social events so that is precisely what we shall do. The only question is where she should be seated to minimize any awkward or uncomfortable situations. Are there any broom closets on this floor plan?," The First Lady cattily inquired.

"There's actually a serving closet behind this movable wall panel," Antoinette responded with a wink of an eye pointing to a section of wall in the White House Mess.

"Looks perfect to me!" The First Lady stated with a laugh. "Alright, that's enough fun. Let's get serious here, Toni. There's got be somewhere we can seat her without too much fear of a cataclysmic social faux pas?"

"How about here?" Toni replied, pointing to a table mostly reserved for a number of Fox News morning celebrities.

"That is wicked but I love it! Offensive drivel loves company," the First Lady gleefully pronounced.

AT PRECISELY 4:59 P.M. ON TUESDAY afternoon, Justice Winchester's cell phone rang while he attempted to fish his phone from his trousers' pocket.

"Justice Winchester, this is White House Chief of Staff Nathan Whitaker calling, how are you, sir?"

"I'm fine, Nathan, thank you for asking," the Justice replied. "I guess you're calling to find out if I will allow the President to name me as one of his three nominees for the Supreme Court vacancy, ain't that right?"

"Yes, sir, that is precisely why I am calling," Nathan affirmed.

"Seems like the press has already decided I'm in the running," Justice Winchester replied with a chortle.

"Yes, sir, you know how the media is today with everyone racing to get the scoop before the other one. Lots of speculation and guessing on their part. And they no longer seem to be in the business of reporting confirmed facts," Nathan sighed in response.

"Well, Nathan, I've been giving your question a lot of deep thought over the last seventy-two hours. This is not an easy decision for me. I know that most of my colleagues would pounce at the opportunity to be considered for the Supreme Court. If you've devoted your life to the law, like I have, there is no greater honor than to serve on the highest court in the land. And, I am humbled and honored that the President of the United States would even consider me for that prestigious position. But on the other hand, my life is so deeply rooted here in New Orleans, my heart sinks at the thought of leaving this amazing city," Stanford Winchester slowly stated as he stared at the partially eaten pecan pie that still sat on the corner of his desk.

"Sir, if I may," Nathan interrupted. "I understand the tremendous sacrifice that we are asking you to make if you are chosen and confirmed to sit on the Supreme Court. However, sir, after eight years of the previous administration allowing our country to retreat into the background of history, to be economically surpassed by China and Europe. For this great land to no longer have the moral integrity and righteous resolve to lead the world like we once did, the Cochran administration is ready to stem the tide of American decay and once again lead the world. We need men, like yourself, on the Supreme Court to fight for the Constitution and to restore our core values and principles."

"Yes, thank you, Nathan, that was quite eloquent," Justice Winchester stated. He cleared his throat and continued, "When I was nominated and appointed to the Fifth Circuit Appellate Court, my beloved wife, LeeAnn, was the happiest I had ever seen her in our thirty-nine years of marriage. At that time, she told me that the only thing that would make her prouder of me was for me to serve on the U.S. Supreme Court. Since she passed five years ago, I have devoted the few years I have left in this world, to the goal of making myself the very best man I can be. I do this in loving memory of my wife LeeAnn. So, to further that goal and to push LeeAnn's dream for me a tad closer to fruition, would you please be so kind as to inform President Cochran that, as unworthy as this simple Southern jurist is, I am honored to have my name considered for this esteemed position on the greatest court in the world."

A few moments later, the telephone call with Nathan Whitaker concluded. Justice Winchester reached over to Bessie's pie and used his index finger to scoop a smidgen of the pecan pie filling into his mouth. He let the sweet buttery flavor fill his mouth as his lips creased into a satisfied smile.

CHAPTER 10

Aaron Rose looked at the official White House press release, and his mind had not changed. He was still convinced that the Cochran administration would inevitably choose Carl Remington to be their nominee for the Supreme Court.

"Aaron, let's button down our research on all three nominees," Senator Douglas stated as he walked down the corridor of the Senate office building with his aide. "All of the nominees have extensive judicial records. None of them are remotely moderate in their political views. Though Brumfield has shown the most compassion and has been the most willing to compromise with his fellow Justices on the Eighth Circuit, don't you agree?"

"Yes, sir, that's probably right," Aaron agreed. "We'll be fully prepared when the administration makes its announcement of their nominee."

Nathan Whitaker sat in the Oval Office, shuffling through papers contained in a manila file folder. "It's right here," he stated, as he handed a sheet of paper to the President.

"What precisely is this?" The President asked his Chief of Staff as he glanced at the sheet of paper.

"It is scoring for the three nominees on how they have ruled on the bench on the issues that we hold most dearly," Nathan quickly replied.

"Nathan, you know that I don't cotton to all this bar graph, pie chart mumbo jumbo. Just tell me the bottom line, please," the President requested.

"On protecting Second Amendment rights, pro-life issues, State's rights, and protecting religious freedom, Justice Winchester ranks the highest of the three nominees," Nathan emphatically stated. "He has been a consistent advocate for those four core issues in his rulings throughout his time on both the State and Federal court bench."

"He is the one person on our list of nominees that I know the least personally," Andrew Cochran stated.

"He comes from a very prominent New Orleans family and is very well-respected. Additionally, one of his family friends was one of the largest Louisiana contributors to our Presidential campaign, Jim Bob McCallum," Nathan added.

"Nathan, we are not choosing a nominee for the Supreme Court based on the whims and connections of political contributors," President Cochran countered.

"Of course not, sir," Nathan responded. "I was only pointing out that in addition to his outstanding judicial record, and his genuine philosophical alignment with our core views, that Justice Winchester is also well-connected to some of the most prominent supporters of our Presidential campaign."

"I'm sure that Justice Winchester would prove to be an excellent nominee for the Court, but you well know, my preference was Artemis Asburger," President Cochran stated with a perturbed tone to his voice. "I do understand that I allowed you and the Republican Senate minority leaders to talk me out of my first choice. What I don't understand, Nathan, is why you are so strenuously pushing for Winchester?"

"Because I believe that he would be the very best choice for the Supreme Court, sir. Nothing more, nothing less," Nathan stated.

"And, we're sure that there is nothing in his past that would cause us embarrassment or question his fitness to be a member of the Court during the Senate confirmation hearings? His judicial and personal history are without reproach?" President Cochran inquired.

"Absolutely," Nathan confidently asserted.

"We don't need another Clarence Thomas-like spectacle in the first one hundred days of my administration, Nathan," the President warned.

"Trust me, sir, that will not be an issue with Stanford Winchester," Nathan assured the President.

"Well, let's get the Chief Judge up here to meet with us face to face. The nomination and confirmation of the new Supreme Court Justice will be the first major accomplishment of this administration. I want to look into the eyes of the person I plan to nominate. In the meantime, the Democrats and the press can chew on the three names we fed them and work themselves up into a lather," the President stated with a short chuckle and a smirk.

SUPREME COURT JUSTICE ALLEN SALLIS called out to his law clerk, Kate Wilson. "Kate, can you come in here for a moment, please?"

"Yes, sir," Kate replied, as she scurried to grab a legal pad and a pen.

"Kate, you've got your finger on the pulse of things around here, what are you hearing about the administration's predilections about who they will tap to fill the vacancy on the Court?" Justice Sallis inquired.

"I'm not sure, sir, I really haven't heard much since the White House press release naming the top three nominees," Kate responded.

"You're very well-connected with the White House, surely you've heard something?" Justice Sallis pressed with a sly grin.

"Truly, sir, I'm not aware of the administration's front runner," Kate stated.

"Well, I'm just concerned that we will get some squish who may have conservative credentials but lacks the backbone and guts to make the hard decisions. Much like our current Supreme Court Chief Justice who lacks the intestinal fortitude to stand by and wholly protect conservative doctrine," Justice Sallis pronounced. "This Court needs a man of conviction such as Artemis Asburger. But our new President clearly lacks the resolve and temperament to make the right choice. They didn't even include Asburger on the short list. Why they haven't placed a call to me to seek my advice is shocking, insulting, and beyond the pale," Justice Sallis railed.

"Yes, sir," Kate politely replied.

"Kate, see what information you can garner from your close relationship with the White House. If need be, I want to intervene to make sure that we get a new Justice that I . . . I mean we, can work with to protect against the constant leftist onslaught on our freedoms and Constitutional rights. I need a partner with resolve to continue the good fight," Justice Sallis stated emphatically to his law clerk.

"Yes, sir," Kate Wilson replied as she exited the Justice's office while scrolling down the contacts list on her iPhone.

ANDREW COCHRAN'S CELL PHONE RANG REPEATEDLY as he sat alone in the Oval Office. Very few people possessed his personal cell phone number. He was in no mood to be interrupted. He thought about his administration's agenda and strategy for their first one hundred days. He braced himself for the long political battles that lie ahead with a Democratic controlled Senate who were gearing up for a philosophical fight with the new President. Anything or anyone else could wait.

SENATOR DOUGLAS LEANED BACK IN HIS CHAIR as he reviewed the files on each of the administration's three nominees for the vacancy on the Supreme Court. He was not as certain as his aide Aaron, that the choice of President Cochran would be Carl Remington. Remington, he thought, lacked the conservative bonafides that the administration would require to push forward a far right wing agenda on the Court. He gave the new President credit for steering away from naming a firebrand like Artemis Asburger. A fight the administration could not win. Not as long as Senator Douglas chaired the Senate Judiciary Committee.

The Senator continued to flip through the dossier that Aaron had compiled on Justice Winchester. Yes, there were the questionable decisions that Stanford Winchester had made not to recuse himself from a couple of cases where his personal connections were at play. But those indiscretions did not disqualify him when he was appointed to the Fifth Circuit. Why would they now? His judicial record was very conservative but not reaching the point of being completely reactionary. His name appearing on the administration's short list was a bit of a mystery. Senator Douglas wanted to know more about Justice Winchester's personal life. He scratched out a few notes that he would discuss with Aaron in the morning. Soon the battle would ensue, and Perry Douglas knew he needed more ammunition.

CHAPTER 11

ANTOINETTE GREEN, THE FIRST LADY'S social secretary, briskly walked towards the office of the First Lady.

"Ma'am, I'm sorry to interrupt but I have an urgent request from the office of the Chief of Staff regarding Friday's White House luncheon," Antoinette stated to Sue Lynn Cochran.

"Oh for land sake alive, Toni, please don't tell me that this has anything to do with where Posy Whitaker is being seated?" The First Lady questioned with a heavy sigh.

"No, ma'am, it has nothing to do with seating for Posy Whitaker," Toni reassured her boss. "The Chief of Staff has requested that we add another guest to the list of luncheon attendees."

"Don't tell me that Nathan wants me to add a friend of Posy's to the list?" The First Lady harshly stated.

"No, ma'am, the Chief of Staff has requested that we add Mabel McCallum to the list," Toni quickly replied.

"And who, pray tell, is Mabel McCallum?" The First Lady queried.

"I was told that she is the wife of Jim Bob McCallum who was a large contributor from Louisiana to the President's election campaign. Apparently, he and his wife are visiting Washington this week, and the Chief of Staff would like us to extend an invitation to Mrs. McCallum for the White House luncheon on Friday," Toni responded.

"Doesn't Nathan know that these luncheons are planned for weeks and are not just some potluck dinner we throw together at the last minute for the wives of contributors to my husband's campaign?" The First

Lady asked with an irritated verve.

Toni chose not to respond. She had been the social secretary and assistant to Mrs. Cochran for years when she was the First Lady of Georgia. She moved to Washington with the Cochran's after the Governor won the election. She knew better than to confront the First Lady when she was in a mood. She was well aware that one of her primary roles was to be the buffer between Sue Lynn Cochran and the Chief of Staff, Nathan Whitaker. Silence was the winning position, and Toni Green knew it all too well.

After several uncomfortable moments of absolute quiet, the First Lady finally relented.

"Fine! You can seat her with the Fox News morning personalities and Posy Whitaker," the First Lady pronounced. "Let her deal with the brainless prattle and the never-ending Posy Whitaker boob job stories!"

STANFORD WINCHESTER SAT ON A BENCH outside of the sliding entrance doors of the United Airlines ticket counters at Louis Armstrong New Orleans International Airport. He let the afternoon sun bathe his face. It had been a couple of years since he travelled to Washington, D.C. It was late February and Stanford was bracing himself for the wintry conditions and low temperatures of the nation's capital. Justice Winchester had passed up an opportunity to fly to Washington on Jim Bob McCallum's private jet. Coincidently, the McCallums were heading to Washington the very same week he had been asked by the President to come to Washington for a face-to-face meeting to discuss the nomination of the next Supreme Court Justice.

Stanford Winchester met Jim Bob McCallum when he was courting his wife to be, LeeAnn, just after graduating from college. Jim Bob McCallum was an old friend of LeeAnn's. They had dated for a short time when they were in high school together in New Orleans. Jim Bob was a close and supportive friend of LeeAnn's since their teenage years up until her death. Stanford always appreciated the gestures of kindness that Jim Bob and Mabel McCallum extended to his wife. However, he was always a bit tentative about accepting favors from Jim Bob and Mabel after LeeAnn's passing. So, he opted to fly to Washington on a commercial airline instead of accepting Jim Bob's offer to accompany the McCallums on their private jet.

Jim Bob McCallum made his money in the consumer products industry. His Lake Pontchartrain Brands had become an internationally famous food and consumer goods conglomerate. Some of his business practices were occasionally called into question by a prying press, but his reputation as a powerful and influential Louisiana king-maker was never in question. If you were a successful conservative politician in Louisiana, chances were that you had the financial and political support of the McCallum family. Ambitious men with access to political power could always find a chair at Jim Bob McCallum's table.

CLAY GROVER SAT IN THE SHADOWS of a corner of the cocktail lounge at Cobalt bar in Washington, D.C.'s DuPont Circle neighborhood. His Washington Nationals baseball cap was pulled down low over his forehead obscuring a good portion of his attractive face. He slowly sipped his vodka and soda as he patiently waited for his friend.

As Chief of Staff for one of the eldest and most esteemed Democratic Senators in Washington, Clay knew that he needed to be discreet. He had learned long ago the lesson that the lions-share of political power laid in perception not necessarily in practice. If people perceived a flaw or weakness in one's character, even if it was wholly unsubstantiated by facts, it could sink a political career faster than an iceberg could rip through the hull of the Titanic. Clay was always careful to keep his personal life private. He sheltered himself, the best he could, from controversy and prurient innuendo. Yet, he was human with needs and desires like anyone else. So, he constantly kept vigil over the balancing tightrope between private needs and public perception. It was a tiresome routine after several years in D.C. politics. He often tried to convince himself that he could leave Washington and live a more open life with the freedom to fully be who he was. But his ambition and the intoxication of power had its own dark allure. Living in the shadows had become an acceptable penalty for participating in the game of power politics played at the highest level.

Clay took another sip of his cocktail. A solitary figure approached his darkened corner of the lounge. They exchanged quick glances and smiles. "Hello, gorgeous," Clay huskily said as his hand traced down the muscled torso of his friend's body.

A FEW SHORT BLOCKS AWAY FROM THE COBALT BAR, Kate Wilson sat patiently in the darkened room at the Ritz Carlton Hotel in DuPont Circle. She sipped her glass of chardonnay as she waited. She spent a good deal of time waiting. Her time was inconsequential when balanced against the schedule of a member of Washington's power elite. But she had a job to do. Her boss required information, and she would do whatever she needed to do to obtain it. It was not a distasteful task, far from it. Just part of the game, she tried to convince herself. Unfettered ambition provides one with many excuses.

Stanford Winchester sat in a window seat of the first class section of the airplane. He enjoyed gazing out of the window as the plane circled New Orleans on its way northeast to Washington, D.C. He slowly sipped at the bourbon in his glass. It was a far cry from the Sazeracs he enjoyed every Wednesday at Arnaud's, but it would have to do.

The city of New Orleans rose up from the swamp lands and the shores of Lake Pontchartrain as the plane began its ascent. He recalled being on a similar flight to Washington just a few days after Hurricane Katrina engulfed his beloved city, as its people, his people, were literally drowning. Then, he was part of a delegation of prominent New Orleans citizens and politicians on their way to Washington to beseech the President and Congress for immediate assistance to save and then rebuild the city. Like many, he could not sit still while his city suffered and the President's administration moved glacially in providing the required assistance. He never felt more ashamed of his party than he did during the days and weeks post-Katrina.

But now, he was on his way to meet a new Republican President, and to potentially be offered a seat on the Supreme Court of the United States. A far different agenda for a well-respected Southern jurist. The more he drank, the better the bourbon tasted.

"What about this one, Nathan?" Posy Whitaker asked her husband as she held a shimmering silver ball gown up under her chin.

"Darlin', it's an afternoon luncheon not a beauty pageant," Nathan Whitaker dismissively said to his wife.

"Well, then I don't know what I'm gonna wear," Posy stated with exasperation.

"Just a simple black dress would probably be fine," Nathan replied while checking the text messages on his smart phone.

"You mean the black cocktail dress you ripped off me when we got back from one of the inauguration parties?" Posy reminded her husband.

"Yeah, I do remember that evening. I still have your bite marks on my ass from that night," Nathan said with a satisfied grin. "Just go buy another dress for the luncheon," Nathan said. "Go tonight to one of those Georgetown boutiques you're always talking about. It's going to be a late night for me anyway. Enjoy yourself, and don't bother waiting up, I'm not sure when I'll be home."

"Well, if you're going to make me a work widow for yet another night, I'm getting me something real expensive," Posy threatened with a chortle.

"Not too expensive," Nathan warned. "Come Friday night after that luncheon I might be tearing that dress off you again."

"I'm gonna hold you to that promise, Nathan, you best believe it," Posy said as she seductively sauntered over to where Nathan was standing and firmly grasped her husband's crotch through the fabric of his well-tailored suit pants.

CHAPTER 12

"Momma, you're only going to Haiti for ten days not six months," Bessie Collins chided her mother Sandra, as she looked at the two over-stuffed suitcases laid open on her mother's bed.

"Hush now, Bessie, you never know when you may need something," Sandra replied. "Haiti is not like New Orleans, there are not shops on every corner to buy things you might need."

"And besides, why are you packed already, you don't leave for another week?" Bessie countered.

"Things come and go, why wait when I have time to do this now," Sandra replied in her lilting French Creole accent. "I might be too busy in a week to take the proper care to pack what I will need. I promised your Auntie Rita that I would help her close down her shop before we leave."

"Speaking of Auntie Rita, how is she?" Bessie inquired of her mother.

"Girl, you have two good legs to walk on, why don't you go see for yourself how she is?" Sandra responded with a vexed tone to her voice. "She's on Rampart, you are not far from her every day. She is your kin, yet you don't have time to go see her. I do not understand this. My sister is seventy-seven years old, how much longer do you think God will keep her with us. Yet, you are too busy to pay her a visit?"

Bessie bowed her head and blushed heavily. "Mama, you are right. I'm ashamed. I promise to go see Auntie Rita tomorrow afternoon," Bessie replied.

"Make no promises to me, Bessie. Do what your heart tells you is right. Just remember, you only have one family and you never know when the Lord will call for any one of us." Sandra brushed her daughter's cheek with the palm of her hand and returned to her packing.

KATE WILSON FINISHED BUTTONING HER BLOUSE as she strode through the kitchen of the Ritz Carlton Hotel. A satisfied grin creased her lipstick red lips as she climbed into the backseat of the waiting limousine. She had gotten precisely what she came for. Kate prided herself on always getting exactly what she wanted from men.

STANFORD WINCHESTER STRAIGHTENED HIS BOW TIE as he stared at his reflection in the hotel bathroom mirror. If LeeAnn were still alive she would be doing this for him, and telling him to "go charm the pants off the new President." After all, he was in Washington for both of them. To attempt to fulfill her dream for him, and of course to bolster his own ego and ambition. His hesitation about leaving New Orleans was beginning to fade away as the prospect of being the potential nominee for the Supreme Court came closer to fruition. As he fidgeted with his tie, his cell phone proclaimed that the "Saints were marching in."

CLAY GROVER ATTEMPTED TO PARSE OUT which clothes were not his by studying the pile of intermingled clothing on the floor at the base of his bed. Jeans, shirts, socks, sneakers, and boxer shorts had quickly been discarded into a heap several hours earlier. The task at hand was to sort through the clothes, so that his companion could dress and leave and Clay could get to work. He was already late, and the hand slowly roaming down his naked torso towards his crotch was not wearing a watch and seemingly had little interest in Clay's ability to get to Capitol Hill any time soon.

NATHAN WHITAKER BROADLY SMILED and extended his right hand. "Justice Winchester, welcome to the White House," he cheerfully greeted Stanford Winchester. "Thank you, Nathan, it's a pleasure to meet you in person," Stanford replied while heartily shaking the Chief of Staff's hand.

"This way, sir, the President is waiting to see you," Nathan replied as he guided the Justice down the corridor.

"Justice Winchester, thank you so much for coming to Washington, it is an honor to meet you," President Cochran greeted Stanford Winchester, as he extended his hand.

"I am moved and humbled to be in the White House and shaking hands with the President of the United States," Justice Winchester replied in his deep Southern accent.

"Please have a seat," the President said motioning towards the couch. "Can I get you something to drink?"

"Tea with honey would be wonderful if it's not too much bother," Stanford Winchester responded. "I'm still trying to acclimate my body to these wintry conditions in Washington."

"I've spent most of my life in Georgia, these temperatures chill me to bone," the President stated with a knowing grin.

Moments later, the President's secretary, Nancy, appeared with a tea service and began pouring cups of tea for the President and Justice Winchester.

"My late wife LeeAnn would never have believed that I would one day be sipping tea with the President of the United States while sitting in the Oval Office," Justice Winchester proudly declared. "I am moved beyond words that you personally invited me to meet with you at the White House."

"Well, I certainly wanted to meet face-to-face with the person who I very well might nominate to be the next member of the United States Supreme Court," the President forthrightly stated.

The President and Justice Winchester talked for over an hour in the Oval Office. They exchanged their personal histories, life philosophies, and discussed Republican Party political dogma and how distorted it had become in the new millennium. The two men shook hands and exchanged pleasantries as Justice Winchester exited the White House. Stanford Winchester came away from the meeting impressed by the forthright, yet friendly manner of the new President. He understood why the American people had taken to his folksy wit and Southern charm. But Stanford was also well aware of his own persuasive ways. He strode out of the White House with the confidence of a man who had just staked his claim to his pie-sized piece of American history.

LATER THAT AFTERNOON, NATHAN WHITAKER WAS waiting for his luncheon companion to arrive at Bourbon Steak restaurant in the Four Seasons Hotel. As Chief of Staff to the President of the United States, Nathan was not accustomed to waiting for anyone other than the President. He fidgeted in his chair as he scanned his text messages and emails on his smartphone. Fifteen minutes seemed like an eternity for a man who wholly believed that he was on a mission to transform American domestic and foreign policies while working at the right hand of the President.

"There you are, you old coon hound," a gruff and distinctly Southern voice greeted Nathan with a hearty slap on the top of his back right shoulder. Nathan began to raise up from his chair to greet his companion.

"Sit down, Nathan, I ain't the President, you don't gotta spring up like some cranked up jack-in-the-box for the likes of me," Nathan's companion stated with a wild cackle. "I've only got a few minutes, I'm taking my wife out to lunch."

"I assumed that we would be having lunch together," Nathan stated with a hint of pique in his voice.

"Sorry, ol' boy, the missus comes first, but feel free to have lunch on me, just charge it to my room, here's my number," Nathan's companion offered. "I just wanted to look in your eye and have you tell me that our arrangement is a done deal," the gruff voiced person stated with conviction.

"Yes, I'm certain that you will have the outcome you seek," Nathan quietly stated as his eyes quickly scanned the other guests who were seated nearby in the dining room of the steakhouse.

"Excellent, Nathan, excellent. That's what I came here to hear you say. We're going to do wonderful things together, Nathan. You're a man with ambition and I'm a man of means who can help men with ambition. Now, if you'll excuse me, I've been taught to never keep a Southern woman waiting. Please enjoy your lunch and order their best steak and best bottle of bourbon on me, Nathan. We'll be in touch soon," Nathan's companion stated as he sauntered away from the table. Suddenly, Nathan had lost his appetite.

KATE WILSON WAITED FOR JUSTICE SALLIS to return from lunch. He motioned to her as he passed her on his way to his office.

"Are you waiting for me, Kate?" Justice Sallis asked his law clerk.

"Yes, sir, I have the information that you requested the other day," Kate responded.

"Go on," Justice Sallis coaxed, as he removed his overcoat.

"The Cochran nominee for the vacant seat on the Supreme Court is going to be Stanford Winchester," Kate Wilson hurriedly stated.

"Are you sure about this, Kate? Does this come directly from the White House?" Justice Sallis quizzed his clerk.

"Yes, sir, it's a done deal," Kate emphatically responded.

"Interesting," Justice Sallis replied as he sat in his large leather chair. "Winchester is no Artemis Asburger, but he's a good conservative who's not afraid of a fight. And he's got that Southern charm where he can be swiftly imbedding a stiletto knife deep between your shoulder blades with his left hand while shaking your right hand and giving you that big Cheshire cat smile as you bleed out. There's something to work with there," Justice Sallis stated with a satisfied grin. You're absolutely sure it's Winchester?" He questioned his clerk once again.

"Absolutely," Kate Wilson confidently replied.

BESSIE COLLINS PUSHED OPEN THE OLD CREAKY DOOR to the shop on north Rampart Street. The small bell attached to the entry way announced her arrival.

"Auntie Rita, are you here?" Bessie called out.

"Ya, Bessie, come to the back, my love," Auntie Rita beckoned to her niece.

Bessie went to the back of the old shop and pushed aside the beaded curtain to find her aunt carefully making a small structure out of dried chicken bones and hemp twine. Bessie approached her aunt and gave her a kiss on the cheek so as not to disturb her actions.

"Let me finish here, Bessie, and I will give you a proper hug," Auntie Rita said while smiling broadly at her niece.

"I've watched you build these here structures for years and I've never been sure exactly what they are for?" Bessie questioned as she watched her aunt carefully interweave the bones and the hemp twine.

"They can be for many things," Auntie Rita began. "Sometimes the chicken bones can be used to ward off evil spirits. Sometimes the bones of a sacrificed chicken can be read like stones or tea leaves are read to tell a person's fortune. Chicken bones can be sprinkled across a doorway to conjure a curse or prevent a curse. And sometimes, chicken bones are used as Black JuJu to summon evil spirits. Back in Haiti, chicken bones were commonly used for many things."

"And what about the structure that you are working on now?" Bessie asked her aunt.

"No worries for that, sweet head," Auntie Rita said as she stopped her work to place both of her arms around Bessie and gave her a long tight squeeze. Bessie squeezed back hard.

"Mama is already packed for your trip back to Haiti and it's still a week away," Bessie proclaimed.

"My sister does not know how to live for the moment. Everything must be planned and planned. She has always been that way, even when we were small children in Haiti. I love her and her ways, but if you do not enjoy today, why bother worrying about tomorrow?" Auntie Rita asked as she resumed her work with the bones and hemp twine.

"Why do you use the twine to connect the bones together?" Bessie questioned as she watched her aunt painstakingly interweave the twine and bones.

"We are all woven together, my dear. Each of us is part of the other, and nature, through the hemp, holds us all in place. If one piece is not steady the whole structure of things falls apart," Auntie Rita explained.

The bell on the front door way rang as a customer entered the shop. Rita walked out from behind the beaded curtain. "Can I help you?" She asked the stranger.

"Hello, yes, uh, I was sent by a friend who said that Queen Rita gives the best readings in all of New Orleans," the customer stammered in response. "Is Queen Rita available for a reading?"

"Yes, if you come seeking the truth, Queen Rita can provide for your needs."

Rita turned to her niece and placed her hand on her cheek and gave her a wink. "Time to get back to work for the both of us," she quietly said.

CHAPTER 13

It was spring in Washington, D.C. as Sue Lynn Cochran glanced around the well decorated White House Mess just a few hours before her initial luncheon as the First Lady of the United States.

"I love the intermixing of Azaleas and Cherokee Roses with a sprig of Dogwood in the table settings," the First Lady effused to her social secretary.

"We wanted to make sure that we incorporated all three of the state flowers of Georgia in the table settings for your first luncheon, ma'am," Toni Green replied with a modicum of pride.

"Just beautiful, Toni, you're the best. I don't know what I'd do if you hadn't agreed to come to the White House with us," the First Lady responded. "And we've successfully segregated the Fox News people and Posy Whitaker from anyone with more gentile sensibilities, who might be offended by their crass comments?"

"Yes, ma'am, their table is in the back of the room, far away from the ambassador's wives, and the clergy," Toni replied with a vigorous nod of the head.

"Good. Let's try to keep the intermingling to a minimum, shall we?"

"Nathan, help me with this clasp," Posy Whitaker called out to her husband.

"Posy, I'm already late, I should have been at the White House an hour ago," Nathan Whitaker protested to his wife.

"I don't recall you complaining about being late when I had your cock in my mouth less than an hour ago," Posy retorted. "Just help me with the clasp on this pearl necklace, and you can go to your precious job."

"Should you even be wearing a full string of pearls to an afternoon luncheon?" Nathan asked with an exasperated tenor to his voice.

"Since when are you a fashion consultant? Ain't you just supposed to save the free world, like you're always tellin' me?" Posy challenged back.

"Pearls are perfectly fine with a black cocktail dress. Heck fire, Nathan, I already took off the gold ankle bracelet you told me to remove," Posy stated. "A girls gotta have some bling to show off. You don't want all them uppity Washington women to think that you don't take care of your wife, do you?"

"I'm pretty sure that's not gonna be a problem, darlin'. They'll just be staring at how you're the most beautiful woman in the room," Nathan complimented his wife. "There the clasp is clasped," Nathan announced. "Now, I've got to run. Have a nice time, and try not to be late. You know how precise Sue Lynn Cochran can be," Nathan reminded Posy.

"Yeah, I know what a bossy bitch she is!" Posy exclaimed in response.

"Behave yourself. Just a couple of glasses of wine, at the most," Nathan interjected as he walked towards the door.

"We'll see," Posy mumbled to herself with a grin.

AARON ROSE STOPPED AT STARBUCK'S on his way to work to pick up a large coffee for his boss and one for himself. His cell phone vibrated in his pants pocket as he attempted to juggle the two large coffees in one hand and fish his phone out of his pocket with his other hand. Aaron smiled as he read the text message from Clay Grover.

"Miss you madly. Can you meet me for drinks after work tonight?"

Aaron using only his right thumb to navigate his phone keypad replied, "Sure. Meet you at JR's at 8:30."

An added bounce in his step accompanied Aaron on his way up Capitol Hill.

STANFORD WINCHESTER PACKED HIS SMALL SUITCASE in the bedroom of his hotel suite. After a good meal and an excellent bottle of bourbon, he had slept well after his meeting with President Cochran. His doubts about leaving his home in New Orleans, and his initial indifference about the Supreme Court vacancy had now given way to a full throttled pursuit of the position. He felt that he had developed a friendly and open rapport with the President during his one hour meeting. He had answered the President's inquiries with a good portion of the truth, spiced with just a hint of Southern political mendacity. Stanford was pleased with his performance. As he would often expound from the bench, "Counselor, black and white are only variations in a gray world. You are not arguing the facts but rather your variations of the facts." Stanford Winchester may not have fully informed the President of all of the facts but rather his variation of the facts. After all, it was a gray world for Stanford Winchester. The only thing to do now, was to head back home to New Orleans and wait for the President's call.

"Mr. President, please excuse my tardiness, there was a small emergency at home," Nathan Whitaker lied to his friend.

"Oh no, is something wrong with Posy? Is she alright?" The President asked with concern.

"It's Posy's grandmother, she had a stroke. So, we spent a good portion of the morning attempting to coordinate things with her mother in Savannah by phone. The doctors are hopeful of a full recovery," Nathan fabricated.

"Well, please give Posy my best and tell her that I'll say a prayer for her grandmother tonight before I go to bed," Andrew Cochran offered.

"Thank you, sir. I will surely pass that on to Posy, who will be so grateful for your kind words and prayers," Nathan responded.

"I've got to tell you, Nathan, I was very impressed with Stanford Winchester yesterday. I'm beginning to see why you are such a staunch advocate for Winchester being nominated for the vacancy on the Court."

"Yes, sir, Justice Winchester is guided by his faith, his family, and his love of this country. Not to mention decades of meritorious judicial service on the Louisiana and Federal bench," Nathan energetically added.

"I've got an afternoon meeting with Brumfield today, and a morning meeting with Remington tomorrow. I hope to have a final decision on our nominee by Monday morning. Let the press run with the story all day long and into the week," the President explained.

"Yes, sir, that's an excellent strategy. We'll put the Democrats on their heels by rolling out an exemplar nominee and dominate the next few news cycles with praise for your thoughtful and outstanding choice of the man who will be the next Justice on the Supreme Court," Nathan stated effusively.

The guests arrived and began moving into their assigned seats in the White House Mess dining room. Posy Whitaker stood along a back wall and spied a well-known country music singer. She immediately made a beeline to his table, where a former Disney child film star was also seated. Steps away from where the country singer was seated, Posy was intercepted by Toni Green.

"Mrs. Whitaker, I believe your table is over there," Toni Green politely stated to Posy Whitaker while using her body to block Posy's access to the country singer.

"Yeah, I know where my table is, I just wanted to say 'hey' to Clint. I'm a big fan of his music," Posy explained as she attempted to maneuver past Toni Green.

"Ma'am, we're about to start the luncheon with a short prayer delivered by Reverend Billy Joe Tolliver, so we require that all of our guests be seated. Perhaps, there will be an opportunity to express your best wishes after the conclusion of the luncheon," Toni insisted.

Posy Whitaker begrudgingly went back to her assigned table. She continued to peer over at Clint's table as the Reverend requested that everyone bow their heads as he recited a prayer and a blessing.

The Reverend concluded his comments with, ". . . and may God bless our wonderful hostess, Sue Lynn Cochran, the First Lady of the United States and our beloved President, Andrew Cochran. Amen."

In a tenor well above a hushed "church voice," Posy Whitaker declared to the seven people seated at her table, "I'm only sayin' Amen, when they finally open them bottles of wine."

A slightly stunned Mabel McCallum, quietly uttered, "Oh my."

Posy turned her head in Mabel's direction, stared at Mabel for a few moments and blurted out, "Hey, I know you! I met you and your husband in Louisiana at a fundraiser for Andy's campaign for President last year."

"I'm sorry, I don't recall," Mabel McCallum politely but cautiously responded.

"Heck yeah, we sure did meet. Hi, I'm Posy Whitaker, my husband is Nathan Whitaker, Andy's Chief of Staff. We were seated at a table together at some campaign event in Baton Rouge. Remember now?" Posy questioned Mabel.

"I apologize, Mrs. Whitaker, my memory isn't what it used to be, I'm afraid," Mabel McCallum replied.

"Oh, come on now," Posy encouraged, "Nathan and your husband went off and had a lengthy conversation and left us two gals all alone, so we went to the bar and had us a few mint juleps together. We had a good ol' time."

"I'm sorry, I'm ashamed to admit that I simply don't recall," Mabel apologized again.

"Well, that's alright, I forget where I put my car keys just about every day," Posy said. "But, we're back together again now. We should see if they'll make us some juleps. Between you and me, I'd rather drink juleps for lunch than eat them dressed up little chickens they plan to serve us."

"I believe that they are serving roasted squab with banana leaf wrapped rice, ginger tofu, and grilled zucchini," Mabel politely corrected Posy.

"Whatever. It won't go down as smooth as a nice julep. Ain't that right, Mabel? It is Mabel, right?" Posy questioned.

"Yes, Mabel McCallum, Mrs. Whitaker," she replied.

"Hell, Mabel, Mrs. Whitaker is Nathan's mean as an old angry junkyard dog of a mama. Call me Posy. We're already friends, you just can't remember. But that's alright, I feel a whole lot better having you at my table," Posy excitedly stated.

Mabel McCallum nodded her head politely and provided an uncomfortable smile.

Posy Whitaker moved closer to Mabel McCallum at the table. She motioned with her head towards the woman sitting on the opposite side of their table and whispered to Mabel, "Ain't that the Fox News morning show girl? She's as dumb as the day is long, ain't she?"

Mabel McCallum sat in stunned disbelief, as Posy wildly motioned to a server to ask for a couple of mint juleps. Posy smiled broadly, content in her belief of a rekindled friendship.

CLAY GROVER STOOD IN THE CORNER at JR's Bar and Grill on 17th Street. His morose facial expression turned into a wide grin when he spotted Aaron Rose walking towards him.

"A little late but definitely worth the wait," Clay kiddingly chided Aaron, while giving him a big hug.

"Been that kind of a day, but I'm glad to be here now," Aaron replied with a smile. "I need a Grey Goose and soda," he quickly added.

"You got it, be right back," Clay responded as he turned on his heels and headed to the bar.

"Happy Friday, cheers!" Clay announced as he handed a cocktail to Aaron.

"I'll drink to that," Aaron replied with a smirk.

"So, I've got some news for you," Clay informed Aaron between sips of his drink. "You know Ben Carroll, right?" Clay queried.

"Yeah, he's a law clerk to Supreme Court Justice Susan Goldberg, right?"

"Bingo!" Clay exclaimed. "Nice guy, Ivy League-cute, great sense of humor, and a good progressive liberal just like his boss. I see him around every now and then. I ran into Ben last night and he told me about a conversation he overheard at the Court yesterday afternoon."

"OK, you've got my attention," Aaron stated.

Clay continued, "So, Ben said he was delivering a draft of an opinion written by Justice Goldberg to Justice Sallis' office, when he overheard Justice Sallis' law clerk, Kate Wilson, telling the Justice that she was absolutely sure that the Cochran administration was choosing Stanford Winchester as the nominee for the Supreme Court vacancy."

"No way, it's going to be Remington," Aaron protested. Are you sure?"

"Ben said that Justice Sallis asked her twice, and Kate told him that it was a done deal and that her source came directly from the White House," Clay explained.

"Well, I guess we'll find out in a couple of days. The administration won't sit on their decision for too long. They want to get their nominee confirmed and on the bench within their first one hundred days," Aaron surmised.

"Yep, you're probably right," Clay replied. "Interesting news though, isn't it?"

"Sure is, if it's true," Aaron confirmed before taking a large gulp of his cocktail.

"So, what do I get for sharing this information with you?" Clay coyly asked with a sparkle in his eyes.

"We'll see. We'll see . . ." Aaron responded with a wide smile after finishing his drink.

CHAPTER 14

"For Christ's sake Posy, I just walked in the door! Can you please give me a minute so that I can loosen my tie and pour myself a little bourbon before you tell me how much you despise the First Lady of the United States?" Nathan Whitaker implored his wife.

"She's never liked me, Nathan. Not from the first minute she met me. She looks down on me, she thinks I'm just a vulgar hillbilly," Posy Whitaker stated angrily.

"That's not true. Sue Lynn has done some lovely things for the both of us over the past twelve plus years," Nathan responded between gulps of bourbon.

"She put me in the god damn corner, Nathan!" Posy shrieked.

"No one puts Posy in the corner," Nathan replied in his best Patrick Swayze impersonation, in an attempt to lighten his wife's mood.

"It ain't funny, asshole! At every step that women tries to humiliate me!" Posy shouted.

Nathan had finished his first drink and quickly poured himself another three fingers of bourbon.

"Yes, dear, what did that horrible witch do to you?" Nathan sarcastically questioned.

"First off, Clint Conway was there. You know how much I love his music. So, I'm standing against the back wall of the dining room, with the biggest losers in the world, and I saw Clint a few tables away. The shindig ain't even started yet, so I tried to walk over to his table just to say 'hey' and tell him how much I love his music. As I get a few feet away, here comes one of Sue Lynn's bitches racing over to me to tell me to go sit my ass down. Nobody treats me like that Nathan!" Posy exclaimed.

"You could have just left, Posy, no one was forcing you to stay somewhere you felt you were being mistreated," Nathan attempted to rationalize.

"Well, the day was not a complete disaster. I was seated next to Mabel McCallum. You remember her? We sat with her and her husband at a political fundraiser in Louisiana last spring," Posy asked, as she calmed down a bit.

"Yes, I recall. I have some dealings with Jim Bob McCallum. He informed me that he and his wife were in town this week, so I arranged for a White House tour for Mrs. McCallum as well as a seat at the First Lady's luncheon. Jim Bob was a major contributor to Andy's campaign. I didn't know that they were going to seat you two together," Nathan stated.

"It's the only thing they did right. Thing is, Mabel didn't recognize me from Adam . . . well, I guess that would be from Eve. It's like she didn't remember anything from that night in Louisiana at the fund raiser. Now, truth be told, we had quite a few juleps that night, so I guess I can understand how she could be a little foggy. But looking through me like I was a complete stranger, that just don't seem right."

"Darlin', Mrs. McCallum is substantially older than you are. You can't expect her to have the same memory as you. I'm just glad you had someone to talk to," Nathan replied.

"Once I got a few juleps in her, we was old pals again. She saved the afternoon for me, Nathan. No thanks to that uppity bitch Sue Lynn," Posy spat.

"You went. Got out of the house. You had a good time with Mabel and enjoyed yourself. Case closed," Nathan responded with a grin.

"You keep that up mister, and more than just the case is gonna be closed to you tonight," Posy playfully snarled in return.

"ANDY, THE WOMEN IS A CRETIN! She's a loud uncouth monster!" Sue Lynn Cochran harshly stated to her husband.

"Come on Sue Lynn, surely you're being a bit over dramatic," Andrew Cochran replied to his wife.

"Oh really! You think so! Moments after Reverend Tolliver concluded his prayer, Posy was waving her arms like a lunatic trying to get the attention of one of the servers so that she could order a mint julep. Of course, she didn't stop at one, she never does. And poor Mabel McCallum had to endure her boorish behavior all afternoon long," Sue Lynn described.

"Mabel McCallum, the wife of Jim Bob McCallum was at the luncheon?" Andrew questioned with a quizzical expression on his face.

"Why yes, I thought you knew. Earlier this week Nathan had made a request to my social secretary Toni, to include Mabel at the luncheon. I was told that the McCallums were in town this week," Sue Lynn replied.

"I had no idea that the McCallums were in Washington. Jim Bob was one of the largest contributors to my campaign last year. I'm surprised that I wasn't informed that he was in the city," Andrew stated.

"Well, obviously Nathan knew, since he was the one who made the request to have Mabel included at the luncheon," Sue Lynn responded. "You may want to speak with your Chief of Staff, Andy. And if you do, tell him that he needs to reign in his foul mouthed, liquor ridden, obnoxious wife!" Sue Lynn demanded.

"Sure, I'll have a word with Nathan," Andrew said quietly, clearly distracted and annoyed by the news he had received from his wife.

BESSIE COLLINS HELPED HER MOTHER and her Aunt Rita out of the cab in front of the departure gate at the airport in New Orleans. The flight to Port-au-Prince, Haiti was due to take off in two hours.

"Mama, Auntie Rita, would you like some coffee or tea?" Bessie asked.

"No, girl, I am fine," Auntie Rita replied. "You have already done so much for me. I am grateful that you will keep the shop open for the two weekends that we are away."

"Oh please, Auntie Rita, it is nothing. Unfortunately, I can't tend to your shop during the weekdays. I have my own job. But on the weekends, I'm happy to do it," Bessie stated, beaming with a smile.

"The weekends are the most profitable with all of the tourists that come to the city."

"Well, I can't do readings or conjure up spirits like the famous Queen Rita, but I certainly can sell an amulet, or voodoo book, or mojo bag," Bessie said to her aunt.

"And I told you that a man will come to the shop next Saturday and you are to give him the package that I showed you in the back room?" Rita questioned Bessie unsure of her memory.

"Yes, you told me. The brown package with the initials 'JBM' on it, right?" Bessie stated back to her aunt.

"Yes, Bessie. That is the one. Give him the package and he will give you an envelope. Keep it safe, my love," Rita replied.

"I'll take care of it for you," Bessie promised.

AARON ROSE SLEPT RESTLESSLY that Sunday night. He kept thinking about how he would relay the information that Clay had shared with him to Senator Douglas without violating a confidence. Clay had convinced him that the information about the Cochran administration selecting Stanford Winchester to be the nominee for the Supreme Court vacancy was legitimate. He wasn't sure how he could impart that news to the Senator without fully divulging his source and the means by which the information was acquired. Or, he thought, perhaps he should just wait for the administration to announce their choice for the nomination. It had to be coming soon. Was there much strategic advantage in Senator Douglas knowing a day or two ahead of time? Additionally, the Senator might dismiss his information as hearsay and gossip. After all, it was based on one law clerk overhearing the private conversation between another law clerk and her boss. Aaron continued to flip and turn in bed, as he stared at the ceiling.

IT WAS LATE SUNDAY NIGHT turned to very early Monday morning as Clay Grover walked slowly down the darkened hallways of the Crew Club, glancing into the open doors of the private rooms as he passed by. Nothing but a white towel hung around his trim waist. Lately, the caution and discretion that Clay had always so carefully taken during his years in Washington working for Senator Fitzsimmons had been shunted aside for the titillation of more prurient pursuits. He found it difficult to continue to suppress his sexual desires in order to maintain an image and professional persona that society would find acceptable for the Chief of Staff to one on the most beloved and respected Senators in Congress.

As a young Southern gentleman from a prominent South Carolina family, Clay was taught to be discreet. He learned to inhibit his inner most thoughts and desires and to present a quiet, yet confident and sophisticated demeanor in public. Nothing in life could be worse than to bring shame and disgrace on the well-respected family name. Nothing should ever be done to tarnish the well-established centuries old legacy. And, for most of his life, Clay dutifully adhered to subjugating his needs and wants to protect his family name and his exemplary reputation on Capitol Hill.

For years, throughout prep school and college, Clay denied, even to himself, his true identity. He prayed to be changed, to have his unwanted sexual desires expunged from his life. But that all changed in law school at Duke when he met the love of his life, Sebastian. Sebastian taught Clay how to accept who he was. To embrace his identity and live his life without shame and remorse. Clay knew that he was who he was meant to be. But his ambition and political expediency required discretion and secrecy. Until lately. For a couple of months, the overwhelming desire for clandestine sexual encounters was overcoming his more conservative and socially appropriate sensibilities. It was as if a war was being waged in his consciousness between wanton desire and professional decorum.

Clay stood in the door way of the steam room and watched as several men engaged in a variety of sexual acts. After a brief pause, he entered the steam room and dropped the towel that had hung around his waist. The war might not be over, but there was no doubt about which side had won this battle.

ANDREW COCHRAN COULD NOT SLEEP. His mind actively sorted and filtered through all of the information he had received over the past few days. He was impressed with each of the three candidates he personally met with during the last seventy-two hours. All had certain qualities and personalities he found appealing. All had the lengthy judicial record and mental acuity to serve as a Justice on the Supreme Court. Yet, he desired a more pronounced certainty to his final decision that was still lacking. Additionally, he kept wondering why his long-time friend, his Chief of Staff, was so clearly in favor of one candidate over the others. He had not discerned such a clear cut choice during his interview process. Why had Nathan? And, why didn't Nathan mention anything to him about the McCallums being in Washington? Nathan's job was to keep the President informed. So, this lack of information was perplexing.

Andrew Cochran sat in a chair in the darkened bedroom and watched the silhouette of his wife, Sue Lynn sleeping in their bed. He wouldn't be joining her. Not that night.

CHAPTER 15

AARON ROSE WAS AT HIS DESK in the Senate Office Building at 5 a.m.
If he couldn't sleep, he was at least going to use his time productive-
ly instead of just staring at his bedroom ceiling. Aaron studied Senator
Fitzsimmons' notes from the Senate vetting of Stanford Winchester,
when he was first appointed to the Federal bench. Aaron also looked
carefully at the material he had gathered on the Fifth Circuit intellectual property case that Justice Winchester did not recuse himself from
despite his close ties with the majority owner of one of the parties to
the suit. Aaron shook his head. There was a pattern of judicial misconduct that was present in Justice Winchester's state and federal court conduct. A minimum of three cases in which the proper thing to do would
have been for Justice Winchester to recuse himself from those matters.
Instead, despite the apparent conflicts, he presided over the matters, and
in two instances wrote the majority opinion.

Aaron had a hard time understanding how the Cochran administration would select that man as their nominee to the Supreme Court. His
job was to gather as many facts together as possible to well arm his boss,
Senator Douglas for a challenge to Justice Winchester's nomination.
Anything to use as a political chip to perhaps get the administration to
put forward a more moderate jurist for consideration to the Court.

"NANCY," PRESIDENT COCHRAN BECKONED to his secretary, "Please place
calls to Justice Brumfield, Justice Remington, and Justice Winchester, in
that order, please. Let me know when you have Brumfield on the line."

"Yes, sir," Nancy responded, while adding, "Nathan is here to see you sir."

"Good, send him in," President Cochran stated.

"Good morning, Mr. President," Nathan Whitaker greeted his friend as he walked into the Oval Office.

"Hey, Nathan, have a seat," the President replied. "I'm about to let Justice Brumfield know that he is no longer in consideration for the vacancy on the Supreme Court. Nancy is getting him on the phone now."

"Yes, sir, I'm sure you'll let him down gently," Nathan replied.

"Look, I wanted to speak to you about a few things in the interim," Andrew Cochran began. "Sue Lynn is having a hissy fit over the way Posy acted at her first White House luncheon as First Lady. Now, we both want Posy to be happy here in D.C. and take advantage of the many opportunities to be involved in the White House social life, but . . ."

"Consider it done, sir," Nathan interrupted his friend. "I'll have a discussion with Posy and tell her to tone down her behavior. It won't be a problem," Nathan assured the President.

"Fine, good, thank you Nathan. We both married strong-willed, opinionated women."

"Yes, sir, that would be an understatement," Nathan sighed in return.

"There's something else that's kinda eating at my craw, Nathan. I understand that you made some arrangements to provide social activities for Mabel McCallum, while she and Jim Bob were here in Washington for a visit. I didn't know anything about it. I didn't even know that Jim Bob was in the city," President Cochran related to his Chief of Staff. "Nathan, I rely on you . . ."

"Mr. President, Justice Brumfield on line one, sir," Nancy stated to the President.

"Excuse me, Nathan, just give me a minute or two here," President Cochran stated as he turned his chair away from Nathan and picked up the phone to inform Justice Brumfield that he was no longer in consideration for the vacant seat on the Supreme Court. A few minutes later, the President hung up the phone and pivoted his chair only to find an empty room.

"Nancy, where's Nathan?" Andrew Cochran asked his secretary.

"He mentioned that he had something urgent he needed to attend to and that he would catch-up with you later, sir," Nancy responded.

President Cochran shook his head with a dissatisfied and puzzled look etched across his face.

"Dammit, Nathan," he quietly uttered to himself.

CLAY GROVER OPENED HIS LIPS as wide as he could, as he forked a large portion of sweet potato pancakes into his gaping mouth.

"Damn, Ben, you don't know what you're missing," Clay mumbled to Ben Carroll as he vigorously chewed his breakfast. "How can you come to Pete's Diner and only have a cup of coffee?" Clay asked.

"I'm not very hungry," Ben softly replied.

"Well, I'm famished," Clay moaned in response. "And, Pete's Diner serves the best breakfast on Capitol Hill, hands down."

"I don't eat breakfast very often," Ben stated.

"Well then, that must be how you keep your girlish figure," Clay chided his friend with a wink of an eye.

Ben Carroll's high cheekbone, square jawed face blushed as he looked around at the occupants of the tables nearby to see if Clay's comments were met with any reactions. Ben reached up to his forehead and pushed his dark wavy brown hair out of his deep blue eyes. "Clay, behave yourself," Ben gently demanded.

"That's not what you were saying last week," Clay responded with a sly grin.

"There's no stopping you lately," Ben stated.

"No, baby, there sure isn't," Clay replied between mouthfuls of sweet potato pancakes and maple syrup.

"Changing topics, since we are in a very public place," Ben reprimanded Clay, "The Cochran administration should be announcing their nominee for the Supreme Court any day now."

"Yeah, now that you mention it, why do you put so much stock in what Kate Wilson said to Justice Sallis?" Clay inquired.

"Everyone around the Court knows that Kate is having an affair with someone very high up in the White House. Even Justice Sallis knows it and uses Kate to get inside information for him," Ben replied.

"How do you know?"

"She's not terribly discreet about it. She kind of brags about it to some of the other law clerks. She wants everyone to know that she is well connected and has some political clout," Ben stated. "Kate Wilson is a very ambitious woman. She sees being a law clerk to Justice Sallis as just a stepping stone to real political power and influence in this city. There's not a whole lot she wouldn't do to curry favor with influential, powerful people. I'm told that she can be ruthless."

"Are you friendly with her?" Clay asked.

"I try to be friendly with most people at the Court. We say 'hello' and all that, but I try to steer clear of her most of the time. She can be a bit of a nut job. And you certainly don't want to cross her or get on her bad side," Ben explained. "Her one close female friend at the Court once told me that Kate had a nervous breakdown right after she graduated from law school. She was a bit delusional, I'm told, and she received professional help. She's also got no love for liberals. She often railed against the decisions put forth by Justice Martin before his death. She claimed that he was subverting the Constitution with every word he wrote. Added to that, my boss and hers are each at the far ends of the political spectrum on the Court. We don't have a whole lot in common other than being law clerks at the Supreme Court

"Interesting," Clay said as he finished off the last forkful of his pancakes.

STANFORD WINCHESTER SAT AT A TABLE at Café du Monde slowly sipping his cup of chicory coffee as he stared at his untouched plate of beignets. He reflected on the fact that within the next seventy-two hours he could receive a call from the President of the United States that could change his life and his legacy forever. He was becoming more and more excited over the prospect of being one of less than one hundred and twenty individuals, in the history of the United States, who can claim the title "Justice of the United States Supreme Court." He began to rationalize to himself that his friends could come visit him in Washington. That he could make his way back to New Orleans several times during the year, and certainly when the Court is in recess in the summer. The prestige and the power of the position certainly held an allure that anyone involved in the law for a lifetime would find extremely hard to resist.

Stanford thought about LeeAnn and how extremely proud she would have been being the wife of a Supreme Court Justice. It was her cherished dream for him as much as it now was his ultimate goal in life. Stanford reached out to delicately grasp a beignet off of the powdered sugar dusted plate. He took a large bite as he allowed the warm pastry to dissolve in his mouth. The taste was sweet, but not as sweet as the success he envisioned for himself in Washington. All that was required was a phone call.

"KATHERINE, YOU SHOULD PROBABLY HEAD BACK to Chicago," Senator Douglas stated to his wife as they both sat eating breakfast at their Georgetown condo.

"Trying to get rid of me so that the other woman in your life can move in?" Katherine jested with her husband.

"Am I that transparent?" Perry Douglas inquired with a big smile.

"Cochran will be announcing his nominee for the Supreme Court any day now, so I'm about to become exceedingly busy and wholly preoccupied with the confirmation hearings. I don't want to feel guilty knowing that you're here waiting for my sorry-ass to show up late at night or even early in the morning. I'd feel better knowing that you're back home with friends and family."

"And there's the mistress to deal with as well," Katherine said with a grin.

"Yeah, that part goes without saying," Perry parried in return, while imitating a fencing thrust.

"I made my flight arrangements back to Chicago two days ago," Katherine responded with a mimed thrust of her own.

"Touché, ouch!" Perry jokingly replied, and then reached over to hug his wife.

"I know how obsessive you normally get," Katherine stated. "So, add to that the first nominee to the Supreme Court by the new Republican administration and your need to marshal the troops in opposition as Chairman of the Senate Judiciary Committee. Please, Perry, I know you. I'd rarely see you, and when I did you'd be preoccupied with the Committee work. Been there, done that. For the sake of our happy marriage, best that I get out of Dodge before the gunfight starts blazing away. You've got your job to focus on, and there's a couple of pre-Broadway play openings in Chicago that I'm dying to see."

"Ulterior motives, I love it!" Perry exclaimed. "And I love my brilliant and beautiful wife who understands me and the ways of Washington."

"I've been here for a few years now, and I still don't think that I understand the ways of Washington," Aaron Rose stated to Clay Grover as they walked down the Senate office building corridor. "Why would a powerful man inside the White House share confidential information with a law clerk he's having an affair with? Why jeopardize your career?"

"Because a hard cock has no conscience," Clay bluntly replied. "Throughout history men have jeopardized power, money, titles and prestige for a good fuck. Look no further than King Edward forsaking the British throne for Wallis Simpson. And that's just the tip of the infidelity iceberg."

"Not me. I wouldn't throw away everything that I've worked for just for sex," Aaron stated.

"Why, child, you cut me to the quick," Clay replied in his best southern accent and with a sly smile, as he brushed his hand against Aaron's.

"Stop it!" Aaron admonished. "Jesus, Clay, we're out in the open in the Senate office building."

"You worry too much about what people think, my dear" Clay stated.

"And lately, you don't worry enough," Aaron replied with a shrug.

SEVERAL MINUTES LATER, AARON WAS SEATED in Senator Douglas' office waiting for his boss to finish a phone call.

"Aaron, what can I do for you?" Perry Douglas asked his aide as he hung up the telephone.

"Sir, I've recently received some information concerning the Cochran nominee for the Supreme Court. I'm really not sure if this information is accurate, but I feel compelled to share it with you," Aaron stated.

"So, were bartering in hearsay, gossip, and innuendo, Aaron?" Senator Douglas asked light-heartedly.

"Quite possibly sir," Aaron replied.

"Go ahead, let's hear it," Senator Douglas said encouragingly.

"I've been told that a high-ranking White House source has said that the Cochran administration's appointment to the Supreme Court is Justice Stanford Winchester," Aaron stated.

"Yep, I believe that to be true as well," Senator Douglas responded nodding his head affirmatively.

"You do?" Aaron asked a bit taken aback by the Senator's response.

"Yes, I have my own source, Aaron. However, mine happens to be a waiter at Bourbon Steak at the Four Seasons Hotel. Apparently last week, Nathan Whitaker charged two rather expensive glasses of bourbon to the hotel suite of Jim Bob McCallum. McCallum, as you know, is an old New Orleans acquaintance of Stanford Winchester. So, you have to ask yourself, what is a major Cochran campaign contributor and friend of Justice Winchester doing in town talking with the President's Chief of Staff? Hearsay, unsubstantiated innuendo, absolutely. But sometimes when you add two plus two, you actually do get four," Senator Douglas said with a smile.

"NATHAN, WHERE HAVE YOU BEEN?" PRESIDENT Cochran asked with an irritated tone to his voice.

"I apologize sir, there was an urgent matter concerning Posy's grand-mother," Nathan lied.

"Alright, we'll discuss what I was raising with you later," the President stated still somewhat perturbed. "Nancy has Stanford Winchester on the phone, and I wanted you here to participate in this call."

"Yes, sir, once again I apologize for my absence," Nathan responded.

"Fine, we'll discuss that later," President Cochran snapped in reply.

"Justice Winchester on line two, Mr. President," Nancy stated. The President picked up the phone from its cradle on his desk.

"Justice Winchester, good day sir," President Cochran began.

"Good day to you, Mr. President," Justice Winchester responded slowly, with a heavy drawl.

"Justice Winchester, there's something that I would like to ask you . . .," the President continued.

CHAPTER 16

Stanford Winchester eased back into his comfortable leather chair and gently rocked back and forth. His feet pushed against the floor as the chair moved in a slow rhythmic pace. He stared at the tea leaves floating in the fine china cup he held with both hands and smiled. Fortune smiles on those who seek it, he thought to himself.

"Naomi," Justice Winchester beckoned to his secretary, "Please look into flights to Washington, D.C. tomorrow morning will you please?"

"Yes, sir," Naomi replied.

"What would you say about living in D.C. and working for a Justice of the Supreme Court of the United States?" Justice Winchester asked his longtime secretary.

"Oh my sir, oh my!" Naomi exclaimed.

Aaron Rose raced down the Senate office building corridor on his way to Senator Douglas' office.

"It's official, it's Winchester!" Aaron breathlessly blurted out. "President Cochran will be announcing his appointment of Justice Winchester to the Supreme Court tomorrow afternoon during a press conference."

"Yes, I know, thank you Aaron," Senator Douglas replied. "We've got plenty of work to do in the next few days and weeks. Once the nomination is official, the Senate Judiciary Committee will send the nominee a questionnaire requesting financial and employment information, biographical information, and copies of the nominee's writings, speeches, and written orders and opinions. A week or two after receiving the completed questionnaire and the requested written materials, the Committee will proceed with hearings. After the hearing, the Judiciary Committee will vote on the nominee and send recommendations to the full Senate for either acceptance or rejection of the nominee. The full Senate will then convene its own hearings and ultimately hold an up or down vote on the nominee. So, we've got about three months of long hours and work ahead of us."

"I'm prepared for whatever needs to be done," Aaron emphatically stated.

"Good, I'm going to need your help with our prospective witnesses that the Committee may want to call," Senator Douglas replied. "Let's get busy, Aaron."

"NATHAN, WE WILL BE ANNOUNCING Stanford Winchester as our nominee to the Supreme Court tomorrow afternoon. It will be too damn cold to do it in a Rose Garden ceremony, so work with Lloyd to come up with the best venue and the best optics for the announcement," President Cochran said to his Chief of Staff.

"Yes, sir, we're already working on that, we'll have a few possibilities for you to consider in an hour or two," Nathan replied. "Additionally, I'm coordinating with Justice Winchester. He's arriving at 9:30 a.m. tomorrow morning."

"We need this to be seamless. The optics need to be perfect as we introduce our first nominee to the Supreme Court to the world," President Cochran stressed.

"Yes, sir, understood."

STANFORD WINCHESTER CAREFULLY HELD HIS FAVORITE photograph of his wife LeeAnn in his hands. He placed the framed photograph at the top of his packed suitcase. After all, Stanford could not go to Washington to be named as the President's nominee to the Supreme Court without LeeAnn right there by his side. They had been partners in everything for more than four decades. He was fully certain that this nomination, this honor, would not have been possible if not for LeeAnn. He only wished that she could have been present to hold his hand as the President announced his nomination and presented him to a country who knew very little about the man who was selected to join the most powerful judicial body in the world. Having his better half by his side, would allow the country to see the better side of Stanford Winchester. But five years ago cancer robbed him of that opportunity. He would stand next to the President, alone.

BESSIE COLLINS STOOD ALONE in her modest kitchen sifting flour, baking powder, salt, and sugar together into a large yellow ceramic bowl. She hummed to herself as she began preparing the ingredients for a pie that she would make for her friend. As she worked in the eggs and cream, Bessie remembered the first time she had met Justice Winchester.

Lucius had just been promoted from kitchen staff to waiter at Arnaud's. It was over fifteen years ago, and she was so proud of her husband. He worked his way up through the ranks, working in the kitchen and then clearing tables at Arnaud's. She remembered it like it was yesterday, straightening Lucius' bow tie and brushing off his black tuxedo jacket as he prepared to leave for work.

On his very first day as a waiter, after weeks of training, Lucius waited on the table of a tall, distinguished looking man and his wife. The man had a deep voice and a pronounced Southern drawl. He was patient with and polite to the young, neophyte waiter. He made jokes and witty quips to put Lucius at ease. Every order was proceeded with "please" and every transport and delivery of a cocktail or food to the table was followed by a "thank you very kindly, Lucius, you're the best." Lucius came home to Bessie after that first night and told her about the distinguished, cordial man and his lovely wife who were so kind to him and made him feel comfortable on his very nervous first day as a waiter at one of the finest dining establishments in all of New Orleans.

A few weeks went by as the couple would come to Arnaud's for dinner at least once a week. The kind gentlemen would strike up a conversation, asking Lucius about his life and his family. Lucius would brag about his wife Bessie and what an outstanding baker she was. It wasn't long before Stanford Winchester asked Lucius to bring his wife to Arnaud's so that he and LeeAnn could meet her. By this time, Lucius was aware that the gentlemen he had been serving was from a prominent New Orleans family and was a highly regarded Justice on the Louisiana Supreme Court.

Bessie recalled agonizing over which dress to wear to meet this important man and his wife. Stanford and LeeAnn could not have been more kind and welcoming to this daughter of a baker who worked in a small women's clothing store in the French Market. They made her feel appreciated and important. Bessie would never forget that evening. Stanford made her laugh with his embellished stories of the behavior of

Southern gentlemen. He poked fun at himself, and kept the mood of the evening light and entertaining. But most of all, he made Bessie feel like an equal. Like a new and cherished friend.

Bessie smiled broadly as she continued mixing the ingredients of the pie together in the bowl. She hummed and sang to herself, as she prepared a pie made of love for her friend.

Even as busy as he was preparing for the Senate Judiciary Committee hearings for the new nominee to the Supreme Court, Aaron could not help but worry about his friend Clay. Lately, Clay had eschewed his careful and discreet manner and had become more willing to let the world in on his well-kept secret life. And, though it was Clay's life and he could choose to be less secretive about his sex life, Clay's decision also had an effect on Aaron's ability to keep his own life secret. Yes, it was a new millennium and people's opinions had drastically changed in the last few years. But Aaron had carefully chosen to keep his own personal affairs wholly separate from his professional work on Senator Douglas' staff. That arrangement was being compromised by Clay's recent behavior. It could become a problem.

"I will only be a minute, sister," Rita said to Sandra, as she stepped inside the rickety shop on the outskirts of Port-Au-Prince.

"You have foxglove that you grow, process and sell, true dat?" Rita asked the shop owner.

"Yah, the deep purple hue, tis da most potent," the old woman who owned the shop replied. "You know the power of da foxglove?"

"I know," Rita replied with a sly smile.

"You know the care to take?" The shop owner asked.

"I have used it before, I know," Rita curtly responded growing weary of the questioning.

"Have I sold foxglove to you before? I do not recall," the old woman stated.

"Yes," Rita replied. "I am Queen Rita of New Orleans."

"Oh yes," the old woman responded. "Oh yes."

CHAPTER 17

CLAY GROVER LOOKED FORWARD TO WORKING with Aaron Rose over the next three to four months. His close friend had been fairly distant from Clay for a good portion of the previous election year. But with the impending Senate Judiciary Committee hearings, Clay knew that he would be working closely with Aaron once again. Aaron's boss, Senator Douglas was the Committee chair, and Clay's boss Senator Fitzsimmons was the most senior Democratic member of the Committee.

Clay longed for the days when he and Aaron worked together every day. They had been inseparable. And that close working relationship and bond slowly developed into a very close and loving friendship. But, the past year had taken a toll on their relationship. Still good friends, they saw each other far less frequently. The busy campaign schedule of an election year had kept them apart for a good portion of the previous year. Clay hoped that their work together supporting their bosses during the Senate Judiciary Committee vetting of Justice Winchester would rekindle their loving relationship. Clay felt himself slipping into an abyss of sexual promiscuity. He hoped and believed that Aaron could save him.

"HENRY, WE'VE GOT OUR WORK CUT out for us," Senator Douglas stated over the phone to his long-time friend and Senate colleague, Senator Henry Fitzsimmons.

"Winchester is a radical conservative dressed up as a live and let live old boy from the Big Easy," Senator Fitzsimmons added with a short chortle. "He's as smooth as a fine-aged, single barrel bourbon and cooler than the other side of the pillow. If he is confirmed and seated on the Court, he will fall in line with Sallis and his far right wing agenda."

"That's what I am afraid of," Senator Douglas replied. "I'm worried that Winchester is just Artemis Asburger, but without the radical judicial baggage and the fringe-baiting lunatic rhetoric."

"I think that's correct," Senator Fitzsimmons concurred. "Winchester doesn't shine a bright light on his far right conservative bonafides like Asburger does, which is what makes him a smart choice."

"Perhaps, I've underestimated our new President," Senator Douglas confessed.

"Perry, you know not to overlook the cunning and tenacity of a Southern gentleman," Henry Fitzsimmons laughed. "I thought you would have learned that from years of knowing me and watching me operate with some of our Senate colleagues."

"Henry, I never underestimated your ability to make a sow's ear of a crappy bill seem like the Magna Carta when you were whipping votes," Perry Douglas chuckled in response. "But I know Senator Henry Fitzsimmons, and Andrew Cochran is no Henry Fitzsimmons!"

"I appreciate that Perry, I do. But Andrew Cochran is no one's fool. He proved that during the Presidential election debates. And his Chief of Staff, Nathan Whitaker, is a smart and relentless bulldog who will stop at nothing to gain success and favor for his friend. Whitaker is a man who enjoys power and has little fear of the consequences in the fervent pursuit of it," Henry Fitzsimmons warned his colleague. "Nathan Whitaker will move mountains to ensure the Cochran administration's success."

"Well, tomorrow my office is going to issue the Judiciary Committee questionnaire to Justice Winchester. We've got a couple of weeks to choose the route with which we'll challenge his appointment to the Court. I understand that you talked to my aide, Aaron, and mentioned the conflict of interest matters you uncovered during Winchester's vetting process during his initial appointment to the Federal bench. Perhaps, that is where we should start?" Perry Douglas inquired.

"Yes, that's a fair starting point. But I have a sense that failing to recuse himself from case matters dealing with his friends and family is just scratching the surface of what we may uncover about Stanford Winchester. I have a feeling in my bones that the Winchester waters run far deeper and darker than the glimmering placid surface tranquility with which he attempts to portray himself to the world," Henry Fitzsimmons stated.

"We will dive into those waters, Henry, don't you worry," Perry Douglas reassured his colleague.

"I THINK THAT THE CEREMONY ANNOUNCING Justice Winchester as your nominee for the Supreme Court vacancy went off quite well, Mr. President," Nathan enthusiastically stated to President Cochran.

"Yes, Nathan, I was very pleased with the staging and optics of the announcement. And, Justice Winchester handled himself with dignity, charm, gravitas, and great aplomb," the President cheerfully replied.

"The appointment of Justice Winchester to the Supreme Court will be a major achievement for this administration and solidify our allies on the Court," Nathan pronounced.

"From your lips to God's ears, Nathan," Andrew Cochran responded. President Cochran then shifted and fidgeted in his chair.

"Look Nathan, I want to thank you for all you've done for me over all these years. Heck, we go back to being college freshmen together. You've been a true and loyal friend, and I deeply appreciate it. But I'm getting the sense that you're not completely confiding in me. I keep thinking back to your not telling me about Jim Bob McCallum being in town with his wife. But yet you made arrangements for Mabel McCallum to be at Sue Lynn's inaugural First Lady's luncheon. Jim Bob was a major contributor to my campaign and a loyal ally. If he is in town, I want to know about it and make sure he understands that I appreciate all of his efforts and contributions on my behalf. Perhaps, invite him to the White House as a guest for dinner. By the way, do you know the reason why Jim Bob and his wife were in town?" Andrew Cochran asked his friend.

"Mister President . . ." Nathan Whitaker began.

"Nathan, it's just you and me, talking as friends, you don't have to be so formal."

"Alright then, Andy, you know I love you like a brother. I would never do anything to harm our friendship. I only want to help. And, sometimes, I just want to take some of the load off of you. Carry some of the weight so that you don't have to take it all on yourself. I didn't tell you about Jim Bob's visit to Washington because I felt that I could take care of showing his wife a good time with a seat at the First Lady's luncheon and a White House tour without bothering you with such minutiae. Jim Bob was grateful for the hospitality shown to Mabel and he knows that it comes directly from you," Nathan stated with conviction.

"As to what they were in town for, it was just for a few days of pleasure and tourism. As you may recall, Mabel McCallum is suffering from Alzheimer's. Jim Bob had brought her up to John Hopkins to talk to a few doctors who are launching some experimental drug trials. After a couple of days in Baltimore, they came to D.C. for a weekend of pleasure. Honestly Andy, that is the long and short of it. I would never hide anything from you," Nathan stated while looking his friend in the eye.

"Nathan, I feel like a fool." I should have known that there was a reasonable explanation as to why you didn't say anything to me. I'm sorry for doubting you."

"Just know Andy, that I love and respect you so much that I would never do anything to deceive or harm you," Nathan replied, his voice choked with emotion.

"I know my friend, I know," Andrew Cochran replied. And then with a smile and a quick laugh, "Hey, before we get too deep into moving our economic agenda forward, what say you and I spend a boys night out at Camp David. We can get in a little quail hunting in the morning, down a few bottles of bourbon, and listen to some Lynyrd Skynyrd cranked up loud like we use to do in college?"

"Sounds great Andy, I can't wait," Nathan stated with a huge grin on his face.

"Excellent, I'll have Nancy block out a Saturday in the next week or two. It'll be fun, just the two of us like old times," the President said to his friend.

"Just like old times," Nathan responded with a wink of his eye.

"BESSIE, BESSIE, DID YOU SEE the announcement on the news?" Lucius Collins excitedly asked his wife.

"Yes, I just did," Bessie gleefully replied. "I had no idea that Justice Winchester was being considered for the Supreme Court by the President of the United States. I saw him just over a week ago. I brought him a pie, he didn't say nothing about it."

"Maybe he wasn't allowed to say. You know how secretive them government people can be," Lucius stated.

"Lordy Jesus," Bessie shouted out in happiness, "Our friend Stanford Winchester is gonna be on the Supreme Court!"

Suddenly, Lucius became sullen in the midst of Bessie's revelry.

"Lucius, what's wrong darlin'?" Bessie asked.

"Well, I'm happy for Stanford and all, but I'm sure gonna miss him every Wednesday night at Arnaud's. We been sharing conversation and good cheer every week for over fifteen years now. It just ain't gonna be the same without him there, sippin' his Sazerac and pokin' fun at me," Lucius somberly said.

"I'm gonna miss him too," Bessie quickly added with a shake of her head. "I'd bake him a pie and bring it to him at the Courthouse, and he'd go on and on about having a slice of heaven right there on his plate. He'd make me blush like a young school girl, and I loved every minute of it. But, what a great honor this is for him. And, think about how button-bustin' proud LeeAnn would be of her husband. She'd be all aglow and rightfully so. He'll be back in New Orleans from time to time, and we can make a trip up to Washington, D.C. to see him. I've never been before, and I sure would like to see all them monuments and such."

"Yeah, you right Bessie. I need to focus on what's best for our friend and not dwell on my loss. He's gonna make us all proud," Lucius stated with a faint smile.

KATE WILSON SAT ON THE COUCH in the hotel suite sipping a glass of wine, and waiting, as usual. She had an agenda that she wanted addressed during the course of the evenings rendezvous. In her mind, she had fulfilled the commitments that she had made. It was time to receive the benefits of her services. There were very few things that she wouldn't do to achieve her ultimate goals. Her faithful and unquestioned loyalty to powerful men had to be met with the fruits of those labors. And Kate was ready to demand for and accept her well-earned rewards.

The digital clock on the end table in the living room of the suite ticked away the minutes. And then the hours. Kate was used to waiting for twenty or thirty minutes, but it was well over two hours since the appointed time of her rendezvous. Her restlessness gave way to frustration, a feeling of rejection, and then anger. She routinely checked her phone for text messages or an email, but there was nothing. Finally, three hours had passed. Clearly, there would be no meeting on that night. Kate left the suite, took an elevator to the lobby, and walked out the front door of the hotel into the dark, quiet night.

CHAPTER 18

THE SMALL BELL THAT HUNG over the doorway of Queen Rita's voodoo shop on north Rampart rang as a customer entered the store on a late Saturday afternoon.

"I'll be right with you," Bessie Collins called from the back room of the shop.

"No worries, cher, I'll just look around for a minute" the deep male voice with a pronounced accent called back in response.

Bessie folded the upper corner of the page of the romance novel that she was reading, placed it down on the wooden table, and scurried through the beaded curtain that separated the back space of the shop from the front of the store which contained all of the merchandise that was for sale to the public.

"Can I help you?" Bessie cordially asked the tall gentleman who was wearing a dark wide brimmed fedora.

"Why yes, thank you kindly. I've come to retrieve a package that Queen Rita had informed me she has ready for me," the gentlemen slowly stated.

"Oh yes, I've been expecting you," Bessie said. "I have a package with the initials 'JBM' on it that my Auntie Rita told me about." Bessie studied what she could make out of the strangers face under the low brim of the fedora hat. She thought that she may have seen that face before.

The gentlemen cleared his throat and stated, "Well now, JBM, that would be me. I am Jim Bob McCallum."

"My goodness, yes, Mr. McCallum, we've met before, sir," Bessie said excitedly. "I'm Bessie Collins, my aunt is Queen Rita. We met a number of years ago when you invited my aunt and her family to the party launching your company's product line of 'Queen Rita's Cajun Jambalaya'. It was a lovely party at the Hotel Monteleone. I still talk about it with my friends to this very day."

"I do remember you," Jim Bob replied with a big smile. "Why, you're as pretty today as you were back then. You haven't changed one bit. On the other hand, I've gained twenty pounds and lost a considerable amount of hair."

"Thank you kindly for saying so, Mr. McCallum, but the mirror in my house tells me that you are just being a very kind and polite gentlemen," Bessie laughed while blushing.

"You know Bessie, that in addition to your Aunt Rita, we also share a common friend, Stanford Winchester," Jim Bob said with a grin. "Oh my word, that's right!" Bessie exclaimed. "I recall now that you and your wife were friends with Justice Winchester. Ain't it just a small, small world?"

"Then, I'm sure you know that Stanford has been nominated by the President to sit on the Supreme Court," Jim Bob stated.

"Yes, my husband, Lucius, and I were just talking about that the other day. We are so happy for him and Lee Ann would have been so proud," Bessie replied.

"Yes, she would be. That was LeeAnn's dream for Stanford, to one day be on the Supreme Court of the United States. LeeAnn was a very special woman, who I would do anything for. We knew each other in high school. We were great friends and we actually dated for a little bit. But then, Stanford came along and swept her off her feet. Stanford was a real charmer. Well respected family name, and the money that goes with it. Plus, Ol' Stanford could be slicker than pig snot on a glass door knob!" Jim Bob chortled.

"You've done pretty good for yourself as well," Bessie quickly added.

"Yeah, I got some luck and met the right people, and put out some products that people seem to have taken a cotton to. But I didn't come from the New Orleans high society crowd that Stanford did. Hell, when I was a teenager, I didn't know a cotillion from a vagabond's ratty coattails," Jim Bob responded.

"But look at you both now. Famous and successful businessman and a soon-to-be Justice of the Supreme Court!" Bessie beamed.

"Yeah, we're both living in the high cotton now. We surely are, cher, we surely are."

"Naomi, I could use your help planning a little party with a few friends. I want to share my good news with the people I love and cherish," Justice Winchester said to his secretary.

"It would be my pleasure, Mr. Chief Justice, I think that that is an excellent idea," Naomi cheerfully replied.

"I'd like to reserve a private room in a restaurant in the Quarter. About forty people or so, I imagine," Justice Winchester stated. "Could you look into that and send out the invitations?"

"It would be my utmost pleasure to do so," Naomi responded.

"Thank you, and do make sure that one of those invitations is addressed to Virgil and Naomi Cutler, if you please," Justice Winchester said with a grin.

"Oh my word, Justice Winchester!" Naomi exclaimed.

Stanford Winchester's guests began arriving at Muriel's in Jackson Square around 7 p.m. The Cotillion dining room and the Séance lounges on the restaurants second floor had been reserved for the Winchester party. A jazz trio played Dixieland songs in the corner of the ornate room as guests enjoyed cocktails and hors d'oeuvres served by waiters in tuxedos. Front and center welcoming his guests, was Stanford Winchester, with an extended right hand, a well-prepared Sazerac in his left hand, and a beaming genial smile etched across his weather worn face.

The large dining room looked gorgeous, with huge splayed arrangements of colorful local flowers decorating the banquet tables as dozens of long white candles flickered throughout the hall. On each of the two mantles of the fireplaces in the room were carefully arranged silver framed photographs of LeeAnn Winchester. There was never a festive occasion celebrated by Stanford where LeeAnn was not present in at least photographs and memories. And it was hardly by coincidence that Stanford had chosen Muriel's for the celebratory party. The building is well renowned in New Orleans as a habitat for harmless and entertaining ghosts.

After an exemplary meal of turtle soup, smoked peach salad, blackened redfish with lump crab meat, and bread pudding with candied pecans and rum sauce, the satiated guests milled around the Séance rooms while some of the banquet tables were cleared to make room for a dance floor. In keeping with LeeAnn's wishes, after a fine meal, LeeAnn and Stanford would go dancing to Dixieland jazz. And so, the tradition continued. A few of the men, including Stanford and Jim Bob McCallum, went out to the wrought iron balconies encircling the second floor of Muriel's to smoke a Montecristo cigar and sip a snifter of fine brandy.

"Well, you did it, you old coonhound, you've made it to the very top, the United States Supreme Court," Jim Bob said to Stanford as he gently slapped his back with his left hand.

"Well, let's not count our chickens before they're hatched," Stanford Winchester cautioned. "I've still got Senate Judiciary Committee investigative hearings as well as full Senate confirmation hearings ahead of me. My guess is that the Democrats will not take kindly to having a Conservative Southern judge being the first appointment to the Supreme Court by a new Conservative Southern President."

"Them feckless bastards? I wouldn't worry myself about the Democrats. They're still licking their wounds after being beaten like a dog in the election. They're all hat no cattle and the American people saw right through them and their liberal ways," Jim Bob responded with a sneer.

"Maybe so," Stanford said between puffs of his cigar, "But I understand that the chair of the Senate Judiciary Committee, Perry Douglas, is a very smart, ambitious man. He's looking to make a mark for himself and put his name high on the list of Democratic hopefuls for the next presidential race. He's gonna be a hard dog to keep under the porch. And despite his advanced age, Henry Fitzsimmons, who is also on the Judiciary Committee, is gonna be up for a tussle."

"Ha!" Jim Bob exclaimed with a grunt. "These days that old man makes about as much sense as tits on a bull. I understand from my Republican friends in the Senate that most of the time he reeks of bourbon and is as drunk as Cooter Brown!"

"I don't think we can take the Democrats too lightly. They may act dumb, but they ain't stupid," Stanford said in return.

"Speaking of, what did you think of our new President?" Jim Bob inquired.

"Seems like a good man. We had a very nice chat together when he was speaking with each of the final three nominees. I was also very impressed with his Chief of Staff, Nathan Whitaker," Stanford replied.

"You should be!" Jim Bob stated with emphasis and a sly smile.

"Why is that?" Stanford questioned.

"Well, all I'll say on that account is that if you're walking along a fence and you spot a turtle atop a fencepost, you damn well know it didn't get there by itself," Jim Bob said with a wink of an eye.

Stanford looked at his friend slightly askance. And, then suddenly he heard the jazz band launch into a rendition of "When the Saints Go Marching In."

"Excuse me, Jim Bob, they're playing my song, and I must seek out a dance partner," Stanford stated as he turned to go back into the dining room.

"Have fun finding your Ginger Rogers," Jim Bob called out as he lifted his brandy snifter to his lips.

Stanford surveyed the room of gathered friends until his eyes landed on the pretty smile of Bessie Collins.

"Lucius, would you do me the honor of allowing me to dance with your beautiful bride?" Stanford asked.

"With her permission, why of course, sir," Lucius responded with a smile.

"Well, then, Mrs. Collins would you allow an old and unworthy gentleman the pleasure of a dance with the most beautiful woman in New Orleans?" Stanford asked Bessie while bowing deeply at the waist.

"It would be my pleasure," Bessie stated while blushing and taking Stanford's hand.

The band played as Stanford twirled Bessie around the dance floor. Bessie laughed heartily as Stanford repeatedly dipped her to just inches above the floor only to elevate her again to a vertical position so that he could spin her back into his arms. The other guests clapped rhythmically as Stanford showed off the dance moves that he and LeeAnn used to dazzle the regulars with at Fritzel's. After the song ended both Stanford and Bessie smiled widely and took a deep bow to the applause of the others in the room.

"My word, Stanford, I haven't danced like that since my senior prom," Bessie said with a giggle as she attempted to catch her breath.

"And I haven't had that much fun since LeeAnn and I use to shake and shimmy together," Stanford replied. "God rest her soul, LeeAnn taught me to appreciate a good dance after a fine meal. It is a wonderful combination. Now, if you'll excuse me, I need some fresh air and some more brandy. Thank you, Bessie. And thank you Lucius. You just made an old man very happy."

"POSY, THEY'RE OUR FRIENDS, not to mention being the President and First Lady of the United States. If we're invited to dinner at the White House, we have to go," Nathan Whitaker pleaded with his wife.

"I know you and Andy go back to being friends when you was just teenage boys, but Sue Lynn ain't no friend of mine," Posy forcefully responded. "She's always got her nose so high in the air she could drown in a rainstorm!"

"Posy stop!" Nathan insisted. "It's part of my job to attend these social functions, and I would think that you would want to be there to support me. Once you're there, you'll have fun. It's not like it's just the four of us, there will be plenty of other people there to talk to. All you need to do is say 'hello' to Sue Lynn when we get there, and 'thank you' and 'goodbye.' It's not that hard to be a little polite."

"Easy for you to say, she don't put you down like she does to me," Posy retorted.

"She won't do that to you when you're with me," Nathan encouragingly stated. "We'll have a nice meal, and a few drinks and then I get to come home with the most beautiful woman in all of Washington. C'mon what do you say?" Nathan sweetly asked as he nuzzled up against Posy's neck while he placed his hands on her shapely hips.

"Alright Nathan, I'll go. But if she looks cross-eyed at me just once . . ."

CHAPTER 19

"You see there, sugar plum, that wasn't so bad. Sue Lynn was a perfect angel. She complimented you on your dress in front of all of those Washington muckety-mucks and then introduced you to one of your favorite fashion designers," Nathan stated to his wife.

"Yeah, well, even a blind squirrel can find a nut every now and then. She don't treat me like that when you're not around," Posy slurred.

"I'm glad we went and had a nice time. It may be a while before we get another night out together. I'm gonna be very busy for a couple of weeks as Andy rolls out his economic agenda for this year," Nathan informed his wife. "There's going to be late nights when I might not even make it home. So, let's enjoy it while we can," Nathan whispered as he unzipped Posy's dress, pulled it off her shoulders and past her slim waist and then slid his right hand below the elastic band of her panties.

"You're such a dirty little pig," Posy moaned.

"Oink, oink, baby, oink, oink," Nathan huskily groaned.

"You better call me back, you son of a bitch!" Kate Wilson demanded into her cell phone. "No one treats me like that! If you think that you can stand me up and then ignore my phone calls, you've sorely underestimated what I can do to your precious career!" Kate fumed as she ended her voice mail message and slammed the phone onto her desk. Kate took a few minutes to attempt to compose herself. She seethed with anger and resentment. She had been made promises. She had fulfilled her side of the agreement. It was time for her just reward.

Senator Perry Douglas hung up the phone on his office desk, rose up from his chair, and hurriedly put on his overcoat as he moved through the corridors of the Senate office building with alacrity. He entered the office of his friend and colleague, Senator Henry Fitzsimmons.

"Henry, you ready to go?" Perry beckoned as he peaked his head into the office doorway.

"Come have a drink before we go," Henry said to his friend.

"Henry, your secretary made 7:30 p.m. reservations," Perry stated.

"Oh hell, Perry, one drink. You think that when we show up they're going to rebuff someone who's been serving in the Senate for thirty-six years? Sorry Senator we gave your table to Buffy and Scooter over there," Henry challenged with a laugh. "C'mon Perry, help me finish off this outstanding bottle of bourbon that your aide Aaron gave to me."

"Aaron gave you a bottle of bourbon?" Perry questioned with a modicum of surprise in his voice.

"Not just any old bottle of bourbon, it's a bottle of Elijah Craig 21 year old single barrel straight bourbon. It's like drinkin' silk," Henry stated as he poured a couple of fingers worth of the bourbon for both Perry and himself. Henry handed a glass to his colleague.

"This is a gorgeous crystal glass, Henry," Perry commented.

"What did you expect Perry that I'd be drinking out of a red Solo cup?" Henry chuckled in return. "I didn't drink out of anything but fine crystal even when I was in college. It could have been homemade moonshine that could blind an eagle from a hundred yards, but I'd still drink it in a crystal glass. Hell, if I didn't my old pappy, the Merchant of Death, would have tanned my hide. Wealthy Southern gentlemen have standards to uphold. So, Cheers. To old friends and even older booze," Henry said with a grin.

"Wow, this is outstanding," Perry said after a long, slow sniff, and sip of the bourbon.

"Your aide has exquisite taste. I've already tried to pry him away from you, but unfortunately he's too damn loyal to you," Henry chortled.

"He's never given me a gift like this," Perry replied.

"Aw shucks now, Perry. Is that little green devil coming out of you?" Henry laughed. "Aaron's an outstanding young man. He asked for a little of my time to talk about Winchester, which I was happy to give to him. And, he showed up at my office door with this lovely token of gratitude. I tell you truthfully, Perry, I was touched. I was moved by the honor and purity of his thoughtfulness. For a Northerner, he was raised right. It was his way of honoring an old war horse, who everyone knows is on his last leg. I know he's a rough and tumble Chicago boy like yourself, but he has the refined social graces of a proper Southern gentleman. Might have gotten some of that from hanging around my Chief of Staff, Clay Grover."

"I didn't know that Aaron spent much time with Clay. I mean, I know they have worked together in the past on a few matters that we coordinated on, but I didn't know that they socialized together," Perry responded.

"Well, I'm an old fool that don't know much about these new lifestyles or such, but from the way they act around one another, I'd say that they're sweet on each other," Henry matter-of-factly stated.

"No, really?" Perry inquired, surprised at the revelation.

"I know homosexuals have been around since Adam and Eve got this whole shebang goin'. Heck, back in South Carolina, you knew that when a couple of young lads went into a dark barn together it wasn't always to fetch the plow. You just looked the other way when they came out thirty minutes later wiping their mouths on their sleeves and picking the straw out of their hair. I saw and heard a lot of things when I was an officer in the Army. So, I've been around boys that've been sweet on each other, and damn if I don't see the same thing when I watch Aaron and Clay interacting," Henry said slowly, raising his crystal glass to his lips.

"God made all of us as we are. And God don't make mistakes. So, here's to both of them. May they find whatever joy and happiness they seek," Henry toasted. "As good progressive liberals, that's what we're supposed to say, ain't it?" Henry challenged Perry.

"Indeed," Perry acknowledged with a raised glass.

"Mama, it's so good to have you back," Bessie said as she gave her mother, Sandra, a big long squeeze. "Tell me all about your trip."

"I will darlin', but a little bit later. Please go help your Aunt Rita with her bags."

"Of course," Bessie declared as she took hold of the heaviest suitcase from the hand of her aunt.

"My lovely girl, could I bother you for a glass of water," Rita asked her niece, as she put down her suitcase and sat on a cushioned chair.

"Certainly, I'll be right back with something to drink for you and mama," Bessie stated as she turned to head back towards the kitchen in her mother's home.

Rita quickly turned towards her sister Sandra.

"Bessie does not need to know about everything that went on in Haiti," Rita quietly but firmly said to her sister.

"Rita, I'm not about to tell my daughter about your business. It's not my place. Spirituality, voodoo, whatever you want to call it, is an aspect of your personal and business life. You practice it and get paid for your services. I don't believe in it. It's not part of my life. Bessie doesn't need to hear from me about your affairs. That is up to you to tell," Sandra replied softly while looking directly at her sister.

"Irie," Rita whispered with a slight smile.

Bessie returned to the living room with a tray containing a large pitcher of sweet tea with fresh mint and lemon slices, and a plate of pecan pralines that she had made that morning for her mother's arrival.

"Thank you, my dear, you are so sweet and attentive," Sandra said while stroking Bessie's face with her hand in a loving caress.

"Oh, I almost forgot to tell you, Auntie Rita, Jim Bob McCallum came to the shop last Saturday and picked up his package," Bessie relayed to her aunt.

"Did he tell you who he was?" Rita questioned with a puzzled expression on her face.

"Well yes, and I also recognized him from the party he threw a few years ago when Pontchartrain Brands came out with the 'Queen Rita' line of Cajun products," Bessie responded.

"Oh yes, the party, I had forgotten that you were there," Rita replied a bit dismayed.

"We talked for a while. We both share a friendship with Justice Winchester. I hadn't realized that Mr. McCallum was so close to Mrs. Winchester. He spoke so lovingly about her. It was a bit sad. He clearly still mourns her loss five years later," Bessie told her aunt.

"Yes, he would do anything for LeeAnn or her memory. Sometimes he comes to me for a séance. He speaks to her through me," Rita offered. "Did he talk to you about anything else?" Rita questioned.

"No, we mostly spoke about Justice Winchester and LeeAnn," Bessie replied.

"Good. I'm glad he has the package. It is a good thing to have friends with power and money," Rita said with a wry smile in her lilting Haitian/Creole accent.

"A PLEASANT GOOD EVENING TO YOU, Justice Winchester," Lucius stated as he approached Stanford Winchester's regular table at Arnaud's on Wednesday night.

"Lucius, my friend, wonderful to see you. I want to thank you and your lovely wife for doing me the honor of attending my little soiree on Saturday night. And, of course, I want to thank you again for permitting me the pleasure of enjoying a dance with Bessie."

"Sir, we should thank you for the invitation. It was a lovely evening. We both enjoyed ourselves immensely. Bessie is on cloud nine. She do go on and on talking about the food and the music and dancing," Lucius stated beaming with a big smile.

"Well, we've shared our lives together for fifteen years, I couldn't have a celebratory affair without both of you in attendance," said Stanford.

"Yes, sir, fifteen years, where has the time gone?"

"Lucius, my friend, I haven't a clue. Time seems to move faster than green grass through a goose!" Stanford said with a laugh.

"Speaking of time, is it time for a Sazerac, sir?" Lucius asked with a sly smile.

"Lucius, if it's a time that I can tell on this here watch," Stanford said while pointing with his finger at the watch on his wrist, "then it's time for a Sazerac!" Stanford and Lucius shared a good hearty laugh.

When Lucius returned with the cocktail, Stanford was in a quieter, contemplative mood.

"You alright, sir?" Lucius asked Stanford as he sat quietly for several moments without acknowledging the drink on his table. It was odd behavior given that Stanford would normally profusely thank Lucius for providing him with a Sazerac made exactly the way he liked it.

"Oh, oh, yes, thank you Lucius, you're the best," Stanford mumbled barely audible. And then, with a bit more conviction and bearing to his voice, Stanford added, "I'm fine, truly I am. I was just thinking about leaving all of my friends. All of these pleasant little rituals that I've become so accustomed to. Having dinner here at Arnaud's every Wednesday night, made even more satisfying with your fine company, my friend. Strolling to Café du Monde every morning and enjoying a sugar powdered beignet. The very special, loving, life-affirming visits from your Bessie, when she comes to my office cradling in her arms a warm, not long out of the oven pie draped with a clean cotton towel to preserve its inner warmth. Bless her sweet heart."

"You know how much we'll all miss you as well sir. But you're gonna be a Justice on the United States Supreme Court. They're more customers in this dining room right now than there has been people who have sat on that Court in the entire history of this country. When I think about that, my chest swells with pride and I can feel my heart trying to beat its' way outta my chest," Lucius replied with heartfelt emotion.

"Now, don't you go turning this old man into a public waterworks, Lucius," Stanford choked out with a feeble smile. "I reckon I'm just feeling sorry for myself for no apparent reason. I'm thinking about how different it will be living in Washington. In the winter it's colder than a witch's tit in a brass bra. I surely ain't looking forward to that, I'm here to tell ya, Lucius," Stanford said with a grin, his mood rising by the moment.

"I love it here in the deep South where sushi is still rightfully called bait. But you're absolutely correct as usual, Lucius. I'm being given an opportunity that precious few people have ever received. It is the honor of a lifetime."

"It surely is sir, it surely is."

CHAPTER 20

"NATHAN, THAT WAS SOME OF THE WORST shooting I've seen in my life. My daughter was a better shot than you when she was nine years old," Andrew Cochran ribbed his friend.

"How could you expect me to hit a damn thing, when you kept yelling, 'look out here comes Dick Cheney,' every time I was aiming to shoot," Nathan Whitaker complained.

"You've always got an excuse, or alibi, Nathan. Sometimes you gotta just say, 'I'm no good at this.' It's alright to be fallible. We all are. It's also okay to get stupid drunk once in a while. I recommend that we set our course for that exact destination," Andrew stated with a wide smile.

"Now, you're talking some sense," Nathan agreed.

The beer and bourbon bottles littered the living room of the Aspen Lodge at Camp David. The Southern rock music loudly blared out of the speakers. Andrew and Nathan stood in the middle of the room with their arms wrapped around each other's shoulders as they sang into a bourbon bottle that was substituting as a microphone.

"Sweet home Alabama. Where the skies are so blue. Sweet home Alabama. Lord, I'm coming home to you. Here I come Alabama."

Nathan simulated playing air guitar, while Andrew shook his head and smiled. After the song concluded, the two friends laughed as they fell back onto the couch in front of a large stone fireplace.

"The Secret Service boys must be thinking, what the hell have we gotten ourselves into for the next four years," Andrew said while taking a sip of bourbon.

"Eight years, Andy, eight years," Nathan corrected his friend with a grin.

Andrew grabbed the iPad that was on the coffee table and asked Nathan, "Alright ol' buddy. Which song do you wanna make a fool of yourself to next? We've been through three Lynyrd Skynyrd songs, we played air guitar to the Allman Brothers 'Ramblin' Man'. We danced to Little Feat's 'Dixie Chicken', and, if I do say so myself, we absolutely killed on 'The Night They Drove Old Dixie Down'. I sounded so much like Levon Helm, I scared myself that I had raised the dead," Andrew said with a hearty laugh.

"Yeah Andy, folks will confuse your singing for Levon Helm when they start mistaking me for Brad Pitt," Nathan responded.

"Oh, I know what song to play!" Andrew excitedly stated with the enthusiasm of a young boy.

"I swear Andy, if you play, Willie Nelson singing 'Georgia On My Mind' one more time, President or not, I'm gonna smack you upside your head," Nathan jokingly threatened his friend. Moments later, Andrew stood up, holding the bourbon bottle up to his lips like a microphone, looked Nathan straight in the eye, and crooned:

"Georgia, Georgia. The whole day through. Just an old sweet song, keeps Georgia on my mind. I'm say, Georgia, Georgia. A song of you. Comes as sweet and clear as moonlight through the pines. Other arms reach out to me. Other eyes smile tenderly. Still in peaceful dreams, the road leads back to you."

"That does it!" Nathan shouted as he reached out and grabbed Andrew around the waist and wrestled him onto the couch, playfully fighting his friend for the iPad and control of the music. Both friends laughed as they fell back onto the couch with their arms around each other.

The ruckus caused a Secret Service agent on the other side of the door to politely knock as he asked, "Sir?"

"It's alright Billy. Nathan is just trying to kill the President of the United States!" Andrew laughed, and then followed with, "We're good. Just a couple of over grown adolescent idiots acting like fools."

"Yes, sir," the agent responded through the closed door.

"Land sakes, Nathan. If people knew what was going on here. Two of the most powerful men in the free world rough housing like a couple of hooligans over picking the next song to play, they'd be calling for a re-election tomorrow. And I couldn't blame them one bit," Andrew chortled, and then took a large swig from the bourbon bottle.

"Amen to that. Now pass me that bottle!" Nathan demanded, as he pulled a well rolled joint out of his jeans pocket.

Aaron Rose and Clay Grover sat on the leather couch in the middle of Clay's Capitol Hill apartment, each sipping a glass of wine. The dry wood in the fireplace crackled and hissed as the fire glimmered throughout the cozy living room.

"Judiciary Committee hearings start in two weeks. I've got a number of interns pouring over every book, article, speech, and college paper that Winchester has written in his life. I'm going through his Fifth Circuit opinions, and we still need to look more closely at his Louisiana court opinions again," Aaron informed his friend and colleague.

"Do we have to talk about that now?" Clay sighed.

"No, I guess not. I was just pointing out how much work we have to do in the next couple of weeks to get ready for the hearings," Aaron replied, slightly taken aback by the tone in Clay's voice.

"And we will do the work. And we will be well prepared. And everything will be fine. But I'd rather not talk about work right now," Clay said, while placing his hand on the side of Aaron's head and gently stroking his face. "I'd rather talk about how beautiful you are and how much I want to make love to you."

"That's hard to argue with," Aaron whispered, as the two friends engaged in a sweet, languid kiss. Lips parted and tongues playfully parried in each other mouths. Clay's hand squeezed Aaron's muscular thigh. Their breathing intensified as passion overtook both of them.

"This is what I wanted to talk about," Clay moaned as he began gently biting the side of Aaron's neck and shoulder.

"Oh yeah," Aaron sighed with pleasure.

"Oh yeah, now this is more like it," Nathan croaked, his mouth, throat and lungs filled with smoke after he took a huge drag off of the joint and passed it over to Andrew.

"Christ's sake, Nathan, it looks like cumulus clouds are being exhaled from between your lips," Andrew stated with amazement as he watched Nathan blow the marijuana smoke out of his mouth.

"Andy, we should be the first administration to have the balls to legalize weed," Nathan announced while coughing. "Sure we'll get push back from our Bible thumpers, but most of the country and more folks than you'd imagine in our party would support it. Hell, the

Libertarians in our caucus would declare you the best President ever!" Nathan proclaimed.

"Sometimes you're as crazy now as you were when you were sneaking through the window of the professors' lounge at Vanderbilt and coming back to our dorm room with $50 bourbon," Andrew said while slowly shaking his head.

"Hell Andy, if I'm gonna break in, I sure ain't gonna steal the rotgut shit. Even thieves must set some standards," Nathan said with a devilish grin.

"You are something my friend," Andrew replied. "It was nice that you and Posy could join us at the White House last week for dinner. It was a good gathering of folks, I thought. Posy looked lovely and seemed to be having a good time."

"Oh, the girl can have a good time, that's not the problem. The good times are real, real good. It's all the other times that's the problem. I swear Andy, that girl can start an argument in an empty house. If she was a huntin' dog, you'd have to put her down for being too aggressive and mean. She can be so stubborn and willful, you can't imagine. When I married her, I thought I was getting this pretty little thing with a body that just wouldn't quit, and the staying power of a $2 whore on a Saturday night when the fleet was in. Only to find out that she's one of the most demanding, confrontational, obsessive, mean-spirited people that God made a mistake in making. The girl could make a preacher cuss!" Nathan exclaimed.

"Well, if we're being truthful here, I gotta admit, when I first met Posy, I said to myself, what an amazingly gorgeous woman. All the right curves and those bright eyes and that sparkling smile. How the hell did Nathan get so lucky? Then she opened her mouth, and I thought, uh-oh, this pretty little gal's only got one oar in the water," Andrew confided to his friend.

"It's not that she's dumb, that's not the problem," Nathan conceded. "At work, I have high level, complex, strategic conversations all day long with some of the most brilliant people on the plant. Sometimes, it's nice to come home to simple. The fact that she is not a terribly learned person is not an issue with me. It's the willfulness and spiteful attitude that drives me up a wall. It was so much easier when we were a couple of horny kids at college, just you and me drinking bourbon and smoking weed and talking about our future. How I long for those days."

"Well, we got it back for at least this night, my friend," Andrew stated as he took a long hit off the joint.

"Hey, puff, puff, give," Nathan stated in mock protest.

"Here you go," Andrew said as he passed the joint to Nathan and exhaled.

"This is real nice, Andy. Thank you for inviting me along," Nathan said as he reached over and gently rubbed the knee of his longtime friend.

"THAT WAS AMAZING!" CLAY EXCLAIMED AS he collapsed in total exhaustion and laid in his bed next to Aaron, both men soaked in sweat. "That is what sex is meant to be," Clay gasped. "Without the connection of love, the passion can never be the same. I endlessly search for this. I crave this. And with you, Aaron, I finally have it."

Aaron just laid quietly on his back next to Clay, their legs still intertwined together. He was happy to be silent and let his friend talk. He enjoyed listening to Clay's refined Southern accent. Not harsh or jarring like some Southern accents. Clay's accent was dignified, almost aristocratic in tone and verbiage. Aaron stared at Clay's trim and tight torso. Clay kept himself in excellent physical shape, all sculptured muscles and sinew. Aaron gently brushed his hand over Clay's abdominal muscles, tracing the pronounced cuts with his fingertips.

"I want the rest of my life to be just like this," Clay sweetly declared. "Lying in bed with you, completely spent and satiated after having had the best sex in my life. Once you find this, Aaron, you never want to let it go. Especially, after years and years of searching for real sexual gratification and fulfillment."

Clay readjusted his pillow to prop his head up, so that he could look into Aaron's eyes while he spoke to him.

"Growing up as Baptist in South Carolina, the only son of a wealthy and influential man, does not easily lend itself to living a carefree gay lifestyle. I hid my desires for years. I actually tried to pray the gay away. I dated girls during prep school and undergraduate studies at Duke, and had sex with them, but it was meaningless to me, and sexually unfulfilling. I received far more pleasure looking at pictures of men in the 'Playgirl' magazine that I swiped from a 7-Eleven, while I dry humped a pillow, than I ever had with a girl. Prep school was pretty much endless masturbation including several circle jerks with my classmates. It wasn't until law school, that I really understood how good sex can be with another person. That's when I met Sebastian," Clay related to Aaron.

"You've briefly mentioned him before, tell me about him," Aaron asked, as he propped his head on his hand his elbow braced against a pillow, now fully facing Clay.

"Sebastian Booth, six foot one of dark haired, blue eyed, handsome and built, Charleston high society Southern charm. I fell in love at first sight," Clay began. "We were both freshmen at Duke Law School's orientation weekend. Sebastian was smart, sophisticated, charming and wealthy. He was the boy that every mother wanted their daughter to date and marry. But unlike me, Sebastian was very confident about who he was and what he wanted out of life. And marrying and settling down with some pretty little Southern gal who came from the right type of family, was not on Sebastian's dance card of life.

But very fortunately for me, I was. In retrospect, I guess you'd have to say that he pursued me. Though truth be told, I was just as interested in him as he was in me. I just wasn't bold or confident enough in myself and my sexuality to press the matter. Sebastian pressed and then pressed some more. And, it didn't take long for me to commit to the program and realize that I never wanted to have sex with a woman again . . . ever! Sebastian taught me how to accept and love myself. To be proud of who and what I am. And for that special gift, I will forever be indebted to him."

"Where is Sebastian now?" Aaron asked.

Clay lowered his head for a moment and sighed.

"Sebastian was always the life of the party. And he loved to have a good time. One night after having been drinking and doing some coke, Sebastian got behind of the wheel of a car when he shouldn't have. I was devastated. I buried myself in my studies just to keep from falling into crushing depression. I knew Sebastian for a little over twenty months. But they were twenty of the best months of my life."

"I'm so sorry," Aaron said. "I feel horrible for asking."

"Why?" Clay replied. "We all make mistakes. Sebastian made one of those types of mistakes that you can't erase. He knew better. But that's the past. You, my gorgeous friend are the present and hopefully the future. We've got an old sayin' in South Carolina; 'You better give your heart to Jesus 'cuz your butt is mine!'"

CHAPTER 21

"CALM DOWN KATE, this is all a misunderstanding," the male voice beseeched on the other end of the phone line.

"Standing me up is not a misunderstanding, nor is ignoring my calls for days on end," Kate Wilson shouted into her phone. "Nobody treats me with that kind of disrespect!"

"Kate, darling. It was all my fault. I got the dates mixed up. You can be mad at me, but please know that it wasn't intentional. I wouldn't willfully do anything to make you upset," the male voice attempted to reassure Kate.

"Then why didn't you return my calls?" Kate curtly inquired.

"Honey, I've got three different phones with different numbers. I was wildly busy at work and I was just checking my work-related phone. Once again, it was my fault. I'm sorry," the male voice apologized.

"You owe me, Kate interjected.

"Of course, I do. And trust me, Kate, I'm a man of my word. You'll get everything that you so justly deserve. Please give me a few days and we'll meet again at the Ritz. You tell me when it's most convenient for you and I will be there on time," the male voice promised.

"OK, I'll give you one more chance. But don't disappoint me ever again," Kate warned.

"No worries, my love, no worries."

STANFORD WINCHESTER SELDOM DID SEARCHES ON the internet. He was an old dog that had little personal use for learning new electronic tricks. He still drafted his Court opinions in long hand and had Naomi convert his writings into Word documents. As for researching legal precedent, that's what his cadre of young and perky technologically proficient law clerks were for. And, Stanford didn't give a hoot about, nor much understood social media. So, it was rare, to say the least, to find Stanford behind the screen of a computer. Yet, there he sat, laptop cover open, as he slowly hunt and pecked his way around the computer keyboard.

Stanford knew enough about the internet to know that you could find out information about people through using a search engine such as "Google." His eyes scanned the keyboard and his fingers pecked at the appropriate keys as he typed into the Google search window: "Senator Perry Douglas." Stanford pushed the "enter" key as he watched the results of his search populate his laptop screen. Pages and pages of result links became available for his perusal. Stanford began to select certain result links and scanned the accompanying text. When he found something to his liking, he sat and read the article. With his reading glasses precariously perched at the tip of his nose, Stanford spent the better part of an afternoon, reading about Perry Douglas.

Stanford Winchester was a bit of a Civil War buff. He had read extensively about the war when he was a teenaged boy. He was particularly invested in reading about Robert E. Lee. Stanford admired General Lee's tenacity and relentlessly aggressive nature on the battlefield. During the Peninsula Campaign, Lee's audacious tactics drove George McClellan's Army of the Potomac from the gates of Richmond during the Seven Days Battle. Lee's brilliant counter-offensive turned the tide and won him the devotion of his troops. Within 90 days of taking command of the Army of North Virginia, Lee had driven McClellan off the peninsula, and the battle lines had moved from 6 miles outside of Richmond, to 20 miles outside of Washington. During a two-year period, Lee invaded the north twice, keeping the Union forces on the defensive.

Stanford, as well, believed in counter-attacks and the tactics of offensive defense. Keep your opponent guessing and off kilter. He continued reading article after article about Perry Douglas, at times, stopping to jot down a few notes. Much like his boyhood hero, General Lee, Stanford knew that you needed to be aggressive and cunning and attempt to gain a strategic advantage over your adversary. Stanford Winchester was preparing well for battle.

AARON ROSE SAT AT THE HEAD OF A CONFERENCE ROOM TABLE populated by young Senate staffers who were reading books, articles, speeches and legal opinions written by Stanford Winchester. Each staffer had a yellow highlighter in their hand, highlighting relevant passages within a document and then passing the highlighted document to Aaron for review.

There was a knock on the conference room door, as one of Aaron's colleagues on Senator Douglas' staff peeked his head through the doorway.

"Aaron, Senator Douglas would like to see you for a minute," the staffer stated.

"Sure, I'll be right there," Aaron replied.

"Come in, Aaron. How are things going?" Senator Douglas inquired of his aide.

"It's going well, sir. We're finding some contradictory opinions and stances in Winchester's written materials and a few inflammatory quotes from some of his speeches to Conservative organizations that we can use during Committee hearings," Aaron responded.

"Good, that's good Aaron, but I want you to pass that review on to someone else for the time being," Senator Douglas stated. "After we received Winchester's responses to the Committee questionnaire, I had an investigator do some background checking on potential witnesses we may call at the Committee hearings. Here is a list of people we may have some interest in talking to," Senator Douglas said as he handed the list to Aaron.

"I would like to have you go to New Orleans for a couple of days and dig a little deeper into Judge Winchester's past. Talk to a few of his colleagues, friends, and acquaintances and see what you can find. I'll forward the investigators report to you. Take a look at it, and let's see if we can flesh out some of the findings. We need to go further into certain details than the superficial information we have so far. Are you up for a trip to the Big Easy?" Senator Douglas asked his aide.

"Yes, sir," Aaron eagerly replied.

JIM BOB MCCALLUM SAT BEHIND THE LARGE ORNATE dark mahogany desk in his Lake Pontchartrain Brands office building. His crossed cowboy boots pressed against the top of the desk, as his leather chair reclined backwards and his telephone was cradled between his head and shoulder.

"Look here," Jim Bob bellowed into the phone, "I don't give politicians millions of dollars because I'm just a sweet guy. Like any other investment that I make, I expect a reasonable return on my money. And, y'all know what my expectations are with respect to my many contributions. So, when am I going to see some action?"

Jim Bob rocked back and forth in his chair as he listened to the caller reply to his question.

"That ain't gonna cut it," Jim Bob assertively stated. "That's about as useful to me as a steering wheel on a mule. You better come up with something better than that."

Jim Bob fidgeted in his chair and became increasingly more agitated as he listened to the caller's response.

"Now, you're just pissing on my leg and tellin' me that it's raining. I need to see results, and I can't wait forever. I need the funding for the research institute to be taken care of soon and the plan announced while Mabel still has the ability to comprehend what's going on. Her memory ain't getting any better. So, get off your ass, and cut through the damn bureaucratic red tape. You best be given me the answers that I desire the next time we talk. You hear me, boy?" Jim Bob angrily spat.

"YOU RECOVERED FROM OUR LITTLE WEEKEND ESCAPADE?" Andrew Cochran inquired of his friend.

"Mostly, I reckon. The fact is that the next morning I felt like I'd been rode hard and hung up dry," Nathan confessed with a grin.

"Well, we had our fun, now it's time to get back to work. Do you have the preliminary cost estimates for the major items on our economic agenda?" Andrew asked his Chief of Staff.

"Yes, sir. I've got the CBO scoring and will get that over to Nancy once we finish up here," Nathan replied.

"Excellent. Let's make sure that we're not handing any ammunition to the Democrats with our budget numbers, and then we can present our economic vision for this country to the American people," Andrew Cochran stated.

"Yes, sir, I'll have our number geeks take one more look," Nathan responded.

"Have you heard anything about how the Democrats are going to question Justice Winchester during the Judiciary Committee hearings?" Andrew inquired.

"Just the usual, sir. They're going to claim that his views are too extreme. That because of some of his non-mainstream opinions that he is unfit to sit on the Court. But they've got nothing, because there is nothing to be had," Nathan confidently replied.

"OK. Let's ask the Republican Senators who are on the Committee to poke around and see if the Democrats have anything that we are unaware of relating to Justice Winchester. We don't want any surprises," Andrew Cochran said.

"Yes, sir," Nathan affirmed.

CHAPTER 22

Ben Carroll sat at the small table at Pete's Diner on Capitol Hill, holding his warm coffee mug with both of his hands. He watched with amazement as Clay Grover devoured a four egg mushroom omelet, a large side of bacon, and a short stack of buttermilk pancakes.

"How the hell can you eat like that and still maintain six-pack abs?" Ben questioned his friend.

"Not sure. I've always had a very fast metabolism and I do work out regularly. At least, when I can," Clay offered. "All I know is that I sure do like to eat. And, I always clean my plate like a good boy."

"I'm not sure 'good boy' is a term that I would use in relation to you, my friend," Ben replied with a sly grin.

"You should talk!" Clay laughed in response.

"Alright now, let's change the subject. We are in a very public place after all," Ben said as his eyes glanced around at the other patrons in the diner.

"Any new Supreme Court gossip?" Clay asked.

"Well, since you mentioned it, there was an episode a few days ago," Ben began, as he lowered his voice and made sure that no one he knew was in the diner.

"A couple of clerks overheard Kate Wilson having a hissy fit on the phone a few days ago. They weren't sure who she was talking to, but she was screaming into the phone. She kept saying that 'you can't do this to me' and something about threatening to 'ruin someone's career.' Very loud and very dramatic from what I've been told," Ben related to Clay.

"You told me that she's a bit of a nut job, didn't you?" Clay inquired.

"Oh yeah. She's having an affair with someone with clout in the White House. Maybe that is who she was screaming at on the phone," Ben guessed in response.

"Well, nut job or not, you don't want to mess with the new administrations' good ol' boy Southern mafia, that's taken up residency in the West Wing," Clay replied. "From what I've heard some of those Georgia country boys are as crazy as rabid dogs. Not a crowd you want to be making threats to."

"All of you Southern boys are a little touched, if you ask me," Ben stated with a smile.

"Spoken like the damn Connecticut Yankee that you are. With all of the smugness and superiority that your precious Harvard law degree can muster," Clay kiddingly chided Ben in return.

"Well, speaking of Harvard law degrees, I've got to get to Court, it's almost 8:30. I've got a staff meeting with Justice Goldberg at nine," Ben stated, while glancing down at his watch.

"Alright then, we'll revisit our little civil war at my place on Friday night. May the soldier with the biggest sword prevail," Clay shamelessly offered with a wink of an eye.

"YES, I OBTAINED WHAT I NEEDED IN HAITI," Queen Rita said into the phone. I can have it ready for you in a few days. But this one will cost far more than the other one back in January. I had to go through much trouble this time around. You understand, it is only fair. Alright then, we speak soon," Queen Rita said as she laid down the telephone in her small voodoo shop. She turned around only to find her niece Bessie standing in the doorway of her shop.

"Oh child, you frightened the spirits out of me!" Rita proclaimed, while placing her hand over her heart. "How long have you been standing there?"

"I'm sorry, I didn't mean to frighten you," Bessie profusely apologized. "I've only been here for a few moments. I was on my way to mama's house, and I just wanted to stop by and see how you are?"

"Oooh," Rita moaned. "Once my heart stops beating like a jungle drum, I'll be fine." Rita took in a deep breath. "My word, I wasn't brought up in the woods to be scared by owls. But girl, I surely was not expecting to find you over my shoulder."

Bessie walked over to her aunt and encircled her arms around her in an attempt to calm the old woman's frayed nerves. "I'm so sorry that I frightened you," Bessie repeated. After a few moments of gentle embrace, Auntie Rita began to breathe normally and stopped shaking.

"Who were you talking to on the phone?" Bessie inquired of her aunt.

"It was a customer. Of no concern to you, my child," Rita stated firmly.

"Ok," Bessie replied, clearly aware her aunt did not want her pursuing that line of questioning.

"Is there anything that I can get for you?" Bessie asked. "How about I bake you a pie tomorrow and bring it by the shop in the afternoon? We can share a couple of slices together," Bessie asked.

"That would be a lovely treat. I would enjoy that," Rita replied.

"It's a date!" Bessie declared with a short giggle. "I'll stop by with a pie tomorrow afternoon, and I'll be sure to knock or holler when I'm at the door."

"Yah, sweet girl, yah," Rita quietly said.

CLAY GROVER WAS WALKING PAST HIS BOSS'S OFFICE when he heard Senator Fitzsimmons call to him.

"Clay, can you please get one of the interns to take a draft outline of the Winchester questioning and a stack of documents over to Senator Douglas' office?" Henry Fitzsimmons asked his Chief of Staff.

"I'll do it," Clay offered.

"Nonsense. I'm not going to have my Chief of Staff act as an errand boy. Just get an intern to do it," Senator Fitzsimmons stated.

"Really Senator, I don't mind, and I was headed in that direction anyway," Clay affirmed.

"Well alright, it's on the corner of my desk. Thank you, Clay."

Clay strode down the hallway of the Senate Office Building with a bounce in his step. He greeted Senator Douglas' secretary and knocked on the Senator's office door.

"Yes, come in," Senator Douglas responded. "Oh Clay, what a wonderful surprise."

"Good afternoon Senator Douglas," Clay said in greeting. "I've got a draft outline of questions for Justice Winchester and a stack of documents from Senator Fitzsimmons for you."

"Are things so dire in Henry's office that he is using his Chief of Staff as a messenger boy?" Perry Douglas asked jokingly.

"No, sir, I was headed this way, and I would have spent more time wrangling an intern, so I decided to just make the delivery to you myself.

Plus, it's always a pleasure to see you Senator," Clay replied.

"Why that's very nice of you to say. Hey, do you have a minute, can you have a seat?" Perry asked.

"Why of course, Senator," Clay stated as he sat in one of the comfortable chairs in front of Senator Douglas' large desk.

"Clay, recently I received a report from an investigator that the Judiciary Committee used to do some background checks on Justice Winchester. I want to follow-up with some potential witness interviews and dig a little deeper into Justice Winchester's personal behavior. I'm sending Aaron down to New Orleans for a few days. But in thinking this through, it's actually a job for two people. During witness interviews we should have someone who does the primary questioning of the witness and also a prover, someone who can corroborate the statements of the witness, in case the witness later recants their accounts given during the interview. I think it would also be helpful to have someone who has a Southern background, and charm, and even a Southern accent to help put some of the witnesses at ease."

"Someone who can help translate some of the more colorful Southern idioms," Clay added with a smile.

"Precisely!" Perry Douglas agreed. "Unfortunately, I don't have anyone fitting that bill on my staff. We're all a bunch of Northerners, I'm afraid. And, of course I wouldn't presume that you would be interested in going?"

"I would love to help out the cause, sir. Of course, Senator Fitzsimmons must feel comfortable in allowing me to go, sir," Clay stated enthusiastically.

"Well, yes, there is that. I know how vital you are to the day-to-day functioning of Henry's office. Though you would be leaving on a Thursday night and returning on Monday. So, in essence you would only be missing half a day of work in Henry's office," Senator Douglas rationalized.

"Why is the trip over a weekend, sir?" Clay inquired.

"We want to incorporate one normal workday to interview the witnesses who work at the State and Federal Court buildings. But most of the other witnesses, work during the weekdays, so their availability for an interview is more conducive over a weekend," Senator Douglas responded.

"Think it over, and of course speak with Senator Fitzsimmons. But if you'd like to help us out, check with Aaron and he can fill you in on all of the logistical details. Thank you for considering this assignment Clay. It would be a great help to the Committee's work preparing for Justice

Winchester's vetting hearing," Perry stated.

"Thank you, Senator Douglas, it would be an honor to assist the Committee in any way possible," Clay stated as he raised himself up from the comfortable chair.

SEVERAL MINUTES LATER, Perry Douglas' office phone rang. "Hello Henry."

"Perry Stephen Douglas what in blue blazes are you up to?" Henry Fitzsimmons asked his friend and colleague. "Clay was just in my office telling me about your little scheme."

"I apologize Henry, I should have talked to you first before I mentioned anything to Clay. It was just spur of the moment. He was here in my office, and I had been thinking about sending another person with Aaron down to New Orleans to conduct a few witness interviews. I think that it's important that we have a prover. Plus it would be helpful to have a Southerner, who might seem more approachable to some of the witnesses. Clay was in front of me and I just blurted it out, I apologize," Perry explained.

"Oh hell Perry, I've got no problem allowing Clay to go to New Orleans for a couple of days. You're absolutely right. We need a prover and it helps to have a Southern boy along to relate to some of the witnesses. But my gut tells me that you have ulterior motives. If I'm reading this right, after our conversation last week about Clay and Aaron, I get the feeling that ol' Perry Douglas is sprouting wings and is trying to play Cupid," Henry stated with a chuckle.

"No, of course not," Perry feebly protested.

"C'mon Perry, I know you. You are trying to show me that you're a better, more open-minded progressive than I am. And, on some level, I appreciate that. But them boys can find their way around each other without you trying to be a pimp for my Chief of Staff," Henry laughed. "That said, if Clay wants to go, I surely will not stop him. So I guess you've got your prover and Southern charmer all wrapped up in one," Henry said.

"Thank you, Henry. I can never be the progressive that you are. You were championing liberal human rights causes in the Senate when I was chasing baseballs in Little League," Perry acknowledged.

"You know Perry, if this Senate job don't work out for you, you can always get a job at the 'Love Connection,'" Henry chuckled.

CHAPTER 23

B EN CARROLL ANSWERED HIS SMARTPHONE, "HEY you, can't wait until Friday night?"

"I'm sorry, my friend, but the Civil War is going to have to wait until next week," Clay stated to Ben. "I've been asked by the Chair of the Senate Judiciary Committee to go down to New Orleans to conduct some investigative interviews in preparation for the Winchester vetting process."

"New Orleans, the city of Mardi Gras, Southern decadence and go-go boys dancing on bar tops," Ben replied.

"It's purely a business trip. Of course, if I just happen to find a few minutes at the end of a long hard work day, there's nothing wrong with enjoying a Sea Breeze or two at a local watering hole on Bourbon Street while pushing a few rumpled dollar bills into a well filled jock strap."

"Just as I suspected. You will always try very hard to mix business with pleasure," Ben chuckled.

"Speaking of pleasure, sheath your sword, my dear. We'll have to resume our sword play after I return," Clay stated.

"You're incorrigible!" Ben laughed.

AARON ROSE HAD JUST BEEN TOLD BY HIS BOSS that Clay Grover would accompany him to New Orleans for the Winchester witness interviews. On the one hand, Aaron was excited to have Clay along for the trip. But, yet, on the other hand, Aaron was afraid that Clay would attempt to monopolize the interview process and thereby reduce Aaron's role in the assignment. And, there was also the possibility that it would be difficult to keep Clay focused on the task at hand in a city whose motto is, "let the good times roll." Clay was already well-schooled in seeking out good times. However, these were all minor concerns. Aaron had been entrusted with an opportunity to perform meaningful Judiciary Committee work. And for that, he was very pleased and proud.

Aaron spent hours going over the investigator's initial findings and committed to memory facts about the witnesses that he would be speaking to. On the list of witnesses, was a former judge who served on the Louisiana Supreme Court during Stanford Winchester's term on the Court, as well as a current justice on the Fifth Circuit Court who was a Democrat, and who had written the dissenting opinion on the *Happy Foods v. Lake Pontchartrain Brands* case. Additionally, on the witness list was the name of a former law clerk to Justice Winchester and a current leader of the Louisiana Bar Association. A couple of names of additional staff workers at the Fifth Circuit building were also included on the witness list. Finally, there were a few names of individuals with knowledge of Stanford Winchester's personal life. A neighbor from when he and LeeAnn owned a home in the Garden District, neighbor from his current residency in the French Quarter and a couple of French Quarter merchants. And, Lucius and Bessie Collins.

BESSIE COLLINS USED HER FINGERS TO carefully press the pie crust dough into the pie plate.

"Umm, what kind of pie are you makin'?" Lucius asked his wife, as he sidled up beside her at the kitchen table.

"Peach, but it ain't for you," Bessie firmly advised her husband. "It's for Auntie Rita. I scared her to death, when I was visiting at her shop on my way to mama's house yesterday. She sure has seemed jumpy ever since she and mama got back from Haiti."

"She's an old woman, Bessie. That trip may have been a little too much for her," Lucius offered.

"Surely, that might be part of it. But there's something more. She just seems more skittish, even secretive around me lately. She was whispering something to mama after I left the room the day they got back from Haiti. And, she had this look on her face when I talked about meeting Jim Bob McCallum at her store. And, when I scared her, she was on the phone with someone, and she seemed concerned that I may have overheard her talking. It's a lot of little things, but it all seems a tad odd. Different than how she acted around me before the trip to Haiti," Bessie explained.

"Has your mama said much about their trip to Haiti?" Lucius asked.

"Just the usual." How much they enjoyed themselves, while visiting with old family members who had stayed on the island. She showed me some photos of the relatives and of some pretty scenery, but that's about it. Though, I will say that I get the sense that something happened that may have put a strain on mama and Auntie Rita's relationship. They seemed a little annoyed with each other. But, I assumed that that was just two older women traveling for several days together and by the end of the trip they were both getting on each other's last nerve."

"Well, don't rule that out. It could be nothing. Sometimes Bessie, you want to read more into things than there truly is. You enjoy too many of them mystery romance books and you think that everything is a mystery that needs to be solved," Lucius cautioned his wife.

"I don't know, Lucius. Call it woman's intuition or whatever you want to call it. I get the feeling that something strange is going on with Auntie Rita. I just don't know what it is," Bessie said with conviction.

"SOMETIMES LIFE IS A MYSTERY," said Stanford Winchester to his secretary, Naomi Cutler. "Here I was, just happy as a pig in slop to be the Chief Judge of the Fifth Circuit. Not a worry in the world, and perfectly content with where I put down my roots and what I did for a living. Then, one day out of the blue, I get a phone call from the Chief of Staff to the President of the United States, and my life has become a snow globe that somebody decided to vigorously shake up and down and scramble everything."

"The picture is not always clear, sir," Naomi began. "Virgil and I enjoy the challenge of putting together a good jigsaw puzzle. Especially, the big ones with over a couple thousand pieces. When you open the box, you pour all of the pieces onto the table. Then you turn over all of the pieces and arrange them face up on the table. But you've got to stare at them for a while. Take it all in before you start matching some of the pieces together. You look for like colored pieces. It takes a while before any shapes begin to match and look like the right fit. And sometimes, you're darn sure you've matched the correct pieces together, but they just don't fit quite right. There's a better match with another piece. Maybe, you just found a better match, sir. Maybe, the Fifth Circuit was a good fit, but the Supreme Court is a better fit. You never know, until the puzzle is completed."

"Yes, you're right, Naomi," Stanford Winchester affirmed. "God lays all the pieces of life in front of us. It's up to us to find the ones that are a match. Whether it's the right college you choose to attend. Or the spouse you pick. Or the correct path to follow in your career. I just can't help but wonder if I've already found my matching piece here in New Orleans as Chief of the Fifth Circuit."

"Is your puzzle complete? Have you used all of the pieces? If not, you'll never know until you finish the puzzle," Naomi stated.

"You couldn't be more right, Naomi." You couldn't be more right."

PERRY DOUGLAS SLUMPED BACK in his leather chair, a puzzled expression crossed his face as he recalled his conversation with Henry Fitzsimmons. Was Henry right, had he gone too far and attempted to meddle in the personal life of his aide Aaron? In retrospect, perhaps that was the case. But, in his mind, Perry thought that his intentions were good and his motivation was reasonable. After all, a prover was necessary for the interview process, and the presence of a fellow Southerner could put some of the witnesses more at ease. But, by the same token, there were at least a half dozen Senate staffers aiding the Judiciary Committee that could fill that bill. Did it have to be Clay Grover?

Granted Clay was in Perry's presence, so he became an obvious and convenient choice. But had the fact that just days before, Henry had surprisingly mentioned to him that he believed that Clay and Aaron were "sweet on each other" as Henry so charmingly phrased it, become a factor in Perry asking Clay to accompany Aaron on the trip to New Orleans? Perry searched his conscience and it became clear that Henry was correct. The spirit of Cupid had occupied itself in the soul of Perry Douglas.

Perry had become very fond of Aaron. From the day he interviewed and hired him, he saw qualities in Aaron that easily related to the personal traits of his mentor and friend, Judge Martin. The couple of years working together had only confirmed and solidified Perry's admiration, appreciation, and affection for Aaron. So, if in the back of his mind, Perry felt that he could do something positive and pleasing for Aaron, then why not act upon the impulse.

Perry's rationale and well-intended motivation spurred his actions. But, as is the case in life, without the knowledge and appreciation of all of the facts involved in a human situation, the most well-intended actions do not always lead to the most desired results.

CHAPTER 24

IT WAS A WARM JULY SUNDAY MORNING in New Orleans. Stanford Winchester sat at the kitchen table in his French Quarter home. He had cleared everything off of the table, creating a blank space. He opened the box and poured the contents onto the empty kitchen table. The puzzle pieces filled a good portion of the center of the table. Stanford flipped over the pieces until all of the colorful sides of the jig sawed components were visible.

It had been years since Stanford attempted to put together a puzzle. He and LeeAnn would occasionally do a puzzle together when they had tired of playing bridge, or Monopoly or some other board games. When he and LeeAnn assembled a puzzle, it was usually a scenic picture of a destination that they had either planned to visit or had recently visited in their travels abroad. A picture puzzle of the Eiffel Tower in Paris, or the Vatican in Rome, or Big Ben in London. LeeAnn was always quicker to find the interlocking pieces that fit together. Her skill set was more visual. Stanford was more acute at word skills. Crossword puzzles or word jumbles were his bailiwick. But, his conversation with Naomi had triggered his desire to see if he could successfully put together a jigsaw puzzle without the assistance of LeeAnn.

Stanford propped up the box cover to the puzzle at the side of the kitchen table. It was the way LeeAnn use to do it, to use the completed picture as a guide to locating shapes and colors among the pieces. The cover of the box proclaimed that there were over 1000 pieces. The picture on the box cover was of the U.S. Capitol building. Stanford surveyed all of the pieces of the puzzle laid out in front of him. He slowly and carefully began selecting and attempting to make the small pieces mesh. It might take a while, he thought to himself, to make the pieces of this puzzle fit together.

KATHERINE DOUGLAS SAT AT THE KITCHEN TABLE of their Georgetown condo, her packed suitcases lined up at the side of the front door. It was Thursday morning and Katherine studied the New York Times crossword puzzle as she waited for the town car that would take her to the airport. She was prepared to go back to Chicago for several weeks while her husband went about the business of preparing to chair hearings to vet the person nominated to take over the vacancy on the Supreme Court.

"A nine letter word starting with the letter "m," meaning "untruthfulness?" Katherine challenged her husband Perry.

Perry Douglas hesitated for a moment, as he sipped his morning coffee. "Mendacity," he offered.

"Yep, that works," Katherine cheerfully replied.

"I have a feeling that I'm going to be experiencing quite a bit of mendacity during the upcoming Judiciary Committee hearings. The preliminary investigative report that I received points to the fact that Justice Winchester is not above stretching or even fabricating the truth. Whether it be embellishing a 'good old boy' story he tells to his friends, to blatant falsehoods concealing the fact that he prospered financially from rulings on case matters he presided over. Apparently, this Southern jurist holds the belief that as long as you lie with charm and in an orotund manner, it can pass as the truth," Perry explained to his wife.

"Orotund?" Katherine questioned with a puzzled expression.

"It means containing extremely formal and complicated language intended to impress people," Perry stated.

"You mean like using the word 'orotund?'" Katherine shot back at her husband with a grin.

"When does your flight leave?" Perry asked with a sheepish expression on his face, trying to change the topic.

"Not soon enough to keep me from calling you out on the fact that you think that you're such an amazing wordsmith when, in fact, you're being an insufferable elitist snob," Katherine countered with a laugh.

Perry just sunk into his chair sipping his coffee. He was through helping with crossword puzzles.

Kate Wilson placed her right foot up on the kitchen chair in her apartment. She leaned over and tied the shoelace on her running shoe. Kate enjoyed a good, long morning run. It helped clear her head and ready her for the work day. She enjoyed getting into a runner's "zone" after the first couple of miles, where your breathing regulates and you push ahead in a type of laser focus determination. And laser focus was something that Kate had in abundance.

As she ran down the streets of D.C. early in the morning, Kate thought about her upcoming rendezvous at the Ritz Carlton. In her mind, she planned how she would put forth her demands for a position at the White House. It was time to move on from her clerk's position at the Supreme Court and become a part of the inner circle of the real political power in the country. Kate's ambition was as relentless and powerful as her accomplished runner's gait. She had made moral sacrifices and taken great personal risk to gain the favor of the Washington power elite. Now was the time to push forward and state her demands. Kate powered on as she raced with determination down Pennsylvania Avenue.

Bessie Collins wrapped the peach pie in a clean cloth towel as she exited her house and made her way to her Aunt Rita's voodoo shop on north Rampart Avenue in the French Quarter.

"Oh my word, girl, what have you brought me?" Aunt Rita asked her niece as she greeted her in the doorway of her old shop.

"It's a peach pie," Bessie cheerfully explained.

"Why, bless your heart child, peach is my favorite pie," Aunt Rita fawned. "Let me get some plates and forks from the back, I'll be right back."

While she waited for her aunt to return, Bessie looked at a chicken bone and hemp constructed structure on the counter top that her aunt was clearly working on. Rita entered the main room of the shop pushing aside the beaded curtain carrying a couple of plates, forks, and a knife.

"I will move that," Rita said gesturing at the structure in progress, "it is not nearly done."

"What's it for?" Bessie inquired.

"I have told you before, there are many purposes. When a chicken is sacrificed in a ceremony to the spirits, its dried bones are used to form either a tribute to the departed or a sign of a curse to be placed on the living. If it is a curse, potions, incense, or other means may also be used to bring harm to the intended," Rita explained.

"Why would you want to harm someone?" Bessie asked her aunt.

"Child, it is not that simple. I am only the servant of the spirits. People ask for my services, which I provide to them. I do not harm anyone. It is up to the loa to determine the outcome of a spell. If a person has offended the spirits by their actions, they may be displeased and act as they wish. Why do you ask such things?" Rita asked with a degree of irritation.

"Mama is a Christian and doesn't believe in your spirits, why is that?" Bessie asked.

"I love my sister, but we are not alike in many ways. Sandra is seven years younger than I. When I was a teenaged girl and Sandra was still a child, I met a man in Haiti who taught me the ways of Vodou. He showed me the love of Bondye, the unknowable Supreme Creator. Unlike the Christian God, Bondye does not intercede in human affairs. Vodouists worship the spirits who serve Bondye. We call them loa. Every loa is responsible for all aspects of life and death. We develop relationships with the loa through our traditions and ceremonies. In your Roman Catholic religion, Bondye, is your God, and the loa are your saints. Sandra followed the Catholic religion of our father. I believed that I was called to go down another path. I chose Vodou, and eventually became a bokor. It is as simple as that."

"What of the man who taught you Vodou, where is he now?" Bessie questioned.

"Too many questions, my love. Some things you need not know. I would rather have a piece of this lovely pie that you so thoughtfully brought for me," Rita said.

Bessie cut a piece of pie for her aunt and served her.

"This is too good for humans," Rita said with great pleasure as she ate the delicious peach pie that Bessie had baked. "You please me no end, child."

Bessie smiled in return, but there were so many questions she wanted to ask her aunt. Though she knew in her heart, some of the answers she would never want to hear.

AARON ROSE AND CLAY GROVER SAT in a conference room in the Senate Office Building going over the list of witnesses that each would call to set up appointments for interviews.

"You should call the federal Fifth Circuit judges and employees, Aaron, and I'll handle the Louisiana Supreme Court witnesses and the friends of Justice Winchester. If I encounter someone on the phone call who has a deep Southern drawl, I can make my accent as thick as Mississippi mud," Clay explained while intensifying and slowing down his speech patterns.

"OK, that's fine with me, I'll call the federal court witnesses," Aaron stated.

"See there, already we have a problem," Clay said with a grin. "In the south we never say we're going to do something, we say 'yes, sir, I'm fixin' to get to callin' them folks.' We're always 'fixin' to do something not actually doing it," Clay explained with a short laugh.

"Keep this up and I'll be fixin' to whoop your Southern ass," Aaron threatened with a sly smile.

"Nope, still not quite right. Better said would be 'I'm fixin' to knock you into the middle of next week, looking both ways for Sunday,'" Clay chortled in response.

"You're a demented Southern idiot," Aaron replied with a shake of his head.

"Well butter my butt and call me a biscuit!" Clay exclaimed in return.

"Oh jeez!" Aaron sighed in mock frustration.

CHAPTER 25

NATHAN WHITAKER STOOD IN FRONT of his bathroom mirror while forming a Windsor knot in his striped tie. He shouted to his wife who was in the adjoining bedroom, "I'm not going to be able to make it home tonight."

"Why the hell not?" Posy Whitaker shouted in response.

"Lots of work to do and Andy has asked for a late evening cabinet meeting tonight," Nathan explained, as he walked into the bedroom and donned his suit jacket.

"There you go again, Nathan. You're tryin' to carry water with no bucket. Lie after lie!" Posy spat back.

"Darlin', what are you makin' all this ruckus about? This ain't the first time I got to work late, and it won't be the last. So just settle down girl," Nathan implored his wife.

"I know you're seeing some other woman, Nathan. I can smell her perfume on your clothes," Posy claimed.

"Posy, you're making a mountain out of a mole hill," Nathan replied. "I get hugged by women at work often. Sometimes it's Sue Lynn, who will give me a hug and a little sugar on the cheek when she visits Andy in the Oval Office and I'm present. Nancy, Andy's secretary will give me a hug from time to time. It's nothing. And if I smell of some other woman's perfume, it's because they hugged me for a minute. Ain't nothing more devious to it than that."

"I don't believe you Nathan, you're chasing skirts and I know it," Posy shot back angrily.

"Posy, darlin', I love you and only you. I could never find anyone more beautiful than you are. I hope you know that in your heart of hearts. But, honey, I don't have time for this right now. I've got to get to work. So settle yourself down, and we can spend the weekend together and talk things through. But right now, I've got to go," Nathan calmly stated to his wife as he walked out of their bedroom and left their house.

As Nathan exited his house he was greeted by a member of his Secret Service detail who opened the door of the SUV for the Chief of Staff.

Posy shouted, "You're a lyin' bastard, Nathan!" From the opened bedroom window of their house.

Nathan climbed into the SUV as the Secret Service agent closed the door. Nathan sat in the back seat just shaking his head.

"Get me the hell out of here, fellas. That woman is as mad as a wet hen and as crazy as a loon!" Nathan Whitaker exclaimed to the agents.

"Yes, sir," his driver stated with a slight grin.

AARON ROSE AND CLAY GROVER WAITED for Senator Douglas to arrive at his Senate office. Senator Douglas approached the two as he began unbuttoning his overcoat.

"Good morning gentlemen, I hope I haven't kept you waiting," Perry Douglas cheerfully greeted his guests.

"Not at all sir, we just arrived ourselves," Clay replied. Aaron handed the Senator a cup of Starbucks coffee as they entered his office.

"Thank you so much, Aaron, just what I needed. You really don't have to bring me coffee, but I do appreciate the gesture, and I am going to drink it."

Senator Douglas took off his overcoat and suit coat and sat behind his large desk.

"Sit down guys, this won't take long. I just wanted to see where things are before you head off to New Orleans later this afternoon. I've got a Senate vote this morning and then Committee meetings this afternoon, so this is the only time that I could meet with both of you," the Senator explained. "Have you spoken with all of the witnesses and set up the interviews?" Perry Douglas asked Aaron and Clay.

"Yes, sir, I have spoken with all of the Federal Fifth Circuit judges and staff that we want to talk to and the interviews are all scheduled for Friday morning. There are five witnesses in total from the Fifth Circuit," Aaron stated.

"Does that include the Democratic Justice who wrote the dissenting opinion in the *Happy Foods* case?" Senator Douglas inquired.

"Yes, sir, that would be Justice Charles Sewell. He is giving us a half hour before his Court day begins. We are interviewing him from 8:15 a.m. to 8:45 a.m. on Friday," Aaron replied.

"Excellent. And what about the former Louisiana Supreme Court Justice who served alongside Winchester?"

"Yes, sir, that would be Justice Beauregard Dumaine. We are scheduled to interview him around 5 p.m. on Friday afternoon," Clay responded.

"So, everything is taken care of?" Senator Douglas asked.

"Well, sir, there is one witness that I am still attempting to contact. I will try again this morning. It is a witness who would have knowledge of Justice Winchester's personal life. It is actually a couple sir, who have known the Justice for fifteen years, Lucius and Bessie Collins," Clay replied.

"OK, fine. Try to get them on the schedule," You've both done witness interviews before, and you know what information we're looking for, so be polite but persistent. Good luck gentlemen, bring home some information that the Committee can use for the vetting hearing," Perry stated as he shook the hands of Clay and Aaron.

"We will, sir," Clay and Aaron said in unison.

THE TELEPHONE RANG AND RANG as Lucius scurried up the stairs to the front door of his home. He fiddled with his keys, as he attempted to open the door and get to the ringing telephone. Lucius shoved the door open and was able to grasp the phone from its cradle before it stopped ringing.

"Hello?" Lucius huffed into the phone as he gasped for air.

"Mr. Collins?" The Southern male voice asked on the other side of the line.

"Yes, this is he," Lucius stated as he attempted to control his rapid breathing.

"I am so sorry, have I caught you at a bad moment?" the male voice inquired.

"No, sir. Just was running up the stairs to grab the phone. If you would kindly give me a minute to catch my breath, I'll be fit as a fiddle," Lucius replied while still huffing.

"I understand. You take as much time as you need, Mr. Collins. Get yourself a cool glass of water, if you're of a mind," the voice suggested.

Lucius sat in a chair nearby the telephone, as his breathing began to regulate and his racing pulse began to slow.

"Yes, sir, what can I do for you?" Lucius asked the man on the phone.

"Mr. Collins, my name is Clay Grover. I work for the Senate Judiciary Committee. As you probably know, your friend, Justice Stanford Winchester, has been nominated to fill a vacant seat on the United States Supreme Court by President Cochran. The Senate Judiciary Committee is going to be conducting hearings to determine the fitness of Justice Winchester to be seated on the Supreme Court fairly soon. To that end, myself and my colleague will be in New Orleans over the weekend, and if possible, we would like to sit down for a few minutes with you and your wife Bessie, if she is available, to talk about Justice Winchester. We can meet with you wherever you like and would only take a few minutes of your time. Could we please arrange for a meeting this weekend, Mr. Collins?"

"Why, of course, Mr. Grover. My wife and I would be delighted to meet with you and your colleague and talk about the Chief Justice. We both know in our hearts that he will make an outstanding judge on the Supreme Court. We are more than happy to help him in any way possible," Lucius responded.

"Excellent, thank you so much, Mr. Collins. I will call you back once we are on the ground in New Orleans and we can arrange for an exact time and place for our meeting on Saturday. Is that acceptable to you sir?" Clay asked.

"It surely is, sir, it surely is," Lucius gleefully replied. "I will look forward to your call. Safe travels to you sir," Lucius wished Clay.

STANFORD WINCHESTER SAT AT HIS KITCHEN TABLE, attempting to fit pieces of his puzzle of the U.S. Capitol Building together as he sipped a cup of coffee that his housekeeper had brewed for him. His lips curled upward and his eyes winced as he took a long sip from his coffee cup.

"Lordy Jesus, this surely ain't gonna cut it," Stanford mumbled to himself well out of Clara's earshot. His hand slowly moved and then pushed puzzle pieces into place. He was making progress but was far from being done with his puzzle. He took one more sip of coffee, and quickly determined that he had enough of the coffee and the puzzle.

Stanford snuck into his usual seat at Cafe Du Monde. Perfectly content to savor his chicory coffee and plate of beignets. He reached into his briefcase and removed a manila folder. As he enjoyed his coffee, he leafed through the papers in his folder. They were printouts of Google searches that he had conducted on every Democratic Senator who was a member of the Senate Judiciary Committee. Once he began reading about the

Committee chairman, Perry Douglas, Stanford became more interested in knowing background information about the other Democratic members of the Committee as well.

Stanford knew that he had allies in the Republican members of the Judiciary Committee. First and foremost, the Republican Minority leader on the Committee, Senator Cletus Sawyer from Alabama. Stanford had met Senator Sawyer while traveling in Southern political circles. He sat next to him at a fundraiser just about a year ago during the Presidential campaigns. They both understood the political expediency of developing a mutually beneficial working friendship. And that they had. Stanford knew that he could count on Cletus Sawyer to attempt to deflect whatever criticism the Democrats may throw his way during Committee hearings. Yet, he knew that the Democrats would provide a difficult challenge. So, best to know the most you can about your enemies.

Stanford came to the realization that his two most staunch adversaries on the Judiciary Committee would be the chair, Senator Perry Douglas of Illinois, and the most senior member of the Committee, Senator Henry Fitzsimmons of South Carolina. Senator Fitzsimmons, like himself, was a born and bred Southerner from a wealthy and well-respected family. Stanford recalled the dogged questioning that he received from Senator Fitzsimmons when he was being vetted for the Federal bench. He considered himself lucky that the Senators had to adjourn from the Committee hearings to take up an important vote on urgent foreign policy matters, and that his appointment was confirmed without further challenges to his record.

Stanford knew that Henry Fitzsimmons understood the ways of Southern political men and their families. Fitzsimmons understood that Louisiana politicians did not always consider the legitimacy of the means that they used to achieve the ends that they sought. Fitzsimmons knew that the rough and tumble ways and means of the departed Senator Huey Long of Louisiana were not buried with his human remains. Huey Long had once famously said, "One of these days the people of Louisiana are going to get good government—and they ain't going to like it." Henry Fitzsimmons knew that Stanford Winchester was well schooled in the Louisiana ways of political advancement. And, that knowledge made the Senator from South Carolina a threat to Stanford Winchester at the Committee hearings.

Stanford grasped a buttery sweet beignet off the plate and briefly studied it in his hand before devouring it whole. What to do about the challenge of Henry Fitzsimmons, Stanford thought to himself.

KATE WILSON WALKED THROUGH THE FRONT DOOR of the Ritz Carlton Hotel in DuPont Circle. Two minutes later, right on time, her companion for the evening meeting was also present at the hotel. Kate was barely at the hotel elevator when she was joined by a lone male.

"Hello gorgeous, right on time as promised," the male stated.

"Well, I guess there's a first time for everything," Kate said with a smile. And in fact, it was the first time they had entered the hotel at the same time. Their arrival was usually carefully staggered.

The couple boarded the elevator and proceeded up to their usual hotel suite.

BEN CARROLL LIVED IN THE DUPONT CIRCLE neighborhood of Washington. He was out for a late evening run, when from across the street he recognized Kate Wilson walking towards the Ritz Carlton Hotel. Ben hesitated and then came to a complete stop as he watched Kate enter the front door of the hotel. Moments later, Ben saw a black SUV pull up to the door of the hotel. Ben moved across the street closer to the entrance of the hotel. He noticed a male figure get out of the SUV. Ben was close enough to easily see the man as he turned to enter the hotel. Illuminated under the bright lighting of the hotel entrance, Ben recognized the man and audibly gasped. Ben turned quickly and began running in the opposite direction.

Ben knew then what others had only speculated about. And, possessing that information sent a chill down his spine.

CHAPTER 26

Aaron Rose and Clay Grover briskly walked through Louis Armstrong Airport after having deplaned the flight from Washington, D.C.

"I haven't been in New Orleans since attending Mardi Gras while I was still in college," Clay told Aaron with a big smile. "And I'm telling you right now, Aaron, on the way back, I'm gonna buy some of the frozen alligator they sell here at the airport. I do love some good home-fried gator."

"We're here for business," Aaron quickly reminded his traveling companion.

"Yeah, well, there's nothing in the business handbook that says you can't take some gator meat home with you," Clay countered. "Lighten up Aaron, we're in the Big Easy now. We will get all of our work done and have a little fun as well." Aaron shook his head and quickened his pace.

Clay and Aaron checked into the Omni Royal Orleans Hotel in the French Quarter. The hotel was located directly across the street from the Louisiana Supreme Court Building, a few short blocks from Justice Winchester's home and within easy walking distance of the Fifth Circuit Court Building. A perfect location from which to get to all of their scheduled witness interviews. Not to mention being in the bustling center of the famed French Quarter.

As they approached the lobby desk of the hotel, Clay mentioned, "It's a pity that we waste taxpayer money on two rooms when we really only need one."

"Clay, Senator Douglas' secretary made reservations for two rooms, we will inhabit two rooms. This is a business trip after all," Aaron scolded his colleague. Clay just smirked. He had other plans.

The first witness interview on Friday morning was at 8:15 a.m. at the Federal Court Building in New Orleans Business District. Justice Charles Sewell was a Democrat who had been appointed to the Fifth Circuit Appellate Court fifteen years ago. Justice Sewell authored the dissenting opinion on the *Happy Foods v. Lake Pontchartrain Foods* case. This was the case that Aaron had discovered where Justice Winchester had failed to recuse himself from despite having a friendship with the defendant company's owner, Jim Bob McCallum, in addition to the financial holdings of his wife and her family in the defendant's company.

Aaron questioned Justice Sewell about the case matter, and the Justice explained that he believed that not only had Justice Winchester been wrong on applying the governing laws and his interpretation of the Lanham Act, but also that he was aware of Justice Winchester's conflict of interest in the matter and had spoken to Justice Winchester about recusing himself from the case when it was assigned to the Appellate panel.

"One thing you've got to understand about Stanford Winchester is that he is a stubborn old bird," Justice Sewell noted with a shake of his head. "He was born and raised as an entitled child of an old and powerful New Orleans family. His mother's father was governor of Louisiana. There aren't many people in these parts that have the fortitude or lack of common sense to say 'no' to the Winchesters."

"So, you agree that Justice Winchester should have recused himself from the *Happy Foods* matter?" Aaron asked Justice Sewell.

"Yes, of course. His friend was the CEO of the defendant's company and his wife and her family owned a fair share of stock in that company. He had no right sitting on that panel. But old Stanford is very fond of arguing that his family roots run far and deep in Louisiana and if he recused himself from every case that he had a tangential relationship with one of the parties, he would never preside over any cases. Plus, he likes to add that he relies on his God given ability to judge the facts objectively and apply the governing law fairly. Here in Louisiana, the track record for good, above board governance and judicial restraint is, to say the least, lacking," Justice Sewell related to Aaron and Clay.

"Do you believe that Justice Winchester applies the law fairly and impartially?" Aaron inquired.

"Sometimes yes, sometimes no. Stanford is not a stupid man. Far from it. He knows what he can get away with and where he needs to pull back for the sake of professional decorum. His application of legal doctrine is usually within the confines of an acceptable interpretation of the law. But, he operates on the edges, taking advantage of the least bit of ambiguity in the language of the law in order to achieve the ends he seeks. Stanford possess cunning, a keen intellect, and the charm to disarm even his most avid critics. He is a man not to be taken lightly. Our relationship on the Court is cordial and collegial. He is a pleasant person to share a conversation with, but there is an aggressive side to Stanford Winchester that you don't want to cross," Justice Sewell warned.

Aaron looked at his questioning outline as Clay finished taking notes. "Is there anything else that you'd like to add?" Aaron asked Justice Sewell.

"Good luck to you. Senator Douglas has his work cut out for him. Stanford Winchester is a tough nut to crack. He has a judicial agenda that is staked at the far right reaches of the Republican Party. I sincerely hope that he does not gain Senate confirmation and a seat on the Supreme Court. I say this with no personal animus. He has always treated me with collegial respect. I just do not think our country would benefit from some of the radical viewpoints espoused and pursued by Justice Winchester, not to mention his proclivity for conveniently ignoring his personal conflicts of interest."

Aaron and Clay thanked Justice Sewell for his time and moved on to their next interview with a Fifth Circuit staffer who worked with Justice Winchester, Filbert Montague. Mr. Montague had worked at the Federal Court Building for ten years as an administrative clerk. Aaron asked him several questions about his daily contact with Justice Winchester and his general impressions about working with the Chief Justice.

"Well, I reckon I'd have to say that overall I have a decent working relationship with the Chief Justice," Filbert began. "He's always treated me fairly, but make no mistake he expects you to do things his way. He's got certain routines that he expects you to follow and if you don't do things the way he wants it done, y'all gonna hear about it. Most of the other justices are a tad more flexible and accepting of deviations in routines, not the Chief Justice."

"Have you observed Chief Justice Winchester showing favoritism to any of the parties that appear before him in case matters?" Aaron asked Filbert.

"The Chief is a Southern gentleman in public, so he is very polite and refined in the way that he deals with the attorneys who appear before him in the open courtroom. But, I've seen him light into a few attorneys in chambers. Them boys leave his chambers shaking like a cypress tree in a hurricane."

Aaron pressed Filbert with several more direct questions about the *Happy Foods* case as Clay took copious notes.

"Yes, sir, I was working the day of the oral arguments on the *Happy Foods* intellectual property suit. Chief Justice Winchester was the most active of the three Justices on the panel questioning the attorneys for the parties. He was giving the attorney representing Happy Foods fits, challenging pretty much everything he said. That boy could barely get out a full sentence response without being aggressively questioned by the Chief. Just from watching the oral arguments in the courtroom, if I was a betting man, I surely knew what horse I would have bet on to win that race," Filbert acknowledged with a sly smile.

Clay and Aaron thanked Mr. Montague for his time. They still had two additional witnesses at the Federal Court Building to interview before moving on to the Louisiana Supreme Court.

JIM BOB MCCALLUM STOOD ON A SMALL BLUFF overlooking a vacant parcel of land in Baton Rouge, not far from Louisiana State University. Jim Bob had met his wife Mabel while they were both students at LSU. Jim Bob was born and raised in New Orleans. Mabel was the daughter of a prominent doctor in Baton Rouge. When he met Mabel at college, Jim Bob was on the rebound, having just been gently letdown by his high school sweetheart, LeeAnn. Several years later, Lee Ann married Stanford Winchester. Once LeeAnn was no longer available, Jim Bob married his college girlfriend from LSU, Mabel.

Jim Bob loved Mabel. She was a sweet, innocent young woman who whole heartedly loved him. But, LeeAnn was and would always be the first true love of Jim Bob's life. And for that fact, Jim Bob often felt guilt and shame. He could never give himself as fully to Mabel as she did to him. There was always his longstanding love for LeeAnn that would not allow him to be completely and utterly in love with Mabel. Once he became a very successful businessman, Jim Bob would attempt to compensate for this by giving Mabel all of the material things a woman could possibly desire. He was a devoted husband to Mabel, he just felt that he couldn't be as emotionally committed to her, as he believed she deserved.

When Mabel was diagnosed with Alzheimer's disease a little over two years ago, Jim Bob was devastated. He blamed himself and felt ashamed that he had not devoted all of his emotions to his ill wife. In an attempt to offset what he regarded as the treachery of his heart, he pledged to himself that he would do everything in his power to honor his wife and promote her name. To that end, he used his money and political influence to endeavor to have a medical center built devoted to the research for a cure to Alzheimer's. The medical research institute would be built next to LSU, where he and Mabel had met, and would be named the Mabel McCallum Alzheimer's Research Center. Some of the funding for the research center was directly provided by Jim Bob, with additional money to come from Louisiana state funds and the Federal government.

Recently Mabel's disease seemed to be progressing. Despite the medical treatments that she was receiving from a host of prominent doctors, Mabel was having a harder time remembering people and places. Jim Bob was determined to have the medical research center named after his wife completed while she was still able to recognize the honor that her husband was bestowing upon her. It was paramount to him that this be accomplished within the next two or three years. And he would do anything necessary to fulfill this promise he made to Mabel and himself. Anything.

LATE ON FRIDAY AFTERNOON, AFTER INTERVIEWS with staff and clerks at the Louisiana Supreme Court Building, Aaron and Clay met with former Louisiana Supreme Court Justice Beauregard Dumaine at Pat O'Brien's main bar. Aaron initially was taken aback by the hundreds of beer steins that hung from the ceiling of the dark wood and ornate iron bar. Aaron inquired with a bartender and was pointed to a table along a far wall where a distinguished gray haired gentleman sat alone sipping a cocktail.

"Justice Dumaine?"

"Why yes. You must be the gentlemen from the Senate Judiciary Committee," Beauregard Dumaine replied. "Please gentlemen, have a seat."

After brief introductions and handshakes, Aaron and Clay settled into a couple of chairs. Aaron caught Beauregard's eye as he glanced around the room taking it all in.

"I take it that you've never been to Pat O'Brien's before?" Beauregard asked Aaron.

"No, sir, first time," Aaron replied.

"This use to be a refined old-fashioned private gentlemen's club, but then they decided to open it to the tourists. I've been coming here for over thirty years, and well, let's just say that old habits die hard," Justice Dumaine said with a laugh.

Aaron looked at a framed picture hanging on the wall directly over the head of Justice Dumaine.

"Yes, that's a photograph of me and my wife, Lenore, some twenty or so years ago. Many of the locals have their photographs up on the wall," Justice Dumaine offered. "Before we get to talking about Stanford Winchester, you gentlemen should have a drink," Justice Dumaine stated while gesturing to a waiter dressed in a green jacket.

"I'll have an iced tea," Aaron said to the waiter.

"Mr. Rose, you are at Pat O'Brien's in New Orleans. It's 5:15 p.m., you should reconsider your choice of beverage," Justice Dumaine stated with a smile.

"I'll have a Hurricane," Aaron corrected himself, and of course, Clay joined him in his cocktail selection.

"When in Rome, Mr. Rose, when in Rome," Justice Dumaine drawled slowly.

Justice Dumaine took a hearty sip of his cocktail and stated, "I'm guessing' y'all didn't come all the way to New Orleans just to have an evening cocktail with a tired old jurist. You want to hear about what a no account lying s-o-b Stanford Winchester is, ain't that right?"

"Well sir, we would just like to hear your impressions and opinions about working on the Louisiana Supreme Court with Justice Winchester," Aaron diplomatically replied.

"Hmm, Northerners are always seeking the plain facts and the simple truth, but the South ain't the place to find them," Justice Dumaine said with a chortle. "As a colleague, I had few problems with Stanford Winchester. Lord knows, he and I had our share of cocktails at a few bars on Bourbon Street after a day on the bench. We weren't exactly friends but from time to time we enjoyed each other's company. Stanford is, as I'm sure you have already heard dozens of times, a charming man. Smart, clever and with a good sense of humor. He's also a fine judge, for the most part. He wrote some of the most eloquent opinions you're ever going to read from any jurist. But the problem with Stanford was that, in some matters, he didn't know how to separate his personal life from his professional decisions. Stanford never thought that it might seem unethical to let his personal relationships or sympathies color his judicial reasoning. He would argue with me that a man's decision making is dictated by who he is and where he comes from. That they are inseparable from how he perceives the world. That all facts are only interpretations of events as seen through one's own history. And that the law is a tool to be used to craft a personal conception of truth. So, it's hard to see bias when you look at it through the eyes of a man with such a self-centered philosophy."

Justice Dumaine sighed and took another long sip of his cocktail. Aaron and Clay continued questioning Justice Dumaine for another hour and another two Hurricanes. At the end of the interview they thanked him for his time, paid the bill, and went back to their hotel to review their notes and prepare for the next day of interviews.

CHAPTER 27

AARON AND CLAY WENT FOR AN EARLY SATURDAY morning walk together to have breakfast before meeting with their first witness interview of the day. The morning air on Bourbon Street smelled of an acrid mix of garbage, spilled liquor, urine, and street cleaning disinfectant.

"I don't have much of an appetite, let's just get some coffee and beignets," Aaron suggested to Clay, who was squinting in the morning sun.

"Sure buddy, whatever you want," Clay replied, as they walked toward Decatur Street. A line had already formed at Cafe Du Monde. It was a lovely Saturday morning and the tourists were out in force.

"I'm in no mood to wait in line for coffee," Clay said to Aaron. As they were about to turn to go somewhere else, Aaron spotted a lone customer sitting at an outdoor table sipping coffee.

"That's him!" Aaron exclaimed to Clay. "It's Justice Winchester!"

"Are you sure?" Clay asked.

"I've been building a dossier about him and studying articles and photos of him on the internet for weeks, I'm sure," Aaron replied.

"So, now what?" Clay asked.

"I don't know, I just want to watch him for a moment," Aaron replied. "It's kind of weird. Stanford Winchester has been the center of attention for me for a few weeks now. You develop this portrait of the man in your mind's eye. You see him for his rabid right wing philosophy and his misdeeds as a judge. Someone you surmise is wrong for the country and unfit for the job he seeks. You see an enemy that must be politically defeated. But in person, he is a tall, rather elegant, elderly gentlemen who looks peaceful and lonely sitting by himself drinking his morning coffee. There's no radical monster here set on forcing his ultra conservative agenda on the American public. It makes me question a little why we're here, why do we participate in this never-ending game of power politics?" Aaron asked with a bit of sadness in his voice.

"NATHAN, I'M GETTING TIRED OF YOUR LITTLE GAMES," Posy Whitaker sighed angrily.

"Posy, it's Saturday morning, I'm going to spend the entire weekend with my beautiful wife, why do we need to start it with yet another argument?" Nathan wearily questioned his wife.

"Because you're a liar and you're cheatin' on me, and you think you can play me for a fool," Posy snapped back.

"Darlin', I'm running out of ways to convince you that I love only you and would never do anything to hurt you," Nathan gently responded. "I send you flowers once a week. I take you out to dinner and movies. I arrange for you to attend luncheons and events at the White House. I buy you new dresses and jewelry. I tell you how beautiful you are and how much I love you. And how much I want to make love to you, like right now. C'mon baby, give me a little sugar," Nathan cooed to his wife as he placed his hands on her shapely hips.

"Well, you do do all them things for me," Posy conceded, her anger subsiding. "But I'll tell you now, Nathan, if I ever find out that you've been lying and cheating on me, there will be hell to pay," Posy threatened.

"Ain't never gonna happen, sugar," Nathan said, as he lifted Posy into his arms and moved towards the bedroom.

"IT SURELY IS A FINE DAY," Lucius Collins said to his wife Bessie as he gave her a kiss on the cheek. Bessie was in the kitchen working on a pecan pie.

"Good morning Lucius," Bessie replied with a smile. "I'm just fixin' a pie for our company later today. What time did them Washington fellas say they'd be stopping by?"

"Around four this afternoon," Lucius responded. "I'm not quite sure what we can tell them about Stanford that they don't already know."

"They probably just wanna hear from some folks that've known him for a good bit, about what a fine and wonderful man that he is. What a great judge he will be on the Supreme Court," Bessie assuredly stated.

"You're as right as rain, as always, my pretty wife," Lucius said while placing his hands on Bessie's hips and nuzzling against her neck from behind.

"Quit that now," Bessie giggled. "You're gonna get flour all over your clothes."

Kate Wilson stared at the large, gorgeous arrangement of flowers that she had just received from a delivery man. There was a small card with the flowers. It read, "From a man who always keeps his word, beautiful flowers to christen your exciting new career. Thanks for an unforgettable evening. Next time, your place, so we can get even louder! XOXOXOXO."

Kate sat on her couch with a satisfied smile creasing her lips. Despite her doubts and fears, she had managed to get what she wanted. She looked forward to the new challenges and opportunities of working in the West Wing. She knew that the job transition would take some time. After all, she couldn't just up and leave Justice Sallis in the middle of a Supreme Court term, she didn't want to burn any bridges. She did feel a sense of loyalty to the man who hired her out of law school and brought her to Washington. But, now she knew that she was on her way to an important role at the place that was the pinnacle of political power. Her excitement grew as her imagination wandered through the possibilities that may lay ahead.

Kate unable to control the nervous energy that was overtaking her, quickly donned her running clothes, laced up her shoes, and headed out for a long run on a glorious sun swept Saturday morning.

Aaron and Clay arrived at Cochon Butcher in the Central Business District of New Orleans a little before their appointed meeting time for their next witness interview. After a fifteen minute wait, they were able to secure a small round table near the window. Moments later, they were met by a young woman, Emily DuBois, who was a former law clerk to Stanford Winchester. After initial greetings and introductions, the trio engaged in some small talk.

"Just the smell of this place has my mouth watering. What can you tell us about the food here?" Aaron asked.

"It's one of my favorite places in New Orleans for lunch," Emily mentioned. "I've had most of the sandwiches here, and they are all excellent. But the pork belly with mint, the pressed duck pastrami, and the fried oyster sandwiches are to die for. That's what I do know. What I don't know is why you gentlemen wanted to speak with me today?"

"Well, Ms. Dubois," Clay began, but was quickly interrupted.

"Please call me Emily, if you will."

"Of course, Emily. As I mentioned to you on the phone, Aaron and I work for the Senate Judiciary Committee, and we have been interviewing a number of people here in New Orleans who have worked with Justice Winchester in the recent past. We would just like to ask you a few questions about the Justice and get your overall impressions," Clay stated.

"So, you're looking for positive feedback in support of Justice Winchester's confirmation to the Supreme Court?" Emily questioned.

"We're looking for feedback in general," Clay replied. "But before we launch into some questions, why don't we order some lunch. Neither Aaron nor I have had breakfast, and the food here looks and smells sensational."

After they savored their large sandwiches, house chips and orders of sweet tea, Clay was ready to begin questioning Emily.

Did you enjoy working with Justice Winchester? Clay asked.

"Why yes. The Justice was a perfect gentleman and treated me exceptionally well. Of course, he had high standards and he expected his clerks to meet those standards. He was not one to tolerate ineptitude or laziness, but if you did your work well, he treated you with kindness and respect," Emily responded.

"Did you ever witness Justice Winchester being cross or angry with attorneys or staff?" Clay inquired.

"Well . . ." Emily started before she hesitated. "I did see him lose his temper with a few attorneys in chambers, but never in open court. As I mentioned, Justice Winchester had expectations about how attorneys should acquit themselves in his courtroom, and if someone did not meet his standards, the judge was not hesitant to let them know about it. He would not reprimand them in open court, but would invite them to join him behind closed doors in his chambers."

"Did Justice Winchester ever have chamber conversations with attorneys who were presenting legal or political viewpoints that he did not agree with?" Clay pressed.

"There were a few times, though usually it was because the Justice found their arguments to be wholly inappropriate or unnecessarily contentious or rude," Emily answered.

"Did Justice Winchester ever ask you to focus the legal research you preformed for him with a certain political persuasion in mind?" Clay asked.

"I'm not sure I understand what you're asking," Emily replied. "But if you are asking if the Justice wanted research that supported a Conservative and strict constitutionally based line of reasoning, the answer is yes. Justice Winchester is a hard line Conservative, that is not a point of debate or a secret," Emily added with emphasis.

"And the research and writing that you did for him incorporated Justice Winchester's Conservative beliefs and values?" Clay inquired.

Emily smiled. "You've never clerked for a judge have you?" She asked Clay.

"Sure haven't," Clay responded.

"Clerks are extensions of the judges that we work for. You don't include liberal and progressive tenants in a draft argument that you write for a staunchly conservative judge. You serve the master well who chooses you," Emily replied.

"That sounds biblical," Clay stated.

"I think it's a line from Star Wars," Emily said with a wide grin.

Clay blushed, knowing he had been one upped.

"Point taken," he replied.

"Let me ask you, have you ever witnessed Justice Winchester attempt to tailor an opinion or order to serve the interests of family or friends?" Clay inquired.

Emily sat for several moments without responding. She took a long sip of her sweet tea, and restlessly fidgeted in her chair, clearly attempting to collect her thoughts and frame her answer.

"Justice Winchester is an honorable man. He cherishes nothing in this world more than his family and friends. I started clerking for him less than a year after his wife LeeAnn died. He could barely utter her name without tears welling up in his eyes. There is precious little that he wouldn't do to protect and promote the well-being of those he holds dear," Emily somberly replied.

"Does that include twisting judicial ethics for the benefit of those he holds dear?" Clay persisted.

"I think I've said everything that I care to say about Justice Winchester," Emily countered. "It was a pleasure meeting both of you, but I need to attend to a few weekend errands on this Saturday afternoon. A young associate at a law firm has precious little time of their own, as I'm sure you both can attest to. Thank you ever so much for lunch. Safe travels back to D.C." Emily rose up from the table, shook both Aaron and Clay's hand, nd departed the restaurant.

"That was the most telling non-answer I've heard since moot court in law school," Clay said with a stunned look on his face.

"Sure was," Aaron confirmed.

CHAPTER 28

"WELCOME GENTLEMEN, welcome to our humble home," Lucius Collins graciously announced as he shook the hands of Aaron Rose and Clay Grover. "I'd like to introduce you to my beautiful wife, Bessie."

"It's an honor to meet you ma'am, thank you ever so much for the hospitality of inviting us into your lovely home," Clay responded, his Southern accent heavy as maple syrup.

"Y'all have a seat in the parlor. I'm gonna fetch some pecan pie and chicory coffee," Bessie proudly stated as she headed towards the kitchen.

"Now, don't go fussin' over the likes of us," Clay responded. Aaron looked at his friend with a smirk on his face.

"No trouble at all," Bessie cheerfully called back. "It's my pleasure to do so."

"Bessie gets excited when company pays a visit," Lucius admitted in a hushed voice. "Gives her a chance to show off her pies. And let me tell you, Bessie bakes one mean pecan pie."

Seated around a rectangular coffee table in the parlor, Aaron and Clay removed pads of paper and pens from their briefcases as they waited for Bessie's arrival from the kitchen.

"Y'all in town for long?" Lucius asked his guests.

"Until Monday morning," Clay replied.

"Well, then you should come to Arnaud's for jazz brunch on Sunday morning. I work there as a waiter. I'm off today, but I'm working the Sunday brunch. It would be my honor to serve you fine gentlemen. We got a wonderful jazz quartet that plays some of the best Dixieland you'll hear in all of New Orleans. As well as an excellent chef, and outstanding service, if I do say so myself," Lucius chuckled with his head bowed.

"Lordy Jesus, you braggin' on yourself again Lucius," Bessie called out as she entered the room with a large coffee tray. Aaron stood up out of his chair to assist Bessie with the tray.

"See what a gentleman does, Lucius," Bessie said admonishing her husband.

"Your mama raised you proper, Mr. Rose," Bessie sweetly said to Aaron.

"Please, Mrs. Collins, call me Aaron," he asked.

"Well alright, but only if you call me Bessie, and you can refer to that braggin' lazy bag of bones as Lucius. We all friends now," Bessie declared with a wide grin.

"Speaking of friends, Arnaud's is where I first met Justice Winchester," Lucius added, while mock scowling at his wife. "It was fifteen years ago, and me and Bessie been friends with him ever since."

"That's lovely," Clay replied. "Well, since you brought up Justice Winchester, would you mind if we take a few minutes to discuss him?"

"Of course, what would y'all like to know?" Lucius replied.

Clay interviewed Lucius and Bessie about their friendship with Stanford Winchester for over thirty minutes. Lucius described how they met at Arnaud's and how their relationship progressed through the years. Bessie talked about her visits to bring the judge pies at the Federal Courthouse. Both Lucius and Bessie praised Justice Winchester for being a "generous, kind-hearted man who is caring and protective of his friends and family."

"Thank you both, this has been most helpful," Clay stated. "May I ask, when was the last time you saw Justice Winchester?"

"I see him every Wednesday night around 7 p.m., when he stops by for dinner at Arnaud's. Last time both Bessie and I saw him together was at his party at Muriel's to celebrate him being nominated by the President," Lucius replied.

"Can you tell me a little bit about the party? Who some of the guests were?" Clay inquired.

"It was a lovely affair," Bessie offered. "All them beautiful flowers and flickering candles. That food was so very tasty. And, Jesus forgive my vanity, but I just have to tell you, that Justice Winchester got me out on that dance floor and spun me around like a top. He is such a wonderful dancer. When his wife LeeAnn was still living, God rest her soul, they would go out dancing at least once a week. And, I'm here to tell you, them two could cut a rug," Bessie laughed and smiled.

"There were plenty of folks there," Bessie continued. "I recall seeing Jim Bob and Mabel McCallum there, which was real nice because she don't get out as much anymore 'cuz of the Alzheimer's, you know. They seemed to be havin' a good time. Then there was Pastor Roberts and his wife, Virgil and Naomi Cutler, his housekeeper, Clara, Justice Winchester's brother Malcolm and his family, another couple of judges from the Courthouse, I didn't catch their names, and some of the retailers from Royal Street. I don't know them folks very well. They got some very fancy shops."

"Thank you so much for that," Aaron interjected. "You said that Jim Bob and Mabel McCallum were in attendance?"

"Yes, sir. It's kind of funny," Bessie began. "I had not seen the McCallums since they hosted a party for my Auntie Rita several years ago when they introduced the 'Queen Rita Cajun Jambalaya' products on the Lake Pontchartrain Brands," Bessie continued, as Aaron quickly jotted down notes.

"Mr. McCallum had met my Aunt at her shop on north Rampart years ago. They had a business relationship but also developed a friendship. He named a product line of his business after her and it became quite a hit with folks. My aunt is the famous 'Queen Rita of New Orleans,' even though, truth be told, she was born in Haiti. So, as I was sayin' I hadn't seen hide nor hair of the McCallums since the jambalaya shindig and then in less than a week's time I ran into Jim Bob at my aunt's shop and both of the McCallums at Justice Winchester's lovely party at Muriel's," Bessie explained.

"And what business is your aunt in?" Aaron followed up.

"Well sir, that might take some explainin'," Bessie said with a puzzled look on her face. "I once heard some polite folk refer to it as 'the spiritual arts.' But, truth is, my Auntie Rita practices Haitian Vodou."

"That is very interesting," Aaron said. "I have a bit of a fascination with the occult and astrology, I would love to visit your aunt's shop before we leave and maybe have my palm read or a tarot reading."

"Auntie Rita does not do palm reading, she says that is for the silly pretenders in Jackson Square. But, I'm pretty sure that she would do a tarot card reading. Let me write down her address for you," Bessie offered.

"Thank you, that is most kind," Aaron replied. "One more thing about the McCallums. You said that Mrs. McCallum has Alzheimer's?"

"Yes, Jim Bob mentioned it to me when he stopped by my aunt's shop to pick up a package. We talked about many things including his wife, and the fact that he use to date Mrs. Winchester when they were in high school. He said that they were very close. I could tell just by the way he talked about her. It was kinda sad," Bessie related to Aaron.

"Thank you again, this is all very interesting," Aaron said as he finished taking his notes.

"Alright, then if we're finished talking, it's time for some eatin'," Lucius pronounced, as he began slicing into Bessie's pecan pie.

"Well, I sure couldn't say no to pecan pie," Clay grinned.

After the pie and coffee, Aaron and Clay said their thank you's and goodbyes to the Collins' and walked towards their hotel.

"The whole Jim Bob McCallum having been in love with LeeAnn Winchester and add to that the Queen Rita dynamic is fascinating," Aaron stated as they strolled through the French Quarter. "We've got a lot more research we need to do when we get back to D.C."

"Tomorrow morning we need to pay a visit to Queen Rita. I'm intrigued as to how she fits into this whole puzzle of a story. What business does she have with Jim Bob McCallum? On the surface it seems like an odd arrangement of characters. I had no clue that the Queen Rita of jambalaya fame was an actual person. I just assumed it was a fictitious character like Aunt Jemima, Uncle Ben, or Betty Crocker. Nothing more than a trademarked company logo," Clay added.

"Our last two interviews aren't until two tomorrow afternoon, so we will have plenty of time in the morning to stop at Queen Rita's shop," Aaron affirmed.

"We're done for today. How about a nice dinner and a few drinks?" Clay asked.

"Sure," Aaron responded. "But not too late of a night."

"Well, let's play that by ear, shall we?" Clay replied, with a huge Cheshire cat grin spreading across his lips.

KATE WILSON COULDN'T HELP BUT SMILE every time she walked by the enormous floral arrangement sitting on her living room table. She would stop to smell the fragrant aroma of the flowers as she glanced again at the card so full of promises. Including the next romantic liaison taking place at her apartment. Kate made a mental note to herself that she needed to stock up on condoms and lube.

Kate walked to the kitchen and grabbed a bottle of Fiji water from her refrigerator. Bottled water dominated Kate's refrigerator. A fitness fanatic, Kate kept herself well hydrated throughout the day.

Kate went into her bedroom and sat at her desk. She opened her laptop and began drafting an outline of a thank you letter that she would at some point give to Justice Sallis. It would need to be a few months until she could deliver said letter, but she wanted to put some words to paper while she recalled fond memories of her clerkship with the judge. Kate thought that she would miss working with Justice Sallis, but opportunity was knocking at her door. And, Kate was ready to welcome it in.

CHAPTER 29

CLAY GROVER ORDERED A SAZERAC as he and Aaron sat on the balcony of Muriel's enjoying after dinner cocktails. Earlier that evening, Clay and Aaron had devoured crawfish cakes and drank hearty Cajun Bloody Mary's at Chartres House Cafe. A gentle breeze caressed their skin as they enjoyed sitting out of doors in the fall, something that one couldn't do with any degree of pleasure in Washington.

"There is something magical about this city," Clay stated with a contented sigh. "I can see how it would be easy to lose yourself here. Leave the pressure and bustle of Washington behind, and surrender to the languid pace. Allow yourself to be enraptured by the jazz, indulge in the plethora of outstanding food, and wholly acquiesce to the non-judgmental creed of a city that places pleasure above all else."

"You sound like Tennessee Williams waxing about the virtues of unfettered self-indulgence," Aaron replied with a smile.

"Probably more like F. Scott Fitzgerald, old sport," Clay corrected Aaron with a whimsical grin while he finished his drink.

"Are you not drawn in by the intoxication of this place?" Clay asked.

"Perhaps, but clearly not as intoxicated as you, old sport," Aaron countered with a chuckle. "Time to pay our bill here and head back to the hotel. Tomorrow presents a new challenge and the opportunity to begin to fit more pieces of the Winchester story together."

SUNDAY MORNING, AARON ROSE pushed the front door of the old shop open as the small bell registered his arrival. Clay followed directly behind his colleague.

"How can I help you?" the old woman asked Aaron.

"Hello. I'm looking for Queen Rita," Aaron replied.

"Then my son, you have found who you seek. I am Queen Rita."

"My companion and I are from Washington D.C," Aaron began, but was quickly interrupted by Queen Rita.

"You are the Washington government man?" Rita questioned loudly, clearly agitated. "It is not ready yet. I told him to give me a few more days."

"I'm sorry, I think there must be some confusion," Aaron stated attempting to calm the old woman.

"Who sent you?" Rita demanded. Aaron perplexed by the question did not immediately respond.

"Who sent you?" Rita demanded again.

"No one sent us. Well, Bessie Collins mentioned you to us when we met with her yesterday afternoon," Aaron blurted out in response.

"Bessie, Bessie!" Rita exclaimed, clearly bewildered. "How do you know Bessie?"

"Ma'am, my colleague and I work for the Senate Judiciary Committee. We've been interviewing some folks here in New Orleans with respect to the nomination of Justice Stanford Winchester to the Supreme Court," Clay interjected in an attempt to clarify the situation.

"You are not the man for the package from Washington," Rita declared.

"Ma'am?" Clay asked befuddled.

"I am sorry to confuse. Please forgive an old woman whose mind has seen greater sunshine," Queen Rita apologized as she realized that Aaron and Clay were not the people she thought them to be. "So, you met with my niece Bessie yesterday?" Rita politely asked now calm and behaving more lucid.

"Yes, ma'am. We met with Bessie and her husband Lucius at their lovely home yesterday afternoon," Clay confirmed. "We asked them a few questions about their friend Stanford Winchester. They mentioned that you had a business relationship and friendship with Justice Winchester's friend, Jim Bob McCallum."

"Yes, I have known Jim Bob for many years. He was a regular patron of mine. We developed a friendship. He named his jambalaya product after me for which I was proud and thankful. I have served him well, and he supports my business. It is good to have powerful friends," Rita explained.

"May I please ask, what services do you provide to Jim Bob?" Clay politely asked.

"No. It is not your concern," Rita replied with a stern expression on her face. Then after a moment, she added in a friendlier manner, "People have grief in their lives for their losses. They seek peace for the spirits of their departed. Sometimes they come to me. I try to give them comfort that their loved ones are content in the spiritual world."

"Bessie mentioned to us that Jim Bob McCallum was once in love with LeeAnn Winchester," Clay bluntly stated.

"Bessie sometimes speaks when no words are required. My lips do not speak of another's heart. But what is known is known," Rita responded.

Clay understood that his questioning was beginning to irritate Queen Rita, so he began just browsing around the shop.

"What are these?" Clay questioned.

"You know gris gris?" Rita replied.

"I'm from South Carolina, I had a grandma who believed in spirits, so yeah, I know a little."

"Then these are part of gris gris. They are wanga amulets for spiritual and aura cleansing. They protect against negative and evil energy," Rita informed Clay.

"And what of all these potions on this shelf?" Clay inquired.

"Many things," Rita replied. "The world is filled with many powers, both good and evil. Everything here has a purpose in the realm of the spirits. Nature provides what is needed to do the work that the loa require."

"Does Jim Bob McCallum ask you for help with respect to his wife's Alzheimer's disease?" Aaron asked Queen Rita.

"When you love someone who is ill and your heart hurts, you do anything to chase the evil away. Western medicine does not heal the spirit and soul. What is needed is not always provided by a white coat. The mind can kill the body. The spiritual world knows this," Rita responded.

"Bessie mentioned to us that Jim Bob told her recently that he would do anything for the memory of LeeAnn Winchester. Has he mentioned anything to you about this?" Aaron asked.

"I do not speak of others' hearts. But love and commitment do not leave us when our beloved is in the cold ground. Spirits live among us and they possess great power over us. This I know to be true," Rita solemnly stated.

Clay and Aaron bought a few items at Queen Rita's shop more as a token of thanks for her time than anything else. Clay purchased an amulet. Aaron, a book on the origins and uses of Vodou potions. They left her shop with a bit more information and a shared sense that there was far more to Queen Rita's involvement with Jim Bob McCallum than she would ever allow them to know.

STANFORD WINCHESTER SAT IN A ROCKING CHAIR on the balcony of his home in the French Quarter. It was Sunday afternoon and the streets were bustling with people. Off in the distance on Bourbon Street, he could faintly hear a brass band playing "When the Saints Go Marching In." It was commonplace for an impromptu parade of musicians, dancers, and revelers to take place in the Quarter. Stanford tapped his toes in beat to the music, as he continued to read articles and background material about the Democratic members of the Senate Judiciary Committee. The more he read about Perry Douglas the greater his apprehension grew. But Stanford Winchester never shied away from a challenging confrontation in all of his life. He was not about to begin now.

JUST A FEW SHORT BLOCKS AWAY, Aaron Rose and Clay Grover were meeting with another former colleague of Justice Winchester's on the Louisiana Supreme Court. Clay cautioned Aaron as they approached the home of former Justice Leland Calhoun.

"Just from five minutes on the phone with this guy the other day, I'm pretty sure he still believes in segregation. He may not be politically correct, ya know, so try not to show offense. Let me handle this one," Clay suggested.

"Sure thing boss," Aaron replied affecting a Southern plantation workers accent.

"That's not going to help," Clay warned ramping up his own refined Southern accent.

"Good afternoon Justice Calhoun," Clay slowly drawled as the door to the house opened.

"Why you must be Mr. Grover from the Senate Judiciary Committee, and is your boy here takin' notes?" Justice Calhoun questioned.

"This is Aaron Rose, he is my colleague on the Senate staff," Clay firmly stated.

"Well come on in and ask me whatever you want about that no account liar Stanford Winchester," Leland Calhoun offered.

Clay and Aaron sat together on a small tufted couch as Leland

Calhoun perched himself in an overstuffed large upholstered arm chair. His bald head gleamed under an antique torchiere floor lamp.

"What was your relationship like with Justice Winchester when you were both serving on the Louisiana Supreme Court?" Clay asked.

"I couldn't stand that pompous ass," Justice Calhoun said with contempt.

"You were both Republican members of the Court, isn't that right?" Clay asked, somewhat startled by Leland Calhoun's reply.

"Just 'cuz someone shares your political affiliation don't mean you got to like 'em," Justice Calhoun offered. "Look, Stanford Winchester presented himself as this high and mighty jurist. He thought he was smarter and better than the rest of his colleagues. Spoiled brat grandson of one of the most corrupt governors that the State of Louisiana has ever known. And if you got a spit bucket worth of knowledge about Louisiana politics, you know that's saying something. I got my law degree from Loyola University, right here in New Orleans. Stanford, with his fancy Harvard degree would try to treat me and a few of the other justices on the Court like daft red-headed step children. He always thought he knew better. Only thing that he knew better than us was how to twist and contort the law to suit the best interests of Stanford Winchester and his friends," Leland Calhoun bitterly stated.

Aaron's hand flew across his legal pad as he quickly took copious notes.

"You believe that while on the Court, Stanford Winchester used his influence to affect decisions rendered by the Court?" Clay asked.

"Ain't no belief needed, just read the opinions he wrote. There was a real estate case where one of his cronies was a defendant. It boggles the imagination on how you come to the judicial conclusions that ol' Stanford reached. And believe you me, his friends on the Court went right along with him. Pandering lot, all hungry for more power and money. Not an honest one in the bunch. Man, should be impeached not nominated to the highest court in the land," Justice Calhoun spat with invective.

"There were no complaints about his behavior or a judicial review?" Clay inquired.

"When the Governor of the State, the State Attorney General, the President of the State Bar Association, a few well-heeled businessmen, and a handful of very prominent politicians in Washington all gather lint in the pocket of your suit pants like so much loose change, you can get away with murder if you want to," Leland Calhoun summed up. "This is Louisiana after all. Lady Justice ain't blind down here fellas. Her eyes are wide open, she's wearing a diamond Rolex watch, and her bra is stuffed with hundred dollar bills. She knows damn well what time it is. You can shoot somebody in the head and successfully claim a defense that their head got in the way of your bullet, if you know the right people. Wake up son, life ain't fair or kind. I learned that lesson well, which is why I'm sitting here talking to you instead of being nominated to the Federal bench."

Clay spent another twenty minutes questioning Justice Calhoun while Aaron could barely keep up with his note taking. After handshakes and salutations they both left Leland Calhoun's house shaking their heads.

"Witness number one," Clay simply and definitively stated.

CHAPTER 30

AARON ROSE LOOKED AT THE WITNESS LIST and the interview schedule that he had prepared just prior to the trip to New Orleans. The last name on the list was Linda Dunham, a former law clerk to Justice Winchester while he served on the Louisiana Supreme Court. During a very short interview, Ms. Dunham was less than forthcoming and hesitant to say much about her time working with Justice Winchester. She offered very little more than obsequious platitudes about the Justice.

"Last witness, we're done," Aaron stated while glancing at his wrist watch. "4 p.m., now what?"

"A well-earned round of Sea Breezes and some music videos at a gay bar?" Clay offered with hope in his eyes.

"Why the hell not. I think we earned it!" Aaron allowed with a sheepish grin.

Aaron and Clay sat at the back of the bar at Bourbon Pub near the back entrance. The doors were open as the warm breeze wafted through the establishment. It was a good crowd for a Sunday afternoon. A mix of gay men, straight women and couples, and the curious tourists. Clay had ordered double shots of Tito's vodka in the Sea Breeze cocktails. Cher's music video "Woman's World" played on the large video screens and blared from the bar's speakers.

"Look at her face and body," Clay commented with amazement. "They were exactly the same when I first saw her music video, "If I Could Turn Back Time" on MTV in 1990 at the age of seven."

"What were you doing watching Cher at seven years old?" Aaron asked with a grin.

"Hundreds of sailors in dress whites standing under those huge phallic guns, oh please," Clay smiled in return. "Just because I fought my sexuality for years, that doesn't mean that I wasn't visually stimulated, even at a young age. Heck, when I was a teenager I didn't ride my bike past the naval base in North Charleston on the Copper River just because I wanted to see the boats!"

"You're amazing!" Aaron laughed while looking at his friend.

"C'mon, there wasn't anyone in music videos that you lusted after when you were young?" Clay asked.

"Well, I sure wouldn't change the channel during a Lenny Kravitz or Backstreet Boys video," Aaron offered.

Clay laughed heartily, "Me neither." Focusing again on the Cher video, Clay said, "I know Cher probably has plastic surgery once a month, but still look at her . . ."

"Guess she really could turn back time," Aaron chortled between sips of his Sea Breeze.

Less than a couple hundred yards away from Bourbon Pub down Bourbon Street, Stanford Winchester sat at the bar at Fritzel's talking to friends and enjoying a little Dixieland jazz on a late Sunday afternoon. Stanford often sought out the companionship of friends on weekends, as he was well-known to the locals at Fritzel's.

Calvin Putnam was a longtime friend of Stanford's. He and his wife, Lucille, would often go to dinner and dancing with Stanford and LeeAnn. Calvin was a retired attorney with a well-respected Appellate Court practice in New Orleans. Calvin entered Fritzel's and noticed Stanford sitting at the bar.

"Well, good afternoon, Mr. United States Supreme Court Justice," Calvin addressed Stanford with a polite slap on the back.

"There are many miles to go before we can put that horse in the barn," Stanford said with a sly smile.

"Speaking of miles, I saw Beauregard Dumaine this morning at church. He looked like ten miles of bad road. You thought that old boy could drink when the two of you were on the Supreme Court, now that he's retired, I'm not sure he has a sober moment," Calvin chortled.

"I'm not sure he had a sober moment when he was on the Court," Stanford allowed.

"What you drinking, Stanford?" Calvin asked.

"Just a little bourbon on the rocks," Stanford replied.

"Eddie, two more," Calvin called to the bartender pointing at Stanford's glass.

"So, I ran into Beau at church this morning and he was telling me that there were a couple of young fellas from Washington snooping around asking questions about you," Calvin related to Stanford.

"I'm not surprised. I figured the Senate Judiciary Committee would send someone down here to do some investigating. They're just doing their due diligence. Not sure what they thought they'd find talking to Beau Dumaine other than the bottom of an empty liquor bottle. Did Beau mention anything that they talked about?" Stanford hesitantly inquired.

"No, not really. Just asking about you and some of the cases you ruled on while on the bench," Calvin allowed. "You got nothing to worry about," he added.

"Do I look worried?" Stanford asked while raising his glass of bourbon and smiling.

Calvin finished his drink and looked at his watch.

"Look here old buddy, I got to skedaddle. Lucille is making Sunday supper and has invited her old witch of a sister over to join us. If I'm late, there'll be hell to pay. I'll talk to you soon," Calvin said as he raised off the bar stool and walked out the door.

Stanford watched as Calvin left Fritzel's. He took a big gulp of bourbon from his glass and under his breath he angrily muttered, "Tarnation!"

"OUR LAST NIGHT IN NEW ORLEANS, what do you want to do?" Aaron asked Clay. "Wanna go to Tipitina's and catch some zydeco music?"

"I was thinking more of a quiet, elegant dinner," Clay stated. "In fact, I made 8 p.m. reservations for us at Bayona."

"Clay, I was thinking more in the line of shrimp and oyster po-boys. Isn't Bayona a little too pricey to be putting on a government expense report?" Aaron asked.

"Probably, which is why dinner is on me," Clay replied.

"No. Why?" Aaron protested.

"Aaron, please let me do this. We've done some good work this weekend. It's been a great learning experience. I wouldn't have had this opportunity if not for your boss. I got this, really. Let's just have a wonderful dinner and a nice relaxing evening together," Clay explained.

Bayona is located in a romantic creole cottage in the French Quarter.

Clay and Aaron were seated in the intimate courtyard beneath banana fronds and olive trees. Aaron and Clay enjoyed cocktails before dinner and an excellent bottle of wine with dinner. The setting, the food, and the weather were perfect.

"It is so amazing to have dinner outside at this time of year. And in such a gorgeous courtyard," Aaron nearly moaned as he spooned into his chocolate bourbon panna cotta dessert. "This is pure decadence!"

"I'm glad you're enjoying yourself," Clay responded. "And I'm glad that I can share this dinner and this place with you . . . with someone I love. You, Aaron, are the only person I truly want to be with."

Aaron looked deeply into Clay's eyes. "Are you sure? Are you really ready to settle down into a monogamous relationship? I know how it's been the last several months with you."

"I've never been surer of anything in my life. I don't need anyone else but you," Clay whispered as he took hold of Aaron's hand.

That night, Clay's earlier teasing statement at check-in at the hotel proved to be prophetic. For that night, Clay and Aaron only needed one hotel room.

Nathan and Posy Whitaker settled into their bed together late Sunday evening.

"Did you enjoy our weekend together?" Nathan asked his wife. "Just the two of us."

"Yeah, it was real nice, Nathan," Posy admitted. "And I got to thank you for buying me them new clothes at that cute little Georgetown boutique. What was that pretty African girl's name who owned the place?"

"I think it was Fatima. Was she pretty?" Nathan replied with a grin.

"You ain't got to play that game with me, Nathan Whitaker. You know that girl was beautiful. She reminded me of that tall model. Shoot, what's her name now?" Posy asked while scratching her head.

"You mean Iman?" Nathan asked.

"Yeah, that's her! She was the tall drink of water that was married to David Bowie, right? Heck, that man wore dresses as much as she did. I always thought that boy was queer as a three dollar bill. But, then most of them English boys seem a little faggy don't they?" Posy snorted. "Anyway, my point was, shoot, what was my point?"

"Darlin' I've got no idea. You were talking about the black woman who owned the Georgetown boutique," Nathan responded with a sigh.

"Oh yeah, my point was that you don't got to act like you can't recognize if another woman is beautiful for my sake. You can look all you want, Nathan. You ain't dead and buried in the deep ground. And you sure ain't one of them faggy English boys. Honey, look all you want. Just know that if you touch, I'll cut them nice big hangin' balls of yours off," Posy laughed and snorted.

Nathan shot his wife a furtive glance and just shook his head.

"Lucius, you comin' to bed?" Bessie called to her husband from their bedroom.

"I'll be there in just a minute, sugar," Lucius replied.

"Was it busy at Arnaud's today?" Bessie asked.

"Oh, it surely was," Lucius responded as he walked into the bedroom while removing his black tuxedo jacket.

"Did them nice Washington fellas show up for the jazz brunch?" Bessie asked.

"Well, I don't rightly know. Folks was waiting for tables, so they might have slipped in when I was busy and sat at some other waiter's station. I tried to keep an eye open for them, but you know how it gets for Sunday brunch with all them tourists in town."

"Probably for the best then. You wouldn't have had much time to be hospitable to them fine gentlemen. They seemed so nice. And coming all this way from Washington just to talk to folks like us about Stanford and hear what a lovely, caring person he truly is. Makes me proud of our government," Bessie declared.

"It surely does," Lucius agreed. "Though, I saw that you were a little sweet on that good looking black fella, Aaron."

"Hush now, you silly fool. Why I'm old enough to be his mama!" Bessie declared. "He was too light skinned not to have one of his kin being white. But whichever the case, as you say, he was a fine mix of whatever," Bessie laughed and blushed.

"I wonder if they made it over to your Auntie Rita's shop?" Lucius asked.

"Oh, they made it there alright. I got me a call from Auntie Rita this afternoon giving me an earful about talking too much and being boastful to strangers. She told me don't go saying too much to folks from Washington snooping around. I got to tell you, Lucius, I'm a little worried about Auntie Rita. She been acting real strange and secretive lately. I think I'm gonna say something to mama, see what she knows."

"Careful now, Bessie. Last thing you wanna do is get in between them two old sisters. Ain't nothin' good gonna come from it," Lucius warned his wife.

"So, I'm just supposed to let Auntie Rita's strange behavior be, and not try to see if there's something I can do to help?" Bessie questioned.

"Are you asking for my advice?" Lucius inquired.

"No," Bessie said with no hesitation.

"Didn't think so," Lucius replied just shaking his head.

CHAPTER 31

Aaron Rose and Clay Grover sat in their adjoining seats in the Economy section of the airplane as it taxied off the tarmac onto a northbound runway of Louis Armstrong Airport. Clay smiled broadly, content in the knowledge that he was in love with Aaron, and that he had three pounds of frozen alligator meat securely placed in the overhead compartment above his seat.

"What are you grinning about?" Aaron asked.

"Nothing really, just happy," Clay replied.

"I guess, I'm pretty happy as well," Aaron added. "I think we got quite a bit of useful information for the Committee."

"You were wonderful with some of those witnesses. You had Bessie Collins eating out of your hand. You did such a great job with the Fifth Circuit witnesses as well," Clay expounded.

"I think we make a pretty good team," Aaron said with a smile.

"I do to," Clay confirmed. After quickly making that statement, Clay remained silent for a couple of minutes, just staring out of the plane window.

"What are you thinking about?" Aaron asked after what seemed like ten minutes of taciturn hush.

"I'm thinking about what the first thing I want to put in my mouth is after we land and get home," Clay responded with a sly grin.

"What could that possibly be?" Aaron asked coyly.

"Well silly, you know," Clay whispered.

"I do?" Aaron playfully questioned.

"Fried gator! I want me some fried gator!" Clay bellowed in a heavy Southern accent.

Aaron threw his airplane pillow into Clay's face, who couldn't stop laughing.

MONDAY MORNING, AND STANFORD WINCHESTER was seated outdoors at Café du Monde sipping his coffee. Laid out on the table before him was additional research he had done on the Democratic members of the Judiciary Committee. The Senate Committee was comprised of twenty members, eleven Democrats and nine Republicans. Two of the Senate Democrats were women. Stanford glanced at their photographs as he carefully read their biographies.

Hellen Raymond was a fifty-one-year-old moderate from North Carolina. Stanford was impressed that she was born and raised in a rural farming family, and at the age of twenty-four she graduated from Duke Law School at the top of her class. A religious woman with a family of four, Stanford felt that he could use his Southern charm and folksy ways to disarm Senator Raymond. It was just a bonus that she had the same first name as his maternal grandmother, the wife of the former Louisiana Governor. Stanford was not above playing every card in the deck to curry favor with any and all members of the Judiciary Committee.

The task of charming, or even making any positive connection, with the other Democratic woman on the Committee was going to be a far harder reach for Stanford's many talents. Senator Patricia Knetzger hailed from Wisconsin. Born and raised in the suburbs of Milwaukee, Senator Knetzger attended Lawrence University where she acquired a liberal arts degree, and graduated from law school at the University of Wisconsin at Madison. In Stanford Winchester's mind, Madison Wisconsin was one of the nation's hotbeds of progressive Democratic Socialism and about as far opposite of the political spectrum from his own philosophy as conceptually possible. Patricia Knetzger seemed to be the guardian mother of a new generation of young ultra-liberal members of Congress. They often sought her approval and frequently heeded her advice and counsel. Virtually all progressive organizations gave Senator Knetzger the highest scoring of all members of Congress for her 99% liberal voting record. Senator Knetzger's political campaign manager was her out and proud lesbian daughter. She was also the only member of the Senate that described herself as an agnostic. In other words, Senator Knetzger was Stanford Winchester's human embodiment of hell on earth in a pant suit.

QUEEN RITA HELD THE PHONE TO HER EAR while sitting on a hard wooden stool in the back room of her store. She faced the doorway so that she could see if anyone came in.

"You have to tell me exactly when the man will be coming for the package. There were two men from Washington here in my shop yesterday and I almost said more than I should have," Queen Rita explained in a quiet voice. "It is getting dangerous with all these people snooping around and asking questions. We need to soon be done."

She continued her phone conversation for another two minutes, mostly replying "yes" to the statements made by the voice on the other end of the phone. Rita concluded the call by stating, "Loa Ghede's will be done."

Queen Rita ended her first call and immediately made another call to Papa Levi. The entirety of her conversation to Papa Levi was, "Time come soon for a sacrifice. Steal a chicken. Prepare the others."

BEN CARROLL WAS DOING HIS BEST TO AVOID Kate Wilson Monday morning in the corridors and office hallways of the Supreme Court building. So, as he glanced over his shoulder, he turned a corner and almost ran smack into Kate Wilson.

"Excuse me, Ben, I didn't mean to mow you down. Been one of those manic Monday mornings and I'm running around like a chicken with its head cut-off," Kate apologized in the hallway.

"No worries, I just took a glancing blow. No harm," Ben said a bit shaken up and very nervous.

"Great! I wouldn't want to hurt you," Kate offered. After a short pause, Kate asked, "Hey, you live in DuPont Circle don't you? I thought I noticed that you lived in that area while I was glancing at an office address book when I sent out Christmas cards last year. Did you get yours?"

"Yeah, thanks. Yes, I'm just off Connecticut Avenue," Ben said.

"Gee, I'm in that area all the time. I'm surprised I've never run into you," Kate stated.

"Well, I'm here so late most of the time," Ben replied.

"Yeah sure. Sure, that's it," Kate said with a grin. "Well, gotta go. As I said, just another manic Monday."

Ben turned the corner and was out of Kate's eyesight. His entire body trembled and he could feel his pulse racing. He quickly fished his cell phone out of his suit pants pocket and began scrolling through his contacts list. His right thumb flinched as he alphabetically reached the "G's."

Aaron Rose glanced at the display call screen on his iPhone. He recognized the number as being the number for Senator Douglas' secretary.

"Hey Aaron. Are you and Clay back in D.C. yet?"

"Yes. We just landed. Clay is attempting to get a cab," Aaron explained.

"Great. Senator Douglas wanted me to contact you and see if you and Clay could meet with the Senator in his office at 4:30 p.m. this afternoon for a debriefing meeting on your trip to New Orleans?"

"Of course," Aaron confirmed. "Both Clay and I will be there and fully prepared to meet with the Senator."

"Excellent. I'll send both of you a meeting invite email."

"Great, thanks. Tell the Senator that I'll bring the Starbucks," Aaron happily stated.

"This is why you're his favorite staffer."

I am? Aaron thought to himself, beaming with pride.

"Hey Darling, it's not too early is it? Did I wake you?" President Cochran asked his wife Sue Lynn. "I'm about an hour from London and I don't have Nathan here to remind me what time it is on the East coast."

"Andy, there's no one on Air Force One other than Nathan who can add and subtract time zones?" Sue Lynn Cochran chided her husband.

"Honey, if it ain't written as a requirement in their bureaucratic civilian government manual, the answer would be no," Andrew Cochran joked with his wife.

"Why are you calling me so early, Mr. President?" Sue Lynn asked.

"I think I mentioned to you that the Senate Judiciary Committee hearings for Justice Winchester are scheduled to commence next week. The Justice will be residing here in D.C. for at least a week or two. I thought it would be nice if we have a little White House dinner party honoring our guest. Have one of your gals find out what hotel he's staying at, and let's send him a big fruit basket with some pecans, and a really nice bottle of bourbon to his suite. With an invitation to join us for dinner at the White House. Let's try to make him as comfortable and relaxed as possible. I need him to make a good impression with the Senators on the Committee.

"I'll have Toni and her staff put something together. Toni can get your calendar from Nancy and we can pick a date for dinner. I'm happy to get the ball rolling on this. By the way, that is a wonderful and thoughtful gesture for Justice Winchester. You see how sweet and kind you are when Nathan is not with you?" Sue Lynn kiddingly asked.

"Yeah, I'm just a big ol' softie without mean old Nathan around. But a big ol' softie that has no frickin' clue what time zone I'm in!" Andrew Cochran laughed to his wife.

CLAY SAT PATIENTLY IN A COMFORTABLE CHAIR in Senator Douglas' office, as Aaron attempted to place the cup of Starbucks coffee next to a heating vent, in an effort to keep the coffee moderately warm. Hot stopped being conceivable five minutes earlier.

"You do understand how ridiculous you look holding a paper cup of coffee up to a heating vent, right?" Clay ridiculed his colleague.

"I'm only trying to be considerate," Aaron stated as he glared at Clay.

"You're succeeding at looking stupid," Clay countered.

"How else am I going to keep his coffee warm?" Aaron asked.

"Do you Northern boys have that fancy electric power? And one of them there microwaver machines?" Clay asked in an exaggerated hillbilly accent.

"Remember what I said last night. Never mind," Aaron said with a smile.

"Sorry gentlemen, the Republicans have so many geriatric male members on the Committee, we break every 45 minutes for bathroom time," Senator Douglas apologized while explaining. "But I'm now ready and interested to hear your report on your trip to New Orleans. With respect to Justice Winchester, we'll make this like an Appellate Court oral argument. You start making a statement and I'll interrupt you abruptly, disrupt your speech and speaking rhythm, make self-serving political statements, and then ask you some disarming and inconceivable question. Sound good?" Senator Douglas asked sarcastically.

"Sounds good, sir," Aaron parroted back with a smile.

Aaron and Clay began their recitations about the witnesses that they had talked to and the various facts that they had uncovered during the interviews. Senator Douglas sat quietly listening to the comments and analysis presented by the two young Senate staffers. He understood and appreciated the excitement in their voices and the thoroughness of their summaries and descriptions. When Clay began extolling the importance of the statements of former Justice Leland Calhoun, Senator Douglas interrupted Clay's soliloquy.

"Clay, though I appreciate your enthusiasm with respect to Justice Calhoun's statements, you've got to keep in mind the source and the motivation involved. From my understanding, Calhoun and Winchester, though both Republican's, were enemies on the Louisiana Supreme

Court," Senator Douglas stated. "Calhoun resented Winchester's power and wealth. They fought bitterly for years for control of the Court. After he lost that battle to Winchester, Calhoun lobbied to be appointed to the Federal bench, which he never got. A good deal of what Leland Calhoun told you might have some truth to it, but I can guarantee you that a good deal of what was said was also motivated by resentment, jealousy, and hatred. We've got to be careful to parse out the truth from the animosity and invective."

Clay' shoulders slumped, because he knew that the Senator was correct. Leland Calhoun would have told them anything to derail Stanford Winchester's nomination. There was nothing impartial about the statements that Leland Calhoun made to them. And most of it was hearsay. Clay's enthusiasm dwindled as he realized that he and Aaron were fed a very biased and unreliable account of Stanford Winchester's activities during his tenure on the Louisiana Supreme Court by a man with a personal vendetta.

Senator Douglas was more interested in the comments of Fifth Circuit Justice Sewell, the statements from Emily DuBois, the former law clerk to Justice Winchester, and he found the discussion of Jim Bob McCallum and his relationship to Stanford Winchester and his late wife LeeAnn fascinating.

"So, let me get this straight, Aaron, Stanford Winchester threw an elaborate party for himself and his friends after President Cochran placed his name in nomination for the seat on the Supreme Court?" Senator Douglas asked his aide.

"Yes, sir, at Muriel's restaurant," Aaron replied.

"There's a real arrogance to that, isn't there? Why wouldn't you wait until after you were confirmed to the Court by the Senate before you have a celebratory bash? Sure, sounds like someone who thinks that his appointment and confirmation to the Court is a done deal. That someone has told or promised him that it's in the bag," Senator Douglas posited.

"Yes, in retrospect, that does seem odd. Jumping the gun, as it were. Celebrating something that is less than certain," Aaron allowed.

"Well I hope Justice Winchester had a good time at his victory cotillion. This man will not be sworn in as a Justice of the United States Supreme Court if I have anything to say about it," Senator Douglas stated with emphasis to Clay and Aaron.

"And I do!"

CHAPTER 32

"Lucius, so good to see you," Stanford Winchester addressed his friend while being seated at his table at Arnaud's.

"My pleasure to serve you this evening, sir," Lucius replied.

"It might be a couple of weeks before I'm back here for dinner," Stanford stated. "I leave this coming weekend for Washington. The Senate Committee hearings are set to begin on Monday."

"Well, then I'll have to make sure we do our utmost best to please you this evening sir," Lucius responded. "Bessie and I enjoyed talking to the young gentlemen from Washington about you," Lucius added with a smile.

"Someone spoke to you about me?" Stanford inquired with some surprise.

"Yes, sir. Two young fellas, they said they were from the Senate Committee. They wanted to hear all about what a kind and wonderful person you are, sir," Lucius related to Stanford.

"Do you recall any specific questions about me that they asked you?" Stanford inquired, his eyes squinting as his brow creased.

"Well sir, they just mostly wanted to hear stories about how we met and how our friendship has grown over the past fifteen years. Bessie told them all about the lovely party that you had at Muriel's. Oh, and they asked a few questions about Jim Bob and Mabel McCallum," Lucius added.

"They asked about the McCallum's?" Stanford questioned.

"Yes, sir. Bessie explained about Mabel and her Alzheimer's and talked about Jim Bob knowing LeeAnn in high school and things like that," Lucius answered.

"Well alright Lucius, thank you for telling me. If you hear from them gentlemen again, could you kindly let me know?" Stanford Winchester requested of his friend.

"Most assuredly, Justice Winchester, I'll surely do so," Lucius replied. "Me and Bessie didn't do nothing wrong did we?"

"No, of course not," Stanford assured him. "This is just part of the nomination process. The Committee is just doing what they do to make sure that they put honorable, upstanding folk on the Supreme Court. You did just fine Lucius, just fine."

Sanford Winchester fidgeted in his chair as he waited for Lucius to bring his pre-dinner cocktail. His mind filled with thoughts and concerns.

FRIDAY MORNING AND BEN CARROLL AND CLAY GROVER were back at Pete's Diner, as Ben watched Clay inhale a plate full of scrambled eggs and country sausage patties.

"Are we still on for this weekend?" Ben asked Clay.

Clay downed half a glass of orange juice before responding to the question. "Ben, I'm not sure how to put this other than to let you know that things have changed for me," Clay began. "I adore you as a friend, and I want to make sure that we stay friends for years to come. But the 'benefits' aspect of our friendship has to end. We had a lot of fun together. A lot of fun. But, I'm trying really hard to make things work, and I'm putting all of my energy and devotion into one relationship. I hope you understand."

"Clay Grover settling down? Do I know this boy you're in love with?" Ben asked a bit astonished at the news.

"You know of him," Clay responded. "It's Aaron Rose, Senator Douglas' aide."

"Very cute!" Ben replied. "Didn't you have something going with him a couple of years ago?"

"Yeah, we've been off and on for a while. But we're definitely on now, and frankly, I couldn't be happier!" Clay exclaimed.

"Well, then I'm happy for both of you," Ben said. "I'll miss our little Civil War enactments, but I'm glad that you found someone you love who can keep you in line. You could use some stability in your life. You can't be a tramp forever," Ben smiled.

"No you can't," Clay replied with a big grin. "But I tried, I sure did try."

AARON ROSE SAT AT THE HEAD of a large conference room table in the Senate Office Building. Senate staffers and interns buzzed around him as they busily prepared binders of documents with copies of questioning outlines for each of the Democratic Committee Senator's. Aaron kept going over his notes looking for some aspect of the witness statements that could be germane to the vetting hearing.

The beginning of the Committee hearings was just a couple of days away. Aaron believed that they had done their best to be prepared, but he couldn't help but feel that some pieces to the Winchester puzzle were missing. He just didn't know how to fit them together. He thought that there must be more information about the relationship between Justice Winchester and Jim Bob McCallum that was missing. But what? And how to go about obtaining it?

Clay Grover stopped by the Senate conference room and stood in the doorway watching as his friend was busy marshaling the troops and attending to every detail in the preparation process.

"You need any help from me?" Clay asked.

"Oh, hey, I didn't see you there," Aaron responded. "We're getting there, but it's going to be a long weekend. There's still a lot to get done before Monday morning. Did Senator Fitzsimmons get his questioning binder yet?" Aaron asked.

"Yup, one of the interns dropped it by this morning. I was adding some highlighting to some of the documents in the binder just a bit ago," Clay replied. "Look, it's going to be fine. You've done a remarkable job pulling all of this together and getting your boss prepared, just try to relax a little."

"I will, but I have this feeling that I've missed something. I just don't know what," Aaron stated with a sigh.

"Will I see you this evening? Are you coming by?" Clay asked with a grin.

"I hope so, but it's gonna be pretty late, is that ok?" Aaron asked.

"Sure, late is great," Clay answered with a smile.

NATHAN WHITAKER WAS GREETED walking down a West Wing corridor by the First Lady's social secretary.

"Toni, what's up?" Nathan asked with a cheery smile.

"Hi Nathan," Toni replied. "Do you have a minute?"

"Yes, one," Nathan jokingly responded. "I'm trying to keep all the balls in the air with the President away for a few days at the European Economic Summit. What can I do you for?"

"The First Lady asked me to get the details on where Justice Winchester is staying during the Senate Judiciary Committee hearings," Toni stated.

"Check with my gal, Carolyn she made all the arrangements. Anything having to do with the Winchester hearings just talk to Carolyn or Robert. With the President out of town, I'll be the welcoming committee for Justice Winchester," Nathan related to Toni.

"Great. Thanks for the information, I'll stop by and talk to Carolyn," Toni responded.

"Give my best to Sue Lynn," Nathan called back as he continued down the corridor.

STANFORD WINCHESTER WAS SEATED at his kitchen table on Saturday morning, fitting pieces of his puzzle of the U.S. Capitol Building together. The picture of the steps leading up to the building, the landscaping around the building and the two wings of the building were completed. But there was still a large hole in the building's rotunda where Stanford was missing many pieces. His flight to Washington to attend the Senate Judiciary Committee hearings was late Sunday morning, just about twenty-four hours away. Stanford knew that he did not have the time to spend completing his puzzle. He had a busy afternoon planned for himself.

If LeeAnn was there to help him, Stanford thought to himself, the puzzle would have been completed days ago. He was not quite up to the puzzle challenge, he could not finish it by himself before he left, without LeeAnn. That fact bothered him as he moved from the kitchen table into his bedroom and began selecting the suits, shirts, and ties that he would pack for his journey.

THE GRANDFATHER CLOCK IN STANFORD WINCHESTER'S living room chimed two times. It was 2 a.m. on Sunday morning. Stanford Winchester sat at his kitchen table dressed in his bathrobe and pajamas while sipping a cup of badly brewed coffee that he had made himself. He diligently selected puzzle pieces and snapped them into place. Stanford had been working nonstop on his puzzle since 9 p.m. He was not going to bed until every piece of that puzzle had been successfully formed together. Stanford Winchester had never accepted failure at any time in his life. He was not going to start now.

CHAPTER 33

IT WAS A COOL OCTOBER MORNING in Washington, D.C. Aaron Rose laid in bed attempting to rub the sleep from his eyes.

"Good morning sleepy-head," Clay Grover cooed while handing a cup of hot coffee to his friend.

"What time is it?" Aaron asked still attempting to shake the cobwebs from his head.

"It's about 10:40 a.m.," Clay announced.

"Oh God, I've got to get going. I'm late," Aaron stated with panic in his voice.

"Relax, it's Sunday morning. Take your time," Clay chided Aaron.

"You don't understand, there's still so much that needs to be done before tomorrow morning's hearing," Aaron protested.

"And there is a whole cadre of Senate staffers and interns who are there to help make sure it all gets done. You don't have to do it all yourself, Superman," Clay responded as he reached over to gently stroke Aaron's face.

"I can relax when this is all over, when the hearings are completed. But until then, I've got to get to work," Aaron explained to Clay.

SENATOR PERRY DOUGLAS SAT IN HIS HOME OFFICE at his Georgetown condominium. Binders of documents spread out before him on his desk as he continued making edits to his questioning outline for Stanford Winchester. Perry didn't believe in "gotcha questions," though he did believe in surprising a witness with the sequence of questions to be asked.

He recalled from his days as a trial attorney starting a deposition of an expert witness with the most pertinent question relating to the crux of the litigation at the very beginning of the deposition. Most expert witnesses anticipated spending twenty minutes going over their illustrious professional history before receiving a question of any substance. Which is why Perry occasionally surprised them with the most important issue question following directly after "please state your name." Sometimes, when you ask a question can be as important as how you ask a question.

Perry shuffled papers, as he scribbled notes in the margins of some documents. His cell phone rang. He looked at the display screen. A smile creased his lips, it was his wife Katherine calling.

"Hello darling," Perry cheerfully intoned into his phone.

"Let me guess, you're sitting in your office buried in papers, wearing a t-shirt and sweat pants. You've already been up for hours, had a slice of cold pizza for breakfast, and you haven't showered since Friday morning," Katherine playfully chided her husband.

"Gee, are we on FaceTime?" Perry asked glancing down at his phone.

"No, Perry, I've just lived through the day leading up to a major hearing before, I know what you do," Katherine replied.

"How are things in Chicago?" Perry asked attempting to change the topic.

"Cold, dreary. I think we might need a new furnace," Katherine responded.

"Well, that furnace is twenty-one years old, it might be time. Call Alan, he'll take care of it," Perry stated to his wife.

"How are you holding up?" Katherine inquired, hearing the fatigue in Perry's voice.

"I've vetted my fair share of judicial nominees over the years, but there's something about Winchester that just doesn't add up," Perry said. "He's either a saint walking amongst us or the anti-Christ depending on who you ask. The only thing people seem to agree on is that he is smart, charming and cunning as a fox. He protects his family and friends and vanquishes his enemies with ruthless swift action and steely eyed determination. He is definitely a different kind of cat."

"Do I detect a hint of doubt and hesitancy in that stalwart Douglas confidence?" Katherine asked.

"I don't think so . . . maybe," Perry Douglas admitted to his wife. "I'm just perplexed by the dichotomy of this man. The more I read about him the more confused I become. Stanford Winchester is the grandson of the former governor of Louisiana. His name is well-respected. He comes from wealth, power, and entitlement. Yet, he befriends and holds dear a black waiter and his wife, who has served him dinner for fifteen years. Why? By all accounts this is a man who doesn't move a muscle unless it benefits him in some tangible way. Though here he is fully emotionally invested in a couple that can provide neither wealth nor power to him. For someone whose motivations seem to be unquestionably self-centered, I don't get it."

"You'll begin questioning him and then you'll slowly figure him out Perry. You always do," Katherine confidently proclaimed.

"Yeah, maybe," Perry hesitantly replied.

"I DON'T KNOW, BESSIE, I hope we did the right thing by talking to them gentlemen from Washington last weekend," Lucius Collins said to his wife, as they sat together in the kitchen of their home.

"Why you say that?" Bessie asked with a quizzical look on her face.

"Well, Justice Winchester was at Arnaud's on Wednesday, same as usual. But when I mentioned talking to them Washington fellas he started asking me about what we talked about and such. Then he asked me to give him a call iffin' they come back around asking questions. I don't know for sure, Bessie, but Stanford just seemed on edge after I told him about them fellas," Lucius related to his wife.

"But we just told them the god honest truth about what a wonderful, caring person Justice Winchester is. We didn't say nothing bad. They was there to hear about what a great person he is. Ain't that right?" Bessie asked.

"I suppose," Lucius confirmed. "I'm just saying that Stanford turned white as a sheet when I mentioned that we talked to them gentlemen. I just ain't sure, Bessie."

JIM BOB MCCALLUM LED HIS WIFE by the arm down the aisle of the Baptist church. He made sure that she was comfortably seated in the pew, with her hymnal in hand.

"I'll be right back in a few minutes, Mabel honey, I'm just going to step out to take a call. I'll be back before the preachin' starts," Jim Bob assured his wife.

"Alright dear, but don't embarrass me walking in late in front of the Reverend," Mabel admonished.

"No, ma'am," Jim Bob confirmed as he walked down the aisle and exited the church. Jim Bob selected the call back icon on his cell phone.

"What in Sam Hill do you think you're doing? You understand that you're calling me at church on a Sunday morning while I'm with my wife, so this better be good," Jim Bob angrily spat into the phone. Jim Bob listened to the caller while fidgeting and looking at his Rolex watch.

"Alright that's fine. But you and your boss better make sure that the funding gets through Congress. I can't wait much longer. I'll be in Washington later this week. Tell your boss that I'll be at the dinner. Tell him that he best not disappoint me," Jim Bob warned as he ended his phone call.

"See there darlin'," Jim Bob sweetly kidded Mabel as he slid in next to her in the pew, "back in plenty of time to hear all about the fires of hell and damnation."

"Hush now, Jim Bob, here comes the Reverend. The Lord knows we're all sinners," Mabel stated in a hushed voice.

"Oh that he does, my love, that he does," Jim Bob confirmed without any hesitation.

"Nathan, why does everything fall to you when Andy leaves the country? Why don't the Vice President take care of things?" Posy Whitaker asked her husband as he dressed to go to the West Wing on Sunday morning.

"It don't work like that darlin'," Nathan stated. "I'm the Chief of Staff, it's my responsibility to make sure that everything in the Executive branch functions smoothly while the President is abroad."

"So what does the Vice President do?" Posy asked.

"Not much, my dear, not much," Nathan sighed.

"Oh, I almost forgot to tell you that your drinking buddy, Mabel McCallum will be in D.C. later this week. On Thursday, the President will be hosting a dinner at the White House for his Supreme Court nominee. Justice Winchester will be in town for a week or two as he goes through Senate Judiciary Committee hearings. I've heard that Jim Bob and Mabel McCallum will be here late in the week to attend the dinner in honor of Justice Winchester. We're invited, so you and Mabel will have the opportunity to get a snoot full together," Nathan stated to his wife.

"I like Mabel. We had some fun together after she got a few drinks in her. Well, if you're there with me, then maybe that stuck-up bitch Sue Lynn won't push me in the corner, like last time," Posy spat as she glared at Nathan.

"Don't you worry, I'll make sure that Toni seats us with the McCallum's right up front," Nathan replied.

"I can wear that pretty little dress that you bought me last week from that Fatima gal," Posy enthusiastically said.

"You wear whatever you want dear. It should be a nice evening," Nathan responded.

"Oh, it's going to be some fun once Mabel and I get some juleps in us," Posy promised.

"Well, I gotta get to work now. Somebody's got to keep this ship of state afloat," Nathan said as he kissed Posy on the forehead and headed out the door.

QUEEN RITA SLID THE LATCH CLOSED on the door, as she turned the sign in the shop window over from "Open" to "Closed."

"Why are you closed on a Sunday morning," Papa Levi asked with surprise.

"I need to finish the potion and I cannot have customers in the shop while I do this."

"You need to put this on," Rita said while handing Papa Levi a gauze mask.

Papa Levi donned his mask and Rita placed hers over her nose and mouth. Papa Levi held the small bottle securely in his latex gloved hand. Queen Rita carefully poured the liquid into the vial. She sealed it with a cork stopper and placed the small bottle into a tightly sealed bag.

"We must have a sacrifice, so that I can dry the chicken bones. The loa must have their tribute. All must be done for the spirits," Queen Rita solemnly stated.

"We are almost ready. I have talked to the others. I will get a chicken," Papa Levi replied.

"Soon," Queen Rita confirmed.

CHAPTER 34

THE COMMITTEE HEARING ROOM at the Hart Senate Office Building was filled with aides and staffers placing materials at the assigned desks of the Committee members. Television and klieg lights bathed the hearing room in a bright and stark aura. Aaron Rose led a small procession of staffers and interns down the hallway walking swiftly towards the hearing room.

Clay Grover helped Senator Fitzsimmons with his suit coat, guiding his arm through the sleeve.

"This is probably my last one," Henry Fitzsimmons said to his Chief of Staff. "I don't expect I'll be around the next time we have a Supreme Court nominee."

"That's not true," Clay protested to his boss. "You'll be around for years to come. The Senate cannot function without the Honorable Henry Fitzimmons."

"You're a very good man, Clay. You're an excellent Chief of Staff. You just happen to be an abysmally bad liar," Senator Fitzsimmons chortled. "I can barely dress myself, as you clearly demonstrated. Hell, if I was a horse, they would have put me down years ago, and rightfully so. No, son, a man's got to understand when enough is enough. If good old Albert Martin had grasped that fact, we might not be in this here situation of trying to prevent a radical Conservative from taking a seat on the highest court in the land."

"If anyone can prevent that sir, it's you," Clay replied.

"Well, I'm going to give Stanford Winchester a run for his money.

That, I'll guarantee you. Perry and I will give that gentleman from New Orleans a couple of rounds of liberal buckshot. See how high and mighty he sits then," Henry Fitzsimmons promised Clay.

STANFORD WINCHESTER SAT IN A SENATE BUILDING conference room with his attorney and a few assistants. He believed he was as ready as he ever was going to be for the hearing. He had diligently done his homework on the Democratic Senators on the Judiciary Committee. He identified his most ardent adversaries as Committee Chairman Perry Douglas from Illinois, Henry Fitzsimmons of South Carolina, Patricia Knetzger of Wisconsin, and Cranston Tolliver of California. He also believed that he might find at least a modicum of sympathy, if not support, from Hellen Raymond of North Carolina, and Cole Maynard of Florida. The remainder of the Democrats he surmised as being generally inconsequential to the results of the Committee's findings. Stanford tapped the left inner breast pocket of his suit coat. It contained a small photograph of his wife LeeAnn. After all, a seat on the Supreme Court of the United States was as much, if not more, her dream for Stanford than it was a lifetime goal of his. They were in this together, and he made sure she was with him for every moment.

THE SENATORS BEGAN FILING INTO the hearing room and taking their assigned places. In the middle of the dais sat Chairman Perry Douglas. Flanked to his immediate left was Senator Henry Fitzsimmons and the other Democratic Senators on the Committee. To his right, was the Ranking Republican member of the Judiciary Committee, Senator Cletus Sawyer, followed by the other minority members of the Committee. Justice Stanford Winchester entered the hearing room accompanied by his counsel, staff and a couple of advisors.

Stanford Winchester, attired in a gray suit with a white shirt and red striped bowtie, looked elegant and supremely confident as he pulled his chair up to the table in the middle of the hearing room.

"Good morning Justice Winchester, welcome to our committee room," Senator Douglas greeted Stanford Winchester. "We have more people here than we usually do. That is probably because this is the first time in several years that this Committee has gathered with respect to a nomination to the Supreme Court of the United States. One of the most important roles of the U.S. Senate is to advise and consent to presidential nominations. And that is precisely what we are assembled here today to do. So, once again, welcome."

"Thank you, Senator Douglas, it is an immense honor to be in the presence of this august committee," Stanford Winchester slowly drawled in a deep and commanding voice.

"We appreciate your comments, sir," Senator Douglas replied. "I'd like to take a moment to describe how this hearing will proceed. I will make an opening statement, followed by an opening statement by the Ranking Republican Member, Senator Cletus Sawyer from the State of Alabama. Then in turn, each Senator on the Committee will have opening statements. We will attempt the best we can to limit these statements to five minutes or less. We have twenty members of the Committee, so this process will probably take us to the lunch break. Then sir, you will have an opportunity to make an opening statement. Following your comments, a few Senators will speak supporting your nomination. Eventually, we will get to a question and answer session with the Committee. That will probably conclude our day, and we will resume at 10 a.m. tomorrow. Does that seem reasonable and acceptable to you, Justice Winchester?"

"Most certainly, Senator Douglas," Stanford replied.

"Excellent, let's get started."

"HE SEEMS ALMOST REGAL sitting there, doesn't he? There is no nervousness or outward indications of hesitancy to his manner," Aaron whispered to Clay as they both observed the proceedings from the side of the committee hearing room.

"The Southern well-heeled are taught confidence, that some would describe as arrogance, at a young age. You are indoctrinated into believing that you are smarter, wealthier, more sophisticated, and more entitled than the common man. It starts at an early age, preached by your nannies and your parents. It only gets bolstered when you attend a prestigious prep school. And then, your superior attitude is honed at an exclusive private college. The South is still very much a caste system. Southern aristocracy thrives. You associate with others of your social rank and foster an air of supremacy amongst yourselves," Clay explained to Aaron.

"My lord, you're a bunch of blue-blooded stuck-up snobs, aren't you?" Aaron challenged in return.

"Hell yeah," Clay allowed with a smile. "We've got a saying back in South Carolina, 'if you can't run with the big dogs, you best stay under the porch.'"

"You've got a lot of ridiculous sayings in the South, don't you?" Aaron posited.

"Well shoot howdy bubba, you sure is truthin' on a Sunday! Over the next few days, between Senator's Sawyer, Fitzsimmons, Marthy, and Tibold, and of course Winchester himself, you'll need me to interpret for you," Clay said with a grin.

"Great, Southern Idioms and Colloquialisms 101," Aaron replied with sarcasm and a shrug.

"Bless your heart, ain't that the God's honest truth."

OPENING STATEMENTS BY EACH of the twenty members of the Committee took the proceedings to the lunch break. After the break, the hearing resumed with statements delivered by three Republican members of the Committee in support of Justice Winchester's nomination. The most praiseworthy comments came from the Ranking Member, Senator Cletus Sawyer of Alabama, who extolled the judicial record and even-handed temperament of Justice Winchester. Senator Sawyer described Stanford Winchester as a fair and honest man and a very well respected and highly appreciated jurist. Ten minutes of lavish praise did not elicit even one blush or nod from Justice Winchester, who sat stoically as he listened to the exultant testimonial. After the supporting comments by the Republican Senator's, Senator Douglas asked Justice Winchester one question.

"Justice Winchester, do you know what the definition of the word recusal is in the context of judicial behavior?"

"Mr. Chairman, point of order, what is the point of this demeaning question?" Senator Sawyer objected.

"Senator Sawyer, there is nothing demeaning or insulting about my question. I would just like to know how Justice Winchester, who has been nominated by the President to assume the vacant seat on the Supreme Court of the United States, defines the term recusal," Senator Douglas calmly asserted.

"Mr. Chairman, this goes beyond the pale . . ." Senator Sawyer began to emphatically state before he was interrupted by the witness, Justice Winchester.

"Senator Sawyer," Stanford Winchester began, his voice low and steady and his Southern drawl deliberately slow, "This ain't my first rodeo. Thank you for your concern, but I am happy to answer the Chairman's question."

"Very well," Senator Sawyer hesitantly stated.

"Mr. Chairman, simply put, to recuse oneself means to remove oneself from participation in a decision so as to avoid a conflict of interest.

I'm assuming that you do not require a recitation of all of the paragraphs subsumed in 28 U.S. Code Subsection 455. Is that correct, Mr. Chairman?" Justice Winchester asked with a grin.

"That is correct, Justice Winchester, your definition is sufficient for the time being, thank you," Senator Douglas replied. "Justice Winchester, in all of your years on either the Louisiana State or Federal bench have you ever had occasion to recuse yourself from a matter that you were assigned to?"

"No, sir, I have never shirked my sworn duties as a member of the Court," Stanford Winchester responded.

"That was not precisely my question," Senator Douglas stated.

"Well, Mr. Chairman, that is precisely how I choose to answer your question," Justice Winchester replied.

"Just to clarify the record, sir, you have never recused yourself from any case matter assigned to you over your many years of service on the bench?" Perry Douglas reiterated.

"Mr. Chairman, I assume that you do not want to spend the rest of the afternoon playing word games. I consider it my duty as a judge to take on every case that I am assigned to. I listen to all of the facts presented, consider and apply the standing law, and faithfully render a decision utilizing my God given ability to fairly administer justice," Stanford Winchester stated.

"Alright sir, we'll come back to this topic later," Senator Douglas grudgingly acquiesced.

Stanford Winchester sat back in his chair and patted the left side pocket of his suit jacket which contained the photograph of his wife, LeeAnn. His lips parted into a very slight contented smile.

Dusk descended on the shores of Lake Pontchartrain, as Queen Rita and her assemblage prepared for a ritual sacrifice to Loa Ghede. Her eyes glazed over as she raised her head to the heavens. The rhythmic beating of the drums gained speed and volume, as chants were sung in homage to the spiritual world. As a Haitian bokor, Queen Rita had performed this ceremony several times over the years. She often professed that she "served the loa with both hands." She was well practiced in both dark magic and light magic.

Papa Levi seized the cackling chicken as chimes clanged in frantic syncopation. Queen Rita moaned loudly as her aged body thrashed in a convulsive seizure. The men howled as the women loudly clicked their tongues in unison. Moments later, it was over. Queen Rita's long black dress was splattered with chicken blood. Her hands covered with blood, trembled as she dropped the sickle knife to the ground.

"Now, it is the will of the loa," Queen Rita whispered as she dropped down to the cool ground on her knees in a state of exhaustion.

CHAPTER 35

Late October in Washington, D.C. usually brings a welcome respite from summer's lingering humidity. Temperatures begin to moderate ahead of winter's embrace.

Stanford Winchester exited the cab and walked towards the Thomas Jefferson Memorial. He had been to Washington several times over the years, but never in late October.

"My God LeeAnn, can you believe how beautiful this city looks right now?" Stanford whispered to himself. "It truly is glorious. And standing here at the Jefferson Memorial. I hear tell that they used stone from thirteen states to construct this magnificent edifice. The interior walls are pure white Georgia marble. The floor is Tennessee marble. It's a fittin' tribute to the President who engineered the Louisiana Purchase. It surely is."

Stanford sat on a bench and relished the visual and olfactory resplendence of his surroundings. He quietly spoke to himself as he regaled LeeAnn with the events of his first day at the Judiciary Committee hearings.

"It was a good first day, my darling. Most of the time was spent with twenty Senators making statements. I had to pinch my leg to keep my eyes from closing. I was allowed to speak for ten minutes, and was asked only a few questions. Senator Douglas, he's the one I warned you about. He tried to ask me about them cases, but I was able to step to the side for now. But, he's going to come back tomorrow with guns a blazing, so I best be prepared. He's gonna be a tough nut to crack, but I'll do my best for you, my love. You know that to be the God's honest truth."

HENRY FITZSIMMONS TILTED THE BOURBON BOTTLE towards the edge of the crystal glass and began to slowly pour.

"It's not as good as that bottle of liquid ambrosia that Aaron so kindly bought for me, but it'll still get the job done just the same," Henry stated as he handed a glass to Perry Douglas.

"He's a smug one isn't he?" Perry Douglas asked rhetorically.

"Damn Perry, what did you expect? You ain't seen nothing yet. That old boy is going to try to make us dance to his tune. We gotta let him know who the band leader is at this Senate soiree," Henry cajoled his colleague.

"No worries, my friend, we've just begun," Perry stated. "I wanted to see if I could catch him off guard and hit him with the question on recusal right from the get-go. When he turned it into a wrestling match on semantics, I decided to let it slide. After all, it was the first day, no need to take the gloves off yet. But you don't get to claim you're just doing your job when you rule on cases in favor of your friends."

"I think that's right," Henry agreed. "Let's focus on his writings and speeches over the next day or so. Get him to acknowledge that a number of his professed beliefs are extremely right wing and outside of moderate doctrine. Let me approach him with his egregious behavior on conflict of interest after we've made him acknowledge and defend his radical ideology."

"Patricia Knetzger is ready to go full bore at him on his writings and speeches," Perry added.

"Excellent. She can be a real pit bull on Conservative philosophy. I remember how she dissected one judicial nominee on his espousal that he could apply Ayn Rand Objectivism to a Fair Housing Act case. I think the poor nominee had skimmed the Cliff Notes version of 'Atlas Shrugged' in high school, whereas Patricia had studied Political Philosophy for five years in graduate school and had a PhD. before she obtained her law degree. To say the least, it wasn't a fair match. But it sure was enjoyable to watch," Henry chuckled.

"Where was I when that happened?" Perry asked with a quizzical expression on his face.

"This was during the administration of our last regrettable Texan president. There were four lower court nominees scheduled on the same day. Some of the judicial nominees that man passed our way, you just had to shake your head. Patricia was fairly new to the Senate and brand new to the Committee. I believe that you were out on the campaign trail trying to convince the good people of Illinois that you deserved a second

term as their Senator. It was good theater watching Professor Knetzger
school her inept student."

"Well, then it should be a good show," Perry surmised.

"Stanford Winchester is no green behind the ears shit-kicker from
Braindead, Texas. Patricia will need to bring her 'A' game. We all will,"
Henry stated before he finished his bourbon with one gulp.

Queen Rita answered the ringing phone in the back room of her shop.

"Yes, I am surprised that you are calling me on the shop telephone,"
Rita commented as she listened to the caller.

"When will you be by? OK, and there will be no government man?
Yes, I understand. We will visit when you come," Rita replied as she
hung-up the phone.

Rita began wrapping a small package in brown paper. She tied it
tightly with a strong white string. She placed it in the middle of the
wooden table in the back room and sat on her stool waiting for her guest.

"Good morning Justice Winchester, I hope you had a nice evening in
our fair city," Senator Douglas stated. "Today should be a bit livelier. For
the most part the opening statements by the Committee members and
statements by Senators in support of your nomination have been completed. We are eager to hear more about your judicial background and views."

"Thank you, Mr. Chairman, and good morning to y'all. I had a lovely
evening. I spent some time down by the Tidal Basin taking in the glorious views. It was splendid, just splendid. But now, I am pleased and
prepared to provide whatever information the Committee seeks on my
judicial history and philosophy," Stanford Winchester responded.

"My colleague, Senator Knetzger will begin the questioning this
morning," Senator Douglas stated.

"Excellent," Justice Winchester intoned. "It is a pleasure to see two lovely
ladies seated on the Committee amongst the very distinguished gentlemen."

"Thank you for that, Justice Winchester," Senator Knetzger began.
"Sir, I'd like to call your attention to the document behind 'Tab 23' of the
large binder that you have on your table."

"Yes, ma'am, I have it in front of me," Stanford Winchester drawled.

"Justice Winchester, this document is a transcript from a speech that
you gave two years ago, is that correct?" Senator Knetzger asked.

"Yes, Senator, that is what it appears to be," Stanford Winchester
agreed.

"During the course of your speech, you mention that you adhere to the judicial philosophy of originalism which holds that the Constitution should be interpreted in terms of what it meant to those who ratified it over two centuries ago. Sir, do you not see this type of interpretation as an impediment to progress?" Senator Knetzger inquired.

"Senator, I understand that you and many of your colleagues see the Constitution as a living document. You want to allow courts to take into account the views of contemporary society. I wholly disagree. The Constitution is not supposed to facilitate change, but to impede change to citizens protected basic fundamental rights and responsibilities. A judge should not be seeking change through his or her judicial decision making. We have the people's house in the form of the legislature to implement the mechanisms of change. The legislature is where the will of the people is represented and exercised. Not in the courts," Justice Winchester expounded.

"But by the same token, sir, if you interpret the Constitution in its original form, then any progressive law that is passed by the legislature, you may very well declare unconstitutional because it does not adhere to the original intent of the founders," Senator Knetzger countered.

"Senator Knetzger, with all due respect, are we now going to indulge in a game of conjecture and supposition?" Stanford Winchester slowly asked his voice ringing with a sarcastic tone.

"No, sir," Senator Knetzger shot back defiantly. "Tabs 44 through 51 in the binder in front of you contain court decisions written by you in which you routinely have allowed your conservative views of interpreting the Constitution to influence your legal judgments. Should the law be applied justly and fairly for all or only as it applies to the acceptable judicial philosophy of Stanford Winchester?"

"There is no need for raised voices and pointed accusations," Justice Winchester's attorney stated. "My client would like a ten minute break, if it so pleases the Chair."

"We will adjourn for ten minutes," Senator Douglas acquiesced.

Senator Henry Fitzsimmons turned and spoke quietly to his colleague Perry Douglas, off microphone.

"Patricia's got him on the run. Those cases clearly demonstrate his inability to fairly decide matters that are not in keeping with his narrow conservative view of the Constitution," Henry whispered.

"It will be interesting to see how he responds, that's for sure," Perry Douglas softly replied with a sparkle in his eyes.

CHAPTER 36

JIM BOB MCCALLUM SAUNTERED ACROSS THE TARMAC toward his private plane. He handed a small bag to his attendant as he helped his wife Mabel climb the steps into the Gulfstream G650 jet. Seated on the cream-colored leather couch in the main cabin, Jim Bob took Mabel by the hand.

"Darlin' we're going to John Hopkins. I'm going to drop you off with the fine doctors there. You'll be in the best of care. They're going to run a few more tests. I've got some business to attend to in D.C. this evening, but a limousine will bring you to Washington on Thursday. We can spend the day taking in the sights, and then we will be having dinner at the White House. Stanford will be the guest of honor. You understand? That sounds like fun, don't it?" Jim Bob sweetly asked his wife.

"Why, of course, I understand Jim Bob," Mabel said to her husband. "You don't have to treat me like some fragile china doll. I know that time is coming, but it ain't here yet."

"It's not coming, my love. Not if I can do anything about it. Not if all them doctors at John Hopkins can do anything about it. I swear to you Mabel, I ain't never going to stop fighting this thing," Jim Bob solemnly declared.

"Yes, I know. I surely do know," Mabel quietly replied.

"THIS IS A PLEASANT SURPRISE," Queen Rita exclaimed as she spotted her niece Bessie Collins in the doorway of her shop.

"I have the morning off from work today, so I thought I would stop by to see my favorite auntie," Bessie replied with a wide smile.

"Come sit, I have some rooibos tea brewing in the kettle. An old client from South Africa brought me two pounds. It does not contain caffeine so it is not jittery making. Everything in nature has a purpose. Life is about knowing nature's purpose and using its tools," Rita deliberately stated to her niece.

"And that is what you do, isn't it? You use things from nature to make your potions and such?" Bessie asked.

"Yes, nature provides. The spirits guide my use. But the time has come," Rita allowed with a sigh.

"What time?" Bessie asked concerned.

"I am an old woman. I have been a bokor for many years. Nature tells you when to stop. I am hearing the message. The spirits require a new voice. My calls to the heavens are now a weary rasp instead of a devoted shout. My time has come," Rita slowly stated.

"I don't understand, your time for what has come?" Bessie nervously asked.

"The loa need another mambo to speak the word, to perform the rituals. My voice is not strong enough to praise the spirits," Rita confessed.

"So, you're not going to practice vodou anymore?" Bessie asked.

"I will always be one with the loa, but I can no longer do their bidding. I will keep the shop, but my days serving with both hands is over. I am at peace," Rita responded.

Bessie sat and nodded as she listened to her elderly aunt speak of no longer wanting to be an active high priestess in her Haitian religion. As she spoke, the tea pot on the small stove whistled a high-pitched note as the gusty New Orleans wind banged against the door of the old shop.

SENATOR DOUGLAS SHOOK HIS HEAD as he sat in the office of his friend Henry Fitzsimmons.

"It's 12:15 p.m. in the afternoon, isn't that a little early for spirits?" Perry asked his friend.

"What time is it in London?" Henry asked.

"I don't know, 5:15 p.m., I guess," Perry replied.

"You see there governor, it's after 5 p.m. somewhere," Henry stated with a hearty laugh in a bad British accent. "Besides, I ain't getting a crack at Winchester today am I? It's Patricia finishing up her questioning, followed by Cranston Tolliver and Hellen Raymond, right?"

"Yes, that's the schedule," Perry agreed. "You don't question Winchester until first thing tomorrow morning."

"It's a half a glass of bourbon, Perry. I can't get any kind of buzz off of a half glass. Plus, it helps soothe my stomach after lunch and calms my nerves," Henry replied with a smile. "I'm an old man, my friend. I don't have much time left to enjoy the pleasures of life. This one I'm taking to my grave," Henry stated as he held up his crystal whiskey glass to Perry.

"You're gonna out live all of us, Henry. You're too stubborn and set in your ways to leave this planet anytime soon," Perry said with a grin.

"I'll drink to that!" Henry cackled as he raised his glass.

Stanford Winchester sat in a conference room in the Hart Senate Office building as he ate a turkey sandwich on whole wheat bread.

"I've been in this city for over two days and I haven't had a meal that had any kind of flavor to it. I should have packed some hot sauce," Stanford commented to his attorney.

"Stanford, Senator Knetzger is going to drill home your strict interpretation of the Constitution," his attorney pronounced.

"Even the cheese ain't got no proper flavor," Stanford replied. "And besides, what in tarnation is wrong with defending the Constitution? They've built magnificent monuments in this here city to the men who wrote it. Why on God's green earth should I apologize for defending it?"

"That's not the point. They are going to claim that your judicial philosophy of Constitutional Originalism colors the way you interpret a case. That you do not adequately consider standing law if it is contrary to your philosophy of strict interpretation of the Constitution. They will argue that you put your own philosophy above the law. That you do not adequately weigh facts that are presented that do not coincide with your philosophical beliefs. They will insist that your decision making on the bench is wholly tied to your own dogma not to an application of the existing law and precedence," Stanford's attorney stated emphatically to his client.

"I'm pretty sure that you couldn't find a decent muffaletta in this whole city to save your life," Stanford calmly responded.

"Stanford are you even listening to me?"

"Of course, I hear you. I'm neither deaf nor dumb. If the shoe was on the other foot and one of those pretentious Democrats was sitting in my seat, I could question them endlessly about how their judicial activism is taking a meat clever to the greatest document written by mankind. Documents such as the Constitution, are not to be dressed up and changed to suit the whims of a modern society. Because modern society decides that it is now acceptable to violate the principles that this country was founded on, doesn't mean that I have to accept their changes. We all have beliefs and interpretations of the law. It is not my belief, it is a belief. And, it is a belief that many legal scholars across this nation share with me. They can claim what they want to claim. And, I will defend myself. But I will not cower to unabashed liberalism run amok," Stanford Winchester forcefully stated.

Stanford took a large gulp of his iced tea. He looked his attorney squarely in the eye, reached over and grasped his arm and asked, "Can we have one of these fine young folk that work for y'all, see if they can wrestle me up a spicy salami sandwich with a hearty provolone for lunch tomorrow?"

THE AFTERNOON SESSION of the Senate Judiciary Committee moved briskly as Senator Knetzger went over each case decision that the Committee deemed showed Justice Winchester utilizing his strict interpretation of Constitutional law to support his decision-making in each of the cases. She pointed to inconsistencies in logic and potentially faulty reasoning in interpretation of the facts. For each example, Stanford Winchester provided a defense. He did not back down from his principles and claimed that in each case his judicial conclusions were fair and well-reasoned.

Senator Cranston Tolliver of California, questioned Justice Winchester on his previous writings, including two articles he wrote in law school about his belief that the Constitution does not contain a general "right to privacy." He railed against the Supreme Court's 1973 decision in *Roe v. Wade*. He also wrote an article opposing the 1964 civil rights law that required hotels, restaurants and other businesses to serve people of all races. Each question and comment from Senator Tolliver was met with a calm and well-defended response.

At the end of the day's session, Justice Winchester thanked the Committee for their patience and hospitality. Seemingly unscarred by the torrents of questions and accusations of judicial prejudice, Stanford Winchester remained stoic and unbowed. But then, he was taught at a young age that a Southern gentlemen never shows his adversaries that they have had any effect on him. He strode out of the hearing room with a smile on his face and his hand on his left suit coat pocket, as if to pat LeeAnn and reassure her that everything was going to be fine. And, to reassure himself as well.

Nathan Whitaker walked into "Off the Record," the hotel bar located in the Hay-Adams Hotel. He looked around the well-appointed room in search of the person he was scheduled to meet that evening.

"Nathan, over here," a deep voice beckoned from a red upholstered wing chair in the corner of the ornate cocktail lounge.

"Nice to see you," Nathan cordially stated.

"Can you tell me why a hotel directly across the street from the White House has a Presidential suite? It ain't like he's gonna stay here when his house is 200 yards away, right?" His companion asked, while lifting a cocktail glass to his lips.

Nathan did not respond, surprised by the simplicity of the question.

"Well, I'm staying in the Presidential suite that must make me the President. Ain't that right, Mr. Chief of Staff?"

Once again, Nathan just nervously smiled in return.

"Is the funding going through?" Nathan's companion abruptly questioned.

"It's in the hands of Congress, but yes, we're pretty sure that the Democrats will not remove it from the budget bill. They tend not to oppose federal funding for hospitals and medical research centers," Nathan replied. "We should know conclusively in a couple of weeks."

"Good, that's real good Nathan. You sure you don't wanna stay for a drink?" His companion asked.

"I've got a lot to take care of, I should get back to the West Wing. The President arrives back in the country tomorrow morning. We have an afternoon briefing that I need to prepare for," Nathan acknowledged.

"Well, alright then. There's a Tiffany bag to the left of my chair. Take that with you on your way out."

"Yes, thank you," Nathan stated as he leaned over and took hold of the small blue bag in his right hand. Nathan walked out of the hotel lobby and stared at the White House directly across the street. He straightened his tie and buttoned his suit coat. He had work to do.

CHAPTER 37

"Excuse me Senator Fitzsimmons, with this morning's mail, a package arrived addressed to you sir. It was put through the security scan and it appears to be a bottle," Colleen, Senator Fitzsimmons secretary explained.

"A bottle is a good sign, Colleen, can you please fetch it for me," Senator Fitzsimmons asked his secretary. Senator Fitzsimmons gingerly opened the package.

"Lands sake, it's a bottle of Elijah Craig 21-year-old single barrel bourbon. This here is liquid gold, Colleen," the Senator crowed enthusiastically. "Is there a card or note that came with it?"

"Not that I could tell Senator. Would you like me to ask security about how it arrived?" Colleen asked.

"No, there's no need for that," Henry Fitzsimmons said with a smile.

"Senator, Clay just arrived," Colleen announced.

"Clay, you old scoundrel come on in," Henry Fitzsimmons called to his Chief of Staff.

"Good morning, Senator," Clay Grover greeted his boss.

"It certainly is a good morning," Henry Fitzsimmons chirped. "Any day that starts with a gift of a $300 bottle of bourbon is an excellent day by all accounts."

"Who is it from?" Clay asked.

"I got no clue, but as my pappy use to say, 'boy, never look a gift horse in the mouth.' You know what that means?" Senator Fitzsimmons inquired.

"I assume its meaning is to be grateful for the gifts that you receive, but I don't know its origin," Clay stated.

"Well, neither did I," Senator Fitzsimmons acknowledged. "But after hearing my old man say it over and over again, I looked it up. Apparently, you can determine a horse's age by the shape and projection of the horse's teeth. The longer and more forward projected the teeth, the older the horse. The saying 'long in the tooth' is derived from this fact as well. Some say that the phrase can be traced back to the Latin text of St. Jerome, The Letter to the Ephesians, circa AD 400. The literal translation is 'Never inspect the teeth of a given horse.' Why he thought of that, no one seems to know. But here we are over 1600 years later, still saying the same damn thing."

"Yes, sir," Clay responded, unsure of how to reply.

"Anyhow, I'm gonna put this excellent bottle of bourbon on my desk. A noontime sip or two will be my reward for knockin' the gentlemen from Louisiana down a peg or two this morning. You got my notes and questioning outline, Clay?"

"Yes, Senator, along with your binder of documents. I have Post-Its on the pages and highlighting of the relevant passages," Clay answered.

"Excellent. Let's get this tussle started. Nothing gets the juices flowing like two old Southern horse thieves goin' toe to toe," Henry Fitzsimmons stated with a smile.

"Welcome home, Andy," Sue Lynn Cochran greeted her husband.

"It was only four days, but I surely did miss you," The President said to his First Lady as he kissed her on the cheek. "Has Nathan destroyed the country yet?" The President asked with a smile.

"Not that I'm aware of, but I'm sure it's not for lack of trying," Sue Lynn chuckled in response.

"Well now, that ain't fair Sue Lynn. If Nathan really put his mind to it and wanted to destroy the country, we'd be sitting on a pile of nuclear rubble by now. The boy does get things done!" President Cochran laughed.

"Speaking of getting things done, the White House dinner for your nominee, Justice Winchester is tomorrow night. Nancy has it in your calendar," Sue Lynn mentioned.

"Good. Thank you dear for getting that set-up. Did we send the good Justice a bottle and some fruit and such?" Andrew Cochran asked his wife.

"Done and done. Toni took care of it before he arrived at his hotel in Washington," Sue Lynn stated.

"And what hotel is the Justice at?" Andrew Cochran asked.

"He's just across the street at the Hay-Adams," Sue Lynn replied.

"Excellent, that's convenient. And guest list for the White House dinner in his honor?" Andrew asked.

"There's every Republican member of the Supreme Court, a few of the Republican Senators on the Judiciary Committee, Jim Bob and Mabel McCallum, a few of Justice Winchester's law school classmates and friends that reside here in Washington, the Attorney General, the Solicitor General, and some West Wing senior staff. And, yes, Andy, I invited Posy Whitaker," Sue Lynn begrudgingly added.

"That's my girl, I know I can always count on you to do the right thing. I understand that she gets along with Mabel McCallum," Andrew responded.

"Get along? It's more like torment, constantly pushing liquor on that poor woman. But yes, I had Toni seat the Whitakers at the same table as the McCallums," Sue Lynn said with a heavy sigh.

"You're the best, Sue Lynn. Now come give your president a little welcome home sugar, sugar," Andrew Cochran seductively cooed to his wife.

"GOOD MORNING, JUSTICE WINCHESTER, are you ready to proceed?" Senator Henry Fitzsimmons greeted the witness.

"Good morning, Senator. I'm as ready as I'll ever be," Stanford Winchester stated with a confident smile.

"Justice Winchester, it's a fair statement to say that you have many friends and family in New Orleans, is that correct?" Senator Fitzsimmons inquired.

"Yes, Senator, the roots of the Winchester family tree spread wide and run deep in Louisiana, but specifically in New Orleans," Justice Winchester drawled.

"And of course, you cherish and protect those who are dear to you?" Henry Fitzsimmons questioned.

"Why of course. But I have no idea why you are asking me these questions, Senator?" Stanford Winchester inquired.

"With all due respect Justice Winchester, but who is pluckin' this here chicken, you or me?" Senator Fitzsimmons asked with a slow drawl.

"Point taken, sir. Proceed," Justice Winchester stated with a smirk.

"Alright sir, can you please explain to this Judiciary Committee why in your many years on the bench both in Louisiana and on the Federal bench why you never recused yourself from one single case?" Senator Fitzsimmons pointedly asked the Justice.

"I do not shirk my sworn duties, sir," Justice Winchester promptly replied.

"Justice Winchester, is it your sworn duty to render court decisions in favor of your friends and relatives? To refuse to recuse yourself from matters which you have no right presiding over? To issue substantial financial rewards and judgments to close friends which directly benefit your family and your wife's family? Is that the sworn duty that you are referring to, sir?" Senator Fitzsimmons aggressively challenged his witness.

"Point of order, Mr. Chairman," Senator Sawyer quickly interjected. "Is this a nomination hearing or is Senator Fitzsimmons conducting his own personal Spanish inquisition?"

"More appropriately, that would be a Southern inquisition, Cletus," Senator Fitzsimmons replied sarcastically to his colleague. "But, please inform me, when it became inappropriate for this Committee to question a nominee on his fundamental judicial behavior? The section of the U.S. Code dealing with the subject of judicial recusals ain't there just to be window dressing. Now, unless you have a legitimate objection or point of order, I'm going to ask the witness to respond to my inquiries," Senator Fitzsimmons stated as his face became flushed and his voice grew in volume and intensity.

"Senator Fitzsimmons, as I previously mentioned to you, my family and I are well rooted in the New Orleans community. If I recused myself from every case where I had tangential interests, I would never preside over any matters in Louisiana. I impartially listen to all of the facts presented, and with equanimity and a sense of fair justice I apply the governing law, and render decisions utilizing my God given gifts of discerning truth and equality," Justice Winchester stoically proclaimed.

"Sir, that is not an answer to my question, it is a speech. And it is a tired old speech that you have been giving for years to justify your judicial misbehaviors. It takes courage to admit to one's mistakes in judgment when it comes to one's relations. But a refusal, sir, to exhibit the courage to concede to truth and reality is nothing more than the worthless baggage of delusional misbegotten arguments," Senator Fitzsimmons challenged Justice Winchester.

"Mr. Chairman, my client did not come all this way to be insulted and ridiculed," Justice Winchester's attorney loudly and forcefully interjected.

"All right, let's take a fifteen minute break to allow cooler heads to prevail," Senator Douglas stated. "But let me remind you counselor, that Justice Winchester is here to be vetted as a nominee for the Supreme Court. It is not only this Committee's purview but our duty to ascertain the judicial behavior and temperament of the nominee. Tough questions will be asked. With that, we are adjourned for fifteen minutes."

The Committee members filed out of the hearing room as the guests and press in the gallery buzzed with excitement.

"Henry, you're relentless today," Senator Douglas said to his colleague, just outside the hearing room.

"I've had enough of that obfuscating Southern gentleman. He will continue to tell that tired old tale of his family roots being a legitimate reason for refusing to recuse himself from cases involving his friends and family if no one challenges him on it," Henry Fitzsimmons charged, clearly ready for verbal fisticuffs.

"Well, you're demonstrating a vim and vigor in your questioning that puts the rest of us to shame," Perry Douglas said with a smile, as he patted the shoulder of his friend.

"Just an old coot on his last leg putting on a little show for Congressional posterity," Henry allowed with a wink and a smile.

The Judiciary Committee hearings reconvened and Senator Fitzsimmons questioned Justice Winchester about each of the three matters that he presided over while on the Louisiana bench, that involved members of his extended family or friends as defendants in the matter. In each instance, Senator Fitzsimmons made a reasonable argument why a jurist should recuse himself from the matter. And in every instance, Justice Winchester defended his judgment and impartiality, as he pointed out that in one of the three case matters, he ruled against the interests of his friend. Senator Fitzsimmons was quick to rebut that argument, by noting that the friend in question had been estranged from Justice Winchester for several years. The questions and answers on the point of recusal continued throughout the morning session.

"Mr. Chairman, I will yield my time as we are upon the lunch break. However, I would like to resume with my line of questioning, specific to the Fifth Circuit case matter of *Happy Foods v. Lake Pontchartrain Brands*, after the luncheon break," Henry Fitzsimmons stated to the Committee Chair.

"So noted, thank you Senator Fitzsimmons. We are adjourned until 1:30 p.m." Senator Douglas stated.

HENRY FITZSIMMONS SAT AT HIS DESK in his Senate office going over his notes and scribbling comments on his questioning outline. An untouched corned beef sandwich and bowl of barley soup sat on a tray at the side of his desk.

"Senator, it's almost time to go back to the hearing room, you should have something to eat," Clay Grover said with concern as he entered his boss's office and glanced at the uneaten lunch. Moments later, Perry Douglas arrived at his colleague's office doorway and offered the same advice.

"Henry we're going to start soon, but why don't I go ahead and stall a little while you get some sustenance in you," Perry said to his friend.

"Nonsense, I'm fine. I'm not hungry. I'm too full of piss and vinegar. The *Happy Foods* case is going to be the final nail closing off the nomination of that pompous Southern gentleman. His conduct during that case is a sterling example of why the U.S. Code has a section dealing specifically with recusal. Watch me drive that nail in boys," Henry Fitzsimmons energetically stated to Perry and Clay.

"Go get him, Senator!" Clay exclaimed.

"But first, a little liquid encouragement with the help of old Elijah Craig," Henry Fitzsimmons said with a smile as he opened the bottle of bourbon he had received that morning. He carefully poured a couple fingers worth of the caramel colored liquor into a crystal whiskey glass.

"Would you fine gentlemen care to join me?" Henry asked Perry and Clay. Both shook their heads. Henry quickly downed the bourbon in one gulp. He took a tin of mints out of his desk drawer and placed one mint in his mouth to cover up the smell of the bourbon. He bounded out of his leather chair and joined his colleagues as they walked down the Senate building corridor. Less than fifty feet from the doorway of his Senate office, Henry Fitzsimmons became wobbly and attempted to brace himself against the corridor wall with his outstretched hand. His hand slipped off the wall as he futilely attempted to gain his balance. He went crashing to the floor. Senator Fitzsimmons was splayed across the floor of the Senate Office building corridor. He was clearly no longer conscious. Clay and Perry raced to his side. Clay quickly dropped to the floor and cradled the elderly Senator's head in his lap while he checked his pulse by placing his fingers at the left side of the Senator's neck.

"Henry! Henry!" Perry Douglas shouted in dismay.

CHAPTER 38

Perry Douglas watched with concern as the EMT's loaded
Henry Fitzsimmons onto a stretcher in the Senate Office building corridor.

"Stop looking at me like I'm already dead," Henry Fitzsimmons joked
to his friend as he was being strapped down. "I just got a little woozy, fell,
and banged this old cement melon on the floor. Aside from a little bump
on the back on my head, I'm fine, Perry."

"We'll let the doctors determine that Henry," Perry stated with
emphasis.

"What about the hearing?" Henry asked as an EMT affixed a blood
pressure cuff to his left arm.

"We'll just adjourn until next Monday. We were scheduled for this
afternoon and just tomorrow morning anyway. It's a one day delay that
we can pick up next week," Perry reassured his colleague.

"Alright. I'll be rarin' to go by Monday," Henry said.

"Let's see what the doctors have to say about that," Perry acknowledged. "Rest Henry, rest."

Senator Douglas entered the hearing room after he was certain
that Senator Fitzsimmons was receiving medical care and was on his way
to the hospital. He informed the participants and guests at the hearing
of Senator Fitzsimmons fall and his current condition. He adjourned
the proceedings until Monday morning at 10 a.m. After making his announcement, Perry Douglas went directly to the hospital to be with his

colleague. Stanford Winchester sat quietly for several moments at the witness table shocked by the news about Senator Fitzsimmons. He asked his attorney for a piece of paper and a pen, and he wrote a short note. He beckoned to Clay Grover who was collecting Senator Fitzsimmons hearing materials from the Senator's place at the dais.

"Excuse me sir," Justice Winchester quietly said as Clay approached him, "Do you work with Senator Fitzsimmons?"

"Yes, sir, I am his Chief of Staff," Clay replied.

"Would you do me the kind service of giving this note to Senator Fitzsimmons when he is recuperated from his unfortunate fall?" Stanford Winchester asked Clay.

Clay a bit stunned by the gesture accepted the handwritten note and thanked Justice Winchester. As he walked out of the hearing room, Clay could not help himself. Overcome by curiosity, he unfolded the note given to him by Justice Winchester and read it.

"'I have fought against the people of the North because I believed they were seeking to wrest from the South its dearest rights. But I have never cherished toward them bitter or vindictive feelings, and I have never seen the day when I did not pray for them.' Robert E. Lee. My best wishes and fervent prayers for your full recovery. Stanford Winchester."

Clay carefully re-folded the note, as he softly uttered to himself, "Remarkable."

A COUPLE OF HOURS AFTER HENRY FITZSIMMONS was admitted to the hospital, Clay Grover and Aaron Rose joined Perry Douglas at his bedside.

"How is he doing?" Clay quietly asked Senator Douglas.

"The doctors did a number of tests and checked him out thoroughly. Other than his blood pressure being somewhat elevated and the contusion on the back of his head, he's in pretty good shape. They believe that he may have a slight concussion. They're going to monitor him overnight, but if he passes a concussion protocol in the morning, he could be released tomorrow afternoon," Perry explained to Clay and Aaron.

"Excellent," Clay replied, clearly relieved by the good news. "May I speak to him?"

"Sure, he's awake now, though somewhat sedated, so just a few minutes and then we should all leave and allow him to get some rest," Senator Douglas counseled.

"Senator Fitzsimmons, I'm so relieved to understand that you're going to be alright, "Clay whispered as he took the Senator's hand into his. "You gave us quite the scare."

"Thank you, Clay. I scared myself pretty good as well. But other than being hooked up to all these damn machines and peeing into a tube, I actually don't feel so bad," Henry Fitzsimmons said with a slight smile.

"Justice Winchester asked if I would give you a note," Clay stated as he handed the note to his boss.

Henry Fitzsimmons unfolded the note and read it to himself. After he finished reading the note from Stanford Winchester, he grinned and chuckled.

"My lord, we old aristocratic Southerners are a ridiculous lot. If we are not chivalrous and honorable to our adversaries, we feel like we have dishonored our family name. I would not have expected less and quoting Robert E. Lee was a nice touch."

"Alright, Henry, we're going to let you get some rest, my friend. I'll stop by in the morning to see if they're going to release you," Perry Douglas said.

"Thank y'all for coming. I greatly appreciate your concern for this weak old bag of bones," "Clay, son, may I ask you to do a small favor for me?"

"Of course, Senator, anything," Clay replied while nodding.

"Would you kindly lock that bottle of bourbon on my desk in my liquor cabinet? You never know when the janitorial staff may get a little frisky," Henry asked Clay.

"For Christ's sake, Henry!" Perry exclaimed. "We were scared to death that we may have lost you today, and your only concern is your bottle of expensive bourbon?"

Henry winked at his friend, "A man's got to have his priorities, Perry, a man's got to have his priorities."

"A MAN'S GOT TO HAVE HIS PRIORITIES, and right now, my top priority is finding a refined drinking establishment where I can enjoy a well-made Sazerac or two," Stanford Winchester said to his attorney as they walked out of the Hart Senate Office building.

"I've been told that the bar in the basement of your hotel, the Hay-Adams, has a reputation for crafting a fine cocktail," Stanford's attorney offered.

"You can't get more convenient than that. Would you care to join me?" Stanford inquired.

"Thank you but no, I have plans with my wife. I'll see you Monday morning. Enjoy your extra time in D.C. this weekend," his attorney added before departing.

Stanford went to his room to freshen up before heading to the basement bar, Off the Record. As he walked through the establishment towards the back, Stanford was greeted by a familiar voice.

"Why, the best drunks must inhabit this here establishment," a deep Southern voice announced. Stanford quickly turned around to see the beaming face of Jim Bob McCallum.

"Have a seat and join me for an aperitif, you old rascal," Jim Bob offered with a welcoming smile.

"Greetings Jim Bob," Stanford happily replied. "I knew you were coming to town for the White House dinner tomorrow night, but I had no idea you were in Washington already."

"I dropped Mabel off at John Hopkins yesterday. They're performing a few tests to see if the new drug treatment is having any positive effects on her cognitive abilities. And I had some business to attend to last evening here in D.C. How are things going with the Judiciary Committee hearings?" Jim Bob asked.

"Well, I think," Stanford replied. "The Democrats are making a show, attempting to portray me as some wild-eyed extremist hell-bent on destroying democracy, but that's to be expected, I reckon."

"Ha!" Jim Bob laughed. "That surely is the pot calling the kettle black, ain't it? Nothing but a bunch of god-less closeted Communists and sexual deviants."

"This afternoon, Henry Fitzsimmons had a fall, and they postponed the hearings until Monday morning," Stanford explained.

"Hell, that old drunk can't walk to the pisser without falling all over himself," Jim Bob interjected with a snort.

"Now, don't go cuttin' him short, Jim Bob. Henry Fitzsimmons still has an agile mind and the tenacity of a bulldog. He is still a formidable adversary," Stanford noted with respect.

"Henry Fitzsimmons ain't nothing you should be worried about," Jim Bob said with the wink of an eye. "Now who you gotta kill to get a drink around here?" Jim Bob ranted as he scanned the room looking for the wait staff.

CLAY GROVER TOOK A LONG SIP OF WINE. His legs were intertwined with Aaron's, as they sat on opposite ends of the couch facing each other.

"That old man scared the life out of me today," Clay said with a subtle shake of his head. "I guess I never realized until this afternoon how much I care for him, and how devastated I'll be when he's gone. He's been like a father to me. Encouraging me, supporting me, protecting me when he deems it necessary."

"Do you think he knows you're gay?" Aaron asked.

"In his way, yeah, I think so, Clay replied. "I mean, it's nothing we've ever discussed, and I've certainly never said anything directly to him, but sometimes he just gives me this knowing sly smile that makes me think that he knows."

"You don't think he has a problem with it?" Aaron responded.

"Not at all," Clay replied with emphasis. "Henry Fitzsimmons has taken up the cause of civil rights for decades in the Senate. If you are oppressed or downtrodden Henry Fitzsimmons is your friend and advocate. And that is the beauty of the man. He's an old gentleman of the South. Raised during a time when homosexuals in South Carolina were reviled, ostracized, beaten, and even killed. Yet, his open-mindedness and uplifting spirit comes from a place that is so foreign to his upbringing and circumstances. If he were from New York or Boston or Chicago, you might better understand it. But, he's from a little town outside of Charleston, South Carolina. And from that narrow-minded and bigoted hamlet sprung one of the most progressive defenders of equality this nation has ever seen in one of its leaders."

"He's an amazing man," Aaron chimed in, while holding up his wine glass in a toast. "To Henry Fitzsimmons, champion of the oppressed. May God protect him."

"To Henry," Clay whispered as he raised his glass in salute to his mentor. A tear ran down Clay's cheek, as his head bowed in respect.

KATE WILSON RAN PAST THE TREES and flora that surround the Washington Tidal Basin. She enjoyed the fragrant aroma as she jogged down the path. And she was ready to start her own new career path working in the West Wing. In addition to a new career, she was also focused on her blossoming relationship. What even she had acknowledged started as a mutually beneficial sexual fling, was seemingly becoming a more involved and rewarding relationship. Her past doubts and worries of being taken advantage of by a powerful man were dissipating with every encounter, every text message or phone call. The sweet and loving gestures had continued. There was the delivery of flowers, bottles of wine and gourmet chocolates. And just that morning, a thoughtful and much appreciated gift basket that contained bottles of Fiji spring water, dozens of Clif Bar Energy bars, a half dozen pair of women's running socks, organic cotton sports towels, a Fitbit Surge Fitness watch, and a $250 gift card to Potomac River Running Store. The enclosed card read, "Keep running, don't slow down, devoted love is right around the corner."

Kate truly believed that what had started as a sexual dalliance with power was evolving into a committed relationship. Her paramour had recently pledged that he would leave his wife and carve out a new life with her. His messages and calls motivated her. The perfumed fragrance of the flora ignited the passions of love. Kate was ready to follow that path.

CHAPTER 39

Perry Douglas leaned back in his leather chair as he regaled his wife Katherine with details from the first week of Judiciary Committee hearings vetting Justice Winchester and Henry Fitzsimmons fall.

"Katherine, for a frightening moment I thought that Henry was gone. He was white as a sheet and completely unresponsive as he laid on the floor of the Senate Office building," Perry told his wife. "But fortunately, he seems to be his old feisty self and is now at home convalescing."

"Oh my word, how did it happen?" Katherine inquired.

"That old bird is as stubborn as they come. He hadn't had any breakfast. Then went through a grueling session of questioning Justice Winchester during the morning, and then left his lunch untouched as he worked through the break. But, before we went back to the hearing room for the afternoon session, he had to have a glass of bourbon. As we were walking down the corridor, I was talking to his Chief of Staff, Clay, and we were a few feet ahead of Henry. Next thing I know, there is this loud thud and Henry was sprawled out on the Senate building floor. The doctors think that his glucose levels were so low that he fainted," Perry stated.

"But he's alright now?" Katherine queried.

"Other than a bump on the back of his head, he seems fine. They released him the next day after a night of observation," Perry said.

"That's great news. And you, how are you holding up? How is the Committee hearing going?" Katherine asked.

"I'm fine, a little tired. Henry's accident shook me up a bit. Lots of expended emotional energy over the last couple of days. The Committee hearing is going well. We've scored some points on Winchester's radical political views. Patricia Knetzger and Cranston Tolliver did an excellent job of highlighting the judge's far-right views in his speeches and writings. Winchester didn't deny anything. He just defended himself like he didn't understand why people would have a problem accepting the belief that the Constitution does not establish a person's right to privacy," Perry explained to his wife.

"Truly?" Katherine questioned.

"Oh, he's not alone. Including current sitting members of the Court. That is a well held belief of those who espouse Constitutional Originalism. It's baffling, but they seem to lose sight of the fact that the animating spirit of the Constitution was to protect individual's liberty. They lack the pragmatism to see that the Constitution must evolve to match more enlightened understandings on matters such as the equal treatment of women and minorities. The Constitution was written in 1787, and they hold each word as sacred and unchangeable. The consequences of the progress of time and societal changes are held inconsequential," Perry explained.

"Well, fight the good fight, my darling. I'm sure you will prevail in the end. Progressives have good friends in Perry Douglas and Henry Fitzsimmons. Please give my best to Henry and his speedy recovery," Katherine said.

"Will do," Perry agreed.

THURSDAY EVENING AND AT HIS HOTEL, Stanford Winchester prepared for the White House dinner in his honor. He carefully cinched the knot of his bow tie while in front of the bathroom mirror. His cherished photograph of LeeAnn was firmly tucked into the inner left hand pocket of his suit coat. He thought to himself, how proud LeeAnn would be to see her husband being honored with a dinner at the White House by the President of the United States. He grinned at himself in the mirror. He was surely living in the high cotton now.

THE GUESTS WERE ESCORTED TO THEIR SEATS at the tables in the large dining room. The dinner menu had been planned to accent the flavors and produce of the President's home state of Georgia and the honored guest's home state of Louisiana. A Louisiana crawfish bisque was followed by a smoked Georgia peach salad. The entree was blackened redfish with lump crabmeat. And dessert was petite peach cobblers with vanilla bean gelato and mini pecan tarts with rum sauce.

Posy Whitaker spotted Mabel McCallum and swiftly moved to her side.

"Mabel, sugar, don't you look fine tonight," Posy loudly proclaimed. Jim Bob leaned over and quietly whispered to his wife, "Posy Whitaker, wife of the President's Chief of Staff."

"Yes, Posy, nice to see you dear," Mabel graciously replied.

"I'm so happy that you're here. We're gonna have some fun tonight. I just need to get us started with a nice julep. They got all these folks walking around with trays of wine, but we need to get us some serious drinks. Ain't that right, Mabel?" Posy laughed and snorted.

"Yes, I suppose," Mabel hesitantly replied.

"Don't you worry girlfriend, I got this covered," Posy said as she left Mabel's side to pursue one of the wait staff down an aisle.

Stanford Winchester was busy shaking hands with old friends and Republican dignitaries. Senator Cletus Sawyer pulled Stanford to the side for a moment.

"I couldn't possibly countenance that insulting questioning by Henry Fitzsimmons. He had no right, simply no right," Cletus Sawyer insisted. "God struck him down for his immoral behavior."

"Of course, I appreciate your kind concern and staunch defense on my behalf, but it's all part of the same dance, ain't it?" Stanford responded to Cletus Sawyer. "The Democrats aren't doing anything to me that my Republican friends wouldn't do to a Democratic nominee. We call each other radicals and decry each other as far beyond the acceptable standards of moderate Americans. I'm the frightening ultra-Conservative who shuns modern jurisprudence. Henry Fitzsimmons is the left wing progressive out to destroy the Constitution. It wasn't always like this. Sure, we have always had our differences. But it wasn't this endless dance to demonize the other. However, it is what it has become, and I understand the steps. I reckon, I wish we could just dance to a different tune."

Cletus Sawyer stared at Stanford dumbstruck by his response.

"Sorry Cletus, old boy, at times I become wistful. I am a dancer at heart occupying the robes of a jurist. I long for the days of a simple swing dance and am easily confused by these modern twerks. Ain't that what they call them?" Stanford stated with a smile. "Excuse me, if you will, I see my friend Jim Bob McCallum and it would be insufferably rude for me not to greet my fellow Louisianan."

Stanford walked away from Cletus leaving him baffled and confused.

"What did you say to Cletus, ol' boy looks like he lost his dog?" Jim Bob asked Stanford.

"Nothing really," Stanford replied. "In my own way, I was just trying to explain to him that I'm grown and don't need him protecting me from the nature of politics."

"C'mon now Stanford, let's not be turning our allies into foes. I've done way too much to get you here," Jim Bob brusquely stated.

"I'm sorry, excuse an old man's failing hearing, but what did you just say?" Stanford asked, his back stiffened and his face full of resolve.

"Nothing, just that you worked so hard to get this nomination for yourself," Jim Bob fudged in response.

"You sure you didn't say something else?" Stanford persisted with a steely determination in his eyes.

"It's your night Stanford, enjoy it. Best to let sleeping dogs lie, old friend," Jim Bob sternly advised. "Now if you'll excuse me I should get back to Mabel, Nathan's ditzy wife is hanging all over her like a five dollar suit."

Stanford stood quietly as he collected his thoughts. He knew what he had heard, and he attempted to fully understand its meaning. Moments later he was greeted by an old law school acquaintance and shook hands and smiled convincingly. Yet, Jim Bob's comment lingered in the back of his mind for the remainder of the evening.

LATER THAT EVENING AFTER DINNER, cordials and cocktails were served. Jim Bob McCallum found a quiet corner of the room to have a conversation with Nathan Whitaker. Meanwhile, Posy attempted to have Mabel do tequila shots with her. Stanford, the center of attention, drank bourbon on the rocks, and held court, so to speak, with two sitting Republican members of the Supreme Court.

"Nathan, I may have said something to Stanford that put a tick in his hide," Jim Bob quietly professed. "I had a couple of fast cocktails when I arrived and wasn't thinkin' clearly."

"What did you say?" Nathan asked with concern.

"He was telling me that he was being flip with Cletus Sawyer, and I just reminded him that we need to keep our allies close. I mentioned that I had done a lot to get him to where he is. That's all," Jim Bob stated.

"Nothing more than that?" Nathan inquired.

"Nope. I just let that slip. But he don't know nothing about our relationship or what we've done. I swear," Jim Bob added.

"Well, I don't think it's a big deal. As far as he's concerned, the President nominated him based on his judicial record and his exemplary qualifications to be seated on the Court. And this evening is just testament to that fact," Nathan said with confidence. "We just need to be careful not to let things slip."

"As my daddy use to say, 'loose lips sink ships,'" Jim Bob pronounced.

"Indeed," Nathan replied.

"C'mon Mabel, you ready girl?" Posy Whitaker asked as she handed Mabel a shot glass of Don Julio tequila. "Lick the salt, down the shot, and then suck on the lime, it's easy and so tasty," Posy instructed Mabel.

"I'm not so sure that this is a good idea," Mabel replied, looking uneasy. "I don't regularly indulge in pure spirits."

"Oh, you're gonna like it, I promise you that," Posy stated. "Heck, I was doing shots when I was 17 years old and competin' in Georgia beauty pageants. I won the shot contests with them other girls and won the beauty pageant as well!" Posy laughed.

"Ready, on three," Posy commanded as she counted down and emptied the shot glass into her mouth. Mabel took a small sip and placed the shot glass on the table.

"I'm sorry, dear, this just isn't for me," Mabel apologized.

"That's alright Mabel, we'll just get you another julep. I know you can handle those," Posy assured her as she attempted to frantically wave over the wait staff.

President Cochran made a short speech praising the achievements and distinguished career of Justice Winchester. He led the assemblage in a toast to the "next Associate Justice of the United States Supreme Court." After his speech, a five-piece Dixieland band began playing a number of old New Orleans jazz standards. President Cochran and Sue Lynn Cochran took to the dance floor and encouraged their guests to join them. Stanford surveyed the room looking for a dance partner. He noticed Mabel McCallum talking with Posy Whitaker and approached the two ladies.

"Would either of you lovely ladies do an old man the gratifying pleasure of a dance?" Stanford asked.

"I'm afraid, I'm a bit too unsteady at the moment for dancing," Mabel admitted to Stanford.

"I surely wouldn't mind cutting a rug," Posy Whitaker replied. "My husband Nathan ain't much for dancing."

Stanford took Posy by the hand and led her out to the dance floor. He twirled and dipped her in perfect rhythm to the music. Posy smiled and laughed as Stanford demonstrated his proficient swing step moves on the dance floor. A number of guests noticed the couple on the floor and began clapping in time to the musical beat. By the time the song ended, a large number of guests had witnessed Posy and Stanford's exquisite dance and applauded in appreciation.

"Oh my word, that was fun!" Posy loudly exclaimed.

"May I get you a drink, Mrs. Whitaker?" Stanford asked.

"Heck yeah," Posy replied. "But after dipping and spinning me like a top, you should call me Posy, your judgeship."

"With pleasure, if you will refer to me by my Christian name of Stanford," he responded. Stanford and Posy sat together and enjoyed a couple of mint juleps.

"How did you learn how to dance like that?" Posy asked.

"My beloved wife LeeAnn was a staunch advocate of dancing after a wonderful meal. We took lessons early on in our marriage. After a few decades of dancing together, you can't help but acquire some skills," Stanford explained.

"Is your wife back in New Orleans?" Posy questioned.

"She passed on five years ago," Stanford explained as he removed the photograph of LeeAnn from his suit coat pocket and showed it to Posy.

"I'm so sorry to hear that," Posy quietly replied as she looked at the photograph. "She was a lovely woman."

"Yes, yes, she was," Stanford said as he carefully reinserted the picture back into his breast pocket. "And of course, you have a remarkable husband," Stanford added. "I've been very impressed with Nathan from the time he contacted me on the phone about the nomination, to the few occasions where I've spent time with him here in Washington."

"Yeah, he's alright, I guess," Posy chuckled. "I don't get to see him much since we moved here after Andy won."

"I noticed that he was speaking with Jim Bob McCallum earlier, are they close friends?" Stanford inquired.

"Sometimes them two is like peas in a pod," Posy replied. "Nathan's known Jim Bob for a few years now. Though they got real chummy last year when Andy was running for President. Nathan and Jim Bob would spend so much time on the phone scheming and planning on how to get Andy elected. And Nathan, you know, is so devoted to Andy. They've been best friends since first year of college. He won't stop at nothing to make sure his friend is a successful president. Sometimes I wonder if Nathan is married to me or to Andy. He surely spends more time with Andy than he does with me."

"Well, that is life in politics, ain't it? We never seem to have enough time for our families, we're so devoted to our careers," Stanford replied. "It was a great pleasure sharing a dance with you, Posy. And our conversation has been most illuminating. So thank you for that as well. But as much as I hate to say, I should probably go press a little more flesh and mingle with the other guests."

"That's fine Stanford, it was fun cutting a rug with you. I'm gonna go get Mabel and me another julep," Posy said.

"Yes, you go on and do that. Thank you again," Stanford stated with a knowing smile.

CHAPTER 40

ANDREW COCHRAN WAS GETTING READY for bed while he praised his wife Sue Lynn.

"Sue Lynn, darlin', that was a lovely evening. Thank you for putting that all together. And of course, please thank Toni for me. The room looked lovely, the food was excellent, and the jazz band was a nice touch which Justice Winchester greatly appreciated," Andrew commended his wife.

"Yes, it was a nice affair. But did you see how Posy Whitaker was conducting herself and forcing alcohol on poor Mabel McCallum?" Sue Lynn interjected.

"I thought we both agreed that this evening was a smashing success," Andrew replied with a grin. "You let Posy get under your skin too much. She's not a sophisticated woman, we all have known that for years. But, she's harmless. Generally, she means well. She just isn't well acquainted with how to handle herself in some social settings. She's probably a bit intimidated by the pomp and grandeur of Washington elite society."

"To my dying day I will never understand what Nathan saw in that woman," Sue Lynn responded.

"She was and still is, to some extent, a very lovely woman. Though not as lovely as you, my dear," Andrew quickly added.

"But she has the manners and lack of couth of a trucker driver," Sue Lynn replied.

"Well, in our private moments, Nathan has confided to me that intelligence or sophistication were not that important to him, in a woman who looks like Posy. That he actually enjoyed her simplicity, energy, and zeal for life. In simple terms, she's a trophy wife. She is there to remind other men that Nathan is powerful enough to be desirable to such a beautiful woman despite his older age and less than Playgirl cover looks. It can drive one to distraction to try to figure out what others seek in their mates. As long as they're happy with each other that's all that matters," Andrew surmised.

"Are they truly happy with each other?" Sue Lynn inquired.

"That question, my love, is above my pay grade. I'm only President of the United States," Andrew responded with a sly smile.

FRIDAY MORNING AND JUSTICE ALLEN SALLIS greeted his clerk, Kate Wilson, on his way to his office.

"Good morning Kate, I was at a White House dinner last night and expected to see you there."

"Good morning sir," Kate replied taken aback by the Justice's comment. "I don't get invited to White House dinners. Ever."

"Well, maybe that will change," Justice Sallis offered with a grin. "Anyway, it was a lovely affair in honor of the President's nominee to the Court, Stanford Winchester."

"Yes, sir," Kate replied, unsure of how to respond to the Justice's comment.

"I had a chance to chat with Justice Winchester, I think he's going to work out just fine," Justice Sallis pronounced. "Kind of an eccentric fellow, overly polite, but his politics and judicial reasoning are sound. Senator Sawyer informed me that he's handling himself fairly well with that pack of Democratic jackals on the Judiciary Committee. And the head of their scurrilous pack, Perry Douglas, a former Constitutional law professor, who doesn't know the first thing about the Constitution. They all sicken me."

"Yes, sir," Kate said, once again at a loss for an appropriate response.

"Well, alright then. It's going to be a busy morning. I just wanted to let you know that Winchester seems like a good fit on the Court," Justice Sallis stated as he turned from Kate and proceeded toward his office.

"Thank you, sir," Kate said, shaking her head over the whole awkward exchange.

AARON ROSE SAT IN THE OFFICE of Senator Douglas waiting for his boss to get back from a short meeting.

"Aaron, sorry to keep you waiting. I just wanted to make sure that we were prepared for the Committee hearings on Monday. As you know Senator Fitzsimmons was going to question Justice Winchester about the *Happy Foods* case, Fifth Circuit matter before he had his fall. I'm going to resume that line of questioning when we commence on Monday. You were the one that uncovered that case as being a conflict of interest, so I would like to have you assist me with my preparations. Is that alright with you?"

"Of course, sir, it's my honor to help in any way possible. But, isn't Senator Fitzsimmons going to do the questioning? I spoke with Clay Grover last night and he informed me that the Senator was progressing nicely and was planning on being present and resuming the questioning on Monday," Aaron replied.

"Well, Henry may be present, but I don't want to put the burden of questioning Justice Winchester on him, so soon after his accident. Not to worry, I'll talk to Henry. He'll put up a ruckus, but he'll understand that I'm only looking out for his best interests. So, will you please obtain the materials Henry was going to utilize from Clay, and then we can spend a couple of hours together preparing right after lunch. How does that sound?" Perry asked his aide.

"Excellent!" Aaron exclaimed. "I'll go talk to Clay now and will be ready to meet after lunch."

"OH, HE'S GOING TO HATE THAT!" Clay told Aaron as he began to gather Senator Fitzsimmons hearing preparation materials together.

"What am I supposed to do?" Aaron asked. "The Chair of the Committee wants to do the questioning of a witness. Senator Douglas said he would talk to Senator Fitzsimmons and explain it to him."

"Yeah, I mean, I get it," Clay offered. "Just a few days out of the hospital, Senator Fitzsimmons probably shouldn't be indulging in a grueling verbal sparring match with Justice Winchester. But he's going to hate it! He's such a proud and stubborn man."

"I know, but this is not our argument," Aaron responded.

"No, it sure isn't," Clay acknowledged as he handed a stack of binders, papers, and notes to Aaron. See you later tonight at my place?" Clay asked.

"Mos def," Aaron smiled in reply.

"YOU MIGHT AS WELL JUST BURY ME NOW!" Henry Fitzsimmons spat into his phone, as he sat in a leather chair in his Arlington, Virginia home.

"Henry, you were released from the hospital yesterday," Perry Douglas attempted to reason with his Senate colleague and friend.

"And today is Friday, and the hearing ain't until Monday. I'm a fast healer," Henry cajoled his friend.

"Henry, all I'm saying is that I'll take the lead on questioning Winchester. You can certainly ask a follow-up question or two. I'm not excluding you, I'm just going to take the laboring oar on questioning, so that you don't have the whole burden on yourself. You know how much I respect you. But I want and need Senator Henry Fitzsimmons around for years to come. We don't need you exerting yourself, just days after a nasty fall and hospital visit. By the way, Katherine sends her love and best wishes for a full and speedy recovery."

"Well alright," Henry grudgingly acquiesced. "Please give my best to Katherine. To this day, I have no idea why a smart and beautiful woman like Katherine ever got herself involved with a troublesome varmint like you."

"I love you too, Henry," Perry replied with a smile.

THE WEATHER WAS IDEAL for a leisurely afternoon stroll. Temperatures in the mid-50's, a sunny cloudless sky, with a gentle breeze. Stanford Winchester had an entire weekend to himself in Washington, D.C. He decided to go exploring. He decided that he was going to be a tourist for a couple of days. His previous visits to Washington were mostly business trips. He had flown in for a meeting, conference, or hearing and usually flew out that evening or the next morning. In all of his years, he never had the time to be a tourist in the nation's capital, other than one short afternoon when LeeAnn accompanied him on a trip. The delay of his confirmation hearing allowed him the luxury of free time, and he was committed to taking advantage of it.

Stanford began his peregrination of Washington at the National Archives. He felt almost embarrassed that he had never seen the Constitution in person. As he entered the Rotunda for the Charters of Freedom, Stanford gazed at the Faulkner murals gracing the curved walls of the Rotunda. Like any other tourist, he waited his turn to view the Declaration of Independence, the Constitution, and the Bill of Rights.

Afterwards, Stanford headed towards the National Mall. On a past trip to Washington with LeeAnn, they spent an afternoon together taking in a number of the museums that constitute part of the Smithsonian Institution. Stanford recalled how LeeAnn enjoyed touring the exhibit of the First Lady Inauguration Gowns on display at the National Museum of American History. He smiled to himself as he remembered how she would go on about the silk taffeta gown that Martha Washington wore or Helen Taft's white silk chiffon floral gown. He feigned interest yet he was delighted by her enthusiasm.

Stanford found a bench on the Mall away from the general flow of tourists. He decided to discuss the night of the White House dinner with LeeAnn.

"LeeAnn, my love," Stanford whispered to himself, "It was a lovely affair. It was the first meal that I had in Washington that had any kind of taste and character to it. Perhaps, the fact that it was, for the most part, New Orleans creole, in intent, had something to do with that fact. The President and First Lady were warm and welcoming hosts. After dinner, a Dixieland band played very passable jazz. Not like the fine bands in the Big Easy, but good solid music. It just lacked a tad of that swing that we love so much back home."

Stanford hesitated for a moment, and then resumed his conversation with LeeAnn.

"I've got to tell you, my darling, Jim Bob said something to me that evening that has been sticking in my craw ever since. I know what a wonderful and loving friend he was to you. How close the bond was between the two of you. But, Jim Bob and I do not share the same type of relationship with one another. We couldn't. You were the common denominator between us. Truly, the only thing we had in common. We both loved you deeply, in our own ways. I respect, and will always be thankful for everything that Jim Bob did for you, LeeAnn. But, I can't help but feel like he believes that I owe him some debt of gratitude for what he has done for me. I've asked nothing of him. Yet, he seemed to indicate, that my nomination to the Supreme Court by the President was part of his doing. There is something about his relationship with the President's Chief of Staff that just doesn't sit right with me. I'm not sure of the specifics, but I'm feeling like a pawn on a chess board. I'm just not sure who is playing, and more importantly what the stakes are of this game. I'm sorry to burden you, my dear, but you are the only one that I feel safe talking to about this."

Stanford raised up off the bench and began his stroll back to his hotel. His stomach churned as thoughts continued to fill his head.

"Watch out, Stanford, watch out!" Bessie Collins shouted as she thrashed about in her bed.

"Bessie, you alright girl?" Lucius asked his wife as he nudged her into consciousness.

"What? Huh?" Bessie slurred as she awoke from a state of deep slumber.

"You was yelling in your sleep, kicking about," Lucius informed Bessie, who sat up in bed and rubbed the sleep from her eyes.

"Oh Lucius, I had a terrible dream," Bessie explained. "Stanford and Jim Bob were fixin' to have an ol' fashioned duel. I was on Stanford's side and my Auntie Rita was on Jim Bob's side. We each handed them a gun and they began to pace off their steps. But ol' Jim Bob turned before he was supposed to and was about to shoot Stanford in the back, and I just started yelling at him to 'watch out!' It surely was odd and scary. Why would I dream that two old friends like them would be trying to kill each other? It don't make no kind of sense. And why would my Auntie Rita be on opposite sides from me? Everything in the dream was all catawampus. No sense, no sense at all."

"I don't know darlin', sometimes we just have an odd dream now and then. It don't mean nothing. You ought not let it upset you," Lucius said to comfort his wife, as he lovingly stroked her head with the palm of his hand.

"I don't know Lucius, it seemed so real. I got no idea where I would get such a notion. Even in my sleep," Bessie stated still agitated and confused by her dream.

"Hush now Bessie, it's just a dream," Lucius softly said. "Just a dream."

KATE WILSON ENTERED HER APARTMENT AFTER a good five mile run. She felt energized and happy. She grabbed one of the organic cotton towels and a Clif bar from the gift basket that still sat on her kitchen table. Kate opened her refrigerator and grasped a cold bottle of Fiji spring water. She toweled the perspiration from her face as she gulped the refreshing water. There was nothing like a good evening run, she thought to herself.

CHAPTER 41

Perry Douglas stood at the office doorway of his colleague Henry Fitzsimmons on Monday morning.

"Henry, I don't want to see that bottle of bourbon outside of your liquor cabinet all day long. In fact, I'm going to have your secretary give me the key."

"That is referred to as cruel and unusual punishment, sir. And you dare call yourself a progressive?" Henry kiddingly chided in return.

"Scrapping you off the corridor floor once in a week is plenty good enough for me," Perry replied with a smile.

"If I read my calendar correctly, a new week commences on Sunday," Henry argued with a wink.

"Stop it you old fool," Perry laughed. "You're not getting a single drop today! For Pete's sake Henry, there isn't anything that you would not argue for hours about is there?"

"Nothing comes to mind, counselor," Henry elegantly drawled.

Stanford Winchester walked into the Hart Senate building on Monday morning not having slept one wink Sunday night. He could not get Jim Bob's comments out of his head. He tossed and turned in bed, as he attempted to mentally sort out all of the puzzle pieces that would reveal Jim Bob's statement. Stanford was fixated with coming to know exactly why Jim Bob made his contention. Yes, there were some small favors Jim Bob had done directly for Stanford, but nothing that would overtly lead him to conclude that Jim Bob was in some ways responsible for the President nominating Stanford for the position on the Supreme Court. Stanford never asked Jim Bob for anything. So, the entire premise for the statement was questionable. At least, that is what Stanford Winchester concluded. Stanford took his seat at the witness table and readied himself for the questioning to come.

"Good morning, Justice Winchester, I hope you enjoyed your time in our city this weekend," Senator Perry greeted the witness. "Before we begin, I'd like to explain how we will be proceeding this week. We will have a full day of hearings today. I spoke with your attorney early this morning and informed him that three witnesses who will be flying in from New Orleans to testify at this hearing are unable to be here tomorrow morning as planned. Therefore, after the conclusion of today's session, we will adjourn for forty-eight hours. We will reconvene at 9:30 a.m. on Thursday, and have two full days of hearing testimony to conclude the week. With that, the Committee will adjourn, consider the testimony provided during these hearings, and make its recommendation on the nomination to the full Senate. Do you have any comments or questions, sir?"

"Yes, Mr. Chairman, I do have one question, may I return to New Orleans after today's session as long as I am back here on Thursday morning?"

"Why, of course, sir. You are free to travel. We understand that you probably have other matters you would prefer to attend to than be held captive in Washington for two full days," Senator Douglas replied.

"Thank you, Mr. Chairman, indeed I do," Stanford Winchester responded with a slight smile.

BESSIE COLLINS COULD NOT SHAKE OFF the dream she had about Stanford Winchester the other night. It bothered her as she went about her day. She felt that it was more significant than just an idle dream. She especially could not understand her Auntie Rita's role in the dream assisting Jim Bob McCallum. After her work day concluded, she went to her aunt's shop on Rampart to talk with her.

"Bessie, what a lovely surprise," Rita greeted her niece and kissed her on the cheek. Moments later, Rita backed away from Bessie asking, "What is wrong girl? I can sense the bad juju around you."

"There's something that I want to talk to you about," Bessie stated somberly. "I had a dream two nights ago that I cannot get out of my head. You were in the dream. And I can't help but think that there is more to this dream than I understand."

"Yes," Rita quietly said as she nodded her head. "I knew that they would come to you."

"Who would come? I don't understand," Bessie inquired confused by her aunt's statement.

"The spirits are coming to you. The loa are communicating with you through your dreams. I have dissatisfied the spirits with my selfish actions," Rita slowly said as she placed her hand over the amulet that hung around her neck.

"I don't understand," Bessie countered becoming more bewildered by her aunt's comments.

"Was Jim Bob McCallum also in your dream?" Rita abruptly asked.

"Yes, yes," Bessie excitedly confirmed. "Stanford and Jim Bob were having a duel. It was all very odd. I don't understand it."

"I am not surprised. The spirit world opens the shell and exposes a pearl of truth," Rita sighed as she slowly nodded her head.

"What is going on? I'm so confused," Bessie confessed.

"My sweet girl, there are many things that I cannot tell you. Things that you must not know. I have done what I should not have done. I have betrayed the loa. I am no longer able to serve as a bokor. They will bring me down, as they should. I allowed my own vanity and greed to corrupt the spiritual world. They are seeking a new voice in you. Someone who sees and speaks simple truth. I am nothing but a foolish old woman who can no longer connect the worlds of spirit and flesh," Rita acknowledged as her head bowed.

"None of this makes sense to me. I'm not of your religion. I don't believe in your spirits. Why would they speak to me?" Bessie questioned.

"Ahh. We humans think that we are in control. That we decide what happens in life. It is a great lie we tell ourselves. We cannot know the unknowable, my love. But know this, Bessie, I love you with all my heart. You are protected by your pure soul. No harm will come to you. But the dreams will come. And they will tell you a story," Rita informed her niece.

"What story?" Bessie hesitantly asked.

"Some words cannot be spoken. I can only say that you are seeking the right path. As is your friend Stanford. Let him know. He is so full of doubt. Free his mind so that he can have peace." Rita closed her eyes. She had said enough.

"JUSTICE WINCHESTER, WE HAVE SPENT THE LAST HOUR going over the facts in the *Happy Foods* case and your conclusions as written in the majority opinion. Can we at least agree that there is a legitimate reason why some might see it as a stretch as to how you reached some of your conclusions?" Senator Douglas asked the witness.

"No, sir, I cannot agree to your statement. The Fifth Circuit took up this matter on appeal. There were grave errors made by the trial court. Certain testimony should have been allowed which was not. Of that fact, there is no dispute. The lower court judgement was stricken because of those grave errors. Two of the three panelists, of which I was one, rendered an appropriate conclusion based on a thorough review of the case matter," Stanford Winchester responded.

"At no time, prior to hearing oral argument in this matter, did you consider recusing yourself, given the fact that your friend Jim Bob McCallum was the CEO of the defendant's company, and that your wife's family had significant holdings in his company?" Senator Douglas asked.

"Mr. Chairman, I have told this Committee repeatedly that none of those factors had any bearing on my decision making. I do believe the record bears out that fact. Lake Pontchartrain Brands was wronged by the errors of the trial court, we only rectified those wrongs, nothing more," Justice Winchester insisted.

"Justice Winchester you did not answer my question," Senator Douglas persisted.

"I did my duty, sir. I presided over a case that I had been assigned to preside over in a random lottery. I listened to the arguments. I read the briefing. I reviewed the record from the trial court. I, as only one voice of three on an Appellate panel, rendered a thorough and impartial decision. I was fully supported by one of my colleagues on the panel. If justice is fairly reached and correctly applied, where is there misconduct?" Stanford Winchester forcefully responded.

"Many would disagree with your assessment, sir. We know the plaintiff's in the matter disagree. I don't understand why you would take the chance of there being even the slightest hint of favoritism or impropriety by sitting on the panel, when you could have easily recused yourself. Another Fifth Circuit judge could have taken your place. Is that not true, Justice Winchester?" Perry Douglas asked as he pressed his case.

"I did my duty, Mr. Chairman. I do not shirk my duties and transfer my responsibilities onto the shoulders of others. We are all busy, we must all bear our own burdens. We all do the best we can to interpret the law and deliver justice to the parties who seek it," Justice Winchester calmly replied.

"Well, so be it, Justice Winchester. This Committee will call three witnesses who will provide us with a different interpretation of the facts on Thursday morning. Until that time, this hearing is adjourned," Senator Douglas stated.

"IT'S LIKE TRYING TO GET YOUR ARMS AROUND a greased pig, ain't it?" Senator Henry Fitzsimmons joked with his colleague.

"He's entitled to his opinion, he just happens to be wrong. The U.S. Code establishes guidelines for when a judge must recuse himself from a case matter before him. Stanford Winchester ignores it like it doesn't apply to him. And saying that he was only doing his duty is hardly a justification," Senator Douglas argued.

"My, you're getting yourself all agitated Perry, seems like you could use a good stiff drink," Henry stated with a grin.

"There's no end to you, is there?" Perry laughed in return.

"I hope not," Henry chuckled.

THE LEAVES ON THE WILLOW OAK TREES were bathed with red flashing lights on a cool, late October night. On-lookers stood silently as the EMTs wheeled the gurney down the concrete sidewalk. The body on the gurney had been placed in a bag, indicating that there had been no rescue. No revival. Nothing more could be done, other than the act of transport. The gusty fall breeze shook the tree's limbs as the ambulance pulled away.

CHAPTER 42

S TANFORD WINCHESTER WALKED into his French Quarter home late on Monday evening. Exhausted from a grueling day of testimony before the Senate Judiciary Committee and an evening flight to New Orleans. He wanted to unwind with a glass of bourbon as he reflected on his testimony. After a few sips of bourbon, Stanford listened to the messages left on his home answering machine. One in particular caught his attention. It was from Bessie Collins. The message was fairly vague, just that she wanted to speak with Stanford when he had a chance. Her voice was a bit odd. It seemed stressed and anxious, not at all the tone Stanford normally expected from the perpetually calm and happy Bessie. He would call her first thing in the morning. At that moment, he wanted to finish his bourbon and get to sleep so as to hopefully quiet his overly active mind.

CLAY GROVER SAT AT PETE'S DINER as he awaited the arrival of his friend Ben Carroll. Hungry as always, Clay decided to go ahead and order without Ben. After all, he reasoned to himself, Ben was probably going to only get coffee anyway. Twenty-five minutes passed, Clay had devoured his breakfast and still no sign of Ben. He called Ben's cell phone and left a message. Clay left Pete's and walked to work. It was going to be a busy day. Clay would be assisting Senator Fitzsimmons with preparing the questioning outline for one of the three witnesses that the Senator was assigned to question on Thursday. It was to be Justice Charles Sewell, who wrote the dissenting Fifth Circuit opinion in the *Happy Foods* case.

As he bounded up the stairs, Clay thought to himself that Ben was probably just tied up with some late night pick-up that he couldn't shake until after morning coffee. He relished giving Ben grief over it, much like Ben had chided Clay for his many midnight misbehaviors in the past. It was his turn to be the righteous admonisher of casual sexual dalliances. Clay grinned as he headed to his office.

STANFORD WINCHESTER SAT IN THE QUAINT back courtyard of Croissant D'Or waiting for Bessie Collins to arrive. Just steps away from his French Quarter home, the charming patisserie was a delightful place to enjoy a good coffee and an exquisite pastry. The sun warmed Stanford as he patiently waited for his friend.

"Bessie, there you are," Stanford stated brightly as he rose to greet his friend.

"Good morning, Justice Winchester," Bessie replied.

"Bessie, we ain't in my courthouse, I insist that you call me Stanford."

"Yes, of course, I apologize Stanford," Bessie corrected herself.

"No need to apologize, we're old friends," Stanford reiterated with a gentle smile. "Let's get you set-up here. They have an excellent French black roast coffee, and their Napoleons are exquisite."

"Thank you, Stanford, you are always so very kind to Lucius and me," Bessie responded.

"What are friends for, eh?"

"You know I'm on your side. I'm always on your side," Bessie abruptly stated.

"Yes, of course, my dear," Stanford responded, surprised by Bessie's fervent statement.

"Bessie what's wrong? I was delighted to receive a message from you yesterday when I got home from Washington. But, your voice sounded stressed and anxious."

"You're gonna think me a fool," Bessie started.

"Never," Stanford sweetly replied. "Just have a sip of coffee and tell me what has been bothering you."

"I had a dream a few nights ago. You was in it and so was Jim Bob McCallum. The two of you was feuding and was about to have a duel. I was helping you and holding your gun. My Auntie Rita was helping Jim Bob. You remember her, don't ya? My mama's sister. She's Queen Rita of the jambalaya fame?"

"Yes, of course, I remember her," Stanford replied. He was attentively listening to Bessie, intrigued by what she was describing to him. "Go on."

"Well, both of you took your guns and cocked the trigger. You then started to walk off your paces. But Jim Bob turned before he was supposed to and was going to shoot you in the back, but I started to yell, 'watch out Stanford.' And then I woke up," Bessie related to Stanford. "Strange ain't it? But that ain't the end of it. I was so bothered about my Auntie Rita being in the dream and supporting Jim Bob, I went to talk to her about it. She told me a lot of things, but she told me that I was right to support you. She told me that you were conflicted and so full of doubt. She told me to talk to you so that you could free your mind."

Stanford sat quietly and listened to every word that Bessie spoke to him. He paused and said, "Thank you Bessie. Thank you for telling me that. It is more helpful than you will ever know."

"So, you don't think that I'm just a silly fool?" Bessie asked.

"Not at all. We can learn a lot from our dreams. I hadn't realized that your aunt and Jim Bob had an ongoing relationship," Stanford said.

"I'm afraid that they've done something together that just ain't right. My Auntie Rita has been acting real odd lately, and it seems to have something to do with Jim Bob," Bessie acknowledged.

"Well, don't you worry too much about such things. I'm sure that everything will work out in the end," Stanford said comforting Bessie.

"I surely hope that you is right, Stanford, I surely do hope so."

"NATHAN, DO WE HAVE ANYTHING TO be concerned about with respect to the three witnesses that the Senate Judiciary Committee is flying in to testify in the Winchester nomination hearing?" President Cochran asked his Chief of Staff.

"No, sir. Political theater as usual, pure and simple," Nathan Whitaker responded.

"Well, Cletus Sawyer is concerned," Andrew Cochran noted.

"With all due respect, Cletus is afraid of his own shadow, sir," Nathan replied. "Mr. President, the three witnesses are the Democratic Justice who wrote the dissenting opinion on the Fifth Circuit case the Democrats have been harping about. An old ill-tempered jurist who was Stanford Winchester's chief rival on the Louisiana Supreme Court, who has had a vendetta against Justice Winchester for years. And a young and naive law clerk. The Democrats just need to make a show, and present voices in opposition other than Perry Douglas, Henry Fitzsimmons, and Patricia Knetzger. It's all hat and no cattle, sir," Nathan stated as he attempted to reassure the President.

"That's it? No other surprises?" The President inquired.

"It's all they got, sir," Nathan chuckled. "Nothing from nothing is nothing."

"Alright, thank you Nathan. Have a word with Cletus, will you. Try to put his mind at ease. We don't need the Ranking Member of the Judiciary Committee running around like Chicken Little yellin' about how the sky is falling."

"Yes, sir, we'll put that chicken to rest," Nathan said with a grin.

"WHY DON'T YOU JUST COME TO MY APARTMENT?" Clay Grover asked the caller on his cell phone. "OK, OK, calm down, I'll meet you on the National Mall in twenty minutes," Clay reassured the caller as he pressed "end call" on his cell phone.

STANFORD WINCHESTER SAT ON THE COUCH in his living room, with his legs crossed at the knee and a glass of bourbon on the rocks in one hand as he held his telephone in his other hand.

"No, no, I think that what I have to say is better said in person," Stanford stated into the phone as he gently shook his head from side to side.

"Yes, I can meet you tomorrow afternoon. Do you want to meet somewhere near your house?" Stanford asked the person on the other end of the phone.

"Alright then, the Victorian Lounge at The Columns Hotel at 1 p.m. tomorrow afternoon. I'll see you then," Stanford said as he concluded his phone call.

Stanford took a large gulp of bourbon finishing off his drink. He gazed at the framed photographs of his wife LeeAnn that were carefully arranged on the mantle over his fireplace.

"I'm sorry my love, you may not agree with me, but this has to be done," Stanford quietly whispered to the photographs.

CLAY GROVER SPOTTED A SOLITARY FIGURE sitting on a park bench at the precise location on the National Mall that he had been told to go to.

"Hey, what's up man? You sounded so weird on the phone," Clay said.

"I'm pretty shook up," Ben Carroll admitted to Clay. "I went into work today and spent a half hour being questioned by the D.C. police."

"My goodness, why?" Clay asked with concern.

"Kate Wilson was found dead in her apartment yesterday afternoon. Friends had been trying to contact her without success. They were concerned so they asked her landlord to check on her and the landlord found her lying on the floor of her kitchen," Ben told Clay.

"Oh my God!" Clay exclaimed. "What happened, do they know?"

"I'm not sure. But one of the other law clerks said that he had overheard one of the cops mention that the preliminary autopsy report found traces of poison in her blood stream," Ben reported, shaking his head in disbelief.

"Why were the police interviewing you?" Clay asked.

"They interviewed all of her co-workers at the Supreme Court. They talked to all of the law clerks who knew Kate. We're a relatively small group, so they talked to all of us to see if we could shed some light on their investigation," Ben responded.

"And did anyone mention the screaming phone calls and her connection at the White House?" Clay questioned.

Ben stood up and looked around at the people passing by the bench. "Let's go for a walk," he told Clay.

"Not long ago, I was going for an evening run," Ben whispered to Clay. "I was jogging by the Ritz Carlton Hotel when I saw Kate Wilson walking into the front entrance of the hotel. She lives only a few blocks from the hotel, so I was wondering why she would be going to a hotel a few blocks from her house. Moments later a big, black SUV pulls up to the hotel. A man gets out of the SUV and follows Kate into the hotel. When I saw who it was, I started to run in the opposite direction," Ben said quietly, his breathing increasing with every word.

"Who was it?" Clay eagerly asked.

"Nathan Whitaker, the President's Chief of Staff," Ben stated slowly just above a whisper.

"That's who she was having an affair with. That's her White House connection," Clay said with certainty.

"I don't know that, it could have just been a coincidence," Ben replied.

"Did you tell the police that you saw them together at the hotel?" Clay asked.

"No, I was too afraid to say anything," Ben related to Clay.

"Ben, you've got to say something. It may be a coincidence that they were both at the hotel at the same moment. But you've got to tell the police. Let them take it where they may," Clay offered.

"Will you come with me?" Ben asked his friend.

"Of course, I'm here for you," Clay said as he placed his hand on his friend's trembling shoulder.

CHAPTER 43

BEN CARROLL AND CLAY GROVER WALKED out of the police department together.

"Look, you've been through a lot today, why don't you spend the night at my place," Clay offered his friend.

"You sure you don't mind?" Ben asked, feeling relieved by Clay's offer.

"Not at all. Aaron will be there," Clay stated.

"That's fine. I'll actually feel safer around more people," Ben confessed.

"We'll stop by your apartment so that you can grab some clothes for tomorrow and a tooth brush, and then head to my place," Clay stated.

"Thanks man, I really appreciate this," Ben replied.

"Not at all, it's what friends do," Clay said with affection.

AARON ROSE WALKED INTO SENATOR DOUGLAS' office for a meeting to prepare for the witness examinations.

"My word, what horrible news, what a tragedy," Senator Douglas commented as he watched the local news report about Kate Wilson's death on the television in his office.

"Yes, sir, the clerks at the Supreme Court are all in shock. Clay Grover is pretty good friends with one of the clerks working for Justice Goldberg and we were talking about it with him last night," Aaron responded to his boss.

"She wasn't even 30 years old. She had her whole life in front of her. Just tragic," Senator Douglas reiterated. "Do they know the cause of death? They're not saying anything on the news," Senator Douglas asked.

"I don't know, Senator. There's a lot of rumors going around, but I haven't heard anything from the authorities," Aaron responded.

"Well, alright Aaron, thank you," Senator Douglas replied as he reached over and turned off his television.

"We've got plenty to do prior to Thursday's hearing, we better get started."

"Yes, sir," Aaron softly replied.

THE LOCAL D.C. MORNING NEWS PROGRAM filled the television screen as Posy Whitaker watched intently from the kitchen of her Arlington, Virginia home.

"Ain't that just a shame in this world," Posy said to her husband as he poured himself a cup of fresh brewed coffee.

"What?" Nathan asked.

"I said ain't that just a shame about the young woman that they found dead in her apartment," Posy shouted in return. "She worked for that judge who was at Stanford's dinner last week. What was his name, something 'Salad', I think?"

"Allen Sallis," Nathan replied, correcting his wife. "And yes, it's quite a shame when young people are taken from us so early."

"Did you know her?" Posy asked.

"No, of course not. Why would I know her?" Nathan responded clearly irked by the question.

"She worked for that Supreme Court judge and she's in the government and all," Posy replied.

"Do you have any idea how many people work for the government in this city?" Nathan inquired. "I'm not sure I know all of the names of the people who work in the West Wing, let alone in other branches of government."

"Well, it's just a shame. Pretty young thing," Posy said as she walked out of the kitchen headed to their bedroom.

Once he was certain that Posy was upstairs in their bedroom, Nathan removed a pre-paid Go cell phone from his suit pocket. He crushed it with a meat clever into small pieces and then ground the small pieces of the plastic phone in the garbage disposal located in the kitchen sink. The noise was loud enough for Posy to hear from their upstairs bedroom.

"What's that gawdawful noise?" Posy shouted.

"Nothing. Just grinding some garbage in the sink disposal," Nathan yelled in response. "It's nothing."

LATER THAT DAY, PERRY DOUGLAS KNOCKED on the Senate office door of his colleague, Henry Fitzsimmons.

"Perry, come in, you look tired my friend," Henry commented.

"I've spent the entire day with Aaron preparing for our witnesses on Thursday," Perry responded.

"Yes, Clay and I've been preparing my questioning for Charles Sewell," Henry stated.

"Sometimes, I just don't know what we're doing here," Perry said with a shrug.

"How so?" Henry inquired.

"Where's that fancy bourbon of yours?" Perry asked his friend.

"Now, you're talking my language," Henry chuckled. Henry unlocked the discreet liquor cabinet in his office and poured some of the Elijah Craig bourbon into a crystal whiskey glass for both he and Perry. "Cheers, my friend," Henry toasted Perry.

"Cheers," Perry responded holding his glass up before taking a full sip.

"Now what is bothering you?" Henry asked.

"As I mentioned, today, Aaron and I were preparing the questions for the law clerk we are calling as a witness. We were discussing a certain line of questioning and Aaron told me that we shouldn't ask her a specific question or present a certain set of facts because she will side with Winchester in her answer. Henry, it took me aback. He was selectively framing questions like a litigator. Have we become so partisan that we are teaching these young men and women who work with us to ignore or obfuscate facts in order to make political points? You and I started as litigation attorneys. We were zealous advocates for our clients, and we knew how to present the most advantageous defense. Who are our clients now? Don't we serve the American people and our home state constituents? And, if so, should we be parsing only the facts that aid our own personal political views?"

Perry lifted his glass to his lips and took another deep swallow of the mellow liquor.

"Is Stanford Winchester a radical monster we need to protect the American people from? Sure, his views on Constitutional matters are far different than ours. We view his legal interpretations as wrong, but I'm sure a good number of our constituents would agree with him. Conservative Republicans would contend that our views are erroneous and potentially dangerous. And yes, it appears to us that he should have recused himself from a handful of cases, but his voice alone was not enough to determine those matters. There were other judges who agreed with him in the majority opinion. Other judges that did not believe that his presence on the panel created an egregious conflict of interest. However, we Democrats have viewed it as such, and now are we going to ignore certain facts because they don't align with the 'truth' we are seeking?" Perry questioned, not only Henry, but also himself.

"Are you looking for an argument?" Henry asked his colleague.

"No," Perry solemnly replied. "I'm looking for reassurance that stubborn old war horses like the two of us are not breeding a contentious lot of political warriors that will eschew facts for dogmatic purity. Are we truly doing the people's business by fighting tooth and nail to keep Stanford Winchester off the Supreme Court? Is this what we were elected to do? This hearing is causing me to doubt what we are really championing here."

"If you want me to tell you that Winchester is a monster, I can't," Henry responded. "Both you and I remember a time when we didn't tear down and demonize the Republicans. We had our philosophical differences, but the end game was doing what was in the best interest of the American people. A wholly partisan witch hunt and attempted impeachment of a sitting President for a personal impropriety seems to have changed the way the parties deal with one another. Yes, I'm gonna sit here and tell you that the Republicans started it. But, we are as culpable as they are. Now, we are attempting to take down a Presidential nominee, because we don't appreciate his political views or his failure to recuse himself from a handful of matters over a lengthy judicial career. I think Bork needed to be stopped. Stanford Winchester is very conservative but he is no Robert Bork."

"Politics has evolved into a blood sport. A running tally of wins and losses," Perry conceded. "Who truly wins if we defeat Winchester's nomination? Is democracy preserved if he is not on the Supreme Court? The longer this hearing progresses, the more I wonder what we are actually doing here. I've got to tell you Henry, I admire him, to some extent. Winchester does not apologize for his behavior on the bench because he sees nothing to apologize for. He is a man of strong convictions. We may disagree with his convictions, but by the same token, he disagrees with ours. He is not ill-tempered or hostile. Conversely, he acquits himself in a mild-mannered and very courteous fashion. After a morning of intense questioning from you, after you had a fall, did he take pleasure in your situation? No, he actually takes time to write a handwritten note wishing you well." Perry shook his head and finished off his drink.

"Henry, I'm just not sure I know what we're doing here anymore," Perry confessed.

Aaron Rose relaxed in his apartment after a long day of working with Senator Douglas. He poured himself a glass of pinot noir and sat on his couch allowing his mind to wander. Sitting on his coffee table amongst a pile of books and magazines was the souvenir book he had purchased at Queen Rita's shop in New Orleans about, "Voodoo Potions and Spells." He barely had glanced at the book since his purchase. Aaron perused the pages of the book dealing with potions as he slowly sipped his wine.

He noticed that some of the potions that were designed to cause harm to a voodoo victim called for the use of Foxglove. Aaron was unfamiliar with Foxglove so he reached for his iPad and Googled the term. Aaron learned that Foxglove is a plant also known as digitalis. It has also been called "dead man's bells." Aaron read on. Digitalis has in the past been processed in laboratories and used as an antiarrhythmic agent to control heart rate. However, digitalis when not properly processed is quite toxic, and when mixed with water, can be very lethal. Aaron dropped his iPad on the floor and reached for his cell phone.

CHAPTER 44

Sᴛᴀɴғᴏʀᴅ Wɪɴᴄʜᴇsᴛᴇʀ ᴅʀᴀɴᴋ the entire ᴄᴜᴘ of coffee that his housekeeper, Clara, had brewed for him just minutes before.

"It's so nice to see you enjoy a fine cup of coffee in the morning, Justice Winchester," Clara stated with pride, as she watched him drink the coffee. "You are usually rushing out of here first thing in the morning to get to work, most times. You barely have time for a sip or two."

"Well, Clara, I ain't got nowhere to be this morning, so it certainly is a treat," Stanford kindly lied in response.

"Should I plan to fix you a nice lunch today, since you ain't going to the courthouse?" Clara asked.

"No, thank you Clara. I've got a meeting this afternoon. I'll probably just grab something while I'm out," Stanford replied.

"Justice Winchester, what should I do with that lovely puzzle you put together that's sittin' in the middle of the kitchen table?" Clara asked her employer. "Do you want me to put it somewhere for safe keeping or leave it on the table?"

"Box it up, Clara, it ain't important. Just box it up."

Qᴜᴇᴇɴ Rɪᴛᴀ sᴀᴛ ᴏɴ ᴛʜᴇ ᴡᴏᴏᴅᴇɴ sᴛᴏᴏʟ in the back room of her shop. She carefully intertwined the hemp twine around the dried chicken bones. She had made this type of ceremonial structure a few times in her past. It was a Haitian Vodou tribute to the spirit of death, Loa Ghede. It was a symbol of the intersection between the human world and the spiritual world. A token to the spirits to open the pathway for a departing soul to pass into the afterlife. Such a symbol was traditionally placed at the front doorstep of the departed or soon to be departed.

Rita's fingers moved swiftly as she took each chicken bone that had symbolic significance and appended it with another bone using the hemp twine. Finally, she added the dried wishbone which had to be mounted to the top of the structure and pointed upwards towards the heavens. Once she completed the final twisted knot of hemp, she closed her eyes and sighed. She grasped and gently rubbed with her left hand the wanga amulet that hung around her neck.

"Tis in the hands of the loa. Now, it is done," Rita softly whispered, as a tear ran down her age-worn cheek.

STANFORD WINCHESTER WALKED DOWN THE SIDEWALK towards the entrance of the Columns Hotel in New Orleans Garden District. The St. Charles streetcar rumbled past as the conductor rang his bell. It was a sound that Stanford had missed. A sound so foreign from the street traffic noise of Washington. Stanford walked into the elegant dark mahogany bar of the Victorian Lounge. Seated in a red upholstered wingback chair in the corner of the room was Jim Bob McCallum.

"Greetings Stanford," Jim Bob called to him.

"Good afternoon, Jim Bob," Stanford replied.

"Join me for a mid-day palliative?" Jim Bob inquired.

"What are you having?" Stanford asked.

"A well-crafted Sazerac," Jim Bob responded as he signaled to the bartender. "They don't normally serve cocktails in the afternoon during the week, but a good deal of my money re-stocks their bar, so allowances are made. Wealth does have its rewards, you know."

"Yes, you do live close by," Stanford stated.

"Second Street and Prytania. The large mansion off the corner," Jim Bob confirmed. "It surely has been a while since you've been to our home, hasn't it?"

"At least six years, about a year or so before LeeAnn passed," Stanford acknowledged.

The bartender brought the drinks over to the far corner of the empty room where Stanford and Jim Bob sat.

"Thank you, that's all for now," Jim Bob stated as he dismissed the bartender.

"Yes, sir," the bartender replied as he left the two friends alone in the dark wooded formal room.

"I take it you decided to come back to New Orleans for a couple of days with the suspension of the Committee hearings until tomorrow morning?" Jim Bob asked.

"Yes, I have an evening flight back. How did you know about the two day recess?" Stanford inquired.

"I have Cletus Sawyer report to me daily about how things are going with the hearing. I understand that you are more than holding your own against those scurrilous Democrats," Jim Bob replied.

Stanford looked askance at Jim Bob. "You actually have a United States Senator call you with daily reports?" Stanford asked Jim Bob incredulously.

"As I said before, wealth does have its rewards," Jim Bob stated with a wide grin as he sipped on his cocktail. "So, Stanford, my friend, what was it that you wanted to talk to me about in person?"

"Well, since you put it that way, I suppose I want to know what else your wealth buys you." Stanford stated bluntly.

"I'm not sure I catch your meaning?" Jim Bob asked, with an irritated tenor to his voice.

"I'm not here to play games, Jim Bob. You know as well as I do, that I heard precisely what you said to me in Washington. I want to know what you meant by 'I've done too much to get you here.' I want to know everything!" Stanford said emphatically yet keeping his tone and voice down.

"No, my friend, you certainly do not want to know everything," Jim Bob calmly countered. "But, what I will tell you is that what has been done was done for all of us. We are all in this together."

"I have asked you for nothing," Stanford aggressively claimed, his eyes fixed on Jim Bob.

"Not directly, perhaps," Jim Bob conceded. "But you are the immediate beneficiary of many of the things that needed to be done."

"Look, if things were done supposedly for my benefit I have a right to know what they were," Stanford demanded.

"Then you better be prepared for the consequences of enlightenment," Jim Bob stated. "Are you?"

"Yes, I want to know," Stanford reiterated.

"Alright, you agree that we are all in this together then? Jim Bob questioned, determined to get the answer he sought.

"Have I ever violated a trust or not done my utmost for a friend?" Stanford replied. "I'm being crucified by the Democrats for what I have allegedly done for friends while on the court, including you."

Jim Bob took a long sip of his Sazerac, moved to the edge of his chair and leaned forward to be closer to Stanford.

"A few years ago I met Nathan Whitaker at a political fundraiser on the rubber chicken circuit. He was a smart, aggressive, ambitious man who was also the campaign manager and Chief of Staff of the Governor of Georgia. Andrew Cochran was Nathan's best friend since college and most likely the one person in this world Nathan loved more than himself. Nathan was wholly devoted to Cochran. I was in a position to assist Cochran's run for the White House. Nathan and I came to a mutual understanding. I could help his friend, and from a position of power, Nathan could help me, my friends and family, and my business interests." Jim Bob hesitated as he took another sip of his cocktail.

"But Cochran is the President, not Nathan Whitaker," Stanford stated.

"Oh, Stanford please. You ain't that naive!" Jim Bob chided. "Andrew Cochran is a nice man. Pleasant looking, charming, he can make a rousing speech, and he has a great rags to riches story. Rising from the ashes of the burnt rubble of his childhood home, losing both his parents, and still achieving the loftiest position in the world. He made for a perfect candidate. But Andrew Cochran does not have the savvy, cunning or political backbone to do the work that needs to be done to achieve and keep power. Nathan Whitaker does. If you think that Andrew Cochran runs that White House and the Presidency, you have not been paying attention. Nathan is calling the shots. He has been since he and Cochran were 18-year-old boys. Cochran is nothing without the laser-like focus, acumen, and ruthless determination of his friend and protector."

"What does this have to do with me?" Stanford asked, growing impatient with Jim Bob.

"My money and my connections in the Republican Party helped get Cochran the nomination and ultimately the Presidency. I don't give away my money or utilize my political clout without getting a return for my investment and influence," Jim Bob declared and paused again to sip his drink.

"In her last weeks of life, LeeAnn told me how much she had always dreamed about seeing you on the Supreme Court. You know this better than anyone else, Stanford. It was her dream for you. I promised my dying friend that I would do whatever I could to make her dream come true. I would do anything for LeeAnn. I would have married her and been the happiest man on God's earth, if she had not fallen for the wealthy, refined boy from New Orleans high society. But, alas she picked you, old friend.

That never diminished my love or devotion to her, right up to the end. So, I informed Nathan that I wanted you on the Court. I also wanted federal government funding for an Alzheimer's research institute, that will be built in Baton Rouge and bear Mabel's name. Additionally, I required some administrative assistance on some business deals I have in China. Nathan wanted the presidency for his beloved friend. And once Cochran was president, Nathan wanted a very successful first 100 days. The President's new economic vision and agenda for the country, as well as your nomination and confirmation to the Supreme Court are to be the crowning achievements of Cochran's new administration."

Jim Bob finished off his cocktail. He sat deep in his chair and sighed.

"Albert Martin was an old man in failing health. His train ticket departing this world very shortly, had already been punched. Nathan and I merely arranged for him to take an earlier train. Timing is everything in politics," Jim Bob casually stated.

Stanford stared at Jim Bob in stunned silence. His face contorted in shock.

"I'd suggest that you not say or ask me anything else," Jim Bob sternly counseled Stanford.

"Everyone benefits. You are just a few short weeks from taking your rightful place on the Supreme Court. You get the gravitas and power that less than 125 people in this country's history have ever had. Your devoted wife and my great friend gets her dream realized. Mabel's name will have its own cache and legacy in the realm of mental health research. I have my hands wrapped around the puppet master's strings. We are all winners as it should be. Surely, you can have no objections to that, Stanford Winchester."

Stanford sat motionless in his chair, shocked by what he had just heard. Jim Bob raised up to his feet.

"I should get back to Mabel, surely you understand. Please stay and have another drink or two. They'll put it on my tab. Now you have your answers, old chum," Jim Bob said looking down at Stanford. He turned and walked out of the hotel. Stanford's head dropped into his hands, as he sat in the dark ornate room all alone.

THE DOOR WAS LOCKED AND THE "CLOSED" SIGN hung in the window of the rickety old shop on north Rampart. Inside the shop, the wooden stool in the back room had been knocked over. A mason jar less than one third filled with liquid, its cover off, sat on the small wooden table.

A single handwritten word was scribbled onto the mason jar label, "fox-glove." Outside the shop, just to the left of the doorway was a small but intricate structure made of chicken bones and hemp twine. Its apex pointed straight to the heavens.

CHAPTER 45

STANFORD WINCHESTER STOOD IN FRONT OF THE MIRROR in the bathroom of his room at the Hay-Adams hotel. He straightened the knot of his red and yellow bow tie and buttoned the top two buttons of his navy blue suit coat. He patted the left inner pocket of his suit coat. Gone was the photograph of LeeAnn. In its place was a letter sized manila envelope. Stanford smiled at his image in the mirror. He liked what he saw. Stanford walked across Pennsylvania Avenue headed towards the security booth that fronted the fenced-in grounds of the White House.

"Good morning, officer," Stanford said to the security guard in the booth. "My name is Stanford Winchester, I am a judge on the United States Court of Appeals for the Fifth Circuit," Stanford said as he showed his identification to the guard. "Would you kindly have this letter delivered to the President of the United States on my behalf? Thank you so much for your kindness," Stanford graciously stated as he handed the white envelope to the guard and walked off heading towards Capitol Hill. It was a lovely sun-bathed day, and Stanford wanted to enjoy a leisurely walk.

SENATOR PERRY DOUGLAS STOPPED BY THE OFFICE of his colleague Henry Fitzsimmons on his way to the hearing room.

"Henry, you ready to go?" Perry asked his friend.

"Yes, one minute," Henry said as he gathered his notes and papers together off his desk. "Have you changed your mind since our conversation the other night?" Henry asked.

"No, not really," Perry confessed. "I still have conflicted feelings. I believe a judge with more moderate stances would be a better fit for the Court and the country. But we lost the White House in last year's election. We are not in a position to make that determination or select that nominee."

"Are we wearing kid gloves today or are we lacing up the boxing gloves?" Henry asked.

"We'll see how it goes," Perry said with a shrug. "We'll see."

THE POLICE DETECTIVE ASSIGNED TO INVESTIGATE the death of Kate Wilson sat at his office desk reviewing the final autopsy report that was just sent to him by the Coroner's Office. He carefully read the portion of the report that stated, "Lethal quantities of the poison digitalis were found in the bloodstream of the victim." He slowly shook his head. His workday had only just begun.

STANFORD WINCHESTER ENTERED THE HEARING ROOM and took his place at the witness table. He smiled as the Senators on the Judiciary Committee filed into the room and took their places at the dais.

"Good morning Justice Winchester," Senator Perry greeted the witness. "Before we begin, I'd like to outline what we will be doing today. We will begin today with Senator Fitzsimmons completing a few questions for Justice Winchester. After that questioning is completed, we will have a short recess followed by the Committee questioning a new witness, Judge Charles Sewell. That will probably take us to our lunch break. After lunch we will have two additional witnesses. I anticipate closing statements will commence tomorrow morning. With that, the Chair recognizes the honorable Henry Fitzsimmons of South Carolina."

"Good morning, Justice Winchester," Senator Fitzsimmons greeted the witness. "I will try to keep this as short as possible, sir."

"Good morning, Senator Fitzsimmons," Stanford Winchester responded. "If I may sir, with permission from the Chair, I'd like to make a brief statement to the Committee."

"This is not the normal course of how we plan to proceed sir," Senator Fitzsimmons interjected.

"Please," Stanford Winchester implored. "I believe we can shorten our day here if I may give a brief statement."

"Alright, fine. The Chair recognizes the witness, Stanford Winchester," Senator Douglas responded.

"Thank you, Mr. Chairman, I greatly appreciate your willingness to

accommodate an old jurist," Stanford stated slowly and with conviction. "Firstly, I'd like to express my sincere appreciation for the hospitality and professionalism shown to me by this august Committee and its
staff. Secondly, I would like to personally thank the Honorable Senator
Henry Fitzsimmons. Sir, your statements and questions the other day
gave me pause for deep reflection and personal assessment. You allowed
me to see a different perspective on judicial behavior that frankly I had
not reflected on to any great degree in the past. I inhabit this flawed
human chassis, which I have been given the utmost privilege to dress
in the black robes of judicial responsibility for many, many years. It is
a privilege that perhaps I have been guilty of taking for granted. I concede that I could have done a better job of separating my personal life
from my sworn duties. But, I truly believed that I was as impartial in
my final decision making as I could have been given that we all suffer
from the same affliction of being human beings. So, thank you Senator
Fitzsimmons for assisting me with better assessing my judicial conduct.
Finally, I would like to inform this Committee that less than one hour
ago, I personally delivered a letter for the President of the United States.
In said letter, I informed President Cochran that I am hereby withdraw-
ing my name from nomination to be considered for Associate Judge of
the Supreme Court."

The hearing room erupted in a flurry of verbal professions of shock
and loud banter.

"Order, ladies and gentlemen, may we please have order," Senator
Douglas loudly requested. Once the initial buzz in the room subsided,
Senator Douglas addressed the witness.

"Justice Winchester, are you sure that you want to follow this path?
Would you like additional time to consider your decision, sir?"

"No, I had two full days to come to this decision, Mr. Chairman. I
don't require any additional time. My mind is made up, but I deeply
thank the Chair for the generous offer of additional time for reflective
consideration," Stanford Winchester calmly but firmly stated.

"This is not my place," Stanford Winchester said wistfully. "My place
is in New Orleans. It is where I belong. It is where I find contentment
and happiness. The last few days have shown me that what you may wish
for may not be what is ultimately best for you. Actions taken in the name
of friendship can be truly flawed and cause far greater harm than aid
the service of good. I have no doubt that facts will quickly come to light
that will greatly help you understand part of the reasoning behind the

decision that I have announced to you today. I humbly thank you for your patience with me. It would be a high honor if I may shake the hand of each member of the Committee before we depart today. May God bless each and every one of you."

Stanford Winchester filed by every member of the Committee and shook their hands. Several of the Republican Senators expressed profound disappointment in Stanford Winchester's decision and even a bit of outrage. As Stanford shook hands with Senator Fitzsimmons, he leaned in close and whispered in Henry Fitzsimmons ear.

"Sir, I have the utmost admiration for you and your many years of service to this country. I could not be more pleased that you seem to be fully recovered from your unfortunate fall. You are a true Southern gentlemen and a great American patriot. I hope you enjoy the small gift of bourbon I had sent to your office. I did not feel it appropriate to send a card then, but would like you to know it is but a small token of my personal esteem for you, Senator," Stanford quietly stated, as he looked Henry directly in the eye and firmly shook his hand, while smiling warmly, as if greeting a good old friend.

As Stanford moved on to shake the hand of another Senator, Henry Fitzsimmons turned to his friend Perry Douglas and simply uttered, "Remarkable!"

SEVEN MONTHS LATER, CLAY GROVER, Aaron Rose, and Ben Carroll were seated at an outdoor cafe in Washington on a warm mid-June evening.

"Seven months ago, Stanford Winchester withdrew his name from nomination to the Supreme Court," Clay stated while raising his wine glass.

"Seems like yesterday, and decades ago all at the same time," Aaron replied. "So much has happened since then. Thanks to Ben's tip the police were able to focus their attention on Nathan Whitaker."

"And thanks to Aaron's tip about the digitalis poison being mentioned in the voodoo book, the police were able to trace the poison back to the original source, Queen Rita," Ben added.

"Though, I still don't understand why Nathan Whitaker felt it necessary to kill Kate Wilson?" Clay asked.

"I think he thought that she was too much of a threat to him. I understand that she was making a lot of demands that he was unable to fulfill. I wouldn't be surprised if taking out Kate was part of Nathan's plan all along. He had an affair with her, made all sorts of promises and in exchange, she agreed to slip some of the digitalis poison into Justice Martin's water glass. It was easy enough for her to do. We all come and go freely between the offices of the Justices delivering papers and files," Ben said.

"Because of Justice Martin's advanced age and existing heart condition, his family didn't want an autopsy performed. No one ever considered that his death was from anything but natural causes. It's one thing when an eighty-four-year-old man dies of heart failure, it's quite another when it's a twenty-eight-year-old woman in excellent condition," Aaron stated.

"The fact that Nathan allegedly killed her by using a syringe to inject the poison into the bottom of the water bottle and then used a barely noticeable epoxy glue to seal the pin prick was chillingly devious. The water bottles in the gift basket were factory sealed, no one would have thought twice about it," Clay added.

"Are you at all surprised about how quickly and without a second thought, Winchester turned in his friend Jim Bob McCallum?" Ben asked.

"Not for a minute. He is an old Southern gentlemen. His name and his reputation and honor mean everything to him. Once he truly knew that his nomination to the Supreme Court was part of an arranged deal between Jim Bob and Nathan, he didn't want any part of it. If he didn't fully believe that he earned the position through his judicial service and reputation, and that it didn't come from the President himself, he immediately declined the nomination. He devoted his whole life to the legal profession, he was not going to turn his back on justice to save his lying, conniving and murderous friend. Jim Bob made the tactical error in believing that Stanford would choose friendship and self-aggrandizement over serving the law," Clay explained to his friends.

"When we spoke with Bessie and Lucius Collins down in New Orleans before the hearing, it became clear that Jim Bob was LeeAnn's friend. I don't think that Stanford ever considered himself a very good friend of Jim Bob's. Jim Bob was more of an acquaintance he knew through his wife. Once LeeAnn passed, they only saw each other on rare occasions," Aaron added.

Ben looked at his watch and quickly finished his glass of wine.

"Gotta go fellas, first date, he's really cute, don't want to keep him waiting," Ben said as he left Aaron and Clay.

"Good luck," Aaron called out as Ben walked away.

"The whole nomination process has really opened my eyes to the ugliness of modern politics," Aaron offered, turning towards Clay and placing his hand over Clay's hand.

"I know what you mean. This whole ordeal has irrevocably tarnished the Cochran administration. The President's Chief of Staff is under arrest and awaiting a double murder trial. President Cochran is personally devastated that his best friend, the man who he trusted more than anyone else in the world betrayed his trust. And Nathan Whitaker who did whatever he deemed necessary to get his friend elected President and then attempted to solidify the success of the administration, has in fact destroyed what he had hoped to build," Clay said while shaking his head in disbelief.

"We're all damaged. There are no winners here," Aaron said sadly. "Trust was dealt a severe body blow. The American people trust their elected leaders to do the right thing. The President trusted his beloved friend. Stanford Winchester trusted the system that he thought rewarded accomplishment. No one wins when partisanship runs amuck and the thirst for power and political expediency trumps morality."

"So now what? Where do we go from here?" Clay asked.

"I don't know. I've got to re-evaluate what I want out of life. Try to determine what I truly want to do for a living. In the long run, I'm not sure where we go. In the short term, going back to your apartment sure sounds good enough for now," Aaron replied with a coy smile on his face.

"Sounds good to me. Let's go," Clay affirmed with a wink and a broad smile while taking Aaron's hand into his own.

ABOUT A MILE AWAY at the Office of the United States Attorney for the District of Columbia, Franklin Burrows, the United States Attorney for the District rocked back and forth in his office chair as he reviewed the case file with his two top assistants. His furrowed brow indicated his concern over the pending prosecution of the high profile cases.

"No smoking gun and no eye witnesses, but plenty of hearsay and innuendo. The fact that we were able to get a grand jury indictment in these matters is a minor miracle. And let me tell you that we will be getting all sort of second guessing on overreaching with murder charges. Conspiracy to commit murder perhaps, but first degree murder is such a stretch given what I see in this file."

"Yes, sir, it's hard to disagree with that assessment," one of his assistants stated to Franklin Burrows. "One could argue that there is no there there."

"Well, then we are all in agreement that achieving murder convictions for Nathan Whitaker and Jim Bob McCallum will be a herculean feat for this department."

"That seems to be the case, sir," the assistant responded.

"Gentlemen, this is where political pressure should never interfere with our prosecutorial duties. Yet here I sit as a Democratic appointed United States Attorney, and if I had not attempted to seek murder charges against the Republican President of United States Chief of Staff and his Louisiana King Maker, I would have been chased out of town by my own party supporters. If that doesn't make you hate this job I don't know what will," Franklin Burrows said while vigorously shaking his head. "So with that honest assessment, let this ridiculous farce begin."

STANFORD WINCHESTER WALKED DOWN ROYAL STREET waving to his friends in the shops along his way home. The vibrant bustle of the French Quarter enlivened his spirits. The hibiscus trees were especially fragrant after a brief late afternoon shower. Stanford made it back to his home carrying the fresh pie that Bessie had made for him that very morning. He placed the pie on his kitchen table and gathered a plate, fork, and pie server from his kitchen drawers. Stanford cut a good-sized slice of pie and carefully placed it onto a plate. With a napkin and fork balanced in his hand while holding the plate, he walked out of the kitchen and onto his balcony overlooking Royal Street. It was an early Saturday night in June in New Orleans. As usual, Stanford could hear off in the distance, street musicians applying their craft. The low tuba and trombone parts stood out as the street band played "When The Saints Go Marching In." Stanford sat in his rocking chair. The late day sun still warming his back as he listened to the music. He took a large forkful of Bessie's pecan pie and scooped it into his mouth. The buttery richness of the pecan filing and the perfect crust made his lips curl into a satisfied smile.

"This surely is fine pie," Stanford muttered to himself, wholly contented. "This surely is."

THE BRANCHES ON THE BEAUTIFUL CHERRY TREES near the Tidal Basin in Washington, D.C. swayed and danced in the warm June gusts. While the Spanish moss hung heavy as the gentle breeze whistled through the cypress trees in New Orleans.

THE END

Photo by Molly Johnson

Mʀ. Cᴀᴛᴀʟᴀɴᴏ ʀᴇsɪᴅᴇs ɪɴ Cʜɪᴄᴀɢᴏ, IL. He has Bachelor of Arts and Master of Arts degrees in Political Science. He has melded his life-long fascination and love of politics with numerous years of working in the legal profession, into his first love, that of writing fiction.

CPSIA information can be obtained
at www.ICGtesting.com
Printed in the USA
BVHW030511020321
601385BV00009B/466